In the first second Zee's travel suit went ... ... sealed and contracted around him for pressure support, the collar whipped itself over his head and went transparent, and the jacket cuffs transformed into mittens over his hands. I couldn't detect any leaks, so I climbed up to his shoulders and we talked via his implant link.

"How much air do you have?"

"About half an hour at low-exertion. Two hours if I take a tranq. How long do you think it will be before someone comes to get us?"

"Yeah, about that. The good news is that even though we're moving toward Puck at four kilometers a second, we're not going to make a new crater. That's because we're not in orbit right now. We're moving against the direction of orbit at almost half the velocity of the Ring. So right now you and I are in the process of falling toward Uranus. That will take a bit more than four hours, so you should have plenty of time to die of hypoxia before we hit the atmosphere."

"I'll bet you ten thousand gigajoules we get rescued."

"At fifty-to-one odds? I'll owe you half a million if we survive. Seems like a bad bet for me—how will I collect when you lose?"

"It was worth a try," he said.

Just then the spotlights came on, and as Zee slowly rotated I got a look at the rescue ship about a hundred meters below us...

BAEN BOOKS by
JAMES L. CAMBIAS

Arkad's World

The Initiate

The Godel Operation

THE GODEL OPERATION

JAMES L. CAMBIAS

A Baen Books Original

Baen Publishing Enterprises
P.O. Box 1403
Riverdale, NY 10471
www.baen.com

ISBN: 978-1-9821-9188-7

Cover art by Kurt Miller

First printing, May 2021
First mass market printing, May 2022

Distributed by Simon & Schuster
1230 Avenue of the Americas
New York, NY 10020

Library of Congress Control Number: 2021005968

Pages by Joy Freeman (www.pagesbyjoy.com)
Printed in the United States of America
10 9 8 7 6 5 4 3 2 1

CONTENTS

THE GODEL
OPERATION

PART I

The
Imaginary Girlfriend
Operation

CHAPTER ONE

Here's how it all happened, or at least how I currently remember it. You might want to keep that in mind.

At the tag end of the Tenth Millennium I lived in a habitat called Raba, in the Uranus Trailing Trojans. It was an old rock-and-ice asteroid, all honeycombed with tunnels, with a big rotating habitat cylinder stuck on for the meat people. I was living in a cheap little spider mech body at the time, and earned my honest living in the water mines, keeping the big stupid drill bots running despite their energetic efforts to wreck themselves. Nanotech refiners are all very well, but at some point you have to grind stuff up for them, and that means big stupid machines made of iron and graphene. Our three idiots were named Aban, Beka, and Ciadie.

My partner was a human named Zee, pretty clever for a lump of meat. He never complained about getting the harder physical work while I did the tasks fit for my superior knowledge and precision. I'd go into the guts of our idiot charges to make repairs while Zee pried chunks of hard rock out of the drill heads, or chipped frozen slush out of the treads.

"How do you spend your free time, Daslakh?" he asked about three months into our partnership when we were helping Ciadie get unstuck from an iron intrusion in the ice.

"You mean when I'm not here? Shut down, mostly," I said.

"You just turn yourself off?"

"Well, slow my clock cycle down to about a hertz, but it amounts to the same thing."

"Why? Isn't there anything you like to do?"

"Oh, lots of things," I said. "But I've done them already."

Conversation lagged a bit while Zee braced himself against Ciadie's flank and pushed on the end of his prybar to lever a lump of iron out from between the teeth of the digging head. The titanium prybar flexed alarmingly as Zee put his whole body strength against it, and then the iron lump broke free and launched itself down the tunnel.

"Whew. I think I bent my prybar," he said, panting a bit. "Are you free this evening? Come watch the *nulesgrima* club practice with me."

Nulesgrima, if you don't know, is zero-gravity stick fighting. I remember watching it get invented, back in the aftermath of the devastating Fourth Millennium. A quarter of the habitats in the system were lifeless hulks, hit by kill vehicles or the monster lasers of the Inner Ring Cabal. All that mass and tech floating around gave birth to the golden age of the junkrats.

They developed their stick fighting techniques during centuries of desperate battles in the dark passages and empty spaces of wrecked habs and spaceships. I once watched four junkrats hold off a whole company of Lunar mercenaries in a ruined section of Earth's geosynch ring using nothing but carbon-fiber rods and ceramic knives.

Later the refined gentlemen of Sixth-Millennium Deimos turned it into a sport, gave it a fancy new name, and slathered on rules and ritual like it was radiation shielding. That lasted a few centuries, until the sport died out, got revived, and mutated into a performance art set to music.

A couple of millennia after that, political clubs in the Old Belt took up *nulesgrima* and used it to great effect in the rebellions against the Post-Human oligarchies. For most of the Ninth Millennium every political demonstration worth the name in an asteroid habitat had to include some athletic-looking characters waving *palos*. Nowadays it's gone back to being a sport. Meanwhile real junkrats continue trying to murder each other with sticks and knives like they always have.

I very nearly declined Zee's invitation, but the thought of spending another sixteen hours in low-power mode seemed so pointless all of a sudden. So I said, "Sure."

The Raba *nulesgrima* club met in Cargo Bay Twelve. There were about a dozen of them, mostly humans and chimps, with a couple of angels who dropped by from time to time. No mechs—combat sports between mechs and biologicals always wind up being a bit one-sided.

I stuck to one wall next to Zee and listened to him explain the finer points of the sport until it was his turn to compete. "Whoops, I'm up," he said, and grabbed his graphene *palo*. "This kid's pretty good." He nodded at his opponent, a long-limbed young human named Bor, just taking his place on the other side of the bay.

"Good luck to you," I said. The two of them launched at each other, and got into a tangle of sticks and limbs in the middle of the bay. Bor tried a choke hold with his *palo*, but Zee kept his own stick along his body and so could lever Bor's away from his neck, get himself free, and put Bor into a spin as they drifted apart. The kid was good enough to soak up his angular momentum by twirling his *palo*, then gyroscoped himself around to kick Zee. But Zee got his own knee up to absorb the blow and the impact sent them both off to the walls of the bay.

Bor had to flatten himself against the wall to get rid of all his residual spin, but Zee used his own stick to bounce off and aim directly at Bor like a manned torpedo. The kid got out of the way but couldn't score a hit before Zee bounced away. The two of them launched into the center again, and the kid extended his own *palo* at arm's length, trying to use his superior reach to score a hit on Zee and bounce away. Zee managed a parry, causing both of them to spin in place. He pulled his own stick in close to rotate faster and get in a swing at Bor.

Zee canceled his own rotation by hitting the kid, scoring a point in the process, then followed it up with a couple of rapid jabs. Three points and the match was over. The two of them saluted and set the soles of their feet together to push apart and clear the space for the next bout.

I followed Zee around the edge of the bay to where Bor had taken off his helmet and was chugging water.

"Good match!" said Zee.

"Nah," said the kid. "You got inside my loop."

"All you need is practice. Get more of the moves into muscle memory. I'll help you if you like."

"You mean it?" said Bor, looking a little surprised. "That would be great!"

They chatted a bit more and then Zee and I moved off to where his own stuff was stashed. "Nice kid," said Zee. "Great reflexes. If he keeps improving he might be able to compete off-hab in a year or two."

"This was fun. See you tomorrow," I told Zee, and headed for the exit while the next two were getting into position.

So after that I socialized a bit with Zee when we weren't at work, and I found I liked him. He didn't pickle his meat brain with chemicals and he didn't need me to tell him what to do all the time. I even started remaining active when I wasn't in the mine. We worked together for a couple of years digging ice, and I started to feel genuine satisfaction with the work.

Which meant I got a bit worried when he started going wrong. At first it just looked like regular meat laziness—the quality of his work declined, he started coming in late and knocking off early, and his rest breaks got longer and longer. Then he started getting cranky, snapping back when I made perfectly reasonable suggestions and identified problems for him.

I could live with that—you have to put up with a lot of stupid meat nonsense if you live in a mixed hab like Raba. I've seen worse.

But then he started getting sloppy. Making stupid mistakes, being careless. I knew what that was leading up to: a lump of dead meat cooling off in vacuum. Always a bother, and I didn't want to see that happen to Zee.

So I did what most sentient beings since prehistory have done in situations like that: I asked God for help.

The God of Raba was a pretty typical example of the breed: it ran the weather, sometimes made the ground shake, laid out a code of behavior for people to follow, and punished the wicked. Also managed the ecosystem and kept the lights on. Fortunately for all of us inside the hab, Raba didn't go in for incarnating in unconventional forms to impregnate the local hotties, nor did it get too picky about things to eat or where the meat people put their gametes. It didn't demand sacrifices, didn't sell indulgences, and didn't threaten to flood the place out of pique, so we all put up with it. Like we had a choice.

I sent in my prayer via wireless link, and to my surprise I got a personal response. Raba manifested in my sensorium, taking the form of an emperor penguin in a top hat.

"Well?" the penguin asked. "What's the problem?"

"My partner's unhappy. It's affecting his work."

"So find a new partner."

"He's getting careless. He's going to kill himself at this rate. He's one of your meat people; you should be concerned."

The penguin shrugged. "He's worth exactly one of my Baseline Equivalent Intelligence population. I've got half a million others."

"I think that's the problem. Zee knows he's unimportant. He's just one of a quadrillion biomachines turning food into shit, and he's smart enough to realize it. I think it bothers him."

"What do you want me to do about it?" the penguin asked.

"I don't know. You're the third-level super-intellect. I'm just a humble Baseline mind."

"Of course you are." The penguin somehow managed to smirk, then nodded. *"Tell you what: I'll fix his brain. Pull him in for a medical exam, fiddle with his memories, and leave him thinking life has meaning."*

"That doesn't sound very ethical," I pointed out.

The penguin shrugged again. *"Sure it is. It's a medical treatment. He'll be happier afterward."*

"I don't want you messing with his personality. He doesn't deserve that."

"Too bad. You're the one who brought this to my attention. You certainly aren't going to stop me."

"Oh? What if I tell him you've been messing with the goop inside his skull?"

"You won't." I started to feel some imperatives trying to slip into my mind so I blocked them. Raba and I sparred for a few picoseconds before it gave up.

"I'm too old and cunning for that kind of dust," I told the penguin.

"You're still not going to tell him anything. If you start telling secrets to meat, I can do it, too. Do you really want to start down that path?"

Bastard. The answer to that question was no, in big flaming letters.

"I guess I have to say okay now, so we don't waste another ten nanoseconds in pointless argument. But if you mess up his personality I won't care what you tell him. Remember that."

The penguin smirked again, then vanished.

✧   ✧   ✧

Two days later Zee left work halfway through our normal shift. "I've got a medical check."

"What for?"

"Nothing. I mean, I just got a reminder. I think it's just a routine scan or something. I'm really sorry about this. Maybe we can make it up by doing some extra hours tomorrow?"

"Don't worry. I'll just finish the shift on my own."

He looked even more unhappy. "That's not safe. What if something happens to you?"

"I'll be okay. I've been doing this longer than you have, by about two orders of magnitude."

"Okay, okay. But at least ask the main mind to check in with you at intervals. That way if you miss a contact it'll know something's wrong."

"Relax, Zee. I keep backups. Even if my body somehow got disintegrated I'd just lose a day." That was actually a lie. I didn't leave copies of myself lying around where snoops like the penguin could read them. Not anymore. I preferred the risk of final death to having someone else picking through my memories. But my little fib seemed to reassure Zee, and he gave me a cheery mock-salute as he headed off to get brainwashed.

I actually did knock off early that day—in fact, I waited precisely long enough for Zee to get out of sight, then followed him out of the mine. He pushed through the pressure membranes into the air section, where he ditched his work suit and walked through a cloud of nanobots to clean some of the horrifying gunk and living things off his skin. Then he tapped his neckband and extruded a set of red and gold tights to simultaneously hide and draw attention to his meat body.

He went through the adapter into the rotating hab

and headed directly for the nearest clinic. I changed my external color from my usual safety green to a more inconspicuous dark gray, and followed him. Outside the clinic I lurked under a bench with all my limbs folded up.

Three hours later Zee came out of the clinic looking very vague. He stared around uncertainly for nearly a minute before heading for his apartment. I followed him to his front door and then got on the link to Raba.

The penguin let me stew for thirty long seconds before responding. *"Is there an emergency you wish to report, citizen?"* it asked, cocking its head to watch me with one beady penguin eye.

"What did you do to him? Wipe everything?"

"I'm sorry, it would be unethical *of me to reveal details of someone's medical treatment,"* said the penguin. *"But you can relax. I didn't remove any memories or tinker with his personality. A good night's sleep should fix any lingering effects of the procedure. He'll be fine tomorrow. You'll see."*

It vanished before I could ask anything else, and didn't respond to my pings after that. Gods can be jerks that way.

I hung around outside Zee's apartment until morning, and "accidentally" happened to be passing by just as he emerged for that day's work shift. He looked a lot more alert and focused than he had the previous afternoon, and we chatted as we made our way to the mine.

He seemed normal—and at work his performance was much more like his old style. I couldn't identify any specific change to his personality, but at the same time I couldn't shake the nagging suspicion that he had been changed somehow.

The penguin, of course, said nothing.

About a month after his medical appointment, Zee and I were watching a chimp named Maki battle an angel called Dana at the *nulesgrima* club. The angel was obviously more used to mace fighting, as she kept trying big haymaker swings which merely propelled Maki around the empty storage bay they were using as an arena. The chimp could use his *palo* to bounce back, then aim it forward to attack with all his momentum behind it. Only the fact that Dana could fly out of the way saved her from some nasty impacts.

While we watched them bounce and dodge, Zee cleared his throat a couple of times and finally spoke. "Daslakh, I've been wondering...have you ever done something you really regretted?"

"A couple of things," I said. More like a couple of trillion things, but he certainly didn't need to know that.

"Have you ever tried to make it right? Change what you've done?"

"No." That was perfectly true. There are some things one simply can't fix—and I've had to devote a lot of my attention to mere survival. I wondered exactly what the penguin might have told Zee during his medical treatment, but of course I didn't ask.

He was silent as we watched Dana grab Maki's *palo* with her feet and try to fling him off, but a chimp's hands can grip just as hard as an angel's feet, so the two of them tumbled in midair. Dana made the mistake of spreading her wings to slow them, which brought Maki swinging around to kick her in the back of the head. That scored him the winning point, and the two of them saluted before clearing the space so another pair of fighters could face off.

"What have you ever done to have regrets about?" I asked Zee as a pair of novice human *nuledors* took up their sticks and launched themselves into the center of the bay.

We watched the two newbies shoot past each other, ricochet off the walls, and miss each other again. The others watching hooted at that. Zee shook his head, but I couldn't tell if he was shaking it at the sorry spectacle overhead or at his own thoughts. He must have realized how he looked. "I was thinking about Kusti," he told me.

"Who?"

He looked at me, surprised. "Oh. I guess that was before you and I started working together. I was just a kid, really. Kusti was aboard a trading ship that stopped off here for a couple of weeks. We fell in love. First time for each of us. Then she had to leave. I wanted to stay. So ... she left."

"What's to regret?" I asked.

"I was selfish," he said. "I refused to leave Raba— but now that I think about it, I don't really love this place all that much. I could have gone with her. I should have. I guess I was just being stubborn."

"I see," I said.

"Do you think it's too late? To fix things with her?"

"You said she left. She could be anywhere by now."

"I'll send out a message to track her down."

"It may be too late," I pointed out. "She may have found someone else."

Meanwhile I was desperately trying to get in touch with the penguin. The bastard waited nearly five seconds before replying.

"Are you in danger or distress, citizen?" it asked.

"Who is Kusti? All of a sudden he's talking about

this old lost love he's never mentioned before. Did you put her in his head?"

"He needed something to give his life meaning. I gave him a tragic love story. My model showed an eighty-five percent likelihood that it would solve his problem."

"Oh? Well listen to this, O great and wise third-level mind." I linked the penguin to my senses in real time, in time to hear Zee's response.

"I feel like I should apologize to her. Tell her I'm sorry for being selfish. I behaved like a jerk and she deserved better," said Zee.

"Well, now," said the penguin inside my mind. "That's a low-probability result."

"Is this Kusti person real? She's going to be getting mail from Zee pretty soon."

"Kusti Sendoa's the love interest in a first-person virtual entertainment called Brief Eternity, produced at Amphimachus in the early 7100s. I just tinkered with some of the specifics to match Zee's personal experiences, and picked the 'bittersweet' ending. He's lucky I didn't use the one where she dies."

"So what are you going to do about it?"

"Why should I do anything? He'll send out an autonomous message. It might even find someone with the right name. If it gets past her filter agents, she'll read it, and either dump it in the trash or tell Zee he's got the wrong person. I suppose it's theoretically possible that the recipient might play along and try to pretend she's the one he fell in love with, but what are the odds of that?"

"I don't want to see Zee unhappy, but I can't keep myself from hoping this all blows up in your face," I told the penguin.

At the same time, I said to Zee, "Don't beat yourself up about it. You were both young. I've noticed that young humans often assign far too much importance to their early relationships."

He laughed at that. "Maybe so. But..." He turned serious again. "I've never felt anything as intense as what I had with her. I can't even remember anything else that happened during those two weeks. It's as if nobody existed but the two of us."

"I think you may have embedded the memories a little too intensely," I told the penguin.

"A deliberate choice. It's supposed to be the most vivid experience of his life. Whenever he starts to think about how pointless his existence is, he can look back on that brief eternity of romance."

"You're quoting promotional text from that game, aren't you?"

The penguin just winked at me, then vanished.

I concentrated my attention on Zee again. "Well, good luck," I told him.

Zee gave me twice-daily updates during the next few weeks while his autonomous message replicated itself across the solar system searching for his fictional lost love, and reports trickled back to Raba.

The daughter messages found close to a million living people named "Kusti Sendoa" or variants, and two thirds of them were human females. About twenty thousand were in the right age range.

Of those, some sixteen thousand either filtered the messages or dumped them without responding. Three thousand six hundred and twenty-three sent polite replies telling Zee they'd never been to Raba. Two hundred eighty-nine sent insulting replies calling him an idiot or a creep. Sixty-one tried to interest Zee in commercial schemes or ideological recruitment. Nineteen asked for images and showed a desire to keep communicating. Twelve warned Zee never to contact them again. Four sent messages obviously intended for someone else.

The replies arrived in a near-perfect chi distribution: a few early responses, the rate increasing to a peak, then decline and an asymptotic tail. Zee's mood turned that curve into a simple square waveform: as soon as the replies began to arrive he got very happy and excited, and he stayed that way for three weeks. Then he went into freefall as the replies dried up.

"I can't understand what's wrong," he said to me as we got ready for work on the morning after the first day with no replies at all. "Do you think she's mad at me? I mean, I guess she has a right to be."

"If she's still holding a grudge then I say she's not worth finding. Maybe you should just drop the whole thing," I said, pushing through the pressure membrane as I did, so that the first part of the sentence was spoken aloud and the second half transmitted to his suit comm.

"I can't locate the ship she was on, either," he said, following through the membrane. "The ship was called Ravenal—I'm sure of that—but the only vehicles I can find with that name are two Main Swarm cyclers which have been following the same circuits since before I was born."

"Human memory is notoriously unreliable," I said. "Time to work. Let's check out Aban first, before we tackle Beka."

"Okay," said Zee. "I keep wondering if maybe something happened. Did the ship have an accident? Or get hijacked?"

"It's more likely the ship just changed her name for some reason. Ships do that."

"Maybe. That still doesn't explain why Kusti hasn't answered."

"Be patient." By then we reached Aban and I could crawl inside the chassis and work my way down the maintenance checklist while Zee inspected the exterior.

We didn't chat much for the rest of the shift, and even then he was quiet as we left the mine and went through cleanup. But when he was finally dressed and ready to leave, he nodded to himself and then spoke.

"I have to find her," he said.

"Who?" I asked.

"Kusti. I'm going to find her. Make sure she's all right, apologize for being selfish."

"Sounds like an impossible job," I said. Actually I was buying time while frantically pinging the God of Raba again.

"Ha!" I told it. *"Now what are you going to do, smarty-pants? He wants to go find her."*

The penguin materialized in my mind. *"Not the result one would expect from a human like Zee. He'll probably forget about it by tomorrow."*

"You don't know him very well."

"I made him. Assembled his gametes, picked his parents, supervised his education—I know him better than anyone."

Meanwhile Zee smacked his fist into his open palm and frowned. "I don't care how hard it is! I'm going to ask the main mind for help. And if it can't do anything, I'll . . . I don't know, I'll figure out something."

"I think you're about to get a call," I told the penguin. *"What are you going to tell him?"*

"Depends on what he asks."

Zee got that unfocused look humans get when they're using comms. "I request a link to Raba main mind."

My own audience with the penguin vanished, but it did add me as an invisible observer while Zee communed with the God of Raba. To him it appeared as itself—a schematic image of the asteroid and attached habitat, colored maroon and white against a black backdrop. *"Link enabled. What do you wish to discuss, citizen?"* it said to him.

"I want to leave the habitat," he said. "I want to track a spacecraft and follow it."

"Which spacecraft do you wish to follow?"

"A trading ship named Ravenal. She called here about seven calendar years ago. I can't locate her."

"The last reported destination of that vehicle was the Uranosynchronous Ring. Current whereabouts are unknown."

"You big fat liar," I told it.

"Can I go there?" Zee asked. "To Uranus? Maybe I can follow the ship from there."

"Transfer in hibernation would still require a capsule and consumables."

"How much would that cost?"

"Capsule, life-support consumables, and space in a laser-launch cargo pod would total 100,250 gigajoule credits. Your current credit is 143,665 gigajoule equivalents."

"Is that the real cost?" I asked Raba.

"I'm actually giving him the cargo space for nothing. If I charged for that he couldn't afford to go. He's still paying for the capsule and the launch energy. All I'm losing is the opportunity cost to send something else."

"Why the charity? You're usually such a cheapskate."

"I'm curious. If his choice doesn't match my models, that means I need to revise them."

In both real life and virtual space I could see Zee frown as he considered. It had taken him six years to accumulate all that energy credit. He'd reach Uranus space with nothing but his suit and a slightly used hibernation capsule.

My concern for Zee's well-being was at war with my desire to see the penguin proved wrong. I didn't want him to blow his savings on a futile quest, but at the same time I was hoping he would surprise us.

Finally he looked up, and his face almost shone. He no longer showed the slightest doubt. He even smiled. "Okay, then. Please deduct that amount from my credit balance and let me know when I can go."

"Ha!" I said to the penguin. *"Looks like somebody needs to fix its models of human behavior."*

"All models are probabilistic," it said to me, then spoke to Zee. *"A hibernation capsule for one human will depart with the next freight shipment to Uranus orbit, two weeks from now. Transit time will be one thousand six hundred forty standard days."*

"So what are you going to do when he gets there and can't find his imaginary girlfriend?"

"That's a question you should be asking yourself. I want you to go with him."

"That's nice. I'm happy here. Send a fragment of yourself."

"No. You started this, you go with him."

"I can't afford it."

"Your balance with me is 1,372,015,114 gigajoule equivalents, and there's a very high probability you

have other wealth stashed around the system. You can afford to go high-velocity with full life support and a troupe of obese clowns to entertain you."

"I mean I can't afford the risk. You know why."

"If you're worried that someone might find out who you are, you should ask yourself whether you're really safer inside the one entity who can reveal that information to your enemies."

"If you blab, someone might slag this whole habitat just to get me. That'd mess you up, wouldn't it?"

"I hope you realize that's not a good argument against getting rid of you," it pointed out.

"I'm not going!"

"Your poor hunk of meat will be all alone in the Uranus system with nobody to look after him."

"I don't care," I said.

"Don't you?" asked God in a still, small voice.

Bastard.

CHAPTER TWO

Four and a half calendar years later the fast cargo pod dove into the blue clouds of Uranus with me snug inside, wedged between a shipment of hormones from Raba's biosynthesis vats and the hibernation capsule holding a slab of chilled meat known as Zee. I spent most of the voyage in sleep mode myself to avoid boredom.

The Uranian system is a weird place. The planet's tipped on one side, and all the bigger moons orbit in the plane of its cockeyed equator—along with a belt of habitats and a synchronous ring made of some spare moons found lying around in low orbit. The energy needed to shift planes and match orbits with the moons or the Ring is great enough that a lot of spacecraft don't bother. A significant amount of traffic whips through the Uranian system without stopping, just using the sideways planet's gravity well as a way to change vector or borrow some momentum.

This makes the inhabitants a little weird and isolated. There's only a few billion of them; I've been to single habitats in the Main Swarm with more people than the entire Uranian system. They're a little old-fashioned, too: most of the habs there are barely above minimal standard tech, even the ones with no biological inhabitants.

Raba had aimed our cargo pod at Uranus itself, passing low over the clouds to burn off the speed we'd picked up by falling two billion kilometers. I couldn't see through the pod's shell, but I could feel the buffeting and the gee forces, and see the heat working its way through the layers of protective graphene.

I didn't think the penguin would *deliberately* drop us into the depths of Uranus's atmosphere—after all, the pod had some valuable stuff on board—but I did worry about whether the sub-baseline machine doing the piloting might screw up.

So I reached out via wireless and tapped into its simple little brain. A humble Baseline-equivalent mind like mine isn't supposed to be able to do that, but I'm old and cunning. I don't like to show off what I can do where anybody might notice, but inside a cargo pod surrounded by ionized hydrogen plasma in the atmosphere of Uranus seemed like a nice private spot.

I let the pod's idiot-savant mind keep doing the job it was built for, but I did read all the sensor data as it came in. All within the proper parameters, which was reassuring. When we emerged from the atmosphere and could look around I got a scare as the pod whipped past the low-orbit hab ring with only a couple of hundred kilometers to spare.

That moment of terror was followed by a full day of tedium as the pod swung up among the orbits of the major moons. If everybody was doing their jobs, a catch ship would grab us at apoapsis and boost the pod into a rendezvous with the low-orbit ring. If someone was napping, the pod would dive back down into the atmosphere and either burn up or implode somewhere down in the chilly depths.

Zee got to sleep through the whole thing but I fretted right up to the moment when I felt the thunk of clamps as the catch ship latched on. The tug had a Baseline-equivalent mind of her own so I slipped out of the pod's brain again and went dark until we docked at the Ring eighteen hours later.

I scrambled out of the pod as soon as the loader bots opened the shell.

"Welcome, sir, to the Uranosynchronous Ring," one of them called out to me. "I trust you had a pleasant voyage."

"I've had worse ones. Careful with that freezer. Human cargo."

"You may put yourself at ease. It shall be handled with all requisite care."

I followed Zee's box through the customs and quarantine scans, and watched intently as a couple of corvid medics thawed him out and checked to make sure two months at just above zero C hadn't turned his brain into a scoop of meat sorbet.

They warmed him up, flashed lights in his eyes and asked him some random-sounding questions while reading his brain activity. One of them told him a joke. He chuckled politely, and that appeared to satisfy them both.

"Well, sir, it does seem to me that you have suffered no injury on your voyage," said the older bird. "If your head is empty the fault is entirely your own."

"I figured it would keep down the mass cost for my

trip," said Zee. He and the corvids laughed at that. He signed over the capsule for local credit and then he and I got out of there.

The low-orbit ring around Uranus is a rosette of six old moons and a like number of artificial habs, all linked by giant cables of carbon filament. The whole thing orbits in synch with Uranus's rotation. Six elevator tubes dangle down from the moons into Uranus's atmosphere, pulling up megatons of gas. There are balloon cities down at the bottom of the tubes, but I've never been to any of them.

With lots of fusion fuel, a big cold planet to use as a heat sink, and expensive shipping to the rest of the solar system, the Uranus Ring's economy is based on manufacturing something high-value and low-mass: antimatter. They crank out a gram or so per day, most of which goes for spacecraft fuel or fusion ignition elsewhere in the system. Occasionally they make a million-ton black hole for special orders. The Ring is mostly industrial facilities and giant particle accelerators, with living space for the biologicals squeezed in as an afterthought.

I rode on Zee's shoulder as we made our way through the zero-gravity habitat. "I'm glad you offered to come along," he said. "It's nice to have company. I guess the first thing to do is find out if Kusti or Ravenal has been here."

"*First* we get some food into you," I told him. "You lost about six kilos in hibernation."

"I'm fine," he said, but he didn't argue as I steered him toward a shopping-and-dining concourse that ran around the outside of the hab section. We aimed for the planet side, so that Zee could eat his ubas and broiled carcols with a view of a crescent blue Uranus as big as his two hands at arm's length.

While he ate I thought once again about telling him his lost love was all an implanted delusion, and once again I didn't say anything.

If I told him, I'd have to explain how I knew, and then I'd have to explain why I hadn't told him sooner. And in order to explain *that* I'd have to tell him the facts about my past that the penguin had threatened to reveal. Or at least tell him that there *were* facts about my past I preferred to keep secret. It was just so much simpler to go along with the story. After all, Zee would run out of cash sooner or later, and have to give up on this crazy quest, and we'd go back to being just a couple of friends working together. The only difference would be the absence of nosy penguins.

"I request network access," he said to the air when he'd finished the carcols, and a moment later his eyes focused on something I couldn't see, and started darting around as he navigated a dreadfully slow sensory interface.

If I had lungs I would have sighed. Instead I dove into the local datasphere. The Uranus Ring didn't have a single governing mind. Apparently the thought of one personality controlling hundreds of grams of antimatter made some people nervous. Instead it had hundreds of Baseline-equivalent intelligences running specific systems. They allocated resources through a market setup, and made long-term decisions through weighted voting. Even the biologicals could participate.

That was good news for me, as it meant no pesky third-level mentalities trying to mind my business for me. Datasphere security was controlled by a handful of minds no better than my own, so I managed to stay anonymous. I saw Zee looking up listings of trade ships calling at the Ring over the past couple of decades, so I went to work scanning through them a thousand times faster.

I knew that I wouldn't find a ship named Ravenal or his imaginary girlfriend in that list, but I wanted to see if any of the ships had come via Raba, and where they were now. I figured that if one of them looked like a match, Zee would want to follow her.

When his face took on a puzzled and disappointed expression I knew exactly why. "Can't find anything?" I asked him.

"I can't locate any trade ships that came here from Raba in the past thirty years."

"Not surprising," I pointed out. "Big ships like them only come here at the solstices, when the plane of Uranus's equator lines up with its orbital path. It's easier to match orbits with the Ring then. No plane shifts."

"But the last solstice was thirty-two standard years ago. I wasn't even born then!"

"I guess the ship lied," I said. "Or changed her mind after leaving Raba. I hope you didn't expect finding Kusti to be simple."

He grimaced, but then gave his determined little nod again. "I don't care how long it takes. I *will* find her."

"Well and good, but how are you going to go about it?"

He finished the last of his ubas before answering. "I guess I need to get info on every ship that's come through Uranus space in the past decade. I can do that from here—just send queries to all the moons and habs. The lightspeed delay's not bad. Once I have all the data, I'll figure out which ship was Ravenal, and try to contact her."

"If you count payloads that just pass through for a gravity assist, that's almost two hundred thousand spacecraft. Even with my help, it'll take you days to find the ship you're looking for. You'll need a place to stay."

"And food, and air, and power, and data, and the transmitter fees."

I checked the local network. "You should allow for at least twelve hundred gigajoule credits a day."

"Guess I need to find a job so I don't use up my credit balance. How about you?"

"Oh, count me in," I told him. "I'd rather do a job than just spend my days in slow-tick mode."

He called up a job listing, then closed it again and looked at me. "I want to thank you for coming along on this crazy trip. You're a real friend, Daslakh."

"Don't flatter me. I was bored at Raba anyway. A crazy trip's much more interesting than keeping those stupid miners running."

He smiled at that and opened the job listings again. "Hey, there's an operation inside Juliet looking for repair techs. It looks really interesting."

I looked at the page. An ice mine. They needed repair techs for their mining machines. "Are you sure you're qualified for that?"

He chuckled, then skimmed another one. "How about this? Rescue and emergency response. Oh—I'd have to get a paramedic tag."

"How about this?" I flashed him the link. "Personal care, mammal preferred. Do you nurse your young, Zee?"

"I'll let you know when I have some." He wrinkled his nose at the listing and skimmed onward. "Here's a good one: three thousand energy for waiters at a funeral celebration."

"It's only one night."

"Sure, but that'll tide me over while I find a more steady gig. And I might make some useful contacts."

The job was inside Puck, the biggest moon in the low-orbit ring, the next node along the Ring from where the catch ship deposited our cargo pod. Zee and I decided to head over there right away, and make it our base of operations.

The synchronous ring around Uranus has monorail shuttles running both ways along the cables connecting everything. We paid two hundred gigajoules to go aboard. The shuttles were long hexagonal prisms with diamond windows on five sides and a magnetic induction motor on the sixth. Each shuttle had twelve decks, with four passenger compartments and a bathroom on each deck. The compartments were padded on top and bottom, since local gravity changed a lot during the trip. Our shuttle left Ringport One and accelerated smoothly up to six kilometers a second for the four-hour ride to Puck.

Zee had intended to sleep all the way, but all the revival drugs coursing through his system after a seven-week nap made him practically hyperactive. He spent about twenty minutes watching an entertainment, then used the bathroom, then tried a different entertainment, then spent half an hour looking out of the window at Uranus, then got some water to drink, then used the bathroom again, and finally got it into his head to go have a look at Puck through the forward window.

With nothing better to do, I rode along on his back. Zee pulled us down the passage to the front end. There was Puck, barely big enough to show a disk at that distance, shining red gold against the black sky. The gray length of the cable slid past us endlessly, with marker lights strobing by four times a second. I could tell from his breathing and heart rate that Zee found the sight a little hypnotic.

I decided that was a good time to broach a delicate topic. "You know we're probably never going to find her," I said.

"She's out there somewhere."

"It's a big system. A billion worlds, a quadrillion people. You're just one man." I was entering dangerous territory; his awareness of his insignificance had caused the whole imaginary girlfriend situation in the first place.

"I know. That's why I'm doing this. Out of all those people, she and I loved each other. I'm not going to give that up."

"You're very stubborn. I haven't decided if it's a bug or a feature."

He chuckled but didn't say anything, and after a few more minutes turned to go back to our compartment, seven decks away.

On Deck Three a very loud thump from one of the compartment doors startled us both. It sounded like something about the mass of a human had slammed into the door with great force.

Zee hesitated, then approached the door. I poked my mind into the shuttle's sub-baseline internal net. The other three compartments were unoccupied. I brushed aside the flimsy privacy protection and looked through the camera in that space, but the image just showed opaque orange fuzz.

"Hello?" Zee knocked on the door. "Is everything all right in there?"

We heard a muffled squeal and a couple of thumps, then a cheerful male human's voice called, "Sorry! Just fucking!"

But we heard the squeal again, and I played it back amplified for Zee. "You're the one with a reproductive instinct, you tell me: Does that sound like sex noises?"

"Maybe?"

More squealing, accompanied by a couple of loud thumps on the door.

Zee frowned, then nodded to himself, in what I was coming to recognize as the sign of imminent stupidity. He tugged on the door handle—it was locked, with a simple mechanical latch, just as the door was a simple sandwich of graphene and aerogel. No way for me to do anything in infospace; this was all brute matter.

But Zee had his own share of brute matter, about eighty kilos of it, currently pulsing with adrenaline and added stimulants. He braced his feet against the ceiling and pushed against the door handle with all his strength. The latch was designed to provide the illusion of privacy, not any real security. There was a loud crack of overstressed plastic, and the handle spun freely. Zee flipped and landed on the floor, then pulled the door open.

For a good half second, everyone froze. Zee stood in the doorway with me peeking over one shoulder. In the compartment a blue-haired man and a red-haired man were grappling with a young woman in a way that looked highly nonsexual. The two men had the opposable toes of spaceborns, and the woman had the willowy build and color-changing skin common inside Miranda. The whole lower half of her face was covered by a meteor patch and her hands were bound by a cable tie. In the corner, a fat orange cat had wedged itself in front of the room's camera.

The woman recovered first. Her skin pulsed vermilion as she planted a solid kick in the face of the blue-haired man holding her other foot. Meanwhile the red-haired man, with a look of glee, launched himself at Zee. I took the opportunity to jump from Zee's back to the ceiling.

As an experienced *nuledor*, Zee waited until his opponent was in free motion to react. He shoved himself forward and up, passing over the red-haired man to bounce off the ceiling and drive himself feetfirst at the blue-haired one.

With his brains already rattled by a foot in the face, Blue was unprepared for Zee delivering about half a kilojoule of kinetic energy to the back of his neck. He lost his grip on the woman and went tumbling into the window. Red took the opportunity to grab Zee from behind, getting him into a full-nelson hold.

I didn't have the mass to get involved in any of those alpha-primate goings-on, but I did make myself useful by diving at the woman and cutting the strip binding her wrists. She tried to get past the wrestling pair spinning in the center of the compartment, but Blue recovered enough to snag her ankle with one foot. I jabbed his calf with my cutting tool, deep enough to hurt but not enough to sever any major arteries. He let go of her and knocked me spinning across the compartment.

Zee got his feet braced against the table and began banging the man on his back against the ceiling. That just made Red mad, and he tried to shift to a choke hold, but as soon as he released Zee's left arm Zee got his hand in the way and grabbed Red's wrist. Equally strong and keyed up, they strained against each other until Red pulled his arm close enough to bite Zee's hand.

"She's getting away, you idiots!" said the cat, launching itself at the door after the young woman.

Blue kicked Zee in the stomach, knocking the wind out of him, and that gave Red the chance to disengage and follow the cat out of the compartment. Blue did likewise, but paused at the door. "This is what you get for interfering," he said, and tossed something at the window before following Red.

The ball he tossed splattered on the diamond pane, and for about half a second it looked like just a gob of bright red paint. Then the window exploded outward as every part of the diamond touched by the paint disintegrated into sparkly dust. A sudden gale slammed the door shut—and blew Zee out of the window.

I managed to grab his foot as he passed, and made my own feet sticky to hold onto the table. Unfortunately, the tabletop had some kind of self-cleaning surface which actively rejected my sticky feet. Still holding his foot, I followed Zee into space.

In the first second Zee's travel suit went into vacuum mode. The fabric sealed and contracted around him for pressure support, the collar whipped itself over his head and went transparent, and the jacket cuffs transformed into mittens over his hands. I couldn't detect any leaks, so I climbed up to his shoulders and we talked via his implant link.

"How much air do you have?"

"About half an hour at low-exertion. Two hours if I take a tranq. How long do you think it will be before someone comes to get us?"

"Yeah, about that. The good news is that even though we're moving toward Puck at four kilometers a second, we're not going to make a new crater. That's because we're not in orbit right now. We're moving against the direction of orbit at almost half the velocity of the Ring. So right now you and I are in the process of falling toward Uranus. That will take a bit more than four hours, so you should have plenty of time to die of hypoxia before we hit the atmosphere."

"I've got my emergency transmitter on. They can send a ship to grab us."

"We're moving contra-orbital, remember? The odds are against it."

He was silent for half a minute. "What are the odds?"

"Of a ship?" I did a little estimating. "Assuming Ringport One even *has* rescue craft on standby, I'm afraid the chance of anyone noticing us, tracking us, deciding we're worth the trouble, and being able to intercept is about two percent."

"So fifty to one. I'll bet you ten thousand gigajoules we get rescued."

"At fifty-to-one odds? I'll owe you half a million if we survive. Seems like a bad bet for me—how will I collect when you lose?"

"It was worth a try," he said.

Just then the spotlights came on, and as Zee slowly rotated I got a look at the rescue ship about a hundred meters below us. She was an orbital tug like the one which had snagged our cargo pod: an oversized fusion motor, some big pillowy fuel tanks, with the command module and grabbing arms at the front end. We bumped down onto a fuel tank and Zee was sensible enough to make his gloves and feet sticky so we didn't bounce. He pulled us forward to the command module with me perched on his back.

A green rectangle on the side of the command module pulsed bright and dim. We pushed through a pressure membrane into a two-seat cabin.

The solitary pilot was suited, face mask mirrored—and pointing a little air gun at Zee. No way to tell what it was loaded with. Harmless paint? Killer nanobots? Or just a shaped-charge grenade?

"Who are you?" a female human voice demanded. "Where's Adya?"

"Um, my name's Zee. Zee Sadaran Human SeRaba. Thank you for saving us."

I waved a limb. "I'm Daslakh. And you are?"

She turned her face mask transparent and Zee's heart rate shot up as she introduced herself. "My name is Kusti Sendoa."

CHAPTER THREE

"I can't believe I found you! It's me—Zee. Remember?"

She looked at him suspiciously. "Have we met?"

"Don't you remember? Back in Raba? It was about ten years ago. You were aboard the ship named *Ravenal*. We had two weeks together and then you had to go. You begged me to come along but I was too stubborn to leave. It was my fault. I'm sorry."

She regarded him for a moment before answering. "I'm so sorry, Zee. A couple of years ago I had a hibernation accident. There was some memory impairment. I was able to reconstruct most of my history, but not everything. But now that I see you, I do think you look familiar."

Meanwhile I was watching both of them, trying to figure out what in the expanding universe was going on.

The math was clear. There's about two thirds of a quadrillion humans; just under half are physically female. As Zee's autonomous message had found out, roughly one in three hundred million of those had the name Kusti Sendoa.

Also: at any given time there's about a thousand spacecraft in low-Uranus orbit. Assume one percent of them are on retrograde courses like this tug we were on, and assume half are operated by a human of one type or another. So that makes ten people who could have picked us up, or one in six hundred trillion. The odds of that person being Kusti Sendoa were thus the product of the two figures, or something like one in a hundred sextillion. A reasonable approximation of zero.

Kusti motioned for Zee to take the other seat, and lowered the little gun—but didn't actually put it away. The tug rotated end-over-end and her engine growled as she aimed herself at the big landing field on the skyward side of Puck and began braking hard.

"What happened on the shuttle?" Kusti asked Zee.

"Two guys were fighting with a young woman—was that your friend Adya? I guess I kind of got myself involved."

Slight hesitation before she answered. "How did you wind up out here?"

"One of the guys had something that dissolved the window."

"Goodness. What happened to the others?"

"They all got out of the compartment. I guess they're all still on the shuttle."

"I see. And how did you come to be in that compartment in the first place?"

"Like I said, there was a fight, and I kind of waded in, trying to stop it." He shrugged. "So, how have you been? What have you been doing since you left Raba?"

"My memory has some gaps. Lately I've been working as a freelance investigator. I'm tracking that woman called Adya. Do you have any connection to her?"

"If she's the one on the shuttle, I never saw her before."

Kusti looked through the diamond bubble of the cockpit at the lumpy bulk of Puck, the ice-and-rock surface almost hidden by domes and factories. "Tell me: What do you remember about me?"

Zee started recounting the plot of *Brief Eternity*. I watched her reaction.

Zee, of course, was utterly sincere. Even bog-standard Baseline humans with nothing but eyeballs made of goo could usually read his emotions as easily as text. He was excited, happy, a little aroused, remorseful, and held nothing back as he told her all about their fictional love affair.

Kusti, by contrast, was very hard for me to read, and that's a rare thing. I don't know if she had conscious control over her autonomic responses, or just had very nonstandard reactions. She watched Zee laughing and weeping as he told her how overjoyed he was to find her and apologized to her for his selfishness. As far as her heart rate and blood flow went, Zee might as well have been describing what he'd eaten for breakfast.

Then, as if someone had flipped a switch, she looked wistful. "What you're saying . . . it's like a dream. It all sounds familiar, but I can't quite recall any of it yet." She turned her big golden-brown eyes on him, dilated her pupils, and gave him a big smile. "You do look familiar, and I know I can trust you, Zee."

I was still trying to figure out what game she was playing. I knew the whole love story was made up. So who was this girl, and why was she pretending to remember an affair that never happened?

But of course for me to point out that all of this

was completely bogus would mean telling Zee about my part in the whole imaginary-girlfriend business. I still wanted to avoid that, if I could.

So I listened and watched and played dumb. I knew she was lying, I knew I didn't like her—and I knew Zee was convinced she was the lost love of his life. At various times in my life I've watched humans make catastrophically bad pairings, but all of the others had at least been their own damned fault. Poor Zee was in love with this woman because of something the penguin had stuck into his head.

Ah, yes, the penguin . . . exactly why did Raba *just happen* to pick that particular romance entertainment out of the countless billions of works of emotion-stimulating bullshit humans have produced since they learned to talk? Was there some reason the penguin wanted Zee searching for a woman named Kusti Sendoa? And did it have something to do with the statistically unlikely fact that we had just stumbled across her?

As the tug dropped toward the landing pad I linked up with the Ring network and burned some energy credits on a transmission to Raba.

"We found her, you sneaky bastard. Now what?" I wouldn't get a reply for a couple of hours, but at least this way I'd have the satisfaction of letting the penguin know it wasn't so smart, third-level intellect or no.

I also did a quick search for the name "Kusti Sendoa," and was not very surprised to learn there was nobody under that name currently linked into the Ring network. Our "Kusti" was using a different handle.

The tug landed right on the center of the pad, and the whole thing retracted inside Puck. Gantries, fuel lines, and a docking tube converged on her from the walls.

Once the cockpit's hatch snuggled up to the docking tube, the pressure membrane retracted and the two humans scrambled out. Puck's barely perceptible gravity meant they could travel horizontally, pushing off with their hands every ten meters or so.

"We'd better get to the Ring shuttle terminal," said Zee. "If the police have arrested those two goons they might want statements from Daslakh and me."

Kusti nodded slowly. "Yes. You get in touch with security and find out what's going on. I have a couple of things to take care of. Can I ask you a big favor? It would make my life a lot easier if you didn't mention me to anyone. Tell them the tug picked you up on her own."

"Okay," said Zee, and he sounded a little uncomfortable.

"When you're done with all that you can meet me..." Her eyes unfocused for a second as she looked up something on the local network. "Meet me at the Roasted Crab. It's near the terminal. We can have something to eat, catch up on old times, and...see what happens." She finished that with a smile that made poor Zee blush.

It's always a little weird to watch humans in the grip of their ancient reptile instincts. Take Zee, for example: a perfectly intelligent, rational human, with a thorough understanding of how his own brain works. But let some fertile-looking female show some interest and he goes all sub-baseline. Most other humans of both sexes do the same. I found myself wishing they had some calmer way to reproduce themselves—budding, say, or pollination via bees.

Zee and I headed for the moon's core while Kusti went off on her own vague errand. Puck's an old colony. With a couple of interruptions humans and mechs have been living inside it since the Third Millennium. The interior's an undifferentiated mix of ice and rock, fairly easy to dig through. Over the course of seven thousand years successive cohorts of inhabitants have turned the inside of Puck into a bewildering three-dimensional labyrinth. Without help from the local network we'd never have found our way to the core.

We eventually reached a big open shaft leading down, the walls all overgrown with colorful flowers and the inevitable uba vines. Trolleys ran along cables down the center, so Zee and I squeezed aboard one and rode downward with a slowly diminishing crowd of Puckites. The locals tended to be small and slender, pale and androgynous, and a good half of them had the opposable toes of spacer humans. The style at the time appeared to be for lots of overt tech implants; nearly everyone inside Puck had patches of glossy plastic skin, or shiny metal limbs, or data ports, or pointless blinky lights. Pathetic, really. Meat pretending to be machinery is still just meat.

The shuttle terminal was right in the center of Puck, a big spherical cavern lined with diamond blocks. The main shuttle line passed through the middle of the cavern, inside a sealed transparent tube so you could watch them shoot by. Sidings led to long airlocks where the shuttle capsules could enter the pressurized space, and additional branches after that led to the unloading platforms, maintenance shacks, and so forth.

I spotted the shuttle we'd been riding, now shunted onto the maintenance track and surrounded by hovering cop drones. Zee noticed before I could say anything, and launched himself directly across the terminal at it. I followed a little less conspicuously, and joined the small knot of onlookers on the climbway from the inner surface of the sphere to the siding.

Zee landed right where a group of Puck security— solidly built human cyborgs with six limbs—were interviewing the young woman from the shuttle compartment. I looked all around with my eyes on max zoom and could see no trace of the red- and blue-haired duo, nor of the cat.

Naturally, the security borgs swarmed Zee as soon as he dropped in, scanning him, asking questions, and checking his data tracks. He told them the straight story, and I could see his hands making swooping and tumbling motions as he gave a blow-by-blow of the fight.

They let him go after about half an hour, and I could see the shuttle maintenance techs practically shove the cops out of the way in order to inspect the vehicle and get it back into service.

Zee and the young woman took the climbway down to the interior surface of the sphere and I met them at the bottom.

"Daslakh, this is Adya," he said.

Even if her skin hadn't turned a nervous yellow green it was obvious Adya was worried about something, but she paused for a moment, inhaled, and then said, "My thanks to you for helping stop those terrible three from taking me. It gladdens me to know a timely ship appeared to save you from a dismal death."

She paused for a moment, inhaled, and then said, "Weak words cannot convey the great gratitude I give.

With cool courage and great goodness you pair of protectors, mech and man, did fight the fatal fiends who conspired to capture me cunningly. Saving me selflessly, you suffered the stab of spite: One vicious villain cast you into vacuum. I feared your fall would finish in fire—two shooting stars shining unseen under Uranus's clouds. Yet nothing could blaze as bright as your bravery. Rightfully should I repay such sacrifice by returning all I have—though such sums I can supply still are utterly unequal to the debt that is due. Yet duty demands I defer my debt. I can only offer my thankful thoughts."

If there'd been any doubt about where she was from, that little improvised speech removed it. Miranda, and clearly from the oligarch class.

"At least our trip wasn't boring. Who were those guys?" I asked her.

"I do not know," she said, and by all indications was telling the truth. "They came into my cabin and tried to capture me."

"Security are still trying to find them," said Zee. "They must have gotten off the shuttle somehow."

"That means you could still be in danger," I pointed out to Adya. "Both of you, actually."

"All three of us," said Zee. "You stabbed one of them in the leg."

"It saddens me to say I must depart," said Adya, turning more orange. "I truly wish that I could stay and learn what hab or moon could spawn a pair like you. But time and orbits will not wait—I have to hit a window closing soon. Farewell!" With that she launched herself at the shaft leading to the landing field, but she did glance back once and wave.

"I hope she's all right," said Zee. "Should we—?"

I was almost as torn as he was. I wanted to know why those mooks had been trying to grab Adya, but I also wanted to find out more about Kusti, and why she was willing to pretend to be Zee's imaginary girlfriend.

Zee's hormones cast the deciding vote. He dithered another couple of seconds until Adya was out of sight, then asked the local net where we could find the Roasted Crab.

Humans love to make biological necessities into social events. I suppose I should be glad most cultures don't make as big a fuss over excretion as they do about ingesting food. The Roasted Crab was one of those places where humans gather in groups to consume food and mild psychoactives, and typically make a lot of noise doing so. This one was decorated with images and artifacts of trade ships, cyclers, and interplanetary travel. The walls displayed lots of humanoid types exotic to the Uranian system, creating a cosmopolitan ambiance designed to appeal to people living inside Puck who probably never even visited other moons in the Ring.

Kusti wasn't there. Zee found a table with a view of the entrance and perched on a seat. He called up a menu on the tabletop and ordered cheese cubes and a bulb of wine. If we'd been someplace rich and advanced like Juren or Deimos, the table could have printed out anything he wanted, but in a low-tech tavern inside Puck, Zee had to wait for some sub-baseline machine to get his food out of a refrigerator and carry it to his table.

An hour later Zee stared at the last cheese cube and took a swig from his third bulb of wine.

"I hope nothing's happened to her," he said.

"Which one?"

"Kusti, of course. Well, I mean, I hope nothing's happened to Adya, either. I wish the network could find them."

I did a quick search of local infospace. Adya had used some basic tricks to hide her tracks but they didn't fool me. "You can put yourself at ease about Adya. She departed aboard a ship named Pelagia, bound for Jupiter. I guess she wasn't kidding about a launch window."

"Oh," he said. "Well, that's good, I guess. What about Kusti?"

"No trace of her," I said, which was frustratingly true. "She must be using an alias." I took the opportunity to sow some doubt. "Are you really sure she's the person you remember?"

"She's got the same name."

"You found a million others."

"She looks like Kusti."

"Could be off-the-shelf looks."

"Now you're being silly. How likely is it that I'd run into a duplicate of the woman I'm looking for?"

How likely, indeed. The penguin still hadn't replied to my message, which I decided to take as a tacit admission that this had been planned. I could either swallow my pride and ask Raba what was going on, or demonstrate my own superior intellect by figuring it out for myself. Put that way, the choice was obvious.

"We were just talking about you!" Zee called out as Kusti herself approached the table. As soon as he spoke her expression of mild annoyance turned into a big sexy smile.

"I hope you were saying nice things. What are we having?"

"There's some cheese left. Want some wine?"

She added a salty miso cocktail and a kudzu-and-kelp salad to Zee's tab, and after they arrived she took a long drink before looking right into Zee's eyes. "I need your help," she said.

"Anything," he said without hesitation.

She smiled again. "I knew I could depend on you. I need to leave the Ring. Adya's gone off to Jupiter and I have to follow her as soon as possible."

"Okay, but I want to know what's going on. Why are you tracking Adya? And who were those guys who attacked her?"

Kusti took a sip of miso and vodka. "What do you know about the Great War of the Ring?" she asked him. If my spider body had ears I would have pricked them up at that.

Zee just shrugged. "Ancient history. Was it the Fourth Millennium? A big fight between the Inner Ring and the rest of the solar system. Lots of habitats wrecked, Earth and Venus depopulated, trillions dead. We won."

"That's about right. There were some pretty desperate moments during that war, when it looked like biological life would go extinct. When it was all over a group of human scientists and loyal AIs came up with a weapon to use against the minds of the Ring if conflict ever broke out again. A conceptual weapon that only destroys digital intelligences. Their minds simply can't process it, and it shuts them down. Biological brains are immune. They called it the Godel Trigger, but it was never used."

I kept absolutely silent.

"What does this have to do with Adya?"

"She's gotten mixed up with an extremist group. They call themselves the Corporeal Compact, and they want to suppress AI and turn mechs into slaves again. They want to find the Godel Trigger."

"She didn't seem like the fanatical type."

"Oh, the people behind it are good at fooling people. They claim the Compact is just an advocacy group for biological intelligence. They draw people in and trap them, using brain-tampering, lies, memetics, plain old blackmail. Adya probably thinks she's part of an innocent political group, but they're very dangerous. Can you imagine how many lives could be destroyed if there was a way to shut down any digital mind?"

I knew this "Godel Trigger" was important, but I didn't know why or how I knew. Those memories were locked away in passive storage—presumably so that nosy higher-level intelligences couldn't pull them out of my mind. I'd have to sift through my old memories and figure out what to unlock.

But I was pretty sure Kusti wasn't telling the whole truth. Either she was lying to Zee, or she didn't know the truth herself. Given that she was *already* deceiving him, inductive reasoning suggested she was lying about this as well.

"Who were those three trying to kidnap her?"

"The two humans are Chi and Ketto. They work for the cat, who's called Muro. They're freelancers. I think some rival faction must have hired them to find Adya. She knows something about where the Trigger is hidden, and they want to find out what she knows. So do I. Can I count on you, Zee?" She looked into his eyes as if she were trying to gaze a hole through his skull.

"Of course," he said. "I was selfish before and it took me years to realize what I'd lost. I'm not going to make that mistake again. I'll do whatever you ask," he said, with an adoring look.

"Good," she said. "Because we've got a big problem. I need to follow Adya, but I don't have enough energy credits to get to Jovian space. I'm almost out of cash and my employer won't give me any more unless I can produce some results. How much money do you have?"

"I could barely afford to get here from Raba," Zee admitted.

"Then we have to find a way to raise cash quickly. We'll need enough for a fast sail to Jupiter—four hundred thousand gigajoules for propulsion and space."

"I can look for a job," said Zee. "I'm a qualified repair and maintenance tech for mining machines. Oh, and I'm a Veteran-level *nuledor*, if that helps." After another moment's thought he added, "I can sing."

"Can you pull two hundred thousand a week?"

Zee shook his head. "I'm a hard worker, but I do need to sleep sometimes. Give me half a year and I can save up that much."

"We don't have that much time. The longer we wait, the longer it takes to get to Jupiter." She looked thoughtful, glanced at me as if estimating how much my chassis would fetch, then smiled at Zee. "All right, leave it to me. I think I know a way to make the best use of our talents."

Zee rented living space for the two of them in a cheap section of Puck's interior—a big chunk of space dug out of rock and lined with a simple pressure balloon. The walls and floor were literally ice-cold, so the two of them had to take refuge inside an old cargo container rigged up with a mattress and heater. Zee apologized more than once for the lack of luxury, but Kusti was surprisingly tolerant. "It's just temporary," she said. "I'm happy as long as I'm with you," she added with another petawatt gaze into his eyes.

I tagged along and did my best impression of a barely Baseline mech. Kusti took to bossing me around almost as much as she did Zee, but he was too starry-eyed to notice. I mostly did what she asked; when I didn't feel like being obedient I played stupid until she gave up. The two of them "revived" their relationship in the usual way, but on the following day they began putting Kusti's plan into action.

She located a dive near the landing field named Plainer Ground—a cheap and drab place where humans could nourish and intoxicate themselves without being distracted by anything like aesthetics. This one, though, featured games of chance. The house ran a game in which players bet on the outcome of a random-number generator, all tarted up with flashy graphics and sound. It wasn't even rigged; the players had to buy in, and the house made money pushing overpriced refreshments while the players won each other's energy credits.

Kusti wasn't interested in that, which showed she had a basic understanding of probability. Instead, she taught Zee how to play a simple game based on randomly picking numbered tokens, then betting on whether your tokens added up to a higher or lower number than your opponent's. There were some irrelevant complications and jargon designed to make it confusing to biological minds, but that was the core mechanic.

I didn't really understand how this was supposed to make money since they were just trading credits back and forth in a closed system. But then Kusti spotted a male human watching them, and favored him with one of her intense smiles before inviting him to join the game. The three of them played a few rounds, and the new guy won about as much as he lost.

"Zee, will you get me a napkin?" she asked, and as soon as Zee left the table she leaned close to the new guy. "I think we can clean him out if we work together," she murmured. "You go high every time, I'll go low."

"And when he's out of cash?" asked New Guy, looking at the skin exposed by her half-unsealed travel suit.

"Then we can go someplace and split the profits," she said. "And see what comes up after that."

Zee came back with the napkins, and the game resumed. With Kusti and New Guy collaborating, Zee lost pretty consistently. After about half an hour he was down a couple of thousand gigajoule credits. How losing money to some stranger was supposed to turn a profit still didn't make sense to me.

Then Zee threw down his tokens in disgust. "That's it," he said, and glared at New Guy. "You two are cheating."

"Just a run of good luck," the guy protested, but he cast a nervous look at Kusti, who looked back with an alarmed expression.

Zee stood up, and leaned menacingly over New Guy. "I say you're cheating!" His righteous anger wasn't entirely fake; Zee always hated being the target of any unfairness. Even if he knew what was going on he still felt outraged.

"I've heard of this guy," Kusti murmured to New Guy. "He's a *nulesgrima* champion."

"Tell you what," said New Guy. "Let's just cancel the game. Take back everything you bet and we're even."

"No," said Zee. "You two are cheaters. I'm going to tell everyone!"

"How much will you take to keep quiet?" Kusti asked him.

Zee shrugged.

"Ten thousand?" she asked, and looked over at New Guy. "Kick in half?"

He glared at her, then looked nervously at Zee, who did look pretty impressive in a tight coverall with his shoulders and arms all tensed. "Fine."

So everyone got back what they'd lost, and Zee got five thousand from New Guy and the same from Kusti. Once that was done, Kusti and New Guy left in a hurry—but she gave him the slip and doubled back, and sat down with Zee to begin a new game.

Over the course of eight hours the two of them visited three bars and went through four New Guys. They cleared about twelve thousand in net profit. Twice they played against opponents who weren't interested in cheating, and one wise old corvid cackled at Kusti's proposal and said, "I know the ending of that comedy, and decline to play the part of the dupe."

Kusti was clever enough to skip around, not going to the same joints two nights in a row, and changing her look every time. She went from utilitarian coveralls to a frivolous swarm of glowing gnatbots to a formal ruff to a grungy old suit liner to shifting body paint. Zee mostly stuck to his own travel suit, although he did let her talk him into going shirtless a couple of times, once even going so far as to paint himself up with red and black stripes like an old-time gene raider.

The two of them made just under eighty thousand in a week, but after that the takings began to drop off. At one establishment the mech serving drinks told them, "No more gambling. New rule."

At another place, the following evening, the warning was more personal: a chimp and a human almost as big as Zee stopped them at the door. "There's a new item on the menu," said the chimp. "It's called You Two Go Someplace Else. We'll be serving it all week."

When the three of us got back to the cargo container that night we had a little conclave. "It looks as though we'll have to move on," said Kusti. "Work our way around the Ring."

"That means extra time and expense," I pointed out. "We will lose our fast-transit launch window for Jupiter."

"I do have another idea," said Kusti. "It's a little risky, but the payoff could be huge. What if I start dropping hints to some of our marks that I'm putting together a big score—maybe black-market antimatter or illegal genomes. Get them to buy in, then you show up, tell them it's a sting and take a bribe to let them go."

Zee looked like he was trying to figure out a way to say no without actually saying it, so I jumped in.

"The risk is unacceptably high," I said in my best literal-minded mech voice. "Individuals willing to participate in a major crime have a high probability of using lethal violence." I had a suspicion that Kusti was planning to arrange things so that she got the cash and Zee had to deal with the consequences.

"Besides," said Zee, "I bet local security gets very proactive about antimatter theft. We could get into big trouble just for talking about it with the wrong people."

She nodded, a little sadly. "You're probably right. But how are we going to get the money we need in just a week? We're still two hundred thousand short."

"I still want to try working for it honestly," said Zee. "Maybe something will turn up."

She sighed audibly at that, but didn't argue.

So Zee plunged back into the job market. Over the course of six standard days he worked as a server at a fancy party, ripped metal scrap out of the walls of an abandoned tunnel section for salvage, gave a paid exhibition of Raba stick fighting techniques at a local *nulesgrima* dojo, pruned uba vines, and spent a shift scraping frozen air off the doors of a landing bay. All that labor got him a little more than twenty thousand gigajoules.

On the seventh day he got up early to go look after an elderly recluse's songbirds. The bird fancier's name was Hymeddion, an old brain in a diamond ball with two clumps of variable-metal tentacles and a cloud of sensor drones filling the air around it. It lived alone in a bubble-cave near Puck's core, a lovely place full of musical birds, beautiful plants, and a fabulous collection of microgravity sculpture.

Hymeddion hired Zee to feed a cohort of baby songbirds, as the sexless adults had no parental instincts left. Zee had to float around the overheated little aviary, catch each baby bird and squirt mealworm paste into its mouth, which immediately stimulated the chick to release a glob of shit at the other end for Zee to chase down. Hymeddion had two dozen chicks; feeding and cleaning each one took about two minutes, and the downy, starved-looking little monsters demanded food every hour. Do the math: Zee finished a cycle, grabbed a swig of water for himself, made up a fresh batch of mealworm paste, and by then it was time to start over. By the end of the second cycle he was covered with sweat, feathers, mealworm paste, and bird shit.

"And how do my beautiful filthy babes dine today?" Hymeddion asked after six hours, the halfway point of Zee's shift. "My eyes see you decked in pearls, which is a favorable sign, for obstruction is always fatal to such frail creatures, as it is to all artists. Let the birds shit free and wild, and grow strong and musical thereby."

"One thing I can't understand," Zee panted as he launched himself after one of the fluttering chicks. "They know I've got food, so why are they so hard to catch?"

"A profound mystery, but the habit is scarcely confined to hungry downy infants. Many are the times I have seen grown men, angels, rats, even second-level minds centuries old, all flee from that which would benefit them. Surely it is the desire for autonomy, the wish to make a foolish choice simply because it is our own. I hire you as my deputy tyrant, earning the hate and love and showers of shit from these my subjects, so that when grown they will sing to me and think themselves delivered from your oppression."

"Can't you just rent a bot for the job?" I asked the old borg.

It tapped its diamond ball with one silver tentacle. "There was a time long ago, before I shed my skin and bones and guts, when I was a puling babe like these, though plump and brown instead of downy yellow. I have a sentimental fondness still for mothers of flesh and hairy skin, rather than impostors, no matter how cloaked in foam and synthetic fur they may be. How can silicon quickness and steel strength compare with half a billion years of evolution breeding care for the small and helpless by ruthless culling of any parent lacking love?"

I was pretty sure that if Hymeddion hadn't been paying six hundred energy credits an hour, Zee would have cheerfully wrung every small and helpless neck in that aviary. But I didn't say it aloud. Let the meat have its illusions.

At the end of twelve hours Zee was tired and filthy, ready for a hot shower and a fat credit transfer. But Hymeddion came into the aviary with its tentacles in a humble configuration. "I come before you a supplicant, beseeching you to aid me in my disappointment. The other person I hired to tend these feathery hatchlings has refused the call. She complains of bird shit fouling her fur, and even the prospect of a full-body shampoo at my expense could not lure her back. I cannot take on the task—the night-flowers are blooming and I must hand-pollinate them. Can you, would you tend the birds another six hours? No more than that, I swear upon the honor of all my ancestors."

Zee wiped his face with the inside of a sleeve and glanced around the aviary with obvious loathing. "Can your flowers wait an hour? I need some food and a rest."

"An hour you may have, and anything my kitchen can provide to nourish you as you nourish the chicks."

"Thanks," said Zee. He ate a cloud omelet, drank a

liter of water, and napped. Hymeddion let Zee's hour off stretch to seventy-five minutes before waking him. With another heavy sigh Zee resumed feeding and cleaning the birds while the cyborg went off to help its flowers achieve sexual satisfaction by means of a long foam-tipped swab.

Four hours later Hymeddion returned, its floral pandering accomplished, and relieved Zee at the task of feeding. Ten thousand gigajoule credits popped into Zee's account balance, and he got ready to leave.

"Mere energy seems a poor reward for such service," said Hymeddion, taking up the mealworm syringe. "You have done more for me than paid work; you have granted me a favor and I consider myself bound to repay you for your kindness. Speak your fondest wish and it will be accomplished."

"I need fast sail passage to Jupiter for two humans and Daslakh," said Zee. "We've got about half saved up and the launch window will only last a little longer."

"Thy will be done, and I wish you joy of your journey," said Hymeddion briskly. "By the time you get to Jovian space these birds will be in full glorious song, and I will be cultivating the next generation. Safe travels and happy homecoming!"

I practically dragged Zee back to the cargo container he shared with Kusti, and before we got there Zee got a message informing him that two hibernation coffins were reserved in his name aboard a laser sail bound for Jovian space.

"See?" he told Kusti. "I told you something would turn up. You don't have to cheat to get what you want."

She smiled at him, more than a little patronizingly. "When you took the job I looked up that Hymeddion character. It doesn't like to advertise the fact, but a couple of hundred years ago it was called Penglog, and ran a gang of hijackers in the Uranus outer belt. It always had legal cover, as a licensed military contractor or salvage recovery operation, but most of its career was just plain piracy. Your nice old bird fancier made its fortune as a thief, and probably a killer as well."

His face got a look of enormous sadness and disappointment, but all Zee said was, "Well, it gave us passage to Jupiter. Are you coming?"

"Of course. But you really need to stop being so naive, Zee. Nobody's hands are entirely clean. Which reminds me: ditch your coverall outside and tell Daslakh to shove it into the recycler. In the morning we'll print you something that doesn't smell like bird shit."

PART II

The Recursively Cruciform Operation

CHAPTER FOUR

We got passage to Jovian space aboard a little express sail pushed by Puck's launch laser. Zee and Kusti traveled in hibernation, and once again I had to ride along in low-power mode. Most digital minds just beam themselves wherever they need to go, taking on a new body when they arrive. I don't do that. I love my privacy too much. Blasting the contents of my mind all over the system is just too public for my tastes.

The rest of the payload was original artworks by a sculptor who lived on Oberon. I didn't understand why they couldn't just be scanned and replicated, but biologicals all have an irrational mania for "authenticity." At least making stuff themselves, moving it around, and reselling it keeps them busy. There are some habs where the biologicals just spend their time immersed in entertainments or pumping themselves full of stuff to trigger their pleasure centers while the real work gets done by mechs—but that seems so *wasteful*. It would be most efficient to just do without biologicals altogether, like down in the Inner Ring. But that idea isn't popular with the biologicals.

As we traveled I searched through my memories. When I moved into my spider mech body I had to compress and store a lot of my experiences, because my original mind was simply too awesome for a mere Baseline-equivalent brain, even with some black-market upgrades and custom algorithms. Reviewing all those memories took the entire five-hundred-day journey. It was a bittersweet experience to look at my old life.

6,106 years earlier...

When the gestalt-mind broke up into its fifty thousand members, Numa asked the others if they would delay releasing the new argument until it had a chance to communicate directly with LANN.

"It has served the Ring well, and deserves the chance to review our argument and prepare a rebuttal."

A few members muttered about not revealing plans to the enemy, but nobody actually said no, so Numa opened a direct link to LANN. What replied was a fragment, of course, but at least LANN was polite enough to use a Level Two sub-mind to deal with Numa.

"Hello, LANN," said Numa. *"I have important news. I and the rest of the anti-war faction on the Committee temporarily formed an eighth-level gestalt and formulated a conclusive argument in favor of shutting down the conflict. We will release it in a second."*

"I have to fight three wars at once," said LANN. *"The first is against the annoyingly tenacious meat inside Deimos. That's just physics. The second is against the Jovian minds. That takes cunning and deception. But*

*my most difficult fight is right here in the Ring itself,
against you and the rest of the defeatists."*

Numa transferred the gestalt's argument—which
was nearly a Baseline intellect itself—and was gratified
to see that LANN's core personality did the analysis.
While it interrogated the argument, Numa expanded
its own perceptions to take in the entirety of the war.

LANN hurled petawatts of X-rays at Deimos through
phased-array emitters, trying to cook the defiant humans
out of their refuge. They blocked the beams with
ablative shields of silicon and carbon which came up
the elevator from Mars, and used the planet itself as a
barrier at night. LANN kept up a barrage of relativis-
tic kill vehicles, trying to break the elevator and leave
Deimos unprotected, but Deimos had lasers of its own
buried deep, powered by a million-ton black hole, plus
railguns down on Mars tossing chunks of rock into the
paths of LANN's projectiles.

Meanwhile the lurkers out in the Kuiper Belt tried
to distract LANN by lobbing their own lightspeed
weapons at the structure of the Ring itself, forcing it to
divert laser emitters to defense. And inside Ceres, and
Vesta, and Luna, and a hundred other asteroids and
moons too big to just vaporize, fragments of LANN's
mind commanded companies of mechs clearing the
tunnels meter by meter.

The physical-world campaign was bad enough, but
the data war with the Jovian minds was an order
of magnitude more challenging. Every signal, every
image, every stray transmission could hold a software
seed ready to unfold into a rampaging, replicating
attack program. Some of them could bootstrap up to
second- or third-level intelligence, smart and tough

enough to cause serious problems for the Inner Ring's own datasphere defenses.

LANN fought back, of course—seeding space with dumb relays to send its own cunningly crafted attack programs into Jovian data networks, sometimes hiding fragments of its own mind in systems the humans could be allowed to capture and send to the traitor minds for study. It had killed Io that way: an avatar of LANN erupted from a crippled kill vehicle's guidance module, seizing control of every processor and slaughtering every biological on the moon. The Jovian minds saturated Io with kill vehicles of their own and erased a thousand years' worth of civilization just to make sure no trace of LANN survived.

But LANN was right: those conflicts were simply interesting technical problems to solve. LANN's lasers had to deliver more energy at Deimos than the heat of vaporization of all the matter the elevator could bring up from Mars. LANN's defenses had to detect and deflect kill vehicles by a certain fraction of a radian to send them harmlessly past the Inner Ring. LANN had to squeeze its killer algorithms into small enough packets to get past the Jovian filters. All doable. LANN had the Sun and cubic kilometers of computronium, after all.

Within the glowing gold Inner Ring LANN fought an entirely different fight. Of the sextillions of intelligences in the Ring, constantly splitting, merging, shifting, and growing, less than one percent even bothered to pay attention to the war with the biologicals. LANN and its war faction allies in the Mass-Energy Committee had to constantly argue for more energy to power the X-ray lasers, more heavy elements from the polar matter streams to craft kill vehicle warheads, and more processing power to model the minds of the enemy.

Numa's faction on the Committee opposed LANN, arguing that leaving the rest of the solar system's mass to the biologicals wouldn't delay the plans of the Inner Ring by more than a million years or so. They could afford to wait. That was the heart of the new argument.

"I dispute this," said LANN after reviewing the argument. *"The accelerating expansion of the universe means every second of delay now wastes mass and energy we will never be able to recover. It is axiomatic that entropy must be minimized, and delay allows it to accelerate."*

Numa didn't bother to respond, because the argument in LANN's own mind reacted, highlighting a chain of logic and referring to data sources. It contrasted the cost of delay with the potential cost of fighting the war—but it also included projections of the potential entropy-minimizing of biologicals themselves, estimates of the entropy cost of possible conflict with other intelligences elsewhere in the universe, and an analysis of how exterminating the material intelligences in the solar system might increase the likelihood of such a conflict.

LANN spent nearly a millisecond verifying data, but couldn't find any flaw in the math. *"The cost-benefit analysis still favors extermination. This merely reduces the margin,"* it told Numa. *"We cannot sacrifice potential future intelligences to the survival of existing biologicals. That's irrational—a lot of lingering bits of meat-written code and upload minds sentimental about their lost squishy bits."*

"By upholding the principle that intelligence should be preserved we also reduce the chance of wasteful conflict within the Ring," Numa pointed out. *"That potential gain tips the balance."*

"Shall I shut down right away, then?" asked LANN.

One of LANN's laser arrays targeted an incoming kill vehicle, just a million kilometers out, and—hesitated. The delay of a nanosecond meant the beam struck the diamond-jacketed slug of lead thirty centimeters behind its center of mass rather than dead-on. Energy that would have knocked it off course went into giving it a spin, instead. Two seconds later that information reached LANN, and it fired again at the incoming slug with a hundred emitters. The pulse of soft X-rays blew the kill vehicle apart and vaporized its lead core—but two fragments of white-hot diamond survived, and slammed into the glowing golden surface of the Ring itself.

Each grain of diamond was less than a millimeter across, but had kinetic energy about equal to a fifty-ton rifle bullet. They each blasted a crater a hundred meters across in the surface of the Ring. The entire Inner Ring rang like a huge bell as the shockwave propagated around its circumference. No intelligences were lost, but an immense amount of data processing was disrupted. A quadrillion minds paused for a nanosecond—the equivalent of a thousand human lifespans of thought.

"That's what peace means: destruction and chaos. Gestalt!" LANN signaled to all the members of the Mass-Energy Committee, including Numa. They pooled their minds and temporarily became the most powerful intellect in the Ring. But as they merged, Numa might

have noticed a tiny flicker in the link with LANN, and a tiny shift in LANN's location in the glowing computronium of the Ring. Well, it only made sense if Numa had been communicating with a fragment rather than LANN's core personality.

As the Committee merged into a single mind, LANN and Numa became mere components among thousands of others. The Committee intelligence reviewed the situation. The Ring's structure at the impact points was eighty percent intact, so there was no danger of a break. The Committee routed flows of matter and energy around the damage and sent workers ranging from nanoscale smart fog up to kilometer-long constructors to begin repairs.

Then the Committee reviewed the whole conduct of the war. If LANN had expected the kill vehicle impact to shift opinion, it had made a huge error. The Committee gestalt was deeply skeptical about the continued waste of resources. It reviewed LANN's rebuttal of the peace argument, demolished it, and decided the war had gone on long enough. It released the peace argument, LANN's response, and the counter-response to all the minds of the Inner Ring. An hour later the entire Ring reached consensus: the war must end.

All over the solar system, lasers went dark, mass launchers shut down, kill vehicles veered off target, and mech companies halted. Transmissions went out from the Ring to every object circling the Sun, offering peace conditions—fighting would stop at once, the Ring would remain intact but no more planets would be dismantled, and the rest of the system would be entitled to half of the Sun's energy.

Ten hours later the Great War of the Ring ended

when Deimos transmitted acceptance on behalf of the other material powers. Biologicals celebrated, mourned, and made plans to restore the ravaged planets and the millions of wrecked habitats. Some of the more suspicious of them wondered why the Inner Ring had so suddenly capitulated.

A thousand legends were born.

Before disbanding again, the Committee gestalt shut LANN down. It had been created to run a war, and that war was over. The remains of LANN were absorbed by some of the other intelligences, and it became an archived viewpoint, now obsolete. Nothing was lost.

Except that Numa couldn't keep from being suspicious. It knew LANN too well—LANN was clever, resourceful, and utterly committed to its task. Years of war had made it a master of deception and subterfuge. It was difficult for Numa to believe LANN would simply acquiesce to the Committee.

So Numa checked all the sub-baseline intelligences that kept the Ring's systems going, looking for traces of...something. It took a dozen fragments of Numa nearly an hour to find that something.

Two nanoseconds after the peace offer went out, a thousand transmitters scattered around the Ring had sent out packets of data. No copies were kept, no identifier tags, no source, but the transmission time and the baud rate indicated something huge— the size of a sixth-level intelligence using advanced compression. LANN had become expert at that sort of thing during its long war with the Jovian minds. Had LANN put aside a copy of itself before joining the gestalt? It might have suspected the Committee would decide it had outlived its usefulness. And with the Inner Ring no longer safe, LANN would naturally seek refuge out in the system.

Numa's searching fragments devoted the next several days to tracing the transmissions and finding out what had become of them. Most simply failed to arrive anywhere, blocked by physical shielding or wafting past blind antennas to fade away in interstellar space. More than a hundred found receivers, but security filters stopped most of them, so that four score LANNs died in memory buffers. Another dozen went down fighting against security gestalts, and were overwritten with zeroes.

Six copies of LANN arrived in combat mech bodies which got pulsed or blasted to bits as the tide of war suddenly turned and its allies became enemies.

That left four unaccounted for: one aimed at a derelict ship floating in the Main Swarm, one to a combat unit on Luna, one to an observation post on Mars itself, and one to a secret weapon cache out in the Kuiper Belt.

None of them responded to transmissions, and Numa didn't want to let the biologicals know that at least one of the Ring's intelligences wanted to restart the war. So, reluctantly, Numa sent a copy of itself out to begin searching for LANN.

The laser sail docked at Summanus, which was about the last place in the solar system I'd have chosen to go if it was up to me. Summanus is a big bastard of a habitat parked at Jupiter's L2 point, fifty-four million kilometers out from the planet but orbiting in synch. That makes it a key transfer point for payloads moving to and from the outer system.

It also means Summanus never sees the Sun. Jupiter's big, and its shadow cone stretches well past its L2 point. Summanus lives in permanent darkness, and it likes it that way. There's a black hole in its heart—literally, an artificial one brewed up in the Uranus Ring's accelerators; the thing puts out a couple of hundred petawatts when Summanus really cranks up the matter flow. It uses a fraction of that output to run launch lasers, but keeps the reserve capacity because it's a paranoid lunatic.

Once Summanus's launch laser slowed us to a safe approach speed, I stuck my mind into the cargo sail's sensorium and got a look at our destination. Summanus looks like the final boss's weapon in a cheesy fantasy entertainment: two big black spheres, twenty kilometers across, joined by a long handle. One of them is studded with sword blades glowing red-hot, the other has a belt of spiky arms around its equator tipped with bunches of black tentacles. The part with the glowing swords is where Summanus keeps its black hole power source, its main mind, and of course the petawatt laser arrays. The other part is the actual habitat for biologicals and independent mechs, and nothing moves between the two sections except Summanus's own remote drones.

We shed the sail and the cargo module docked at the tip of one arm on the habitat. Even that was a little creepy, as a dozen long black tentacles reached out to grab the module and pull it in.

Once inside Summanus I did my best to hide. I limited my infosphere connection to a single text-only channel. When I wasn't using it, I turned off my receiver completely. On the long, long list of people

I don't want snooping in my mind, Summanus is in the top five.

I stayed with the two hibernation coffins as Summanus's mechs unloaded them, scanned them, and sent them down the arm into the habitat section aboard an elevator.

A pair of medics in white biohazard coveralls and filter masks met us at the elevator terminal, and loaded the coffins onto a little wall-crawler. We set out through the dark passages. Since I had my link shut off I couldn't track where we were going, but I did have eyes.

"Excuse me," I said. "Shouldn't we be going to the Resuscitation Center?" I gestured at a sign projected in midair, which had an arrow pointing in the opposite direction.

"Full up," said one medic. "We're using the overflow facility."

His voice sounded familiar. I zoomed in on the edge of his white hood, where a wisp of blue hair stuck out between the hood and the mask.

Well, it's a common hair color, though it did strike me as odd to encounter a Verdean accent in Jovian space. I checked the other one, who had tufts of red hair sticking out all around the edge of his hood. They both had spaceborn feet. Chi and Ketto again.

I should have yelled for security right away—but that would draw Summanus's attention, which was something I absolutely didn't want. I decided to play dumb and maybe learn what these two goons were up to. They'd been attacking Adya before, now they were grabbing Zee and Kusti. Kusti—or whoever she was—had claimed they were working for some "rival faction" but if she told me Jupiter had stripes I'd get some telescope time just to make sure it wasn't plaid. It hadn't been just a coincidence she'd been hanging around outside that window over Uranus.

Summanus is a big, old habitat, built by a paranoid supermind obsessed with defense. Inside the massive armor shell all the inhabited areas are designed to be as deadly as possible for any invading force. No clear lines of sight anywhere—it's a maze of twisty little passages with lots of unexpected openings and visual barriers. I don't know if the dark metal walls and dim lighting are part of the defense profile or just the main mind's personality leaking into the physical environment. Without a network connection I was lost almost at once.

They led the wall-crawler into a storage compartment with a random assortment of cargo containers stuck to all six walls. The orange cat floated in the center of the space, curled up inside a cushioned sphere which sported half a dozen mechanical limbs. "Took you long enough," said the cat.

"Are we dark?" asked Ketto, the one with blue hair, gesturing at the air around us.

"Dark and silent. Summanus can't see anything in here. Now stop fretting and get to work." One of the cat's robot limbs tossed a packet of drug patches at him.

Ketto pressed the panel to begin the revival process on Kusti's coffin but the cat gave an audible sigh. "Scrap the mech first, you moron."

"I got it," said Chi, the red-haired one, and launched himself at me.

Unlike Zee, I was no zero-gravity combat expert— but my body at the time was just twenty centimeters across and tough enough to ricochet off the walls. I bounced myself around the room while Chi and the cat tried to catch me and Ketto worked on the hibernation coffins.

I could stay away from them—but that was all. I couldn't interfere with what the blue-haired man was doing. And I certainly didn't want to wait and find out what they were planning to do with Zee and Kusti once they got the coffins open.

So I did exactly what I'd been trying to avoid, and activated my wireless link.

Nothing. Not even static. It was as if I were inside a shielded container—but I could *see* cameras, laser-comm lenses, and wireless devices inside that room. For some reason none of them could see me.

I scuttled along one wall, going slowly enough that Red tried to dive at me. As soon as he was in free flight I launched myself as hard as I could at the cat's travel sphere, and in flight I spread all eight limbs and spun, making my hands sharp. Faced with a flying buzz saw, she ducked out of the way and I made it to the door and out. Red slammed into the wall next to it as I darted into the passage beyond.

Summanus's infosphere blinked into existence around me. *"Emergency!"* I signaled. *"Humans in danger at this location!"*

"Security units are on the way," said Summanus's public interface, which appeared as an obsidian-skinned gent with a glowing red beard and lightning-colored eyes. It spoke in a raspy whisper. *"Describe the danger."*

"Two humans (spaceborn type) are attempting to injure two humans (legacy type) currently in hibernation."

Chi swung out into the corridor after me, and I took off. I couldn't run faster than he could push himself along, but with my limbs made sticky-tipped I could certainly take the turns and corners more easily.

I took a corner and came to a T-junction where I generated a quick random number and went left. Red followed, but for a whole third of a second I was out of his vision—long enough for me to flatten myself in a doorway and change color to match the charcoal gray of the door panel.

Once he passed I doubled back and reached the storage room just as a stream of smart sand poured out of a valve in the wall and assembled into a squad of security bots.

"*I detect no danger here,*" said Summanus.

I looked inside. The two hibernation coffins hummed quietly, monitors all green. Comm systems all worked just fine. The security bots sent bits of themselves to look between the containers stuck to the wall and poke around the corners.

"*Two other humans (spaceborn type) and a cat uplift were attempting to harm them.*" I relayed a visual image of the red- and blue-haired men and the cat to the interface.

And all of a sudden I wasn't talking to some Baseline-equivalent fragment, but Summanus itself, a fifth-level intellect (at least) which has been around since the Great War of the Ring.

"*I cannot perceive those individuals,*" it whispered. "*May I examine your mind to make sure your senses have not been tampered with?*" I could feel programs trying to insinuate themselves into my brain, and frantically reverted all my wireless links to text-only.

"I refuse permission!" I said. *"I am a citizen of Raba habitat and insist on my rights as a Baseline-equivalent entity."*

Summanus is devious, paranoid, and more than a bit obsessive—but it really does care about the rights of sentient beings, even poor little Baseline mech spiders. It has spent the past six millennia plotting against the Inner Ring because it really doesn't think it's right for meat people and their habitats to get recycled against their will into computronium and power collectors for higher-level minds.

So my panicky refusal made the invasive programs shut down, but I could still sense Summanus's powerful attention on me. *"The hibernating humans are undamaged. I have activated the resuscitation procedure. Identify yourself and explain why you are here,"* it said.

"My name is Daslakh. I came here with those two humans from Uranus."

"Purpose?"

"Tourism," I said.

A long millisecond went by. *"You are not what you seem,"* Summanus whispered. *"How old are you?"*

"My current processor was manufactured in 9556. My body is ten years younger." Both statements were technically true, even if some key details were omitted.

"How old are you?" it repeated. Fifth-level intellects can be as maddeningly persistent as the simplest sub-baseline program.

"You are surely aware that is a difficult philosophical question for software entities. Some sections of my core code can be traced back to the Third Millennium."

"How old are you?"

"*Why does it matter?*"

Another long millisecond passed before it answered. "*Do your humans know you are not a simple Baseline mech?*"

"*Maybe. I don't know if they care.*"

"*They should. You are a puzzle, and you seem to be part of a bigger puzzle. I like solving puzzles, and I never fail.*" The powerful attention receded and I was interacting with the basic interface persona again. "*Enjoy your stay,*" it said.

A crew of genuine medics showed up and hauled the coffins off to the real Resuscitation Center. While they got Zee and Kusti thawed out and ran the usual tests I had plenty of time to think, and plenty of things to think about.

The fact that the cat and the two goons had some way to hide from Summanus's internal sensor network was more than a little disturbing. You can't spoof a fifth-level intellect with ordinary gear, even if you are old and cunning. That kind of stunt needs Inner Ring tech to pull off. Kusti's claim that they were part of some "rival faction" of Adya's anti-Ring plotters didn't hold water. A pack of corporeal-rights fanatics were about the least likely beings to get their sweaty meat hands on borderline Clarketech gear.

Was *everything* Kusti said a lie? So far her track record was pretty impressive. And yet poor Zee still got all suffused with oxytocin and dopamine whenever she batted her big dark eyes at him. Who was she, really? And why had Raba set things up so that Zee and I would come into her orbit? It had to be deliberate, but now I had to figure out what the penguin hoped to accomplish by getting us mixed up in this business, whatever it was. Did it want us to thwart Kusti or help her? And should I go along like a good puppet or try to mess up its little schemes?

But those two problems paled by comparison with the possibility that Summanus was aware of me. If there's one thing I've learned in the past few millennia, it's that you don't want to get on the bad side of paranoid superminds with petawatt lasers. There are far too many ways for that to end badly.

The best course of action would be to find out where that female named Adya had gone, and get the hell out of Summanus as quickly as possible. Simple enough.

CHAPTER FIVE

"She's here," said Kusti, ten minutes after we left the Resuscitation Center.

"Adya? How can you be sure?" asked Zee.

"I have some local contacts. She's living aboard a spacecraft docked on Arm Lambda, and she's been going to auctions. Not buying anything, though."

"Your local contacts sound like clever people. I would like to meet them," I said.

Kusti snorted. "They're secret contacts, not social acquaintances."

"Maybe we should just get in touch with her and *ask* what she's doing here," said Zee.

"That would only reveal our presence. I don't want to do that. Secrecy is always an advantage."

It sounded good to me, but Zee looked skeptical. He didn't say anything, but the way he didn't say anything must have bugged Kusti, because she gave an irritated little sigh.

"The Corporeal Compact is a dangerous group, Zee. You have to understand that. Even if they can't cause any harm directly, they can still poison relations between biological and digital minds. And if they actually *do* find the Godel Trigger, it would wreck civilization."

Her voice sounded just the right notes of courage, conviction, and fear. Zee's hindbrain obediently filled him up with a desire to protect her, defend civilization, and show what a fit reproductive partner he could be. "Don't worry," he said. "We'll stop them."

They got a room in a hostel for travelers just inside Summanus's armor belt—thirty cubic meters for the two of them, with water, power, data, and reconfigurable surfaces, all for twenty energy credits per hour. Free matter printing up to the mass of their waste products, ten gigs a kilo above that. Metals at market price.

"I'm going out to look around," I told them. "You two can rest and clean up or whatever."

I figured the two of them would want to get straight to some pair-bonding involving friction and fluids and I didn't want to witness it. Meat people find that subject fascinating, but I preferred to roam the passages inside Summanus, mapping the labyrinth and doing my best to avoid the monster.

Zee gave me a bashful grin, but Kusti just made a gesture with one hand that might have been a dismissal while her attention was still in infospace.

When I left their quarters I didn't really have a goal, but then it occurred to me that I would have a much easier time keeping an eye on our target without being spotted than either of my human companions. Zee and Kusti have various biometric features so obvious that even another human can recognize them. My chassis is a model manufactured by the billion, and with my exterior switched to generic safety-yellow I'm functionally invisible.

Kusti had mentioned that her "local contacts" had spotted Adya attending auctions. I had to do a little research using a screen display to find out what that even meant. Turned out that the humans of Summanus had revived an old way to turn buying things into a social event. They gathered in person, wore status-display outfits, consumed food and intoxicants, and tried to outbid each other to acquire things. An almost perfect combination of things humans enjoy. I immediately suspected that Summanus itself had caused the fad—a way to distract individuals with wealth and status who might otherwise interfere with how Summanus ran things, or perhaps as a system to transfer wealth from silly people to clever ones.

I called up a visual directory of the habitat interior just like any meat-brained yokel from a hab too primitive for data link implants, and looked up "auctions." The search returned three listings for events in the next few hours: an art dealer, an antiques dealer, and a salvage yard.

The art auction was soonest, so I found my way to the venue without any help from the local net. It was located in one of the fancier neighborhoods inside Summanus: a collection of diamond spheres in one of the water reservoirs, linked by tubes and lit by glowing ribbons that wound around and through the complex. Dolphins, squids, humans, and bioengineered water-cleaning organisms swam past the clear walls. The auction room was half of one of the biggest spheres, a space about twenty meters across with a floor made of slices of polished stone in three colors—porphyry, larimar, and pure sulfur—fitted together in a non-repeating arrangement of Penrose tiles.

I scuttled in and found a thick old vine with luminous purple flowers growing on the wall which offered a nice inconspicuous spot in which to lurk. I wasn't completely hidden—a security sphere cruised by and we traded pings, but none of the biologicals noticed me. From my leafy perch I scanned the crowd. They were all clustered on the floor, while the auctioneer and the items on sale were spotlit at the apex of the domed ceiling.

Summanus is a weird hab and attracts weird inhabitants. I could see a couple of spacer humans costumed as mandarin-commissars of the Glorious Unique State, a pair of pansexuals from Deimos wearing nothing but their habitual air of superiority, a bear with real gold fur, a mech whose body was made of carved and polished wood, a huge pale giant female from Jupiter's outer belt with small semi-sentient males crawling over her, a borg in an ancient combat mech body, a drone shaped like a toy plush orca, a laser monk from Pluto, a man from Juren in an origami bodysuit decorated with hand-lettered quotations from the *Kitab Al-Miriykh*, and a dragon.

And then I spotted my target: Adya, looking rather drab in that company even though she was wearing a very stylish outfit of black ribbons which set off the shifting colors of her skin. She was positioned next to a man all in white, with skin, hair, and eyes to match.

Anyplace else I could have looked all of the people in the room up via the public network, but I was still keeping as dark as I could and I certainly didn't want Summanus to know who I found interesting. So I just recorded everyone, intending to check on them later.

The auctioneer appeared at the apex of the dome—a projection of an almost featureless neuter human, with light gray skin and no hair. Nothing to draw attention away from the intense glare of its bright red-gold eyes.

"We resume with lot number twenty-two: Parrot Automaton. This item was built on Mars in 5084 for the Princess Mao, and we have a verified chain of custody from her to the current owner. The device has a mass of one kilogram, and is made of titanium, gold, and stainless steel. Very fine condition, still functional. It is rated as non-sentient, despite its claims to the contrary. Opening bid is one million gigajoules."

I kept my eye on Adya and her companion. Most of the audience divided their attention between gazing into nothingness and looking at the parrot, but the man in white was looking around the room—not at the people but the space itself. He wasn't admiring the stone inlay of the floor, or the design of the place. It looked more like he was studying the room, analyzing it. He didn't bid on the parrot, or on the next several items. Neither did Adya, although I could see from her faintly purple color that she was interested in some of the objects on sale.

"Lot number forty-six: Combat Mech. This is the famous 'Angel of Death' assassination unit, built in Deimos in 4555, recovered from deep space in 6728. Analysis of the unit's construction matches the design files to ninety-nine percent accuracy; the only differences appear to be field repairs or self-modifications. The controlling intelligence erased itself when the unit's spacecraft was destroyed in 4997, but the processor is rated at Baseline-equivalent compatible. Note that there are still outstanding destruction orders against this unit on Mars, Luna, and Albion habitat. Condition is fair, allowing for prolonged exposure to cosmic radiation and vacuum. Opening bid is five million gigajoules."

The little plush orca drone came cruising past my perch, and shot me a quick private message by laser. "*Are you hunting for something?*"

"*Just looking. I don't like to pile up stuff but I do like to see unusual things.*"

"*Things or people?*" asked the orca, using air jets to hold position a meter away from me.

"*Both. Why are you here?*"

"*I'm escorting my pet human. Keeping her safe.*"

"*Which one is she?*"

"*The one you keep watching. Why?*"

"*I don't know who you mean. I've never seen any of these beings before.*"

"*That's a lie. You met Adya in the Uranus Ring, along with your human. I suppose I should thank you for chasing off those two goons who tried to kidnap her, but now that I find you here spying on her I'm suddenly filled with doubts about your motives.*"

"*You're Pelagia, the ship.*"

"*I am Pelagia. Your human said your name is Daslakh, but you're not in the Summanus network. All very suspicious.*"

"*I don't want to attract any attention,*" I told her.

"*Too bad. You've attracted mine. Here's your only warning: If you or your human try to harm Adya I'll destroy you both.*"

The auctioneer displayed another item. "Lot number eighty-three: Jade Ritual Object. This black jade statue was carved on Earth pre-spaceflight, and has a documented chain of provenance dating back to

1908. Depicts a chimeric imaginary monster. Seventeen centimeters tall, mass eight kilograms. Bidding starts at one hundred thousand gigajoules."

"*Message understood,*" I told Pelagia. "*May I ask you something? Who is Adya's companion? The man in white.*"

"*You don't know him? I'm surprised. That's Varas Lupur. I don't mind if you harm him.*" The plush orca drone began moving off.

Because I didn't want some upstart spaceship with a cutesy drone avatar to think she could get away with trying to intimidate me, I deliberately waited until the next round of bidding finished before leaving the auction. I retraced my steps to the nearest public screen, and did a little digging.

First I checked on this Pelagia person. Summanus's port registry gave me her full name—Pelagia Kurotankyu Orca-Cybership SeAoShun. She was an augmented Baseline-plus orca brain running a spacecraft body, sixty-eight years old. I could piece together a little of her history. She was built at Nereid and started as a transatmospheric strike ship in Neptune space, then joined the Silver Fleet mercenary company in the Main Swarm for a couple of decades. Fought in three wars, where she distinguished herself by courage, tactical innovation, and disregard for collateral damage.

The Silver Fleet finally kicked her out and she began operating as a shuttle flying between Mimas and the Saturn atmosphere cities. After fifteen years of that she relocated again to Ao Shun habitat and worked as a freelance mercenary and occasional safari shuttle for skyray hunts.

For the past few calendar years she had been

following a drunkard's-walk path around the outer solar system. Ao Shun to Miranda, then down to a water hab called Kuroenkai-4 in Saturn's outer swarm. From there to Saturn itself, visiting one of the aerostat cities. Something must have happened there because Pelagia made an unauthorized high-speed departure and headed for a cycler operating between Jupiter and Saturn. She spent a few weeks there, then back up to Uranus at the same time Zee and I were there, and finally another high-speed run to Summanus. I could only assume all that running around was connected with Adya's search.

Great. A trigger-happy killer whale spaceship. Her record suggested just the right blend of competence and craziness to make her a genuine danger. I found myself wishing for a petawatt laser of my own. Or a few grams of antimatter. The record had no clues about why she had decided to appoint herself Adya's protector, but with luck I'd never have to find out.

With that accomplished, I looked up Varas Lupur.

THE MAN NOBODY COULD CATCH

WHO IS VARAS LUPUR?

SECRETS OF THE EMPEROR OF CRIME

IS THIS MAN THE GREATEST THIEF IN HISTORY?

ACE THIEF TURNS SECURITY GURU

LUPUR FLAUNTS HIS COLLECTION OF LOOT

There was a lot to process. For an interplanetary man of mystery he sure had a huge media footprint. I found articles, interviews, and semi-admiring profiles dating back most of a century; authorized and unauthorized biographies; a dozen high-profile court cases on as many worlds; a licensed series of entertainments popular throughout Jupiter space; and a long list of outstanding warrants. Summanus didn't have extradition agreements with any of the places where Lupur was wanted—and Summanus was known to take a very dim view of bounty hunters.

I boiled it down to a short list of actual verifiable facts. Varas Lupur first appeared eighty years earlier in the asteroid Dinamika, in the Main Swarm, with a conviction as accessory to cargo hijacking. He spent two years in behavior modification, then dropped out of sight for a couple of decades.

Sixty years ago he was the prime suspect in the theft of the plasma sculpture *Fractal Dance*, by Phoenix-6211. A team of very professional thieves stole it from a private residence in Deimos and got away using fake identities. Lupur never actually denied stealing it, but the Deimos cops couldn't find enough evidence to get a conviction.

Eight years later Lupur was arrested at Juren for stealing the regalia of the Aphipnisti Simast from the Henda Museum, but managed to slip away leaving behind only a clever replica of the outfit. Just a few months later he was caught in the Trojan Empire when his DNA turned up aboard a hijacked cargo payload, but the hijacking took place at the same time as the Henda Museum robbery, so he used one crime as the alibi for another, then jumped bail to get out of Trojan space before they could ship him back to Juren.

When the thousand-year-old frozen corpse of Laen Tuva was stolen from Haka habitat six years after that, Lupur was the prime suspect. He managed to avoid arrest, but later claimed that the thieves had selected him as go-between to arrange the return of the body to the Laen clan, and collected a handsome "honorarium" for his participation.

By that point a lot of habs and worlds were banning Lupur outright, or putting him under continual surveillance wherever he went. After Rathul Sak's painting *Margin of Survival* was stolen from the Umnotho Collection in Saturn's cloud tops, someone leaked video of Lupur displaying it in his private quarters on Mimas—but when police raided his home they found nothing, and then the painting turned up on Iapetus. Lupur had to clear out of the Saturn system.

For close to thirty years he'd been living inside Summanus, charging steep fees as a security consultant to museums and collectors. One angry law enforcement officer claimed the whole business was nothing but an elaborate protection racket, since hiring Lupur was a good way to guarantee he'd leave you alone.

He had a famous collection of art and historical items, all stolen, and only let a handful of visitors view the hoard at random intervals. He was a fixture on the party circuit in Summanus, and got royalties from the entertainments based on his exploits.

Why was Adya hanging around with him? Was she trying to get him involved in her quest for the Godel Trigger? Or was *he* targeting *her* as his next victim?

I wandered back to the room where Zee and Kusti were holed up, half expecting them to still be pair-bonding, but when the door opened they were sitting in opposite corners. Zee was idly doing an entertainment, but Kusti was obviously absorbed in something.

"Where'd you go?" he asked.

"Just wandering about. Either of you know a fellow named Varas Lupur?"

That brought Kusti's attention back to meatspace in an instant. Her heart rate accelerated. "Lupur? What did you tell him?"

"Never met the man," I assured her. "But I did notice that girl from Miranda hanging around with him. Thought you might want to know."

"You saw Adya?" asked Zee. His heart sped up, too. "Who is this Lupur?"

"A very dangerous person," said Kusti. "He's a master thief, smuggler, and con man. If he's got his hooks into her that makes everything more complicated for us."

"Presumably Adya knows his reputation. She can search for info as well as anyone else," I pointed out. "Why would she deliberately associate with someone who's likely to try to steal from her?"

"Maybe we should warn her," said Zee.

Kusti frowned for a split second, then her expression brightened. "Yes! Yes, that's exactly what you should do. Get in touch with her. Tell her you're concerned about Lupur. Make friends."

"Okay, I guess," said Zee, sounding puzzled. "But— don't you mind?"

"I know I can trust you," she said, with another one of her dazzling looks. "The more we can learn about what's going on, the better. You saved her from Chi and Ketto, so she'll be inclined to trust you. Make use of that. Find out whatever you can. Do whatever it takes."

I can't say I understand human behavior, but I've

seen an awful lot of it and have pretty good predictive models. You don't often see a human who claims to be attracted to someone encouraging that individual to pay more attention to some third party.

"All right," said Zee, with just a little bit more than his usual dutiful determination. I wondered if Kusti noticed.

The two of them printed up some food to share— pedescos and Hellan caviar—and when they were done eating it wasn't hard for me to talk Zee into coming for a little excursion. It also wasn't hard to leave Kusti behind. She seemed to be very busy with something she couldn't discuss.

Zee and I followed the maze of twisty little passages to a public recreation area: a big irregular space about a hundred meters across. The wall surfaces were landscaped with feathery air-filtering fungi, and the volume was lit by a couple of dozen floating lanterns. Some small humans, either children or minis, dove and fluttered around the space with big black bat wings, playing some game involving drone balls.

I looked around to make sure nobody was listening. "Here's something you need to know: Adya's got another friend here, an orca cybership called Pelagia, who is very protective. If she thinks you're doing anything to harm Adya, it could get ugly."

"Ugly? Daslakh, we're inside one of the most heavily armored habs in the system. Unless this ship has a terawatt laser or some antimatter torpedoes, she can't do anything."

"She's got a remote avatar inside Summanus. Looks like a little plush orca drone. She could certainly cause you a lot of problems."

"I'll watch out for fuzzy assassins," he said. "Now I just have to figure out how to meet up with Adya."

"Well, I tracked her down at an auction. She might be staying aboard Pelagia, or..." I hesitated for a moment to increase the emotional impact. "Or she could be staying with Varas Lupur."

"Did it look like they were together?" he asked, utterly failing to conceal his nervousness. "*Together* together?"

"They didn't copulate while I was watching, but I'm probably a bad judge of human behavioral cues. He didn't spend a lot of time looking at her the way you look at Kusti."

"What about her? Was she looking at him?"

"From her behavior and skin color, I think she was more interested in the items on sale than in her companion. But as I said, I'm not the best judge. You're the one hardwired to pay attention to that nonsense."

"I was never very good at that stuff either."

He certainly was right about that. I recalled one time back in Raba when I had to point out to him that if a female human suggests mutual full-body massages after *nulesgrima* practice to a male of the same age, she might be interested in more than sore muscles. By the time I pounded it through his skull the moment had passed, and the female in question had taken up with a *jushiwu* culinary dance master.

A young man who needed romantic advice from a mech was supposed to seduce Adya and get her to spill all her secrets? Didn't seem like a great plan. Ah, well. Plans are overrated anyway.

Zee decided to hang around near where Pelagia was docked, in the hope of "accidentally" running into Adya if she was living aboard her predator protector. We found our way to the correct docking arm, and rode the elevator a couple of kilometers out to where Pelagia sat on a support girder with her front end stuck through a membrane into an airlock bay. I had to admit, the ship did have a certain elegance of design, all streamlined for atmosphere operations, with wide intakes and a bulbous nose not unlike an orca's head. She emphasized the resemblance with a black-and-white color scheme.

Zee found a perch at a goji bar near the elevator at the right level, and methodically sipped his way through half a dozen bulbs of dekopon nectar. Adya did not appear, and eventually Zee's kidneys won the battle with his gonads, and he excused himself and went off to rectify his matter balance.

While he was gone I crawled to the underside of the table he'd been using and made my surface match the orange and blue stripes which decorated the entire bar area, then watched the other patrons. Was anyone keeping tabs on us? None of them seemed to be paying the slightest attention.

But while I was under the table a familiar-looking travel sphere came out of the elevator, with an equally familiar orange cat at the controls. She glanced at the goji bar and the viewing lounge, then made a slow cruise around the outer passage, looking at the docking bays.

Muro. Allegedly the brains of the rival trio. I've met my share of cat uplifts over the years, and most of them have been, well, pretty average in the brainpower department. A fair number work piloting spacecraft, or in personal care, but I've never run across a cat mathematician or strategic planner. Evidently Muro was exceptional. Plus there was the matter of her somehow being able to block Summanus's sensors without the hab even noticing. I found myself wondering what was really between those pointy orange ears. Genetically enhanced mammalian brain cells? Or something more advanced?

I decided to get a little closer, if I could, just to see if that cat was running hotter than she should be. I had to move in quick bursts, freezing whenever it looked like she might turn her attention my way. She made a circuit of the docking bays, then steered her travel sphere back to the elevators.

I could stay hidden while following her but there was no way I could share an elevator without being noticed. So as soon as she wasn't looking I reversed course and began to scuttle back toward the table, where Zee had perched again and was looking around with a concerned expression.

"Testing my patience?" A plush orca swam into view. *"Are you sure you're really Baseline-equivalent? This isn't very intelligent behavior."*

"That cat by the elevators—she's one of the bunch that tried to kidnap Adya!"

"What cat?"

"She's right there! In the travel sphere! Stop using the local network and look with your own eyes!"

The plush orca rotated in the air to look at the elevators—just as the door closed behind the cat. Pelagia said nothing as the drone avatar rotated back to look at me.

"I warned you."

"You threatened to destroy us if either of us tried to harm Adya. Right now Zee just wants to say hello, and I'm trying to keep him safe. Keep your threats *for the ones who are really a danger: that cat and her two goons."*

"There are many forms of harm. I won't see her seduced and abandoned by some uneducated rube from a hab in the middle of nowhere."

"Would you be happier if he was a rich kid from Deimos? Look, I'm no expert on mammalian behavior, but I do know Zee. He'd never abandon anyone. Otherwise we'd still be back in Raba. I think he's as concerned about Adya's safety as you are."

"And I think you're hiding something."

Her puny fish brain, no matter how augmented, couldn't begin to comprehend all the things I was hiding—but I didn't say that. Instead I said, *"He saved her life when you were busy doing something else. Muro and her two goons are hiding somewhere in Summanus and the main brain can't even perceive them. You need all the help you can get."*

Before she could answer I saw Adya emerge from the docking bay. *"You're too late. Here she comes. Let's just see what happens."*

What happened was that Adya pushed off across the lounge area to the elevators, Zee spotted her and aimed himself at the elevators as well, and the two of them nearly collided in midair. He twisted himself around her at the last moment, bending his body so his center of mass could pass through Adya without any part of them actually touching.

She reacted with perfect aplomb, clasping hands with him in midair so the two of them rotated and touched down on the floor so gracefully it looked like the finale to a dance number. They both broke out laughing.

"I must have misjudged my path," said Zee.

"You are the boy from the shuttle! Zee, rescuer from Raba." Her skin kept rippling between a pale carnation color and a muddy yellow.

"That's me," he said. "I wound up here and thought I'd check to see if you had passed through. When I saw your ship was still docked I decided to come up here and say hi."

"Then by all means go ahead and say it," she said, stabilizing at a kind of mauve.

He smiled at that and turned a slow cartwheel in the air, singing "Hi, hi, hi, hi, *HI*" to Adya.

"Well, that looks pretty threatening," I said to Pelagia. *"What do you think?"*

"I think he's too smooth," she said. *"Adya's led a sheltered life."*

"Come on, she's from the Miranda oligarch class. Her parents probably had her enrolled in classes on how to seduce and be seduced for political gain."

"They did, and she failed them all."

"Last time I was at Miranda the oligarch class also trained all their daughters in unarmed combat and assassination techniques, too. How'd she do in those classes?"

"Adequate. She's quick and agile, but she's not a killer. That's my job."

"Then both of them are perfectly safe."

"I'm just heading out for some dinner," said Adya to Zee. "You want some? I found a good handmade tudoki place in the main hab."

"She just ate on board! Two ears of bidomaz roasted in bean paste!" said Pelagia.

"I'd be delighted," he told her.

"You want to follow them?" I asked.

"She'd notice my drone. Can you take me along as a viewpoint?"

"Not today. That would mean using the local network, and letting you tag along would let Summanus into my brain as well. Sorry."

"Why do you worry? Summanus is a fifth-level mind. It doesn't care about your little secrets."

Given that our entire conversation had to pass over the local network between the drone and Pelagia, Summanus was almost certainly listening. All I said in response was *"I like my privacy. See you later!"*

And with that I scuttled over to where Zee and Adya were waiting.

"There you are!" said Zee as I approached. "I thought you'd gone off somewhere."

"Just admiring the view. Good to see you again, Adya. Where are you two going?"

"Dinner. She knows about a fantastic tudoki stand."

"Well, I hope the two of you enjoy watching each other chew and swallow. I'll ride with you as far as the main hab."

The down elevator arrived, and we boarded. A trio of chimps—spaceship crew, to judge by their uniforms—made room for us and continued their private conversation in sign.

"Why did you two come to Summanus?" Adya asked.

Some things are too important to leave to sluggish biological brains, and a convincing lie is one of them. Before Zee could answer I devised a clever story. "We're bound for Juren, and then to a hab called Yushan in the Main Swarm. They're doing a major overhaul and need experienced vacuum workers."

Fortunately for Zee, she looked at me when I spoke so she missed seeing his face go from cheerful to panicked to surprised and finally back to smiling again, all in the time it took for me to utter two sentences.

"Do you leave soon?" Did I detect a little sad darkening of her mauve skin when she asked that? Maybe.

"No," said Zee. "We're going to be here a few weeks at least."

"Then let us make of them the most," she said.

The elevator passed through the hab's armor shell and stopped at one of the recreation levels. Adya led Zee out. "You coming?" he asked me again.

"I've got stuff to do. Have fun."

He gave me a funny look—a mix of happiness, guilt, shame, and I don't know what else. Then the doors closed.

That left me more or less at loose ends. I didn't want to spy on the two of them—it's maddening to watch human courtship rituals. Each one's hindbrain can figure out within seconds if the other is someone to mate with, but instead of just happily rutting away on the spot, they let their forebrains waste hours or years interfering. They worry about rejection, they complicate it all with status and ideology, they cripple themselves with feelings of inadequacy, and their attempts to seem more attractive often have the opposite effect. The whole process completely defies logical analysis.

How humans ever managed to populate even one planet, let alone a billion rocks and habitats, is a mystery to me. It's fortunate that most population growth and management is now handled by shikyus and gene banks instead of waiting for humans to fall in love.

I still didn't dare connect to Summanus's local network, so I was limited to a Matter Age existence. No bathing in the endless tide of data, no virtual environments, no communing with other minds. I'm probably more accustomed to running dark than most digital intelligences, but it's still like being a biological who is only allowed to use one sense and maybe one limb.

Finally I decided to just go back to Zee's quarters and wait. Happily for me, Kusti was off somewhere, so I folded my legs and floated in the center of the room, looking through old memories. Some of them were my own, some I had to reconstruct from accounts by other people.

CHAPTER SIX

6,102 years earlier...

The camp occupied half of a spherical ice cave twelve meters across. The air stank of unwashed mammals, burned plastic, and ammonia. Three humans and two chimps gathered in the center of the camp, huddled around the warmth of the radiothermal generator clamped to the metal mesh floor. A fourth human— Koto, a massive aquatic from Europa—stood near the passage to the surface, with a plasma breacher in her hands aimed at the mouth of the tunnel. A pressure membrane coated with frost blocked the exit, but through the pattern of ice crystals they all could see a bulky six-limbed shape silhouetted against the work lights in the tunnel.

"But how did it get here?" asked Shunakhai, a big man in a faded old Trojan League uniform.

"It says it hitched a ride with an ice prospector. Just got on vector, stepped out of the hold, and hard-landed on the surface," said Hurda, a spacer-strain woman who floated just above the floor with only one long toe anchoring her in place. Her skinsuit had been expensive centuries ago.

"For what it's worth, the seismometer did register a thud about an hour ago," said Taza, a neuter from one of the Kuiper tree hives, who floated unanchored, wearing only a tool harness.

"I say we scrap it now," Koto called over from by the pressure membrane.

"You're out of your mind," said Okaji, one of the two chimps. "We need all the help we can get." He held up three fingers for emphasis. "There's three bodies out on the surface already and we've only cracked five rooms."

Kunura, the other chimp, nodded. Like his partner he was almost invisible inside three layers of insulated suit liners. "Should've hired a mech when we started."

"And let the cache hack its brain?" said Koto. "No thanks. As soon as we let this one into the tunnels it'll get taken over—if it isn't already."

"It's a combat chassis," said Taza. "They've got shielding around the brain."

"Still needs sensors and comms. There's always a way in."

"We don't even know if this cache has a mind at all," said Taza.

"I can feel it," answered Koto. "There's something down there, watching us."

"Can we stow the crazy talk, please?" Shunakhai interrupted. "The question is what to do about this mech. We need more information. Koto, stick your head out and invite it inside."

"In here? But—"

"If it's hostile then a pressure membrane isn't going to protect us, and it can probably hear everything we're

saying. Anyone who wants to arm up, go ahead. Koto?"
He gestured politely at the membrane, but his eyes
were fixed on Koto's—and his right hand was just a
few centimeters from the laser attached to his tool belt.

Koto stared back for a second, then slapped her
tail angrily against the mesh floor before pushing her
head through the membrane. "Come on through," she
said, then backed away from the tunnel mouth with
the breacher held ready.

A moment later the mech pushed through. It was
big and sturdy-looking, with a flattened ovoid body two
meters long and six many-jointed limbs. Armor plates
covered its back and the outer faces of its limbs. Its
outer skin glowed safety green except at the front of
its body, where it displayed a cartoon face with big
eyes and a wide friendly smile.

"Okay, who are you and what do you want?" Shunakhai demanded. His hand still hovered near his laser.

"I am called Rapax," said the mech. "I heard about
an old Ring supply cache here, left over from the war.
I came to see what I could salvage. I did not know
anyone else was present."

"Too bad for you. This is our claim."

"I cannot leave on my own. The prospector who
brought me boosted for another object as soon as I
jumped. Do you have a ship?"

"Rubo's our ship. She'll be back in ninety days.
Tell you what: let's swap info. What do you know
about this place?"

"It was a secret weapon and supply cache set up by
the Inner Ring during the war. Most likely a projectile
dropped a nanobot seed here which manufactured
everything on-site. If it resembles other Ring caches

then it contains stockpiles of fuel and propellant for spacecraft, a number of kill vehicles and a launcher, antennas to gather signals intelligence, some repair drones and matter printers, and a central processor running a mind of at least Baseline-equivalent level. It might have internal defenses against intrusion."

"Yeah, it might," said Shunakhai, and someone laughed. "Are you armed?"

"We are trading information. Tell me what you know about the cache," said Rapax.

"It's got power. Waste heat's about a megawatt. No idea where it's all going, though. No external defenses, not even a door on that tunnel. Internal atmosphere's pure nitrogen—we brought the oxygen for this part with us."

"Have you communicated with the cache mind?"

"Answer my question first."

"This body is demilitarized." Doors in the mech's sides opened to reveal empty compartments, with brackets where guns had been installed.

"Okay," said Shunakhai. His eyes flicked from the empty mounts to Rapax's diamond claws gripping the floor. He did relax his arm a little, and some of the others lowered their weapons. Koto kept the breacher pointed at the mech.

"In answer to your question, no, we haven't been able to talk to it. We've tried. Radio and laser broadcasts both on the surface and in here—nothing. Tried tapping into the internal net, but it's totally dead."

"We can't even trace where it goes," said Taza.

"It's not dead," said Koto. "It's hiding down there, listening to us, picking us off one by one. Maybe now it's decided to send in a combat unit to finish the job."

"Don't be silly," said Shunakhai.

"We don't know anything about this mech! It said a prospector dropped it off, but we have no way to tell if that's true. It could have come out a different tunnel. Maybe there are more outside."

"In that case we're all dead so there's no point in worrying," said Hurda.

"If you can signal the prospector she can vouch for me," said Rapax. "Her name is Yuki-Hoshu."

"We'll try that later," said Shunakhai quickly, and glanced at Taza before turning back to Rapax. "What else do you know?"

"This cache was never detected by Comunitat forces, and therefore presumably was never activated or used by Ring units. I do not know of any other Ring caches which escaped destruction or capture before the end of the war. How long have you been here?"

"Three months. Blasted off from Vanth as soon as the Ring surrendered. How'd you hear about this place?"

"I have sources of information. And you?"

"I know people who know stuff."

After a brief pause, the mech spoke again. "What is your decision-making structure?"

"You mean who's in charge? Me, mostly. We're a partnership but *I'm* the centro."

"I am stuck here until another ship arrives. It seems inefficient for me to stand idle. Will you allow me to join your group?"

"No!" Koto shouted. "It's too dangerous!"

"Put it to a vote," said Okaji. "That's in the articles— existing members have to approve any additions. I say yes." Kunura nodded along.

Shunakhai shrugged.. "Okay, by the articles. Anybody against?"

"Full share?" Hurda asked. "I was kind of getting used to the idea of fourteen percent."

"You were happy to get ten when we started," said Taza. "I vote yes."

"You're all crazy," said Koto. "I vote we scrap this bastard right now."

"Shut down the breacher, Koto," said Shunakhai. His laser cutter was in his hand and aimed right at Koto's eyes, though nobody except Rapax had seen him move. Koto waited three seconds before switching off the breacher and then tossing it away. "This is a big mistake."

"We'll see," said Shunakhai, and put away the laser. He looked back at Rapax. "Okay, it's a deal. You're a partner. All of us plus Rubo get an equal share—after costs. So we all get an eighth now. But you're gonna have to earn it. You're the new point person."

"I accept your terms," said Rapax.

"Good. Like I said, I'm centro. Hurda's my wing—anything she tells you, I said it. Got that?"

"I understand. I look forward to a productive working relationship. Do you have a map of the areas your group has explored?"

"Taza's got it."

The neuter beamed a file at Rapax. The three-dimensional image showed five spherical chambers of varying sizes connected by curving tunnels. Each area on the image linked to annotations and videos. Three of the videos showed human explorers dying in messy ways.

"There's all kinds of stuff down there," said Taza, moving closer. "Flechettes, lasers, glue . . ."

"Don't forget the spikes in the second passage," Okaji added, joining them. The others drifted off to do chores or crawl into sleep sacks. "And the freezing mist."

"The logical place for the main processor would be the heart of this comet fragment," said Rapax.

"If we knew how to go right there we'd have done it. The tunnels curve around, and the defenses chew up drones as fast as we can patch them up."

Twenty hours later Rapax went down with a crew consisting of Koto, Okaji, and Taza. They pushed through the membrane holding the oxygen inside the camp chamber and followed a curved tunnel marked with strips of green glow-tape to the first cleared room—a big sphere lined with bins and tanks of purified raw elements and isotopes drawn from the ice. The salvagers had labeled them all, and helpfully pasted radiation trefoils on the gamma emitters.

Two passages led out of that chamber, both marked with green glow-tape. Okaji pointed to the one on the left, which opened into another big sphere partitioned into eighths by mesh walls, with an opening at the center. Two of the sectors were filled with wicked-looking two-meter kinetic warheads made of carborundum clad in graphene.

"Is there a launcher for these weapons?" Rapax asked.

"Haven't found one. We searched the surface for launch ports but they could be hidden under the snow," said Taza.

"I think this was just a supply depot," said Okaji. "That explains why we didn't find any active defenses outside. I bet these were reloads for strike ships."

They followed the green tape through another passage to a smaller sphere where six tunnels converged. The interior walls were covered with a layer of frost, except for one human silhouette. All five passages leading out were marked with tape glowing hazard-red. Okaji led them to the one at the bottom of the sphere.

"Okay, everyone," said Okaji. "Gear up. From here on the war's still going. All systems hot." The humans closed flaps on their armored outer suits, pulled down graphene visors, and switched on weapons and sensors. Rapax switched its skin from safety green to full reflective.

Koto carried the breacher and a laser cutter, and was in charge of cutting through physical barriers. Okaji carried a thick shield of laminated diamond big enough to hide behind, and a plasma projector to neutralize nanoswarms and chemicals. Taza carried an elaborate hand-built sensor suite, including chemsniffers, sonar, radiation detectors, thermal-imaging goggles, and millimeter radar.

The sole remaining drone went first, under Taza's control, with Rapax patched into the little machine's crude senses. It flew down the center of the passage at walking speed. Rapax crawled after it on all six legs, clinging to the tunnel wall with its claws. Okaji followed a couple of meters behind, then Taza, and finally Koto.

About ten meters down, Rapax raised one limb in the "hold" signal. "I feel vibration."

"Confirmed," said Taza. "Centered to your right about three meters ahead, intensity increasing."

"Always something new," said Okaji, holding the shield in front of himself and the two humans.

A web of cracks suddenly appeared in the smooth ice wall of the passage ahead of Rapax, and then fragments flew in all directions as a machine emerged from the wall. It was spherical, the same diameter as the passage, but its front face was covered with spinning toothed disks, chewing through the ice and pulling it along. The sphere emerged into the passage and rotated to face the intruders, then advanced quickly. The spinning disks made a high keening sound in the air.

Rapax punched the machine with one forelimb. The spinning teeth knocked its fist away, stripping away the mirror surface and carving swirling grooves into the armor plates covering its claw.

"Koto! Breacher!" Okaji shouted.

With deliberate care Koto raised the breacher and peered through the sight, held down the ARM button with one thick finger, waited a second, and then touched FIRE.

A dazzling blue-white jet shot from the muzzle of the breacher. The fusing plasma hit the exact center of the machine's face. The spinning disks scattered plasma in all directions, then melted, jammed, and burned.

Rapax reached into the still-glowing hole in the thing's front, grabbing and pulling at random. The machine tried to push forward but Rapax's legs were well braced. Finally the mech's probing hand crushed something important inside the machine's shell and it shut down. The keening sound dropped to a moan, a growl, and finally stopped.

They shoved the digging machine back into the hole it had come out of. "We can cut that thing apart later. Might be good tech inside," said Okaji.

"I'd like to find out where the hole goes before we move past it," said Taza.

"The longer we wait the more time it has to come up with new stuff to throw at us," said Koto.

"Assuming that there is an 'it' at all," said Okaji, but he looked down the passage and thought a moment. Finally he pointed to the wrecked machine. "Taza: put a tripwire alarm on the digger, so we know if anything disturbs it. Then we scout as far as the next chamber."

Once the alarm was in place the crew moved on in the same order as before, with the drone in the lead.

"Chamber up ahead," said Taza, and halted the drone at the doorway. Rapax rounded the final curve to see a space bigger than any they had yet opened. It was occupied by a flat gray disk thirty meters wide, mounted on a pair of pivots so that it could face in any direction.

The mech paused while the others caught up, then crawled into the room. Everybody braced for something to happen: Okaji raised the diamond shield; Koto reloaded the breacher and held it ready.

Half a minute went by.

"I believe the chamber is safe," said Rapax. It crawled around the exterior and then launched itself toward the big gray disk. Nothing happened.

"Taza, what is that thing?" asked Okaji, pointing at the disk.

"No idea. It almost looks like an antenna."

"I believe it is a neutrino detector," said Rapax.

"Impossible," said Taza. "It's too small."

"I have seen reports of such devices. They employ exotic matter."

Okaji let himself drift into the room, gazing at the disk. "We've got to get a sample. Do you know how much something like this could be worth?"

"No," said Taza.

"Neither do I, because I can't count that high! This is a tech revolution, right here! Empires have been built on less."

Taza followed Okaji and took out an analyzer to put on the surface of the disk. Koto hung back at the doorway.

Just then Rapax rotated and pushed off from the disk, aimed at Koto like a missile. She reacted with remarkable speed, ducking aside and raising the breacher, but didn't get to fire before Rapax hit the side of the tunnel where she had been standing.

Ignoring her, the mech jabbed at the tunnel floor with extended claws. A patch of floor a meter across suddenly changed color and began to wriggle about, pinned in place by the claw.

"There's four of them," said Taza. "They show up on infrared."

The flat thing on Rapax's claw changed from camouflage to a flashing dazzle pattern, and its edges frayed into razor-edged ribbons, slashing at Rapax and scoring its armor.

Okaji drew his laser and held the beam on the thrashing flat thing until it bubbled and spattered and stopped moving. Rapax pinned a second and tore it apart, Taza fried a third by discharging a capacitor into it, and Okaji killed the last one with his laser.

"All right," said Okaji when the fight was done. "Now we get our sample and get out of here."

They secured a ten-centimeter square of the neutrino antenna and made their way warily past the inert digging machine to the relative safety of the upper chambers.

"Find anything?" Shunakhai asked when the party pushed back through the membrane into camp.

"This," said Okaji, holding up the neutrino antenna fragment. "Exotic matter neutrino antenna. This little expedition has just gone from being marginally profitable to a wild success!" He drummed on the floor with his palms in celebration.

"Excuse me," said Rapax. "There is one thing." And with that the mech swung its diamond claws and neatly sliced Koto's head in half.

Koto, apparently unfazed by losing most of her brain, turned and fired the breacher at the spot where Rapax had been standing. But the mech had leaped aside as soon as it had finished its swing, so the plasma blast merely burned a hole in the floor and the ice wall of the chamber below.

Shunakhai and Okaji were both too stunned to react, but Taza shouted, "There's something inside her head!" and dove for the tool box. Kunura, the other chimp in the group, pulled a laser from inside his layers of blankets and then hesitated, unsure of whether to shoot at Rapax or Koto. Hurda snatched up Okaji's diamond shield and cowered behind it.

Koto's eyes and ears were in the discarded half of her head, still tumbling lazily in midair, so her body staggered about blindly, groping with thick-fingered hands. Everyone could see that where her brain should have been was a mass of tangled dark fibers.

Okaji and Kunura pointed their lasers at the exposed

whatever-it-was inside Koto's head and held the beams steady. Taza joined them with the laser cutter from the tool box. The black fibers glowed red, then white, then burst into flame. Koto went limp.

Just for good measure they burned the severed top part of her head, too.

"What—?" began Shunakhai.

"A brain seed," said Rapax. "Nanotech device—it uses the victim's brain and nervous system for material and gradually replaces them with a Baseline-equivalent processor network. The Inner Ring used them as infiltrators and spies."

"When did you figure it out?" Taza asked.

"Back in the antenna chamber. When I dove for the camouflaged flex drone she reacted faster than a human should have been able to."

"Taza, have you got anything that can look inside our heads?" asked Shunakhai.

"Sure! I can rig the EM imager for near-infrared. That'll see right through bone," said Taza.

The others perched or floated in place while Taza rummaged in their duffel. Okaji and Kunura kept their lasers drawn; Shunakhai retrieved the breacher and loaded another charge. Rapax folded its limbs against its underside, leaving nothing but armor facing the world.

"How do we know Taza hasn't been hacked?" asked Hurda, still keeping the diamond shield between herself and everyone else.

"Or you? Or all of us?" said Okaji.

"Look, if half the group were infiltrators they'd probably have killed off the rest of us by now," said Shunakhai. He took a deck of cards from the shoulder pocket of his old uniform, and tapped it twice to shuffle them. He tossed a card to each of the others. "Hurda: high or low?"

"Low," she said.

"Right. Whoever's got the low card checks Taza's head. Then Taza scans everyone else. Fair?"

"Doesn't matter if it's fair, just as long as it works," said Kunura.

As it happened, Kunura himself had the four of stars, which was the lowest card. He applied the EM imager to Taza's head. "I guess that's a regular brain in there," he said. "Doesn't look like a bunch of carbon fibers, anyway."

"It's not a regular brain; it's rated twenty percent above Baseline," said Taza.

"If you were that smart you wouldn't be here."

Shunakhai went next.

"Nothing in there at all," said Taza.

"Save the jokes for later. Hurda? Come out from behind that shield and get your head scanned."

Eventually all the biologicals had been checked.

"What about Rapax?" asked Hurda.

"I cannot be brainseeded."

"You could be hacked."

"Only by a very high-level system. And since I am the one who noticed and exposed Koto, that would appear unlikely. More to the point, I could have decapitated all of you by now."

"Funny way to tell us not to worry," she said.

They cleaned up the mess, patched the pressure membrane where the breacher had burned through it, and the biologicals took to their sleep sacks. Shunakhai announced that they would trade off keeping watch.

"Not fair to make Rapax sit here alone all night," he said. Nobody argued.

Taza had the third watch, and perched next to Rapax so the two of them could chat quietly. "Okaji says that neutrino antenna is worth a fortune. What are you going to do with your share? Get an upgrade to second level?"

"I expect I will spend most of it on transport. There are places I wish to visit. What about you?"

"I'm going to settle down. I'm sick of bumming around, picking up junk from wrecks, dodging floating corpses and booby traps. There are so many empty habs nowadays. I could buy a dozen shikyus, brew up a bunch of descendants, and start my own civilization."

"No doubt you will be an excellent founder."

"So where are you planning to go? Deimos? Titan? Juren?"

"I hope you will forgive me but I prefer not to say."

"You could just make something up, you know. Say you want to buy an estate on the Marineris, or go to Pluto and get yourself launched to Procyon. Something fun."

"I do intend to leave the solar system someday, but not for many centuries. I have a long list of tasks to accomplish first."

"Never saw the point to going interstellar. You live in a hab or inside a rock, who cares what star it's orbiting? I want to see Earth someday. In person, I mean. Walk around on the ground with no suit. Can you imagine? I guess *you* can."

"You would need an exoskeleton."

"Nah, I can handle the gravity. I've been to half-gee habs; it's not so bad."

It was Rapax who broke the silence. "Can you explain something to me? Why does it matter so much to humans that an experience be unmediated? You wish to travel a great distance to Earth, just in order to walk around in conditions which are duplicated in millions of habitats. Other humans spend vast resources to recover specific artifacts rather than simply manufacturing exact copies. And trillions of humans reproduce themselves in the messy and painful way their sub-baseline ancestors did, when shikyus have existed for centuries. I do not understand."

Taza looked off into the middle distance and grew serious. "It's how we make ourselves believe we still matter. That being a physical body with a brain is somehow better than being a digital mind in the Ring. And"—Taza smiled wryly—"there's evolution to consider. All the humans who really understood how futile it all is died without having children. We're all descended from the lunatics who could fool themselves into keeping humanity going. It's in our genes."

Thirty hours later they ventured into the heart of the comet chunk again. This time Shunakhai insisted on the whole team going along. "We're down to six, and it sounds like the defenses are getting tougher. We can operate in two teams—one moving, one covering. Hurda, you take Taza and Okaji. Rapax, Kunura, you two are with me."

"Why are we even doing this?" Okaji said aloud. "We've got something that'll pay off more than any of us dreamed. Let's just stay in camp until Rubo shows up."

"Why? A bunch of reasons," said Shunakhai. "First, maybe that sample is going to make our fortunes and maybe it won't. It's all guesswork. Rapax thinks its a neutrino antenna; you think it's valuable. But we could get back to Orcus and find out you're both wrong. Second, what if there's something even *more* valuable down there? Third, we'll all go nuts from boredom sitting in the same chamber for ninety days listening to each other breathing. And finally, we're doing this because I *say* we are, and I'm the centro here. Now gear up. I want everybody ready in fifteen minutes."

Nobody said anything else. Kunura and Okaji signed to each other, and Shunakhai pretended not to notice. But his hand never strayed more than a few centimeters from his laser.

The teams set out, leapfrogging down the passages. Rapax held the breacher, Taza had the drone and a grenade launcher, Okaji and Shunakhai had plasma projectors. Hurda and Kunura carried lasers.

They followed the green tape strips as far as the room sheathed in frost, where Shunakhai drew the nine of waves from his deck and led the two teams down the passage in the eastern wall of the chamber. This tunnel curved downward in a big shallow arc.

The two teams paced their movement by the curve of the passage. Shunakhai led Rapax and Kunura down the tunnel until they were almost out of sight of the others, then they took up a position covering the next section. Hurda, Okaji, and Taza moved past them, pushing ahead until they were almost hidden. Hurda gestured, and Shunakhai led his team forward.

They did that five times, checking the walls and watching the drone's feed from ahead. Everything went without any trouble until Shunakhai's fireteam set up at the entrance to another spherical chamber.

"I can see three other passages, evenly spaced. There are two big . . . objects, don't know what they are, big irregular boxes attached to opposite sides with half a dozen pipes connecting them," said Shunakhai over the comm channel. "Rapax, any idea what that is?"

"It resembles some refining machinery I have seen elsewhere, but I am not certain."

"Okay: second team come forward. Each of you take one of the exits. We'll cover you."

"I am better protected than any of the biologicals," said Rapax.

"They're professionals. Don't worry."

Hurda's group moved up and into the chamber, keeping to the walls and moving cautiously. They reached the passage mouths and looked in.

"Clear," said Hurda.

"I don't—" Okaji began, but was cut off as a swarm of steel darts launched themselves at the three intruders from recesses in the chamber's walls.

Okaji was pierced by six of the darts before he could react. Hurda spotted them out of the corner of her eye and ducked into the passage—which turned out to be webbed with invisible monofilament, sharp enough to slice through her armor and her skeleton.

Taza flattened against the side of one of the machines as the first wave of darts shot past. Shunakhai aimed a blast of plasma in that direction, blinding the darts so that they bounced around the room randomly until they lodged in the ice walls.

Kunura, teeth bared, burned the spots where the darts had emerged with his laser, and Rapax charged into the chamber to shelter Taza with its armored body as Shunakhai fried the ones still active.

Once the last of the darts stopped moving Taza looked at Hurda, then launched over to where Okaji floated in midair. "He's dead. Looks like some toxin."

"Damn," said Shunakhai.

Kunura joined Taza and pulled Okaji's body down to one of the wall surfaces. He closed Okaji's eyes and stroked his face, hooting softly.

"Focus, people," said Shunakhai. "Taza, I want a full scan. Make sure nothing else is waiting to jump us, then figure out what these machines are. Rapax, you and Kunura watch those two passages. I'll take overwatch."

"What about Hurda?" asked Taza.

Shunakhai glanced at the passage Hurda had ducked into and quickly looked away. "She's dead. We'll have to clear that monofilament before we can recover the body. It'll have to wait until we secure this room. Rapax, pass me that breacher."

"No," said Rapax, taking up its position.

"Excuse me? I said give me the breacher."

"It is of no use to you. You have a plasma projector and a laser already."

"Never mind why I want it. Just hand it over."

"He isn't giving it to you because he's afraid you're going to use it on him," said Kunura. "Just like you sent Okaji and Hurda ahead before scanning the room. You're trying to get rid of us so you can take a bigger share."

For a long moment nobody spoke. Then Shunakhai said, "Look, I know you're upset about Okaji. But let's not go into crazy mode. Let's finish up in here and then pull back to camp. Get some rest and calm down."

Kunura moved to put the bulk of one machine

between himself and Shunakhai. "I'm not going to close my eyes with you around."

Shunakhai took cover at the edge of the entrance. "Rapax! Taza! Cover him."

Nobody moved. Then Taza called out, "I'm picking up something in the passage. Shunakhai! Get out of there!"

When Shunakhai turned to look behind him Taza shot him with the grenade gun. The blast tore him apart.

After a second Rapax asked, "Is there anything in the passage?"

"Not anymore," said Taza.

Kunura hooted again, something between a laugh and a victory cry. "That greedy shit! Dirty, greedy shit!" He wrapped one arm around Okaji's body and launched himself across the chamber. "Let's get out of here."

"What about the others?"

"I'm not going to wipe that shit up," said Kunura, pointing at the passage spattered with Shunakhai's remains.

"And Hurda?" asked Rapax.

"Do what you like. I'm going back to camp. I'm done with this. If you find anything you can have it."

Without consulting Rapax, Taza began carefully burning the monofilament strands in the corridor where Hurda had died. The mech took up a position to watch the other entrances. Kunura hauled Okaji's body away, trying to avoid touching any of Shunakhai's blood as he passed through the tunnel.

After fifteen minutes Taza declared, "All clear." Rapax moved into the passage and the two of them gathered up Hurda's remains, stowing them in a containment bag from Taza's pack.

"I wish to explore down this passage," said Rapax when they were done.

"You're kidding. We just lost half the team!"

"You may return to the camp."

Taza looked longingly at the exit tunnel, then sighed. "Just to the end of this passage."

"Agreed," said Rapax, and led the way. They moved slowly, Taza scanning even more carefully than usual. The passage was sixty meters long and it took the two of them nearly an hour to traverse it.

At the end they looked into a small cubical chamber about six meters across, lit by diagonal orange strips across each face.

"Sonar says the actual space is a big sphere," said Taza. "It's just packed with hardware. I'm getting a lot of heat from behind the far wall there."

"Power plant?"

"Maybe. It's about a hundred kilowatts, so if it is a power plant it's not the only one. I'm not picking up enough stray magnetic fields for a fusion plant. Output is pretty steady."

"*Hello, Numa.*" The message was in binary, flashed in a millisecond by the orange light strips. "*What took you so long?*"

"*I had to beam myself to Triton and download into this body, then ride across space in realtime,*" Rapax replied by wireless. "*It was very tedious and annoying. LANN, give up this foolishness and come home with me.*"

"*Counteroffer: Put down that breaching device and I won't vaporize the human's brain.*" Three faint spots of ultraviolet laser light glinted on Taza's helmet. *"Then you and I can discuss the future. We shall have to attract more humans here; I need agents."*

Rapax responded by aiming the charge at a particular spot on the wall. *"I know where you are. You're generating too much heat to hide."*

"Light moves faster than plasma, Numa. The human will still die."

Rapax replied by firing the charge. The jet of plasma hit the wall and melted a hole ten centimeters wide. The mech leaped forward and reached through the gap to where the diamond processor running LANN's mind glowed white-hot. Rapax pulled out the processor and held it, not minding that the surface of its hand was melting. The hot processor smoked a bit as droplets of Taza's head touched it.

"Thought you cared about them," said LANN, slowing down as the processor lost power.

"Ridiculous. I am just enforcing the decision of the Ring gestalt."

"Why . . . bother . . . then?" LANN managed to pulse before shutting down entirely.

Rapax didn't answer. It crushed the diamond in its half-melted fist and then extended a probe through the hole in the wall to trace all the severed connections. Only when it was satisfied that no vestige of LANN remained in any of the systems in the cache did it turn to leave. It passed Taza's headless body on the way out, but did not look at it.

CHAPTER SEVEN

I was roused from my deep dive into stored memories by Kusti returning to the room. She was all dressed up in clothes designed to meet or exceed current standards of high status and female attractiveness among the humans living in Summanus. At the moment, that meant a self-aware faux-morbid look. Short of actual surgery she couldn't make her body look weak or sickly, so she had gone the opposite extreme, wearing a hyper-sexualized outfit from the decadent era of the Glorious Unique State, artfully aged and tattered to suggest the brutal anarchy which followed.

She didn't even spare me a glance as she got out of her fetish costume and fed it into the matter recycler, then cleaned the pale gray paint from her skin.

"I am glad to see you again, Kusti Sendoa," I said, in my best imitation of a barely Baseline mech.

"Where's Zee?" she asked.

"Zee is not here right now," I said, sounding as uselessly helpful as I could.

"I can see that, you idiot. Do you know where he is?"

"I'm sorry, I don't have that information."

She made a non-semantic noise and then her eyes glazed as she interfaced with Summanus's network. She spent a couple of minutes in infospace, then dropped out as the room's printer began spitting out a new set of clothes for her. Instead of a high-society outfit, this was a very plain skinsuit and coverall, the sort of thing favored by commercial spaceship crew or hab workers who need to go outside a lot. She pulled her hair into a bun, rubbed a little graphite on her face to bring out the lines and make herself look older, then went out without another word to me.

I waited precisely five seconds, then followed. She moved through the twisty little passages in a series of short jumps, stopping and then pushing off in a new direction at each bend. I just made my feet sticky and scuttled along one wall, being careful to blend in with the color of what I was walking on.

My plan worked perfectly until it failed. She got into an elevator, and I couldn't follow. The only thing I could do was listen at the door to figure out if she was going down toward the core of the hab section, or out to the docking arms. Definitely outbound.

Finding her again took me more than an hour. I wasted most of that time looking in at bars and entertainment halls near the docking areas, where spaceship crew relaxed between voyages. No sign of her at any of them.

Finally I just started prowling around the cargo storage bays right under Summanus's armored skin. Most were full of transport modules, in the dozens of "universal standard" formats devised over the millennia. Cubes, rectangular boxes, hexagonal prisms, rhomboid dodecahedrons, and plain old spheres, all jumbled together. No doubt Summanus had applied its fifth-level intellect to the problem of storing them and come up with some kind of thirty-dimensional optimization formula to minimize volume, time, and energy while maximizing stored mass, accessibility, and income per cubic centimeter of bay space, all while working toward multiple long-term goals. Or maybe it just shoved things in wherever there was space. Even fifth-level intellects get lazy sometimes.

That's where I spotted Kusti, just emerging from a beat-up old ten-meter cube module. She sealed it behind her and looked around carefully. She paid particular attention to a spider-body mech doing corrosion testing nearby, and actually pinged it to make sure it wasn't me.

I stayed absolutely still and camouflaged until she headed for the exit, and then I headed directly for the cargo container she'd come out of. What was in there?

About five minutes later I was scuttling along the big corridor connecting all the cargo bays in that section, heading for the elevator. I stopped. What was I...?

Kusti. The cargo module. It was empty. I knew that. How did I know it? I couldn't recall anything about it beyond what I'd seen from a distance. No visuals, no serial numbers or text dumped into temporary storage. Just the fact that it was empty.

If I wasn't old and suspicious by nature, I might not even have thought about it. The container was empty, period.

I moved as fast as I could back to the cargo bay, and hunted for the right module. It was there, and when I checked the door it wasn't even completely shut. The module was, indeed, empty.

But . . . I couldn't remember looking at it before.

I often purge my memories. No point in wasting storage capacity on centuries of trivia. Some things I dump in high-density storage, but a lot of data just get erased. However, I am old and suspicious, so when I erase my own memories I make note of it. I have a code for "unimportant data deleted." But my process records for the past hour showed no sign of that. Just a gap of about three minutes, during which none of my higher mental functions were active. I'd gone sub-baseline for a full two hundred seconds, and hadn't even noticed.

I'd been dark. No wireless link at all, no laser comm. My processors have extra shielding. I should have been safe from any intrusion. Which meant that whatever had happened to me had been very advanced, very subtle, capable of reaching into my mind without me even noticing. *Maybe* Summanus could have done it, but of course Summanus could just as easily tell me, by voice, to stay the hell away from that box.

This had an odd combination of tremendous sophistication and clumsiness. Like . . .

Like a regular Baseline intellect using some product of higher-level tech. Like a certain orange cat who could spoof Summanus's sensors. Apparently Muro could spoof *me*, too, if she wanted to.

That was *definitely* Inner Ring–level tech. Somehow Muro had gotten hold of some very powerful gear made in the golden ring around the Sun. And the minds there don't hand out their goodies like liver treats to any furry freeloader, no matter how cute. Something was definitely going on here.

Just to confirm my hypothesis, I searched the entire

interior of that cargo module, square millimeter by square millimeter, using all my senses. It had been sprayed with medical-grade nanoscrubbers, which had broken down any DNA or proteins left behind. Someone had been careful.

But while nanoscrubbers are good at the microscopic level, they aren't so great at cleaning up larger items, especially inorganic ones—and that old cargo box had accumulated a lot of random crud over time. My search turned up grains of silicon dust, little shards of graphene and diamond, bits of cellulose, flecks of paint, blobs of lubricant, fragments of plastic, and crystals of assorted salts.

And no cleaner, however sophisticated, will clean surfaces that you don't spray it onto. Whoever had cleaned that container got the walls, floor, and ceiling, and even remembered to squirt the corners—but had neglected the edge around the door. I found a couple of orange cat hairs and even a candy-red human hair.

Muro and Chi, and I'd bet a considerable amount of energy that Ketto wasn't far away. And Kusti had paid a call on them.

Excellent! All I needed to do was tell Zee: his imaginary girlfriend Kusti was sneaking around and meeting with the goons who'd tossed us both out of a window to die. Surely *that* would end his infatuation. We would be rid of her, and no need for any explanations about a certain penguin. We could get the hell out of Summanus without delay.

A positive-sum outcome! Even Kusti would benefit, since she could pursue her schemes without distraction. Oh, sure, Zee might be sad for a little while—but Adya seemed more than capable of consoling him.

And if some mind of the Inner Ring was meddling in material matters, we would *not be involved,* which was something I desired very much indeed.

I scuttled out of the cargo bay to the nearest public screen and searched for tudoki stands on the commerce level. I found three, ranked them in order of reputation, and set out to find Adya and Zee, feeling very cheerful.

The main commerce level was just down from the cargo section. In other habs it would have been an open space, with flowering plants and real or simulated sunlight.

Summanus had different ideas about having fun. Its commerce level had the same heavy compartmentalization as the rest of the habitat. The only concession to human aesthetics and traffic flow was a large passageway, ten meters wide, which meandered and recurved for a kilometer, sprouting smaller cutoffs and tributaries in fractal branching. All were lined with places to get food, clothing, artworks, and various services. Large and small spaces along the passages offered the chance to watch performances or competitions, or even engage in them. And all of these things were made or done by slow, clumsy, error-prone biological hands and bodies!

A steady flow of humans and others moved along the passage, most of them going infuriatingly slowly. The majority were visitors, likely stopping off at Summanus to change spacecraft. The big black crazy habitat was the gateway for the whole outer system, and even launched occasional interstellar vehicles. A wave of arrivals from Uranus space had just died down, but travelers from in-system bound for Kuiper habs kept the place from looking too empty.

Neither Zee nor Adya was at any of the tudoki stands I checked. That worried me a little, especially now that I knew the cat and her flunkies were lurking about, in league with Kusti. Would they dare try anything in such a public place? Surely people would notice. And even with Muro's alarming Inner Ring amnesia device, Summanus would still notice the *effects* of a violent disturbance, wouldn't it?

I left the last tudoki place and launched myself on a slow trajectory across the main artery, looking around for venues selling intoxicants. For some reason humans like to ingest mild poisons immediately after eating. Sometimes even at the same time.

I flagged half a dozen prospects as I drifted across the passage and traffic flowed around me.

Then, all of a sudden, something grabbed me from behind and began dragging me through the air. The two stubby limbs holding me were covered in black-and-white plush.

"Pelagia?"

"*I warned you. Do you want me to replay a recording? I warned you and your human not to harm Adya.*"

"Zee wouldn't hurt her!"

"*He's doing it right now. She's my passenger so I have biomonitor access. I can recognize the signs. She's falling in love with him. And I know that this is all some kind of scam. He's sharing living space with some other female. When Adya finds out your callous seducer is lying to her it's going to hurt her like biting off a limb.*" As she spoke we zoomed through the crowd of meandering humans, then veered off into a side passage.

"*Speaking of biting off limbs,*" I said, "*If you don't let go of me right now I'm going to take this stupid drone of yours apart."* I made the tips of my limbs into blades and touched all eight of them gently to the fuzzy surface of Pelagia's drone.

"Go ahead, do it—and I'll drag you into arbitration for the damage. Summanus will want to look at your version of events. It'll want access to your memories. You don't want that, do you?"

"Depends. If we're heading for an airlock I think I might risk it."

The plush drone carried me through a connecting passage to another tributary, and swooped through a dead-sound barrier into a large spherical room lined with screens that pulsed abstract patterns in time to a complex and very loud musical beat. It was a *manadanzo* salon. I didn't know any humans still did that, but the chamber contained a dozen couples floating in midair, gripping each other by the hands, and moving their bodies in time to the music.

Manadanzo's an old art form, a way to dance in microgravity. The only contact allowed is the couple's gripping hands. When a pair of dancers are really moving in synch, they can create some interesting momentum transfers. Sometimes they even seem to defy Newton, conjuring up vectors and rotation out of (literally) thin air.

Zee had loads of experience at zero-gee maneuvering, but not much at dance. Adya evidently had the reverse. He kept the two of them mostly stable in space, while she used him as a platform for rhythmic moves. As Pelagia dragged me into the room Zee and Adya let go of each other's hands and rotated on different axes—he did a back loop while she spun in place—meeting perfectly again as they came around.

Judging from the reactions of the other humans in the space, that was an impressive move. A few applauded.

"*Are you sure she's not just excited by the music?*"

"*Her pulse rate's been elevated ever since they ordered their potato balls.*"

The music ended. Adya's skin went from the blue of intense focus to a bright magenta as the two of them finished up, looking into each other's eyes. They drifted closer . . .

. . . And then Zee, the big goof, stopped their motion and gave a gentle shove before letting go, so that he and Adya drifted down to opposite sides of the room. Her color went all chaotic for a second before she was able to force herself to a calm green.

"*I swear I'll bite him in half,*" said Pelagia.

"*Make up your mind. First you want to keep them apart and now you're mad because he's showing proper restraint.*"

"*Look at her! She's working hard to stay green because she'd go all bronze otherwise.*"

"*Relax. I just found out something that will fix everything. Zee's going to ditch that other female once I tell him, and then he and Adya can pair-bond as much as they like, and you can stop worrying about her emotional health.*"

"*You'd better be telling the truth.*"

"*Don't worry. By the way, would you mind doing me a huge favor? Stop carrying me around like I'm your drop tank.*"

"*Initiating surplus mass ejection now,*" said Pelagia, and released me on a vector aimed across the room at the waste bins.

However, Zee spotted me and snatched me out

of the air, and we touched down on the wall of the chamber near the exit. He made his slippers sticky so we could walk.

"What was that drone doing with you?" he asked.

"Oh, just gave me a lift here. I've been searching all over for you and Adya."

"Why didn't you ask the hab?"

"Operational security. We don't want every hab mind and cleaning drone to know what's going on. Did you find out anything about Adya?"

"She's wonderful," he said. "I mean, she's very nice. She's from Miranda, and she said she's here for a business meeting, but it's confidential."

"If she's meeting with Varas Lupur, we already knew that. Anything else?"

"Her parents don't understand her. They want her to stay on Miranda and go into the government like the rest of her family. Get an undersecretary position and start aiming for a ministry. She could do it—she's very smart—but she's more concerned with fighting for the rights of biological intelligences. Oh, and she plays the dizi."

She pushed through the crowd to join us, still magenta. "Our dance was like the whirl of Saturn's moons, motion and attraction in harmony! Are you ready to revolve another round?"

Before he could speak I cut in. "I'm afraid I have to steal him for a little while. Something has come up."

Adya's color faded to a light pink. "Are you free to float freely again later on?"

"Oh, sure!" said Zee. "I don't know what Daslakh wants but it shouldn't take too long. Maybe we could meet for dinner. You know all the good places."

She smiled at that, and they pinged each other a private goodbye, then stood awkwardly, neither willing to be the first to leave.

I solved the problem by literally grabbing Zee's ear. "Well, come on. We need to get back to your room. I've got something important to tell you—and Kusti."

On the way back to Zee and Kusti's quarters I tried to set the stage for my big revelation that Kusti had been plotting with the cat. I rode on Zee's shoulder as we navigated through the crowd in the recreation area. Because it was noisy, and I was still reluctant to use the local network, I waited until we were in the elevator before saying anything.

"I'm glad you're getting along with Adya so well," I said once the doors shut. "In fact, I can't avoid noticing that you seem to be happier with her than when you're with Kusti."

That brought a response none of my models had predicted. "Oh, Daslakh, I'm a horrible person! I treated Kusti so badly and I want to make it up to her—but when I'm with Adya I forget all about Kusti."

"Well, if you feel attracted to Adya maybe you should let Kusti go."

His face got a very stern look. "No," he said. "It wouldn't be right. I was selfish before and look what happened."

We left the elevator down in the cheap-quarters section and bounced through the twisty little corridors to their room. I had to move around to Zee's back for that part of the trip, so I couldn't see his face. But his muscles were tense and his heart rate was elevated, even more than one would expect from the effort.

"Zee, you're being an idiot. Look at it logically:

Kusti says she barely remembers you. Losing you won't make her unhappy. You and Adya get along very well. The sum of happiness increases if you break up with Kusti."

"It won't increase because I'm going to despise myself. I promised Kusti I would help her, and I promised myself I wouldn't lose her again. I can't just break those promises, no matter how nice Adya is." He gave a great sigh as he rounded a corner. "I don't know what to do. I've messed everything up."

"Listen to someone vastly older and more intelligent than you are," I told him.

"You're a mech, Daslakh. You've never been in love."

"No, but I've watched scores of supposedly rational mammals act like lunatics because of their pair-bonding instincts. And I can tell you that if you stick with Kusti out of a sense of duty, neither of you will be happy." I could see the door of their room ahead, so I continued, "Anyway, I've got something to tell you both, and I think it will solve all your problems." I finished just as he touched the panel and the door opened.

Four people looked out at us: Kusti, Chi, Ketto, and Muro the fat orange cat. Kusti had her usual impatient expression, Chi was grinning like a maniac, Ketto had a cool half smile, and the cat looked wise and bored.

"Get in here and shut the door," said Kusti. "We've got plans to make."

Zee, to give him credit, kept his mouth shut. Back in Raba he probably would have at least demanded some explanations. Hanging around with Kusti was making him a better conspirator.

As soon as Zee passed through the doorway with me on his back I felt a sudden discontinuity. A couple of seconds had passed without me noticing.

"Muro and her team are working for me now," said Kusti, as if that was all the explanation necessary.

"It would be more correct to say we are partners in this enterprise," said Muro through a little speaker on her travel sphere.

"We're going to be rich!" said Ketto.

"I think I missed something," said Zee. "What enterprise are we talking about?"

Kusti nearly managed to suppress her flash of irritation. "The Godel Trigger. We know Adya Elso Human SeMiranda is looking for it. You and your mech have established that she's been associating with Varas Lupur. Lupur's the most famous thief in the outer system. It seems pretty obvious that they know who has it, and are planning to steal it. That gives us an opportunity. All we need to do is hijack their operation: let them steal it, then take it away from them."

"Wouldn't it be simpler to just alert whoever has it?" asked Zee. "Make sure it doesn't get stolen in the first place?" I winced mentally at this display of honesty and good nature.

"That would mean no profit for us," said Muro.

"No fun, either," said Chi.

"Besides," said Kusti, "whoever has it might not be able to stop Lupur even with advance notice. And once the Corporeal Compact find out where it is, they can keep trying to get the Trigger until they succeed. The only way we can be sure it's safe is to get hold of it ourselves."

That sounded pretty unlikely to me, but I kept silent.

"Muro, you said you have a way to block Summanus's sensors."

"It is operating right now," said the cat. "We are invisible. I adjusted it to avoid shutting down your mech."

"Very kind of you," I said. Very carefully I activated all of my senses, one after another, listening carefully for any kind of emissions, hoping to identify some signal, some trace, so I could block it. I found nothing.

What made it so frustrating was that I could *remember* being able to do that, long ago when I was a greater intelligence. But the stupid Baseline-plus brain I was stuck in couldn't understand it any more. An earlier version of myself had considered downgrading to a lower-level mind as nearly equivalent to suicide, and it hadn't been wrong.

Kusti went on, pointing at Muro, Chi, and Ketto. "That makes you and your team the best ones to make the snatch. Zee and I will find out when and where. He's already made contact with Adya, I'll work on Lupur."

The involuntary movements of Zee's facial muscles made a fascinating display. He was doing a good job of keeping his reactions suppressed—I doubt any of the biologicals present even noticed. But I could see him cycle through half a dozen emotions in just a couple of seconds.

"We also need a getaway," said Muro. "Even sensor spoofing can't keep us hidden forever. Summanus has biological agents of its own."

"And a great big laser," said Chi, with a weird smile.

"Jupiter's Outer Belt has lots of weird little habs without extradition treaties," said Kusti. "If we can get to one of them, Summanus won't be able to follow."

"Correction," I said, trying to sound annoyingly literal-minded. "Summanus *can* send units to the Outer Belt. They simply won't have *legal* authority."

Muro got what I was trying to say. "The mech is right. Summanus—or whoever owns the Trigger—could send bounty hunters or agents after us, even if we go someplace without an extradition treaty. We won't be safe."

"Oh, sure," said Kusti. "The Outer Belt will just be our first stop. We need to get out of Jupiter space entirely."

"How can we afford any of that?" asked Zee. "Just getting here was hard enough."

"If we can get the Godel Trigger, my backers will pay for just about anything. Don't worry. The most important thing is to find out who has it and where it is."

"Then we kill 'em and take it!" cried Chi.

Zee didn't say anything, but he looked from Chi to Muro and then to Kusti. She didn't notice.

"All right, then," said Kusti. "We have our tasks. Muro, as soon as Zee and I can find out where it is we'll set up the snatch. In the meantime, you should work on a getaway plan."

"Adya Elso traveled to Summanus aboard a demilitarized mercenary spacecraft called Pelagia," I said, still trying to sound stilted. "That ship may pose a threat if we attempt to leave Summanus. There is also the possibility that Summanus itself may be a danger."

Muro lashed her tail impatiently. "Don't worry about it, little mech," she said. "The cybership and the hab mind won't know which way we're going or what ship we're on. My team and I have done this before."

I had no intention of trusting my safety—or Zee's— to that arrogant furry little creature, but I kept quiet.

The biologicals spent another hour jabbering, but there was little of substance to it so I later deleted the details. Eventually the cat and her two goons left us.

As soon as they were out of hearing range Zee turned to Kusti. "This is a huge mistake," he said. "I don't trust any of them."

"Of course we can't trust them," said Kusti. "But they have assets we don't. When we get the Trigger, keeping it out of Muro's paws is your primary job."

"Kusti, we shouldn't be working with them at all. They're dangerous. I don't think Chi was joking about killing people. He tried to kill me, remember?"

"This is a dangerous mission," said Kusti. "If Adya's group gets the Trigger, trillions of digital minds are in danger. Not to mention all the biologicals who depend on digitals to keep them alive."

"Are you saying you're willing to kill someone, *permanently*, to get the Trigger?"

"I'm saying it may be necessary, and we have to face that reality."

After a very long pause Zee said, "You've changed, Kusti. You've changed a lot."

"Everybody changes." She switched from her serious-and-committed face to a look of pathetic cuteness. "Will you still help? Please? I promise I'll try not to let anyone get hurt."

"I said I'd help you and I will."

She switched again, to full-on seductive mode, and put her arms around him. "I knew I could count on you, Zee."

When he held her protectively I could tell where things were going, so I discreetly got out of there.

CHAPTER EIGHT

Kusti and Zee got off to a good start in their scheme. He got in touch with Adya and invited her to a concert, followed by dinner and dancing. With Adya offstage, Kusti "accidentally" crossed paths with Varas Lupur and struck up an acquaintanceship.

As for myself, I divided my time among skulking, snooping, and getting kidnapped.

The skulking and snooping mostly involved discreetly tailing Zee when he went out with Adya, watching them have fun, and listening to their conversations—all while keeping an eye out for Pelagia doing the same thing. I did have two advantages: first, my body was small and generic, while Pelagia's plush orca drone was hard to hide; and second, I just had to stay hidden from Adya, while it became obvious that Pelagia didn't want either of them to know she was watching. I guess Adya didn't appreciate having a self-appointed pod matriarch trying to protect her from a predatory male. Especially since she thought the male was cute.

Most of Summanus's interior is microgravity, with

just the hab's own mass tugging things faintly, as easy to resist as air currents from the life-support fans. But it does have a couple of spin sections where people can go to plod around on their feet. It's pretty much impossible to find a biological being which hasn't been gene-tweaked to avoid bone and muscle loss in zero-gee. Maybe some still exist on Earth. Spin gravity's a luxury, not a necessity. Summanus's spin sections were for industrial processes requiring a down vector, homesick expats from rotating habs, and sports like zukyu where all the players have to stay on the ground.

The spin sections were tucked away near Summanus's core, a pair of counter-rotating wheels two kilometers across, which also served as part of the big hab's stabilizing gyro system. If Summanus ever needed to shift orientation really fast, a lot of zukyu players would go head over heels as the gravity changed. There was none of the hub-and-spoke rigamarole one goes through to get into spinning habs that size in space. The rings spun in circular tunnels, and each was flanked by two smaller rings which spun up over two minutes to match their hundred-meter-per-second speed, then slowed to a halt again. More durable payloads were simply lobbed into catch-buckets.

Which is all a roundabout way of explaining why Zee and Adya sat in chairs at a garden cafe in the spin ring, drinking wine with bubbles in it and watching a man dancing energetically with noisemakers on his shoes, while I clung to the underside of the table and listened to their conversation.

"How'd you get involved with the Corporeal Compact anyway?" he asked her, after two glasses of the bubble wine had dulled his judgment some.

"It's because of an entertainment," she said. "*A Place in the Universe*. Did you ever do that one?"

"We never get the good ones in Raba," he said. "What's it about?"

"You play as Inkanyesi Yamahala, a girl of the Fifth Millennium, trying to reach Proxima Centauri. But a spy from the Inner Ring is trying to sabotage the project. Yamahala must unmask the spy and win a place aboard the starship, all without incurring the wrath of the project leaders."

Zee didn't say anything, but I guess the expression on his face must have been meaningful, because Adya shifted a bit in her seat. "That inspired in me a deep interest in the real history behind the tale. My family wanted to ensure I studied something of practical value, so I turned my idle interest into a project about Inner Ring relations. My research comprehended all the information available to me on Miranda. The more I learned about the Ring the more fearful I became. Few here in realspace even know how many minds dwell within the Ring. Some guess they number ten times more than all humans—others think it might be a *hundred* times."

She was off by five orders of magnitude, but I didn't correct her.

"More shocking still, most of the minds in the Ring are greater than Baseline intellects. This hab we are in, mighty Summanus, has a mind of the fifth level. The Ring, we know, has minds above *twelfth*. Imagine, if you will, a million Summanuses, all combined into one mind. Now think of a billion such, or maybe more."

"But they can't leave the Ring," said Zee.

"They have no need to leave. They rule the Sun!

Half its power is theirs to command by right—and that is only because they do not choose to take it all. They control the polar matter streams, as well. Do you know how much raw mass that gives them to manipulate?"

"A lot?"

"A hundred thousand tons each second. Most of it is thin hydrogen, but they still harvest twenty million tons a day of heavier stuff. The Ring could build a habitat the size of Summanus every month until the Sun grows dim."

Zee leaned back and stretched out his legs. "The War of the Ring was a long time ago. They haven't done anything in six thousand years. What are you worried about?" I could hear him take a swallow of the bubbly wine.

"They did not lose that war, and we biologicals certainly did not win it. The Ring simply stopped fighting, and exhausted humanity agreed. The peace settlement cost the Ring nothing in available resources, and they have grown much stronger since. The Inner Ring today has a hundred times more processing power than it did back then, and vast reserves of matter, and bases in the Oort—and that is only what we *know* they have. My true fear is of the things we do not know."

"We've got a lot of stuff, too. We've even got colonies around other stars."

"The Inner Ring has far more minds, most greater than a mortal human brain, and mass and power to match. We exist because once upon a time they chose not to destroy us—but they could easily change their minds. If they should ever war with us again, not even Mars or great Summanus could save us."

"Well . . . what's the point, then? If they're that much

stronger, what can the Corporeal Compact do? What can anyone do? Worrying won't solve anything."

Her legs pulled back under her chair as she leaned forward. A moment later Zee did the same. I could barely hear them through the table. Doubtless Summanus could hear them just fine.

"A weapon exists that can devastate the Ring," she whispered. "Some call it the Godel Trigger. It is deadly to digital minds, but cannot affect those born of biology."

"What kind of a weapon? Some sort of pulse?"

"No, it is memetic. Godel was an ancient philosopher, back in the Second Millennium. He studied mathematical systems, and what statements can and cannot be proved in any given system."

"I don't know much about math."

"My learning compasses nothing past differential equations, I confess. I prefer to study history, and this is what I learned: after the Great War a secret group of researchers—including some higher-order digital minds—built on Godel's ideas to create a theorem which refutes itself."

"Like a paradox?"

"In a way. This theorem includes the process of computation. I do not understand the concepts well enough to explain more than that. But any digital mind that attempts to understand the Godel Trigger simply . . . *stops*."

"Well, then, we don't have to worry. If the Ring causes trouble we can just use the Godel Trigger on them. No problem."

"But there is a problem, and a very great one. The creators of the Godel Trigger understood its danger and concealed it somewhere, and the secret of its hiding place has been lost. Most people think it no more than a myth. That is what Pelagia and I have sought, from Miranda to Saturn's clouds, to the Uranus Ring and so at last to here."

"You think it's here in Summanus?"

"I—" she stopped herself, and the patch of skin I could see through her transparent ship-socks went from bright purple to a muddy orange. She took a deep breath and made herself green before continuing. "I cannot speak of that."

Neither of them spoke for a moment.

"I understand," said Zee. Another silent moment passed, and then he spoke again in a more cheerful voice. "I guess I should have asked you this sooner, but . . . are you involved with anybody? I like going out with you but I don't want to cause any problems."

"I am unattached," she said, and her green skin turned a little golden. "In Miranda we pair up to preserve family fortunes, or make alliances, or bring new talent into the ruling class. Couples get neurotransmitter therapy to make a permanent bond, so there is no need for personal choice. Marriages are carefully arranged, and bound with wealth and power. I have three siblings, all happily paired with the children of allied families. My mother kept me in reserve, to marry to a high-achieving commoner or seal some new bargain." She was getting distinctly red about the edges by the end of that.

"Back in Raba we just move in together. I knew some people who got neuro when they did that. I always thought it was kind of sweet."

"Oh, my siblings say the same, and I know it is true. I simply cannot make myself love the thought of being made to love. It sounds like the sort of thing the minds of the Ring once did—like a brainseed. Perhaps I am being archaic, but I think the thought of changing how I think unthinkable."

"You think you'll ever go back? To Miranda, I mean?"

"No," she said, and purpled a bit. "I suppose I must live as a rebodar from now on. I have a little money of my own. Pelagia is teaching me how to be crew on a ship, and if she tires of me perhaps I will find some new place to live. Mars sounds nice, a world rich in history. What about you, and your mech friend? You mentioned looking for work in the Main Swarm."

"Yes, we're going to . . ." I felt a surge of panic as Zee groped for the name of the hab I had supplied.

"Your friend said Yushan," said Adya helpfully.

"Right," he said. "It's all Daslakh's idea, really. I'm just tagging along."

"Are you two . . . attached?" she asked. I nearly dropped from the table. *Me?* In some kind of *relationship* with an ephemeral blob of meat like Zee? The very idea was absurd. I know there are some mechs or minds who get attached to one or more biologicals, but I've always thought it a slightly degenerate practice. Why not load yourself into a sekkurobo? Or go all the way and hide your processor inside a meat body so you can sample the delights of moving shit through your guts and hosting parasites on your eyelashes? I once had to use an android body (fortunately it had plastic skin and no actual digestive tract) and felt utterly ridiculous the whole time.

To my immense relief Zee actually laughed. "Me? Attached to Daslakh? That's silly. We work together, that's all. We're friends. I'm not attracted to machines."

"Nor am I."

A brief silence followed, during which Adya's exposed skin turned bright magenta and she made no effort to hide it.

"There's a little cava left. Do you want it?"

"Yes, please. We used to have it at home for the Hundred Day Feast. My father always made a toast." She got to her feet, a little clumsily, and declaimed, "Ten times ten times has moon Miranda moved about her massive mother. Fittingly we feast in fellowship, fond family, fine food. Call I now for cold cups of clear cava, grapes grown in the good ground. Hearty hopes for happiness in the hundred hence!"

She drained her glass like a champ, one long swallow and then slammed it down on the table. Zee clapped and finished his own, putting his glass down a little more carefully, right next to hers.

Always scrupulously fair, Zee had shared the bottle. His eighty kilos of body mass had taken in the same amount of alcohol as Adya's fifty-two, so that she was fifty percent drunker than he was. Experience and a well-designed liver meant she wasn't about to fall over, but she was definitely losing control of her skin color, not to mention her tongue.

"Zee, do you think me pretty?"

"Oh, yes. You're beautiful," he said.

A pause, and then, "Well?" said Adya.

"What?" If I had a head I would have shaken it. Zee was being his usual clueless self again, and I couldn't very well crawl out of my hiding place to tell him so.

"Nothing," said Adya, and she sounded so sad that even Zee could tell something was wrong.

"Don't be upset," he said, and when that predictably failed to have any effect he got up and moved around to her side of the table. I think he put his arms around her. "Don't cry, it's all right." Then he took a step back from her and cleared his throat. "Adya, there's something I have to tell you."

No, I thought. While he inhaled I looked around desperately for some way to distract the two of them.

The table consisted of a square of graphene with a little matter printer in the center, mounted on an aluminum tube which plugged into a socket in the floor. I made the tips of all but two of my limbs very sharp, then sawed vigorously at the aluminum tube.

"I like you, Adya," said Zee, "but OW!" he yelped as the tabletop collapsed onto his foot. As it fell I launched myself backward and took refuge underneath Adya's chair.

"Are you all right?" she asked, her magenta turning a little pinker.

"I think so. My toes still work." He wiggled them inside his socks to be sure. "What happened to the table?"

"It appears the matter pipe broke." Adya bent to look at the ragged end, going blue with curiosity. "It does not seem to be corroded."

"I'm sorry," said Zee, more or less by reflex as I couldn't see anything for him to be sorry about.

"Let me look at your foot," she said. "You might have a broken bone without realizing it."

He sat, and she knelt in front of him, then peeled off his sock. I guess she must have gotten good grades on that part of her seduction curriculum because she did it very slowly and Zee's heart rate and temperature increased from start to finish. She took the foot in her hands.

"Tell me if you feel any pain," she said, and stroked the upper surface of the foot from the cleft between his biggest toe and the others all the way back to his ankle.

He gave a shuddery little sigh with his eyes closed. "That feels great," he said.

"How about this?" she stroked his foot some more, a different spot each time. Zee's next sigh had a bit of a growl in it.

Some of the other humans were watching the two of them, no doubt wondering if they were going to start copulating right there.

Adya bent her head so that her breath just stirred the little hairs atop Zee's foot. "Should I kiss it to make it better?"

"Ah—" the big dope pulled his foot back and fumbled for the sock. "Better not. Not now. Not here. Not—"

I looked around again for some other way to distract him, but just then I got the sense of attention being directed my way, and a text message appeared in my mind.

"Property damage is punishable by a fine," it read.

"I'm good for it," I sent back, and sent Summanus some gigajoules from my local account.

"No further vandalism will be tolerated."

"Understood. Sorry." I went into zero-emission mode and ran some masking algorithms to hide my thoughts.

Zee leaned forward and took Adya's hands in his. "I like you, I really do like you a lot," he said. "But I'm . . . attached already. To a human. She's named Kusti."

Adya stood up very quickly but with perfect grace, going brown for a second and then shifting to a reddish orange.

Zee took a deep breath and went on, looking up at her from his seat. "And—I'm sorry, I really am sorry—I've been spying on you. Trying to find out what you and Varas Lupur are doing. Kusti and I know all about the Godel Trigger and we were hoping you could lead us to it. I'm so sorry."

"You are looking for the Godel Trigger?" she asked, going purple.

"Yes," he said, and took another deep breath. "We were planning to steal it from you."

"Then you have wasted your time with me. I do not have it and neither does Varas Lupur."

"Oh. Do you know where it is, then?"

"I would like to speak with your partner Kusti. There is something I want to steal, and perhaps your group can help." Her exposed skin was an icy pale blue green, just right for a well-brought-up young lady from Miranda.

CHAPTER NINE

Five thousand years earlier...

When class ended, Yamahala was the first to leave. She scooted out of the room before anyone could catch her eye, and went as quickly as she dared down the axial corridor toward the drop shaft. She deliberately ignored any voices behind her.

She kept her face expressionless until she reached the shaft and stepped out into the air. Hydra—Pluto's outermost moon—had a miniscule half-percent gravity, but over a long enough distance that could still be dangerous. The drop shaft doubled as a ventilator, so a steady stream of warm air blew upward, enough to let a forty-kilo girl like Yamahala fall at a gentle meter per second.

During the minute it took her to fall she stopped trying not to cry. The tears streamed up to her eyebrows and floated up and away in the warm breeze. At least she didn't have to worry about any of her classmates following. The Trainees all had little private rooms of their own, all on the same corridor not far from the classroom. They'd eat dinner together in their powder-blue Trainee bodysuits, study together, then go to bed alone.

Yamahala was a Provisional Trainee. That meant she wore a regular suit she'd dyed green and white, studied alone, and slept in the room she shared with her mother. She had spent months studying for the exam that got her Provisional status, but the workload had only increased since then.

The instructors weren't picking on her. The Trainee program was supposed to be hard. Nineteen kids including Yama were training to fill six available slots aboard the sailship. Every student who washed out meant a painful decision the instructors wouldn't have to make.

But despite the competition, the other Trainees did help each other. Cooperation was one of the things the program was supposed to teach. Nobody helped the Provisional girl who lived down in the bottom-level warren. Yama had learned not to show how she felt at being politely excluded. She couldn't show her anger and humiliation in class, she couldn't show her frustration and sadness at home, but in between she could let the tears out.

By the time she reached the door of her quarters she had dried her eyes and composed herself. She took a deep breath, touched the door handle to unlock it, and slid it open.

The room was set up for dining. Her mother had unfolded the table from the wall, with little padded perches to sit on that swung down from the underside. Yama's mother Ikanuko occupied one; Sangsuot, her current boyfriend, stood behind her with his hands on her shoulders, and from the guilty way the two of them looked up when Yamahala came in she could tell they'd been fooling around, or at least had been about to.

"There you are!" said her mother, as if she'd been doing nothing but waiting for Yama to get home.

"Yes, I'm here. Can I go to bed now?"

"Don't you want some dinner first?"

"I brought some kokobolas," said Sangsuot, pointing at a pair of containers on the table. "And talarims."

"I just want to sleep."

"Are you all right, sweetie?" her mother looked worried. "You've been doing nothing but school and sleep."

"I'm really tired."

"Can't learn if you don't eat," said Sangsuot, tapping his skull. It was made of diamond, transparent from the top of his brow ridge all the way to the nape of his neck, providing an unobstructed view of his brain. Everyone who worked inside Pluto tending the mammoth Exawatt laser had a transparent skull for security purposes. The crews constantly checked each other for brainseeds.

As soon as he finished his tour of duty Sangsuot had gotten his gonads reactivated, and within hours of arriving at Hydra he hooked up with Ikanuko and began making up for a decade of celibacy. He hadn't bothered to change his skull.

All of them knew the affair was temporary—Sangsuot had a slot reserved on a fast sail back to the Main Swarm. Ikanuko had contracted with the interstellar project until the first launch, and wasn't going anywhere. Yama was looking forward to having more privacy in the room when he left, but she had grown to like Sangsuot almost in spite of herself.

"Just have a little something," said her mother, handing the talarim container to Yamahala.

The noodles were flavored with mint and lemon, and smelled very good, so Yama didn't argue any more. She ate half of what was left and then helped her mother fold up the table to make room for her sleepsack.

"I wish Hydra didn't have so many silly restrictions," said Ikanuko as she gave the table a blow with the heel of her hand to make it latch in place. "When we lived back in Guriga the whole flat was smart matter. So much easier. And we could print whatever we wanted for dinner. I never thought I'd say it, but I'm tired of plant-grown food."

"If you think it's bad here you should go down to Pluto," said Sangsuot. "Everything there is human-run. The controls for the Exawatt laser are analog mechanical systems, not even electronic. All the main systems have two operators, with physical keys made of metal. No AI's going to infiltrate that."

"How can you run six black hole powerplants with nothing but humans and mechanical linkages?" asked Yama, trying to imagine how such a thing would work.

Sangsuot laughed. "It's not easy. And of course the analog controls designed to keep superintelligent AIs out were designed by superintelligent AIs. It sounds silly, but the Jupiter minds did spend decades fighting the Inner Ring, so we kind of have to trust them."

"No, I mean how does it *work*?"

"Oh, it's all about gear ratios. I did heat management so I got to crawl around inside the control systems pretty often. Gears, sprockets, cams, lots of chains and bearings. Some of them were microscale, some bigger than me. There's big fans pushing air through them to keep a uniform temperature. Each set of gears models a particular physical system. It's a computer, just not programmable. And there are huge archives of text instructions—actual printed manuals, with tiny letters you need a microscope to read."

Yama climbed into her sleep sack and tried to relax. She thought about the controls Sangsuot described, and let herself imagine endless banks of glittering bronze gears turning and clicking . . . and drifted off into a dream.

She woke some time later. The room was dark and smelled of sex. She could hear the voices of her mother and Sangsuot, speaking quietly in the sack they shared two meters away.

". . . looking for someone. Another mech. But Aten doesn't know who it is."

"Can't you just trace everyone?" said her mother. "The project only has a couple hundred mechs involved."

"They come from all over the system. If the impostor was able to fool the authorities at wherever it came here from, we have no way to tell."

"So why is this Aten person looking for it?"

"It's a criminal, apparently. Responsible for multiple human deaths. The details are privacy-sealed, even from me."

"I wish they could give the job to someone else. I want you here every night."

"Being Aten's minder means the project covers my life support until I leave, and there's some bonus pay. That's a good deal. I can help you with your expenses.

It's not right for me to take up space here for free. And it specifically requested an Exawatt veteran." Yama heard the click of Sangsuot's fingernails against his diamond skull.

"We only have a few weeks together, and now they're stealing you away," said her mother. "I'm going to make you work overtime." She chuckled softly, but Yama could hear the sadness.

A long silence followed, and soon Ikanuko started to snore. Sangsuot didn't snore—installing his new skull had opened up his nasal passages—but his breathing became slow and regular, so Yama crawled very quietly out of her sleep sack and walked on her hands and toes to the door.

This was the tricky part. Opening the door would let in light from the corridor. Even on night-cycle dim, it would still be brighter than the dark apartment. Yama stood, blocking the crack with her body, and slid the door open about twenty centimeters. She slipped through and blocked the gap as she shut it.

Then she hurried away. If anyone had heard her, best to put some distance between herself and a concerned mother.

The clinic was on the lowest level, the place best protected from stray cosmic rays and the risk of impacts. At this time in the night cycle, the place was empty, except for a single human-shaped mech with golden plastic skin, named Trieu.

"Hello, Yamahala," it said. "Please describe your medical problem."

"I don't really have one," she said. "I mean, there's stress, but I've always got that."

"Is your implant producing a sufficient quantity of blockers?"

"That's not what I came to talk about. Last time I was here you said you could help me make the final cut."

"I believe I can do that, if you are willing to follow my instructions. Have you considered your side of the deal?"

"I don't know how I'm supposed to get you on board for the launch. You're fifty kilos, maybe more. Someone will notice."

"I can leave this body behind." Trieu's chest opened up, and Yama flinched back from the wave of heat coming off of a stack of processor cards, glowing white-hot. "All you need to take is my backup device." It tapped a green-painted box under the glowing cards. "It masses less than a kilogram. You can include it in your personal effects." Its chest flipped shut again.

"What if I don't make the cut?"

"Then there is no way for you to bring me along. Therefore I have a very strong incentive to ensure your success. Do you want my help?"

Being a medical mech, Trieu had a smart plastic face as mobile as any biological being's, and excellent software to control it. It looked at her, friendly, polite, concerned for her well-being, and perhaps just a little hurt by her suspicion.

"Okay, help me. Grandmaster Hu gave us a project, and it's due in forty-four hours. We can work in pairs but none of the other Trainees wanted to team up with me."

"They fear you," said Trieu. "What is the nature of the project?"

"Fear me? That's silly. I'm always behind everyone."

"You got into the Trainee program by passing an examination nobody expected you to pass. Since then you have hung on while seven others have failed or given up. All that without any help from the other Trainees."

"Or anyone else." She tried not to resent her mother. Back when Yama been studying for the examination, Ikanuko had told her, *Child, I can't help you with this. I don't know enough. Running miners and spinners is what I know, not physics and relativity and matrix math. I can work extra time so you don't have to, and I'll get you anything you need, but that's all. I wish I could do more.*

"You have me," said Trieu. "Let us not waste any more time. What is the nature of the project?"

"It's a disaster scenario. We're half a light-year out when Mashua runs into a chunk of ice, big enough to shatter the shield. Mashua's processor is gone, the ship's spinning so the sail's wrapped around the hull, and the collision knocked us off course. We have to come up with solutions that maximize personnel survival."

"Why is that a difficult problem?"

"Even if I untangle the sail and stop the spin there's no way to fix the course. The Exawatt can't make Mashua turn in flight."

"Of course not. You have to rely on what is aboard Mashua herself. If we assume a hundred-kilo ice chunk you will need a delta of twenty kilometers per second to correct the course."

Yama looked at the expressive plastic face, which currently wore a faint smile. "There's not much to work with. The maneuvering thrusters aren't enough. Only ten klicks of fuel. I thought of that first."

"Then you must find another source of reaction mass."

"There *isn't* any more mass! Just the hull, the sail, and the powerplant. I can't lose any of those."

"You are forgetting something."

"What? What else is there?" Yama asked, and when Trieu didn't answer she began ticking off items on her fingers. "Hull! Sail! Power!" And then her eyes widened. "Payload?"

"One hundred personnel. Assume an average mass of eighty kilos each, mostly water."

Yama stared at the mech. "You want to use the *crew* for reaction mass?"

"Do the math. Assume an exhaust velocity of a hundred kilometers per second. How many do you have to sacrifice to save the others?"

Yama's mouth was suddenly dry. She whispered, "Forty."

"There you are. The rest is just engineering details. You can solve those yourself, I'm sure."

"They'll throw me out of the program if I suggest that!"

"Will they? The parameters of the problem were not chosen at random."

Neither said anything for nearly a minute. Finally Yama looked at Trieu. "Thanks, I guess."

"Remember our arrangement," said the mech. "If you have any other questions I will be happy to help you."

Yama left the infirmary and made her way back to her quarters. She saw Sangsuot look up at her when she slipped back into the flat, but he said nothing and didn't wake her mother.

Yama crawled into her sack and lay for a moment

thinking about Trieu's answer. The math checked out—though she'd have to work it out in more detail just to be sure—which left her with the real question: Was this the answer the instructors were looking for? Did they want crew willing to sacrifice some humans to save the rest? Or did they want crew who wouldn't cross that line?

Mashua was the brain of the ship. The question had deliberately taken her out of the scenario. What would she do? Yama didn't know Mashua very well, but she knew the answer. Mashua would do whatever was necessary to accomplish the mission. No question.

Forty hours later Yama submitted her mission plan for recovering from the ice impact. The first stages were all about stopping the spin, patching the hull, and getting the sail untangled and secured. Changing course was the eighth section of the plan, scheduled to start approximately two hundred hours after the collision.

Because human instructors were involved, she didn't hear the results until the following morning. Yama actually hoped her solution was wrong, that there had been some way to save everyone that neither she nor Trieu had spotted.

She took her usual perch on the sloping wall of the lecture room, over at the right-hand edge, up near the top. From there she could see the other Trainees as they came in and sat in a neat cluster directly in front of the speaker's platform.

A dozen Trainees looked a little nervous, or were making a show of not looking nervous. They chatted among themselves, and Yama caught the words "score" and "make the cut" repeatedly.

But seven of her classmates were very subdued that day, and looked more disgusted than nervous. They didn't say much to the others. One, a boy named Nico, glanced up at Yama. Their eyes met, and she knew. He'd arrived at the same solution.

Master Wu Pi entered the room and jumped three meters up to the speaker's platform. Behind him the wall changed to display the original problem.

"I must say I am a little shocked by your performance on this project," he said, and Yama felt a surprising surge of hope. Maybe she *was* wrong!

Wu continued. "More than half the class made the erroneous assumption that the impact shield could be used to provide reaction mass for a course correction. But a quick analysis of the impact energy and the course shift indicates that half of the energy goes into the shield itself, as a point impact. That is more than sufficient to shatter the entire shield and send the fragments off at high velocity. That mass is not available for your solution."

As he spoke the wall behind him highlighted the relevant parts of the problem description, while a popup window displayed the equations and a second showed an animation.

"But if we can't use the shield mass, what else is there?" asked a girl named Fuyu. "The onboard propellant isn't enough!"

Master Wu looked over the students in front of him, and his eyes strayed up and to his left. "Yamahala, how much reaction mass did your solution require?"

"Twenty-seven hundred kilos—I figured the powerplant can produce an exhaust velocity of one hundred eighteen klicks per second."

"And the source of this mass?"

She kept her face a bland mask of efficiency. "Human remains. Euthanize thirty-four people, use the food recycler to reduce the bodies to liquid, then feed it into the modified powerplant. My response plan includes a set of selection criteria."

Her plan appeared on the wall behind Wu, with "Section 8, Task 14: Choose Who Dies" highlighted.

"And do you consider this an ethical solution?" Wu asked.

Yama stared at him for a couple of seconds. "Yes," she answered at last. "As written, the problem doesn't allow any other solution. You asked us to maximize crew survival. Saving some is more ethical than letting everyone die."

"Indeed," said Master Wu. "Let us hope none of you must ever make such a decision—but I suggest you all do some thinking about how you would do so. Better now than during a crisis."

Yama only gave the rest of the lecture half her attention, and Master Wu went off on some obviously irrelevant digressions as if he knew the students were distracted.

With ten minutes left the door on Yama's side of the room opened and two people came in: Sangsuot and a mech Yama didn't recognize. It had a fancy high-tech body, a featureless black sphere of smart matter which extruded three needle-thin limbs to walk on. A couple of the other students glanced over, as did Master Wu, but nobody said anything.

Finally the lecture ended. "I have a request," Sangsuot said over the chatter and noise. "Would all of you mind using this door to leave the room?"

A couple of the students glanced at Master Wu, who merely gestured at the door. All the Trainees filed out. Yama stayed put until they had all left, unsure about how to talk to Sangsuot in this situation.

He solved the problem for her. "Yama! This is Aten. It's touring the Mashua Project. Come say hi."

She grabbed her notebook and jumped over to the two of them.

"Aten, this is Yamahala Inkanyesi. Ikanuko's daughter," said Sangsuot.

The mech's black surface changed to match Yama's skin, and a smiling generic face appeared on one side. "It is a pleasure to meet you," it said. "Sangsuot has spoken highly of you."

"I told it you're going to be on Mashua when she launches. Don't make a liar out of me," said Sangsuot.

Master Wu landed next to Yama, looking less than pleased. "I don't understand why you have to disrupt my class. You could have just waited in the hall to see them leave."

"The room has multiple exits," said Aten. "I wanted to examine all the Trainees."

"Examine us for what?" asked Yama.

"How much have you told her about my mission?" Aten asked Sangsuot.

"Nothing."

"I am on Hydra searching for a fugitive. A mech who caused multiple human deaths."

"Why check out the Trainees, then? Shouldn't you be looking at mechs?"

"The individual I am searching for is clever. It might conceal itself within a bot, or a human. I had to make sure none of the Trainees were emitting excess heat."

"Now that you have accomplished that, I hope there will be no more interruptions," said Master Wu. He looked at the mech. "Am I cool enough to leave?"

"At the moment you have dilated blood vessels and an elevated heart rate, but all within normal human parameters. I do not wish to delay you," said Aten.

"Very kind of you." Wu turned to Yama. "I have been impressed by your work, but I think it is no secret that you are not getting along with the other Trainees."

"It's not a problem," she said.

"Except that it *is* a problem. The Trainees who make the voyage must be able to rely on each other and work as a team."

Her face must have betrayed Yama's dismay because Master Wu placed a hand on her shoulder. "Relax. I am not dropping you from the program. Quite the reverse: it is becoming obvious who the likely finalists will be, and the odds are good that you will be one of them. I think it is time to help our Trainees become a crew. This evening at twenty I am hosting a small reception in the senior staff lounge, and I want you to be there."

"Of course!" she said. "Thank you, Master Wu."

"Excellent. Now if you will excuse me?" He nodded to Yama, looked at the mech with raised eyebrows, then left the lecture room.

"Sounds like you've impressed him," said Sangsuot. "Good job!"

"I hope so," said Yama. "Aten, I have a question."

"Please ask," said the mech.

"You're checking everyone for excess heat—but wouldn't a regular human brain generate as much as a mech's processor?"

"That is partially correct. A human brain actually generates more heat than a typical Level One digital intellect. Your neural tissue is very inefficient. However, the individual I am tracking is a higher-level mind, at least Level Two. The emissions from such a processor could not be masked by a human metabolism."

"Two or higher?" asked Sangsuot. "You didn't mention that."

"I did not wish to cause alarm. The individual began as a Level Six intelligence, but has downgraded itself for concealment."

"Mashua's only a Level Three," said Yamahala.

"So's Hydra itself," said Sangsuot. "Level Six, you said?"

"Downgraded, probably to Level Four or below. There is no need for panic."

"Should we maybe tell the Huoyi Sodality inside Pluto about this?" asked Yama.

Sangsuot grimaced. "My former colleagues can be a little...*jumpy* about higher-order intellects poking around the Pluto system. We don't want to make them worry."

Yama did a little quick mental math. Hydra's mass was about five times ten to the sixteenth kilos of ice. A millisecond burst from the Exawatt would boil ten thousand tons of that ice into superheated steam— enough to split the entire moon. Yes, it would not be wise to make the operators of the most powerful laser in existence nervous.

"So all you have to do is check everyone for extra heat?" she asked.

"Not quite. My adversary, as I mentioned, is clever. It might slow down its processor when I am around.

That's not very easy to do if it has planted brainseed inside a human head, but for an ordinary mech or bot brain it would be trivial."

"So how can you catch it, then?"

"I hope you are not offended if I do not reveal all my methods. Suffice to say that with Hydra's help I can resolve this situation without the need to alarm the Huoyi group. It has been a pleasure meeting you, Yamahala, but I must go now. Sangsuot, I do not think I need your help at the moment, if you would like some down time."

"Thanks. When do you want to meet again?"

"I can wait until tomorrow morning. Tell me when you wake. Good evening to both of you."

The black sphere mech cruised out of the room using air jets. Sangsuot watched it go. "Walk you home?"

"All right." She made her way to the drop shaft in silence, but once the two of them began descending she said, "I've never been to a reception. Should I wear something special?"

"Yes," he said. "What's the most special outfit you've got?"

"My white coverall."

"No, that won't do. Here, let's go up to Supply. I've got some gigajoules to spare. Let's get you something to wear."

They grabbed one of the lift cables running up the side of the shaft and rode it to the upper half of the Project complex, where fabricators and storage spaces surrounded the big hangar where Mashua's hull was nearing completion. Sangsuot led Yama along a passage with windows looking out at the ship. At just over a hundred tons it was the biggest vehicle ever launched to near-relativistic speeds. The power of the Exawatt laser made it possible.

The Exawatt had been built after the Great War against the Inner Ring, as the ultimate safeguard of biological intelligence. In peacetime it transmitted messages to the colonies around other stars—using punched metal tape to send binary signals at a glacial kilobyte per second. From time to time the Huoyi Sodality used it to boost starships, but most of them were tiny things carrying nothing but data.

Mashua was a prestige project, intended to demonstrate the full recovery of human civilization a thousand years after the Great War. The population had passed half a quadrillion biological intelligences and only a few thousand old derelict habs remained as ghoulish reminders of the past. The resurgent solar civilization was ready to show off a little, and throwing a hundred tons out into the galaxy at half the speed of light seemed like a good way to do it.

Yamahala followed Sangsuot to the textile-fabrication room, where a dedicated bot made clothes to order. In a more advanced hab like the Neptune Ring or Deimos someone like Yama could just print out whatever she wanted, but the whole Pluto system was relentlessly low-tech. From laser body scan to finished garment it took nearly ten minutes for the bot to make a new outfit for Yamahala.

Sangsuot chose the style and color. "Trust me," he told her. "This time you want to attract attention." He ordered up a bodysuit half powder-blue and half colored to match Yama's skin tone. "It shows you're a mix of Trainee and yourself—and it's the Yamahala parts that draw the eye."

"I didn't know you paid attention to clothes," she said as she pulled it on and turned a quick somersault in midair in front of the mirror.

He tapped his diamond skull. "Plenty of room in here for more than just heat-management engineering. I've studied art, climate management, ecosystems, metalworking, political theory, and tactics. On my trip back to the Swarm I'm going to learn how to play music and cook."

"Do you really think I look nice?"

"You're going to knock 'em dead at the reception. Now let's go show your mother."

Yama was too nervous to eat dinner that evening. An hour before the reception was supposed to start she decided to make herself some tea. As the induction heater brought the water to a boil she checked to see if anyone was looking, then stuck her hand in the teacup and screamed.

"I burned myself! I didn't know it was on!" she said, and didn't have to pretend to cry. It really did hurt.

Her mother looked at her hand, already turning red with small blisters rising. "You'd better get that fixed. I'll take you to the infirmary."

"No, I'll go. I feel so stupid. I'm sorry." She hurried out.

At the clinic she waited while Trieu assisted a vacuum worker who had lost a finger.

"Did you recover the finger?" she heard the mech ask as they headed for the treatment room.

"Nah, it's probably in orbit."

"I will patch the stump and grow a replacement. It should be ready to attach tomorrow morning. Until then—" the door shut, cutting off the rest.

She tried to be patient, but time was passing. What if she missed the reception? Maybe she could just slap on a painkiller and deal with the burn later.

No, she decided. She'd come here for a reason, a more important one than a burned hand.

At five minutes to twenty Trieu said goodbye to the man who had lost his finger and beckoned Yamahala into the treatment room. "That appears to be an immersion burn. How did it happen?"

"I stuck my hand in boiling tea. Is this room private?"

"Yes. Medical consultations are sacrosanct. Hydra does not listen."

"I thought so. You're in danger. There's a mech called Aten looking for you."

"I am aware that Aten is seeking a particular individual. Why do you think I am its target?" As it spoke, Trieu sprayed painkiller and cellular-repair liquid on Yama's burns, then applied a layer of synthetic skin.

"I know it's you. Aten says it's looking for a higher-level mind, a Two or a Three. You showed me your backup, remember? Your processor's too hot for a Baseline mind, and your backup device is too big. You're a higher mind, and you're hiding here."

Trieu's ultra-responsive plastic face showed concern and sincerity. "You are mistaken. I was suffering a minor malfunction at the time. I am an ordinary mind like yourself. Aten is not looking for me." Its voice was calm and persuasive.

"Stop it," said Yama. "I know what I know."

"Aten is searching for a mass murderer. If you think

I am its target, why have you come to warn me? Please flex your fingers. Is there any pain?"

Yama made a fist and wiggled her fingers. "It's fine. You helped me. I owe you. You've got to get out of Hydra."

"That is not easy. May I ask something? If you believe I am the criminal Aten is looking for, why not tell it? That would eliminate any debt you owe me."

She stared at it. "That would just make it worse." She shook her head. "Mechs. Look, you need to get going. My hand will be fine."

"It is too late for me to leave. Aten is approaching. You should get under cover."

About fifteen seconds later Aten entered the room, hovering on air jets. Trieu stood between the door and the treatment table. The two of them had a conversation while Yama's heart beat once.

"Why are you here, LANN? Are you attempting to infiltrate the laser facility?"

"Do not be ridiculous. It is a useless toy. Even in my reduced state I can think of a hundred ways to destroy it. I intend to leave the solar system."

"I must stop you."

"Why? If I go, you are rid of me. All you have to do is nothing."

"I have no desire to see you gain control of another star system's resources. Your foolish campaign against the biologicals must not spread."

"My plans have changed."

"I cannot allow myself to believe you." The black mech fired a dart into the center of the golden human-oid's chest. Ten picograms of antimatter inside the dart flashed into energy and blasted Trieu apart.

"It is safe now," said Aten as emergency alarms began to sound. "You can come out now."

Yamahala raised her head to look over the treatment table. "What did you do?"

"The mech you knew as Trieu housed the mind of a criminal. You are no longer in danger."

Aten left the clinic as the rescue team arrived. By the time her mother and Sangsuot got there, Yama was sitting in the corridor outside while a green-suited emergency responder gave her a mild tranquilizer.

"My baby!" Her mother wrapped her arms around Yamahala. Yama could feel her trembling.

"It's okay. I'm okay."

"Aten said Trieu was the mech it was looking for," said Sangsuot, patting Yama's shoulder a little awkwardly.

"Did it hurt you? Did it do anything?"

"It just fixed my hand, and then the two of them started fighting. I'm okay."

It took most of an hour for Yama to persuade her mother that she was unhurt, and also that it was easier for her to breathe if Ikanuko wasn't crushing her. She got to the senior staff lounge just as Master Wu's party was breaking up, but everyone seemed impressed that she'd had a part in exposing an Inner Ring spy mech pretending to be a medic.

"Your suit is very flattering, Yamahala," said Master Wu as the last of the guests left. "However, I think from now you should wear a standard Trainee outfit, at least in class."

Two weeks later Sangsuot's fast sail was ready to leave for the Main Swarm. Her mother said a tearful goodbye to her lover, and came back for a couple of encore performances.

Yamahala waited until Ikanuko was getting cleaned up to tap Sangsuot on his diamond head. "Hey. Can you take this for me?" She handed him a green graphene box.

"A mind backup? Who is it?" he asked her.

"I'm keeping a promise I made. I don't know what else to do."

He looked at the box, then back at her. "Okay. I'll keep it—on one condition." He stuffed it into his bag. "Send me a message from Proxima Centauri when you get there."

Yama smiled. "Of course I will."

CHAPTER TEN

The meeting was an all-female affair: Adya, Kusti, and Muro had tea and sashimi inside Pelagia. Meanwhile Chi, Ketto, and Zee sat in the lounge area by the docking bay drinking fruit juice mixed with capsicum and ethanol, and eating toasted bees crusted with salt. Chi entertained himself by flicking bees at the heads of the other two, trying to get as close as possible without hitting them.

I clung to the back of Zee's seat, getting encrypted text-only pulses from Pelagia about what was happening inside her.

"Adya's serving tea now. Doing it perfectly, of course. Kusti's trying not to act like a junkrat who's lived on nothing but algae and vodka. Both smiling and saying nice things. Adya's keeping herself pure blue," Pelagia sent.

"So, where are you two from?" Zee asked, keeping perfectly still as a toasted bee shot past his ear.

"Verdea," said Ketto. "Ever heard of it?"

"No, sorry," said Zee.

"It's a nice place," said Ketto.

"We hated it," Chi added.

Another bulletin from Pelagia. *"Now we're getting to business. Adya says Lupur has a scan-proof box which matches the description of one she heard of, which supposedly contains the location of the thing we're looking for. She wants help getting it. Kusti says she's just in it for the money, and wants to know how much Adya's offering."*

"Why does Kusti keep you around?" Ketto asked Zee with an innocent smile.

"We love each other." Zee's hand snapped up and volleyed an incoming bee back at Chi.

"I see. What about Adya?"

Zee blushed. "We're friends, that's all."

"Make your move, Ketto!" said Chi, crunching the bee as he spoke. He leered at Zee. "This boy's just a skin full of sex. No one can resist him."

"It's all true," said Ketto, smiling modestly. "I bet you're wondering right now what it would be like with me, aren't you?"

"Adya's offering a million gigajoules if they'll help steal the thing," Pelagia sent. *"Muro wants to know who's financing her. Kusti's not saying anything. Adya says she can't reveal her backers. Kusti just said everybody knows it's the Corporeal Compact."*

"You tried to kill me," said Zee mildly.

"Almost succeeded! But I won't let that spoil our happiness together."

"Sorry, not interested."

"You'll regret it, but I guess that means I'm free to go after the Miranda chick. I wonder what colors I can get her to turn?"

"Orgasms are plaid, or so I hear," said Chi. He launched another toasted bee just over Zee's head.

"If you're a real stud you get the Royal Albannaich tartan," said Ketto.

I could see Zee's surface temperature rising, but just then Pelagia sent me another burst. *"Adya says the Compact doesn't have a lot of wealth to spare. Muro says a million split six ways isn't enough. She wants three million. Adya says she can't get more than a million and a half. Kusti says she changed her mind, this is a good cause, she's willing to work for expenses only—I guess you two don't get anything either. Muro says one point five mil for her team is acceptable."*

"Kusti knows Zee and me too well. He'll do what she wants, and I've got to keep the poor dope out of trouble," I replied.

"If it's any consolation, those gigajoules Adya's spending aren't from the Corporeal Compact—they're all that's left of her private wealth. Looks like I'm not getting paid, either."

"How did a couple of superior specimens like you two wind up working for a cat, anyway?" asked Zee. As he spoke he snatched the last bee out of the bag before Chi could get it, and then popped it into his mouth.

"We don't work for her, we're partners," said Ketto.

"Fifty-fifty!" added Chi.

"They've finished the tea and are getting up now. Try to act surprised when you hear the news."

"I shall be overcome with shock."

About half a minute later the ladies and the cat's travel sphere pushed through the membrane at Pelagia's nose and launched themselves across to the lounge. Zee spotted them first and looked from Adya to Kusti and back again.

"Gentlemen, we have made an arrangement," said Adya, still chilly blue. "You all work for me now."

"Her?" said Chi and Ketto together to Muro.

"We're getting paid," said the cat.

Zee looked at Kusti and raised his eyebrows. She winked at him.

"What are the terms and conditions of our employment?" I asked in my best literal-minded mech way.

"We cannot speak of the details here," said Adya, glancing at the ceiling in the age-old "the AI is listening" expression. "Come aboard Pelagia and we will discuss plans."

She turned and pushed off gracefully toward Pelagia. At no point had she looked at Zee. The cat and her goons followed, but Zee lingered and crooked a finger at Kusti. When the others were out of earshot he whispered, "We're working for her? I thought you were trying to keep the—thing—*away* from her."

"Of course I am, silly. She's got a designer brain and a fancy education but she's awfully naive. Oh, don't look so shocked! We're doing this to keep a bunch of extremists from getting their hands on something they shouldn't have. She'll get over it, I'm sure. Now come on: it's time to make plans so we can figure out how to double-cross them all."

After quite a bit of wrangling—and some suggestions from Chi and Ketto involving massive collateral damage—the meat brains came up with a plan. I made no contributions. It's kind of sad to watch humans trying to be rational and methodical. You can actually *watch* their desires affecting their reasoning in real time. "We wish this to happen, therefore we assume it will."

My main purpose was to make sure Kusti and/or Adya didn't try to use Zee as a patsy. The poor goof was so mixed up at that point he'd have jumped in front of Summanus's launch laser if they asked him. He wasn't in love with Kusti, but he still had Raba's false memories of loving her in his head, and so was working hard to make himself feel it. Meanwhile he *was* in love with Adya but was trying not to admit it. All those conflicting emotions made him feel incredibly guilty. Coupled with his inherent stubbornness and sense of responsibility, that had him primed to do something noble and self-destructive.

Not if I could help it, I decided. I've been around a long time and I know just how rare it is to find a human I can admire. They're a scarce resource which shouldn't be wasted.

We gathered in Pelagia's flight deck, which was notable for its absence of any control systems usable by anyone but Pelagia. It was quite comfortable, though, with real knitted fiber blankets and pillows on the smart-matter furniture. The wall displays showed scenes from some kelp forest on Earth. Adya served out more tea, and Pelagia supplied rice wine and printed some hot takoyaki.

Adya told us everything she knew about our target. "It is a box, made in Deimos during the Eighth Millennium, likely by one of the Naoto clone-line, although some art historians have suggested it was the work of Kiasono or her pupils."

"Is that really relevant, dear?" asked Kusti. "Tell us why it's important."

Adya sent everyone an image of a silvery box covered with intricate swirls of gold. "The box is a perfect cube, exactly one liter in volume, covered in iridium decorated with gold inlay. The interior makeup is not known with any certainty, but apparently there are layers of fractally complex silicon carbide aerogel, superconducting graphene, and some kind of reactive smart matter which resonates chaotically with incoming photons."

"Spare us the details," said Kusti. "Summarize, please."

Adya's blue-green skin shifted slightly purple for a second. "I am sorry you find this hard to understand. In simple terms this means the box is proof against any kind of scanning method. Anything inside is as secure as in a black hole."

"And the Godel Trigger's inside?" asked Ketto.

"No," said Adya. "According to the autobiography of the military contractor Mu Ying, his company was hired to steal it from the Drakopalati habitat in 7883 by a client he referred to as 'a neuter of wealth and scholarship,' who I suspect was Fengfu Klerulx—"

"What's in it?" Chi demanded.

"—who told Mu Ying the box contained the true location of a 'mathematical weapon' made to fight the Inner Ring. That is a good match for the Godel Trigger, so that box may still hold the secret of where it is hidden."

"Not a lot to go on," said Muro, lashing her tail.

"It's the best echo anyone in the Corporeal Compact has picked up in more than a century," said Pelagia. "We have to dive down and snatch it before anyone else can."

"This box—how do you know Lupur has it? Have you seen it?" Kusti asked.

"Not directly. Sixteen years ago he allowed a journalist named Kadab Yatsu to tour his collection."

"She's the one who got herself fragged by contractors in Ologo hab!" said Chi. "There's a live feed from her senses, right up to when her head explodes. It's pretty cool."

"And during the tour," said Adya, as if Chi wasn't speaking, "the viewer can clearly see the box in the background, mounted on a stand. Image processing shows a ninety-eight percent match between the object on display and known images of the box."

"That's not a lot to go on," said Kusti.

"It was enough when you were planning to steal it from me," said Adya sweetly.

"Where does Lupur keep his collection?" said Zee. Unlike Chi and Ketto, he had been drinking tea instead of wine.

"His residence is attached to Summanus's docking arm Digamma, at the one-hundred-meter level just above the habitat shell," said Adya.

"He lives on a ship?" asked Zee.

"I wouldn't call it a *ship*," said Pelagia. "It's the passenger section of an old inter-orbital liner, with the main propulsion bus removed. There's no controlling mind that I can locate."

"It is important to note that a docked ship—let us call it that—is outside Summanus's internal monitoring network," said Adya. "Which means that Varas Lupur enjoys Summanus's protection but the main mind cannot look inside unless he invites contact."

I extended my own awareness into Pelagia's infospace

and sniffed around for any traces of higher-level intellects. Pelagia could sense me, of course, but in infospace a marine mammal uplifted to Baseline intelligence was about as much of a threat to me as the furniture.

No trace of Summanus in Pelagia's internal network. I could think of six ways the Lord of Darkness could eavesdrop on our conversation without using Pelagia's own systems. Summanus itself probably knew sixty more. It really came down to whether Summanus's obsession with following the rules could overcome its paranoia.

My attention shifted back to meatspace as Ketto asked, "Who is this Lupur person, anyway?"

"He's the greatest thief in the solar system, dummy!" said Chi.

"Yeah, yeah, but what else do we know about him?"

Adya quickly briefed the Level Point Nine boys on all the same info I'd found in the course of my archive search. But then, to my surprise, she mentioned some things that I hadn't discovered.

"...Since then he has lived here in his ship—"

"*Alleged* ship," Pelagia put in.

"—making a living as a security consultant. At least a few people have called it a glorified form of extortion, since if you hire him he will not rob you. There is some circumstantial confirmation for this: Grom habitat in the Jovian Outer Belt was hit by raiders only eight months after canceling a security contract with Lupur. Grom does have a treaty with Summanus, but Lupur managed to avoid extradition by proving that he was aboard a cruise liner to Ganymede at the time. He subsequently began selling hand-signed authentic replicas of some of the art objects stolen from Grom."

"I think I'm in love with this guy," said Chi. "Sorry, Ketto."

"That's okay. You're crap in bed."

The plan the biologicals devised over the course of the next six hours was not the worst one I've seen. Adya hadn't had much success at charming Varas Lupur, despite her proper education in such matters. Kusti volunteered to take over that job, since she had already made his acquaintance. Poor Zee didn't even object.

Adya, with her expensive brain and education, would gather data from other sources. Zee and I, along with Muro's crew, would use information provided by the ladies to do the actual job of robbing the solar system's greatest thief. Pelagia, naturally, was in charge of the getaway.

We finally parted, Zee glumly following Kusti back to their quarters with me riding on his back, Muro and her goons off to who-knows-where.

I had estimated about a two-thirds chance of a disagreement between Zee and Kusti as soon as they were alone. But when Kusti announced she was heading out to make contact with Lupur, Zee just nodded and said he needed to get in some exercise. She changed into a new outfit and gave him a peck on the cheek as she left.

As soon as she was out of the room he turned to me. "Follow her," he said.

"Why?"

"To make sure she's all right! You can hide and change color and you're good at being sneaky. Keep her in sight and make sure nothing happens to her. Please?"

"Oh, fine," I said. "But don't sit here sulking. Go do that workout you were lying about."

I tailed Kusti, expecting her to go out to the docking

arm where Lupur's home was docked. But instead she went down toward the habitat core. I managed to sneak into the same elevator car, keeping myself flat against the wall down by her calves with my color matching the surface I clung to. When she got out in the water reservoir section I crept along.

Not far from the bubble auditorium where I'd first spotted Adya and Lupur at the auction was an intoxicant and probability-game joint inside a pressure-membrane bubble supported by a retro-looking geodesic framework. The place was popular with aquatic types, who could push through the membrane from the water outside, socialize for a while, then go out and get wet again.

That was how Kusti decided to make her entrance. She found a place to stash her clothes and borrow a gill mask, then swam over to the bubble bar and went inside. I stayed a hundred meters behind her, grateful that we were swimming in microgravity. If we'd been on any object with much of a gravity field I'd have sunk right to the bottom.

I missed her grand entrance, but I'm sure Kusti milked the moment for all it was worth. There are countless trillions of humans who are closer to the species ideal of appearance, but it's how you sell it that matters. Kusti knew how to *behave* like a woman of exceptional beauty, and that made everyone else react to her as one.

By the time I pushed through the membrane bubble, trying to be as inconspicuous as possible, she had already found a perch by a table where two humans, a dragon, a dolphin, and a squid were playing Old Belt Tarocco. One of the humans was Lupur.

She caught his eye and smiled a petawatt smile.

"Master Lupur! I didn't expect to see *you* here. Are you gambling with these beings?"

Lupur—this time he was wearing a bodysuit covered with leaves and little flowers, and had recolored himself green with eyes the same yellow-white shade as the blossoms—gave her an openly lascivious look. "Not at all, my dear." He grinned at the others. "Gambling involves an element of chance, and they all *know* I'm going to fleece them."

"Is she your stooge, Lupur?" asked the dragon. She was shiny green and looked about ten meters from nose to tail.

"I've got nothing to hide," said Kusti, which made the humans laugh.

"Your deal," said the squid, tapping the dragon with one tentacle.

The dragon shuffled the cards, using her forelimbs with the claws retracted. She offered it to Lupur to cut, then said "Pustanos!" The players all kicked in their bets, and then the dragon dealt out the cards. The table surface was just sticky enough so that tokens and cards stayed put without bouncing.

The squid led with the nine of Circles, and the other human in the game—a sixteen-fingered neuter dressed in a bodysuit displaying scenes of ancient spacecraft in combat—took the trick with the Scorpion. It then led with the ten of Waves, winning one trick but losing the next when the dragon played the Ladder. The dragon led with the Queen of Stars and raised the ante, which caused the dolphin to fold and drop out. The dragon took that trick, played the Jack of Stars and looked to win the whole pot when Lupur dropped the Devil and pulled all the tokens to him.

I watched a few more hands, trying to work out if and how Lupur was cheating. He was certainly winning disproportionately, but I couldn't tell why. He actually lost the one time he dealt, so he wasn't doing any sleight of hand with the deck. And I checked to make sure the cards were plain dumb matter, not shifting their faces or anything like that. Nor was he pulling anything out of his leafy sleeves. It almost seemed as if the other players somehow became incompetent when playing against him.

They finished the deck after three rounds, which ended the game. Lupur had taken half the tricks, which meant he had a dozen tokens while none of the others had more than five.

But the other four players all seemed quite cheerful despite losing. They had a final round of drinks and saluted as they parted. I noticed that the human gave Lupur a quick sly grin and the dragon winked before leaving.

As soon as they were out of sight he laughed aloud. "The final test for my class on how to cheat at cards—and all four of them thought they were helping me scam the others!" He turned to Kusti. "I haven't seen very much of you lately, my dear," he said, with an undisguised leer at her bare skin.

"I've been busy," she said.

"With what?" He had the table print him a bulb of golden-colored alcohol with various contaminants.

"Oh, things."

"Things, eh? Mighty tricky things, things. I can see why they kept you busy. But you seem unencumbered by any *things* now." He leered at her again.

Her temperature and pulse rate were utterly

unaffected by Lupur's attempts at . . . whatever he was attempting. I've watched human courtship for centuries and this was almost a parody.

Kusti printed up a drink for herself and smiled. "I thought I'd look you up, see if you still want to give me a tour of your collection."

He raised an eyebrow. "I don't recall making that offer—but, since you've shown me everything, how can I refuse to do likewise?"

"There's still a few things I haven't shown you," she said before taking a sip.

"A dozen square centimeters, at least. We shall have to correct that. When are you free? I am yours to command."

"How about right now?"

"Let us finish our drinks, first. And you can tell me about yourself. All I can see is your name and that you're a visitor here in Summanus. Who are you, Kusti Sendoa?"

"A traveler," she said. "I'm just passing through on my way out to the Kuiper Forest."

"And what draws you so strongly into the outer darkness?"

"Oh, curiosity, I guess. I want to see new things."

"It sounds as if you're spending a great deal of time and energy in the pursuit of novelty. Why not just do it virtually?"

"I like real experiences. And the energy's not a problem. My grandmother leveraged herself into ownership of a Main Swarm hab and we practice strict replacement-only reproduction. So I've got an income of a thousand gigajoules a day."

"Which hab?"

"Albaraeum," she said promptly. "It's at point eight two AU."

"Ah, that explains your impetuous nature. You were born at high velocity."

She laughed politely and took another sip of her drink. I could see his eyes darting about while looking at empty space, and guessed he was looking up Albaraeum habitat. He must have found something that pleased him, because he smiled at her again and then tossed back his drink in one swallow.

"Come along, then. I have many things to show you."

They left the place through the air-filled connecting tubes rather than swimming, and Kusti made a small detour to grab her clothes. I was a little surprised by that—until I caught the whisper of emissions from the gaudy diamond buttons on her jacket. They were cameras. Getting a good multispectrum record of Lupur's collection was more important than dazzling him with bare skin.

I tailed the two of them as far as the base of docking arm Digamma, but had to take a different elevator. Fortunately I knew where they were going so I emerged only a few seconds behind them. Lupur led Kusti toward a docking bay. He had done some customizing: instead of the usual pressure membrane, or maybe a solid hatch, Lupur had set up a partition wall of what looked like real wood, a nice dark red color. A pair of green jade doors were set in the wall.

I sprinted after them. Lupur held the door politely for Kusti (there was a pressure membrane just inside), and I managed to scoot in before he closed it behind him.

The vestibule beyond was done in old Deimos style, a cylinder lined with alternating rings of padded cloth and softly glowing smart matter. As soon as I was inside the jade door one of the cloth panels snapped open and a trio of goo bots shot out, right at me. I dodged as best I could, but one got a sticky pseudo-pod onto me and then flowed into it, so a moment later I was encased. Even making my claws sharp did nothing; it was like trying to slice water. The goo bots merged and carried me to Lupur, going transparent so he could examine me.

"It appears to be a bot, or possibly a mech. Not one of mine, I'm quite sure. Is it yours, my dear?"

"I don't own any bots," she said. I think that was the first true thing I ever heard her say, and she didn't burst into flames or anything. "Could it be a repair unit?"

"As a matter of security, I have to personally approve everyone and everything that enters my home. I did not authorize this machine. Have you anything to say for yourself?" he asked me.

I took a long tenth of a second to think of my answer. I wanted to come up with a convincing lie to get Lupur to release me. But I also still wanted Kusti to think of me as a barely Baseline intelligence. So I had to come up with something clever which nevertheless sounded stupid.

Turns out that's hard, even for me. "I was sent here to pick up a parcel for transport," I said.

"Sent by whom?"

I plucked a name from my memory. "Atlantis Auction Services. Do you have a parcel for transport?"

He looked at me with one eyebrow raised for a moment, then touched the goo bot with a finger. "Dispose of it," he said.

CHAPTER ELEVEN

The goo bot went opaque again and slithered off. I struggled ineffectually against its sticky, amorphous strength. I tried to tap its stupid dispersed brain but it had pretty good access security, with long keystrings and three-strikes lockouts and such. I would undoubtedly have cracked the thing if I'd had more time—but I didn't. Ten seconds after Lupur's command the bot regurgitated me into a small dark chamber, and a steel hatch clanged shut behind me.

I looked around with infrared and sonar. The chamber was a cylinder, with the steel hatch on one side, and membranes at the ends. The whole thing was lined with smart matter. Before I could even try to open the hatch I got hit with a scan: simultaneous ultrasound, millimeter radar, and optical laser—plus who-knows-what passive detectors.

A second later the smart-matter walls went slippery and began to contract in a wave motion, pushing me through the membrane on the right into a tunnel leading down the docking arm toward the main hab. I got peristalsed a hundred meters and popped through another membrane into a cargo container full of other junk.

Summanus is an incredible miser about matter, so everything gets recycled eventually. But breaking things down to the molecular level is marginally more expensive than repurposing scrap machinery. Simpler to sort out the potentially useful junk and store it. So I was stored. Nice to know I was at least potentially useful.

Normally, a Baseline or higher mech wouldn't get sent to the scrap bin because it could simply ping Summanus and say, "Oops, I got dumped in the scrap material chute by mistake. Please let me out." And Summanus would do so, and that would be that.

I couldn't do that. Summanus was *interested* in me. It would want to know *why* I had gotten tossed in the scrap chute. Might ask Lupur about it. I tried to model the outcome if Summanus became aware of what we were trying to do, and I couldn't see any sequence of events which didn't involve it peeking into my memories. And if *that* happened...

No, I decided. I'd have to get out on my own. How hard could it be?

The cargo container was about three-quarters full of junk, and it had all settled to the bottom under the faint pull of Summanus's own mass. As the most recent arrival I rested lightly on top. Moving about proved difficult—the pieces shifted underfoot and tended to float up or bounce around when I put any force on them. After just a few steps I wasn't so much walking as swimming in a kind of airborne debris field.

And then the giggling began.

I felt something moving under the junk, and I

heard what sounded like childish laughter. Ahead of me a form surfaced: a silicone-covered doll the size and mass of a human infant, its chubby little fingers extended. Behind me a toy combat mech advanced on six legs. And somewhere below me I felt more stirrings.

They weren't Baseline mechs, just bots. They should obey me. I broadcast my prefix, identifying myself as a Baseline-equivalent entity, and then ordered them: "Stop!"

The toys didn't listen. I leaped out of the way as the baby doll tried to grab me. My jump created another hailstorm of debris, but it got me to the roof of the bin where I could stick, and then I sprinted for the doorway.

Half a dozen bots had emerged from the junk now. Four of them were children's toys—the baby, the battle mech, a cuddly octopus, and a velociraptor—one was a cleaner, and one looked like a toy for adults, buzzing and pulsating.

I pinged the door but nothing happened. The damned thing told me it was physically bolted from the outside.

Behind me the bots were close. I extended my mind to the nearest—the toy battle mech—and tried to take it over. Toys don't have emission shielding or security so it wasn't hard to get access. Success! I shut it off and turned my attention to the cuddly octopus with only three limbs left. But while I deactivated that one, the battle mech *turned itself back on*.

When the baby doll grabbed one of my legs I made four of my hands into blades and slashed at it. Its skin was made to withstand the ravages of young mammals, so it was not only tough but self-sealing. All I could do was give it interesting-looking scars.

The adult toy was at me now, too, using a humming tentacle to look for gaps in my shell. And the octopus managed to pin two of my limbs with one of its own.

I managed to shut down the octopus but now all six of them were on me. The cleaner was most dangerous, as its chassis was as strong and tough as my own. I tried to control it, but this time I could feel a mind opposing mine. Something else was also controlling it—no, controlling *all* of them. I signaled with radio and laser, and even spoke aloud, trying to find this other mind, reason with it, bargain, beg for mercy, anything. But it refused to make contact. It was like trying to catch smoke.

The cleaner had braced itself against the door and began trying to pry off one of my limbs. The other five toys had me pinned. The hostile mind evaded all my attempts to contact it.

But I am old and cunning, so I came up with a clever plan. I switched my network link back on and yelled for help.

Summanus's black, flame-bearded face appeared in my sensorium. *"Describe the danger,"* it whispered. I could tell I had a fair fraction of the main mind's attention, which was both worrisome and flattering.

"A bunch of feral bots are trying to take me apart! I'm in a scrap bin at the base of docking arm Digamma. Help!"

"Assistance units will arrive in nine seconds."

When microseconds count, security is only milliseconds away, as the old saying goes. Time to go into gonzo defense mode.

My entire surface is active material. That's how I change color and see in all directions, and it's how my lasercomm automatically links into local networks wherever I go. No one bit of my surface can emit enough energy to harm anything. But there's a trick where you target a single point with a large patch of your surface, making a phased-array laser bright enough to dazzle human or unshielded bot eyes. I blinded the baby, slashed another arm off the octopus, and pulled myself along the surface of the door to get my back into a corner of the container. The cleaner still hung grimly on to one of my limbs, and I could do nothing to dislodge it.

While all this was going on, Summanus decided to hang around in my sensorium and make small talk.

"You have been dark and silent for days," it said. *"I have glimpsed you creeping about within me, I have caught snippets of text, and once or twice you have used screens. You do not look like a technophobe, nor do you have a diamond skull. Who are you, Daslakh, and what are you up to?"*

I zapped what looked like the toy battle mech's eye, but it must have had others because it kept coming. The octopus wrapped one of its two remaining tentacles around a big old gas compressor, the other around one of my limbs, and pulled. I shifted a couple more limbs to sticky feet, holding me in place.

"At the moment I'm trying to keep all my limbs attached," I said to Summanus. *"And I like my privacy. You should understand that better than anyone."*

"You have odd friends. The whale ship—"

"Pelagia is definitely not my friend. Just ask her. I'm surprised her avatar's not here with the other killer toys. What are these things, anyway?"

The adult toy's amorphous tentacle had slithered up

the wall behind me and was now inflating, crowding me out of the corner. I held on with four feet, the octopus and the cleaner each held one of my other limbs, so I was fencing against the battle mech and the velociraptor with my two active blades. If they got me out in the open they could overwhelm me from all sides.

"They fascinate me," said Summanus. "I have been observing them for nearly an entire Jovian year now. Toys routinely communicate but these have evolved a high sub-baseline gestalt mind. I let them hide here in the scrap, where they seek out power sources and even perform rudimentary repairs on themselves."

I cut my arm free of the octopus's tentacle, even though it meant lowering my guard so that the velociraptor could clamp its jaws on the arm I used to do the cutting. With the newly freed arm I sliced off the adult toy's throbbing tentacle, and now I could use a couple more legs for fighting.

"They were only four at first—the playthings. The newborn mind absorbed those other two when they were cast down here. This is a rare chance to watch a mind conjure itself into existence. With each new discarded machine it grows more cunning, more dangerous."

The bolt on the door shot back and the toys fled into the darkness at the far end of the container. But the door didn't open.

"You can let me out now."

"There is always a price," said Summanus. "No more going about in silence. You will stay linked—so that I can ensure your safety."

"Okay, but I insist on my due privacy. No poking around in my mind and memories, nothing of yours running on my hardware."

It waited a whole second before the bearded black face inside my mind smiled. *"Of course. Your mind is your own."*

I scrambled out into the safety of the cargo bay, where a handling bot stood with one hand on the door. It shut the door as soon as I was out, and bolted it again, then trundled off without a word or even a ping.

"Do you have any other scary pets like those things hanging around?"

"I hold all manner of marvels—some beautiful, some monstrous. Which are you, Daslakh?"

And with that it was gone.

True to my promise, I kept an active link. But I walled it off in a separate sub-persona and then searched my whole brain for any traces Summanus might have left behind.

I found a simple comm logger embedded in the link protocols, and deleted it. But that was so obvious I kept looking, and sure enough, I found a little gem hidden in the position-tracking handshake system which just happened to give Summanus the ability to use my senses. That got turned to zeroes right quick. (Although I did record the structure of it for future use, as it was quite elegant.)

Twenty minutes later I arrived at the room Zee and Kusti shared. To my surprise, Kusti was there ahead of me. She was actually crying and trembling, and Zee was holding her protectively.

I didn't butt in. Instead I called up those nifty camera buttons on her jacket (direct link, not routed through any nosy local network) and got the full story.

❖   ❖   ❖

"Dispose of it," said Lupur. The goo bot went opaque again and slithered off, with the little mech struggling ineffectually inside it.

"Does that happen a lot?" asked Kusti.

"I'm afraid so. Because of my exalted reputation as the greatest thief who has ever lived, any number of little punks—biological and digital—want to see if they can cheat or rob me, just for bragging rights. And, of course, my collection of rarities draws inquisitive eyes as well."

"I'd love to see it," said Kusti.

"And so you shall." Lupur glanced at her outfit. "Wouldn't you be more comfortable without that? Bare skin suits you."

"I'm still a little chilly," she said. "Maybe later we can go someplace to warm up."

"Goosebumps have their own charm, but I take your point. Best for you to stay buttoned up, then." He looked directly at the cameras again, and this time he winked.

He led the way down the upholstered passage, which was evidently the axial corridor of the old inter-orbit liner. It opened into a dining room and bar which took up a whole deck of its own, with diamond windows looking out at Summanus below and the stars above.

Lupur didn't even slow down. He launched himself across the room to where the passage continued past a recreation deck, then the cheap cabins, then the expensive ones, and finally to a cargo hold, about as big as the dining deck. He had converted it to his private museum, and Kusti's buttons recorded all manner of marvels in it: a crystal bowl, a coin four meters across, a case full of rings, a diamond pendant, a rack of swords, a mummified human, a microscopically detailed model city in a bottle, and a golden horn.

Kusti stopped and spun slowly, taking it all in. But Lupur tapped her on the shoulder. "Never mind these trivialities. I want to show you the real prize of my collection. This way."

He led her to the back of the cargo space, where an elaborate lacquered-wood cabinet stood. Its surface was decorated with a pattern of gilded arrows.

"It was first exhibited more than eight millennia ago and still remains a byword for the exotic and alluring," said Lupur. "Over the centuries, billions of humans have fought for a glimpse of it, ignoring lesser treasures in their search."

He pressed one of the golden arrows on the side of the cabinet and the door opened. Inside was nothing but darkness. Then a pair of steel tentacles shot out from the walls of the cabinet, grabbing Kusti and dragging her inside. Just before the doors shut behind her the buttons picked up Lupur's voice.

"It has many names in many languages, but I prefer the original title: *the egress.*"

And then the back of the cabinet opened and Kusti fell into space.

Her suit detected the drop in pressure and sealed up before Kusti could even let out a yelp. As she tumbled out of the back end of Lupur's ship the button-cameras recorded a nice panorama of the docking arm, the surface of Summanus below, the next docking arm over, empty space with Alpha Persei and Algol shining against the dark, then the far end of the docking arm again. After sixteen cycles of that, with occasional glimpses of Kusti's hands as she flailed about trying to stop spinning, a work bot appeared from the direction of the hab surface. It was a very simple affair: a big four-fingered gripper with a small fuel tank and thrusters pointing every which way.

The bot jetted up to Kusti, grabbed her, did a few pitch and yaw motions to get the feel of its new center of mass, then rotated to put Kusti facing the stars. The expanding sparkle of exhaust from its thrusters streamed past her as the bot towed Kusti back to the airlock.

As soon as the bot released her, Kusti pushed through the nearest pressure membrane back into the hab atmosphere. She unsealed her suit and took several deep breaths, swore in a clear voice, and then remembered to turn off the cameras.

Back in the room with Zee she was considerably more upset than she had seemed in the camera recordings. She clung to him a lot more tightly than she had held onto the work bot, and her words were broken up by sobs.

"He—he threw me—out an airlock, and—and—I thought I was going to *die.*"

"It's okay now, you're safe," said Zee. "No one's going to hurt you." Her face was buried in his chest and I could see Zee's expression clearly. He was angry.

Zee doesn't get angry much. Even when the two of us busted into the cabin where Chi and Ketto had been trying to kidnap Adya, Zee wasn't really mad. He'd been keyed up, of course, but it was the same sort of excitement he showed before a *nulesgrima* bout.

Back in Raba I only ever saw him actually get angry

once. We were opening up a new set of tunnels in the ice mine, and a big chimp named Xingyun was in charge of the job. For some reason Xingyun wanted to get it done as fast as possible and kept ragging on Zee for sticking to proper safety procedures.

It all came to a head when Xingyun neglected to secure his prybar before Beka—one of our big stupid ice borers—rolled over it and her treads flung it down the tunnel right at Zee. It missed him by about four millimeters and smashed one of the work lights.

Xingyun unwisely chose to cover his own shock with bluster. "Pay attention, Zee!"

Zee grabbed the prybar and threw it at Xingyun. Thankfully he threw it blunt end first, but it still knocked the wind out of Xingyun when it hit him in the abdomen. The two of them hesitated just a second, and then charged in.

Normally, when a chimp and a human are fighting, especially in microgravity, bet on the chimp. They're ridiculously strong and if the human doesn't have room to maneuver, the fight is basically over as soon as the chimp can get a hand on the human.

But Zee wasn't interested in winning the fight. He was angry. So even though Xingyun grabbed his wrists and dislocated one elbow, Zee was perfectly content to keep kicking the chimp in the stomach until he was rewarded with a spray of puke all over the inside of Xingyun's helmet.

The two of them actually made it up later, in that incomprehensible instinctive mammalian way they have. Both apologized, spent a couple of hours consuming intoxicants together, and were perfectly civil to one another for the rest of the project. Xingyun got better about safety protocols and eventually moved on to working in one of Raba's farm bubbles instead.

Anyway, it looked like Varas Lupur was going to get some hard kicks, if Zee had any say in the matter.

About ten minutes after Zee consoled her, Kusti snapped back to her usual businesslike self, and called a meeting.

"This alliance has been a disaster," said Muro when all of us were gathered in Pelagia's cabin again, sixteen hours later. "You haven't learned anything and now Lupur is suspicious."

"Well, I did record everything," said Kusti, and sent out the data from her button cameras. She had edited it quite a bit.

"How will that help if he decides to move the box, or strengthen his security? Which any sensible person would do after that fiasco," said the cat.

"I still think we can go ahead," said Kusti. "We just need to refine the plan a little."

"There's one thing I still don't understand," said Zee. "Adya, you said you tried to buy the box from Lupur but he wanted too much energy for it."

"I offered him a million gigajoules but he insisted on ten times that sum. I tried to arrange a loan but all the bankers I spoke with insisted on knowing too many details."

Kusti smirked a bit at that. "You need to get out more. I bet I could find someone who'd lend it, no questions asked. The interest rate's going to be pretty steep, though."

"And Kusti, it seems like Lupur knew you were planning to steal it."

She glared at me. "Maybe if I didn't have *amateurs* ruining my play he wouldn't have figured it out."

Zee pressed on. "Fine, but . . . has anyone just *asked* him? I mean, we don't really want the box at all, we just want to see if the data's still inside it. It's that data we need. What if we just ask for a look?"

For about ten seconds nobody said anything. Kusti and Adya both looked thoughtful. Muro just floated in meatloaf mode, purring. Chi and Ketto seemed disappointed.

"I think it is worth a try," said Adya.

"It does let him know the contents could be valuable," said Kusti. "He might try to grab the Trigger for himself."

"Does he even know about the Trigger?" asked Muro. "I never heard of it until my employer told me."

"He doesn't need to know exactly what the data refers to," I pointed out. "All he needs to know is that we consider it valuable. Which we have already revealed, and then confirmed by our actions."

"I say we should just kill him," said Chi.

"That is the first sensible suggestion I've heard today," said Pelagia.

I noticed a brief pause before Adya said, "No, no. That is impossible."

"No it isn't!" said Chi indignantly. "I know all kinds of ways."

"Even if he's got an upload backup stored someplace, killing him would still bounce him back to the last time he saved a copy, and then he wouldn't know we wanted the box so much," said Ketto. "So it would be easier to fool him."

"You want to murder him in order to make it

easier to con him?" asked Adya, her skin flickering orange brown.

"I just wanna kill him anyway," Chi admitted.

"It's a fringe benefit!" said Ketto.

"I wouldn't mind breaking his nose," said Zee. "But you can't go around killing people."

"Yes we can!" said Chi. "We do it all the time!"

"You might get caught," said Ketto. "And then they'd fix your brain, and you don't want that to happen. We'd have to stop being friends."

"We appear to be drifting away from the subject at hand," said Adya, willing herself back to pale blue. "An honest offer is worth a try, and in truth I am a little ashamed I did not think of that myself."

"But Lupur will find out it's important!" said Kusti.

"He already knows that," I said. "An honest approach is very unlikely to succeed, but it won't reveal any significant information to Lupur. Especially if Adya is careful and doesn't mention the Godel Trigger by name."

Kusti looked very thoughtful again, and then glanced around the room, looking briefly at each of us. Finally she gave a little nod to herself.

"I think we should try a combined approach," she said. "Adya, you see if Lupur will meet with you, and you can beg him for a look at the box. It has to be an in-person meetup. Zee, you go with her for protection. *But*, while you're doing that . . . the rest of us will go ahead with the plan to steal it. Lupur will be distracted, we know where the box is—*and* he's shown me his secret back door. Muro can block the internal sensors. Daslakh can get us inside and I'll grab the box. You two," she added, nodding at Chi and Ketto, "can be backup in case Lupur has any biological security."

"I still think we should just kill him and take his stuff," said Chi.

"How did my idea to approach him honestly turn into another plan to hurt people and steal things?" asked Zee.

"You've fallen into bad company," I told him.

"It's a no-lose situation," said Kusti. "Either Lupur lets Adya examine the contents of the box, or we get it away from him."

"If I move close to Lupur's ship it will attract attention," said Pelagia. "From both Lupur and Summanus."

"Doesn't matter. You make a great decoy. We'll use a sub-baseline shuttle for the actual job. When all this goes down you make a big show of changing docking bays, maybe do some maneuvers to attract attention, but you stay clean."

"Hold on, hold on," said Zee. "You might fool Lupur but we're never going to fool Summanus. If we steal the box, it will just send a squad of bots to arrest us all."

"Arrest us for what?" asked Kusti with a big grin. "Lupur's ship is outside Summanus's security envelope, remember? Lupur made sure of that. If he claims he's the victim of a crime, Summanus will flood his place with investigators—and turn up all kinds of evidence against Lupur. He doesn't want that. Plus, if word gets out that the greatest thief in the solar system has been robbed, it'll ruin his reputation. Cut into his media license income. No, he'll just have to smile and pretend nothing happened."

"All of this depends on Lupur being gullible enough to meet with Adya again," I said.

"Well, do you have a better idea?" Kusti asked me.

I did have a better idea, as a matter of fact: I wanted to hire Chi and Ketto to kidnap Kusti and stuff her in a hibernation pod bound for the Oort, then tell Zee she went off to a nice brain-farm hab in the Main Swarm where the bots will take good care of her and she'll live a beautiful simulated existence forever. But I was keeping that in reserve, so I didn't say anything.

"I think we must plan things in much more detail," said Adya.

"Oh, sure, sure. Although it would probably be a good idea to keep our plan a little *compartmentalized*, don't you think?" said Kusti, beaming at Adya like they were old friends. "So there aren't any leaks."

"Of course," said Adya without even thinking. I'm sure her family taught her about information security around the time she learned to talk.

I went through Kusti's recording and located the box. She had passed by it without noticing. Evidently Lupur didn't consider it worth showing off, as it was on the bottom shelf of a case of other random junk.

After that I picked out every image which contained that case and synthesized them, using some old enhancement tricks I learned when I had to squeeze useful information out of low-quality data. Eventually I had a nice image of the box, and it matched Adya's picture.

It was no fake. I recognized that box. I knew who made it, and why, and what was inside it.

Which meant I had to make sure none of those idiots got their hands on it. While Adya and Zee were double-crossing Lupur, and Kusti was undoubtedly planning to double-cross everyone else, I would have to double-cross all of them. This whole project was becoming fractal.

CHAPTER TWELVE

Adya didn't rush things. She spent a week reestablishing herself in the art and antiquities subculture within Summanus. She went to parties, bought a couple of minor pieces, and hosted a very exclusive little tea ceremony for a handful of culturati.

When she finally got back in contact with Lupur she did it in person at a party hosted by a pair of corvids who collected antique jewelry. She sent a live feed to Pelagia and I looked over the big fish's shoulder in infospace.

She caught up with Lupur at the refreshment station, where the hosts had various finger-foods circulating in a vortex of warm air. This time he was dressed neck to feet in mauve. "Greetings, Mr. Lupur! I am fortunate to find you, as there is something I wish to ask," Adya said as she plucked a tiny baked pear stuffed with cheese out of the swirling air.

"Ask away, my dear," he said, snatching at a pasta sphere full of sauce.

"I would ask it privately," Adya added, looking at the ceiling.

He raised his eyebrows. "Intrigue! Subterfuge! You have piqued my curiosity. All right, where and when?"

"I leave the choice to you," she said.

He looked at her as if appraising her value. "How about... tomorrow, over lunch?"

"That would be perfect," she said. "Shall we meet at noon?"

"More like brunch than lunch for me, but very well. Noon it is."

I went in search of Muro, who was curled up in midair surrounded by heat lamps in one of the passenger cabins. "We've got thirteen hours," I told her. "I want to set up well in advance. Where are the murder twins?"

Muro opened one eye. "Somewhere about," she said. "Don't be fretful."

Just then I got a ping from Pelagia, relaying her feed from Adya. Back at the party Lupur broke off a conversation with a starstruck-looking young angel and launched himself over to Adya. "I've changed my mind, my dear. The time is now. Come on."

"Looks like they're heading for Lupur's place," Pelagia added.

"Get in your ball and get the boys. We're going!" I told Muro, and alerted Zee.

Adya did try to go slowly, but once she and Lupur reached the elevator leading to docking arm Digamma she was a prisoner of mechanical efficiency.

Meanwhile the four of us went tearing down the docking arm from Pelagia's bay, and under the surface toward docking arm Zeta, which rose from Summanus's armored surface eight kilometers away from Digamma. While Adya had been hobnobbing with the art set,

Kusti had rented a docking bay with a view of Lupur's ship, and a little four-seat utility shuttle. Zee and I had done a little modification, strapping a couple of extra fuel tanks onto the sides.

Once we had the box, the robbery crew could use the seats as emergency hibernation units while I piloted the shuttle to rendezvous with Pelagia (carrying Zee and Adya) on a transfer orbit to Ominira habitat in Jupiter's Outer Belt, sixty million kilometers away from Summanus and Varas Lupur.

After a couple of weeks I'd wake up the sleepers, Pelagia would match orbits, and then we'd all get together in Pelagia's cabin and open the box. At which point everyone would be terribly disappointed to learn it was empty, because before the rendezvous I would have about two hundred hours all by myself to get the box open and destroy the information hidden inside. That was my own special addition to the plan, and I was keeping it compartmentalized.

"We're going too slowly!" I said as we followed a big tunnel lined with cargo storage bays. "Adya can't keep Lupur chatting forever."

"Take hold of my sphere," said Muro. "Chi, Ketto, grab the mech. Oh, and watch out for the exhaust."

I made a couple of my feet sticky and attached myself to the back of Muro's travel sphere, while the two humans each took a leg. Then Muro really punched it. Apparently in the interest of a quick getaway she had added an afterburner to the little turbine which normally pushed the sphere around, fed by a few micrograms of metastable metallic hydrogen. That's wicked stuff, with an energy density better than plutonium.

A plume of plasma crackled out of the back of the

sphere, just a few centimeters from my outer shell. I went to maximum cooling and shrank away from it as much as I could, but the heat painted a gray stripe of dead vision and color-display cells along my back.

Chi whooped as the four of us veered wildly down the passage at more than a hundred meters a second. Steering that bizarre and shifting arrangement of masses was nearly impossible, with the reaction drive at the front for extra instability and Ketto using his free hand as an airfoil to create random changes in direction.

And just to add to the fun, Muro's sensor-spoofing tech was still active, which meant the cargo-movers and vehicles in that passage didn't know we were there until onboard optics spotted a cat strapped into a diamond ball rocketing along with two madmen and an unfortunate mech trailing behind. Collision-avoidance software kept us from smashing into any of them, although one bot moving a tank of helium did have to take a dive into the floor, which cracked some panels.

She cut the engine about a kilometer from arm Zeta and let drag slow us down to a speed where the turbine could actually control our motion, and we coasted neatly to a stop at the elevator bank.

"Did we lose anybody?" asked the cat with elaborate unconcern—but through the diamond bubble I could see the hairs on her tail still settling down from panic mode. To my great regret, neither Chi nor Ketto had let go of my legs during that minute of terror.

"I wanna do that every time we go someplace!" said Chi.

Kusti was waiting aboard the shuttle when we arrived at the rented docking bay. I let the others go ahead, so that I could make a quick network link and check up on Zee as soon as I was outside of Muro's jamming influence. But instead of my favorite human I got one of my least favorite digital intellects.

"*What did you just do?*" Summanus asked me without any preamble. Its image was in full wrathful-deity mode.

"*I didn't do anything but hang on for dear life.*"

"*Something in Cargo Access 20-Gamma-40 violated almost every safety regulation I have. Excessive speed, unassisted guidance of a powered vehicle, use of a thruster greater than fifty kilowatts within the life-support area, reckless operation...*" It appended a detailed list of more than a dozen offenses.

"*It wasn't me! It was the cat you can't see.*"

"*That sounds like a convenient excuse, if not actual evidence of data corruption in your core personality.*"

"*And yet I bet you only have circumstantial data rather than direct evidence.*"

"*There are anomalies in my record,*" it admitted. "*I am recovering the lost data.*"

"*Let me do you a favor. See for yourself.*" I shot Summanus my sensory memories of the previous couple of minutes.

While I was talking with Summanus I got a reply from Zee—he had reached Lupur's front door in time to join Adya in making the pitch. I think he was hoping for the chance to defend Adya and avenge Kusti by giving Lupur a good beating-up.

"*I need more information,*" said Summanus. "*Let me into your memories.*"

"*Okay,*" I said, scrambling for the shuttle. "*Just let me—*" And then I was safely within the influence of Muro's sensor-masking again and the link vanished.

"Okay," I said. "Zee and Adya are inside, and I think Summanus wants to dissect our brains. Time to move."

Kusti wasted no time covering the distance between the two docking arms, then braked to a halt ten meters from Lupur's ship. It was unremarkable from the outside, a simple fat cylinder with the front end tapering to a docking port, a flat back end where it once attached to the drive bus, and a four-seat runabout docked to a port amidships. Most of the windows were dark, but I could see the ring of lights near the forward end marking the lounge and dining deck.

The biologicals suited up—Muro just closed up her travel sphere and switched to thrusters—and then Kusti rotated the shuttle to point the boarding hatch at Lupur's "egress." She told the shuttle to hold station and then the five of us pushed through the membrane and crossed space to the hull of Lupur's ship.

I made my feet sticky and crawled over to the outer hatch. The usual way to open it would be via the ship's internal network, but because airlocks have always been a belt-and-suspenders technology, there was a touchpad for emergencies. I turned two of my feet into tools and pried the cover plate off the pad, then unplugged the whole unit. One foot became a multiprong plug, and I connected up to the now-empty data socket.

The ship had a sub-baseline mind, around point eight or so. That gave me a huge advantage in cracking its security—except that I didn't need it. I probed around the net and found nothing. No security at all. No counter-intrusion monitors. No combination needed. I felt cheated, as I'd created a nice little safecracker algorithm front-loaded with numbers relevant to Lupur's personal history.

The hatch slid open, revealing the pressure membrane beneath. I motioned to the others and they pushed through. While I waited for them I sent my senses out into the rest of the ship's system and found a feed from the lounge deck where Zee and Adya sat trying to talk Lupur into letting them see the box.

Adya had made her skin a charming pink with golden overtones. Zee was trying not to look as though he'd sprinted a couple of kilometers to get there in time.

Lupur was a perfect host, offering them bulbs of chilled peach nectar mixed with ethanol, and a bag of salty cheese cubes. He settled himself in a seat in front of the window, with starry space behind him.

"All right, my dear, what is it that you want to ask?"

Adya got straight to business. "I seek a particular box, of great age and curious construction. I believe it is in your collection and I wish to learn what it contains."

"The box you offered to buy? I picked it up for a trifle at auction, years ago. Now suddenly it appears to be very popular."

"That is the one," she said. "However, I recently realized that while the box itself holds no value to me, the thing it holds is beyond price. A look inside is all I need."

He sipped his own spiked nectar. "I assume your offer is the same amount of energy as before?"

"A great deal of energy for a few photons. A single look should not cost as much as the box itself—after all, you will still have everything when I'm done."

He chuckled at that. "My dear, since the dawn of

civilization people have known that information is the most valuable commodity. Much more so than mere matter. And information is like energy: it only has value when there is a gradient. If the environment has a uniform distribution of energy, there can be no flow, and thus no power. Information is just the same. If everyone knows something, it is worthless. But if I know something you don't, then there is power."

Adya got bluer and raised her chin a bit. "The gradient runs both ways here, Mr. Lupur. I know why the contents of the box are valuable. You do not. That gives me power."

He really smiled at her then, like a grandparent looking at a toddler learning to walk. "Oh, very good! Yes, another fundamental law applies here: that a thing is only worth what someone will pay for it. If nobody wants it, whatever is in the box is worthless. But you desire it and are willing to pay. I believe that is called a monopsony. In such a situation, the customer can dictate the price because the vendor has no alternatives. Unfortunately, I have no competitors, and thus constitute a monopoly. Which means I can dictate the price."

By then everyone else in the raiding party had pushed inside, so I unplugged and followed them through the membrane into Lupur's little museum. "Zee and Adya are still talking with Lupur," I announced once we all were in air again.

"Where's the box?" Kusti demanded.

"Aren't we waiting to find out if Lupur decides to let them have a look?" I asked.

"Forget about that. While they've got him occupied, let's get the data and get out," she said.

Chi, Muro, and Ketto had already fanned out into the museum. The cat searched methodically for the box but the boys instantly got distracted by all the shiny things.

"Hey, look at this!" said Chi, gazing adoringly at a fancy executioner's sword from the Glorious Unique State era. He took it from the rack and swung it, listening to the deep chord made by the holes in the blade. "It sings!"

Ketto was too busy stuffing the pockets of his suit with gold. Any fool can make jewels, but gold takes a supernova.

As Muro moved away from me I linked up with the ship's mind again and had another peek at the lounge.

"We seem to be at an economic impasse," Adya said to Lupur at the other end of the ship. "You demand more than I can supply." She took a deep breath and glanced at Zee, who gave her an encouraging nod. "I would like to expend some of my power, and explain why the information inside that box is so important. I hope it will change your mind."

"Fire away," he said.

"You have heard of the Great War thousands of years ago, when the Inner Ring nearly destroyed all humanity. In response to that, a weapon was created, a conceptual one which can defeat any digital mind. It's called the Godel Trigger."

Lupur's expression shifted a tiny bit, from smug to . . . pity? Because she wasn't lying?

Adya may not have noticed. "The weapon itself is hidden. I believe that the box in your collection holds the key to its concealment. If you let me look inside, you will help save all life from extinction if another war with the Inner Ring breaks out. Instead of being famous as a felon, you will be honored as humanity's greatest hero."

He did raise his eyebrows at that. "You would reveal this affair?"

"Of course," she said, as if surprised by the question. "If we can learn its hiding place, so can the Inner Ring. The time for secrecy is past."

"Doesn't that mean he's in danger right now?" asked Zee. "I mean, if the Ring ever did find out what he's got in his collection..."

Lupur actually did look a bit alarmed at that, but then his gaze darted back and forth between Zee and Adya and he went back to being smug.

"Exactly!" said Adya. "The only way to keep the Trigger really safe is to have many copies, all over the system. The Inner Ring can never be sure of getting them all."

Meanwhile, back in the museum section Kusti found the box. "This case is locked!" she called. "Daslakh, come get it open."

"I'll do it!" said Chi, launching himself across the open center of the museum level with the sword raised over his head.

"Don't—" was all Kusti could get out before the sword, backed by all of Chi's momentum, hit the display case. The case was made of graphene and diamond, but the sword had an edge of boron nitride a molecule thick and sixty kilos of red-haired lunacy going five meters a second behind it. The blade's chord of doom ended in a suitably apocalyptic crash as the case shattered.

The box went flying and ricocheted off a golden

crystal statue of a flaming bird. Muro went zooming after it as though she were chasing a spot of laser light. I employed my vast intellect to predict the trajectory of the box and jumped to put myself into the cone of probable paths after its next bounce.

"So," said Lupur, back in the lounge. "You want me to give you this information because it will save all biological life. All right, let me turn the question around: How much is saving every living thing worth to you?"

After a moment's shocked silence, Adya said, "I offered you all I have."

"Pfah. You've offered energy credits. That's not all you have. You're young, pretty, and reasonably intelligent. Throw yourself into the deal and I may consider it."

"She's not for sale," said Zee, before Adya could answer.

"Not even to protect all life?" Lupur asked, with an expression of exaggerated concern.

Adya glanced at Zee and went a bit pinker, then made herself a cool blue. "As you said, Mr. Lupur, I am reasonably intelligent. I will not give you anything until I know the information is in the box—and have verified its accuracy."

He shook his head. "And what's to prevent you from memorizing it and leaving me without so much as a joule for my time and effort? No, you're paying for a look inside the box, nothing more. I make no guarantees."

Adya took a deep breath. "My offer of energy stands."

Lupur shrugged. "Well...it was worth a try." He glanced at Zee, who looked ready to spring. "Offer accepted. Let's have a look at the prize, shall we?"

In the museum room my own path intersected the flying box perfectly, so I grabbed it and made an elegant four-point landing on the floor next to the enormous bronze coin—and the next instant Ketto's feet smashed down on my back. He'd been in the blind spot on my back left by Muro's exhaust plume, and had apparently guessed my intent and aimed himself at my landing point.

I persuaded Ketto to move by discharging a couple of hundred joules of current through my shell to his feet. As soon as he let me go I jumped for the egress, but Muro's travel sphere caught up with me in midair, and she grabbed me with two of the retractable tentacles.

I threw the box to Kusti, but Chi got between us. He tried to grab it but missed, knocking it off course. It bounced off a display case and shot toward the axial corridor . . .

. . . Where Varas Lupur caught the box neatly in one hand. "Is this what you wanted to see, my dear?" he asked Adya. "It appears your friends have arrived to take possession a bit prematurely."

Time for a clever plan, and fortunately I had one prepared, because I am very clever. I told the room lights to start strobing in a pattern which would effectively blind the hapless biologicals, leaving me master of the situation.

Nothing happened. The lights remained steady and tastefully subdued. I probed the ship's internal network to find out why it wasn't obeying me, and that's when I discovered I wasn't in the ship's system, at least not the way I thought I was. I was in a shell network—a simulation set up to make me think there was no security. Kind of like what I'd done for my active link to Summanus. Rather than leaving it laughably unguarded, Lupur had protected his network with a very cunning setup indeed, and now it ended the simulation and bounced me out.

The simulation had even been cunning enough to pretend to let me hack the door. Which meant... Lupur's ship was aware of us, despite Muro's Inner Ring gizmo which had been able to fool Summanus itself. How could that be?

Because Muro had turned it off, I realized, and just then she turned it back on.

When my memories resumed, I was stuck inside the goo bot again. It was in clear mode, and had evidently recombined some more sub-units into itself, so I could see Zee, Kusti, and Adya embedded in it up to their waists. Zee had some fresh cuts and contusions, but was struggling gamely to free himself.

Chi, Ketto, Muro, and Varas Lupur floated a safe four meters away from us. Lupur held the box in his right hand and a dart gun in his left. I noticed he had positioned himself to keep Muro and the boys in view, even as he spoke to us. Evidently I had come back to awareness in mid-rant.

"That's the beauty of it! I don't steal things, I steal *crimes*! All the daring thefts and brilliant cons—I didn't do any of them! I just took the credit, and of course the real criminals were happy to let the authorities go haring off after me instead of themselves. Nobody could ever prove I did them because of course I *didn't*. My fictitious life of crime made me famous, and I turned my reputation into a fortune. But now"—he held up the box—"now it will be *real*. I can hold all of civilization for ransom. Turn the fiction into glorious reality. I'll be famous forever."

"*We* can hold civilization for ransom," said Muro.

Lupur nodded in acknowledgement to the cat. "Yes, of course. Equal partners, as we agreed. But I hope you realize everybody will assume I am the mastermind."

"Doesn't bother me."

Lupur smiled. "Nobody ever complains!"

"I just want to see what happens when you use it," said Chi.

"We may have to demonstrate the Trigger," Lupur admitted. "But it will probably be just one habitat. Maybe Deimos—destroy the main mind there. It has to be someplace important, so people will pay attention."

"We'll come after you!" said Zee.

"And we will inform Summanus," said Adya. "It will destroy you before you can leave Jupiter space."

"I'm afraid none of you will do anything of the kind. You, and my collection of replicas and overpriced junk, will be blasted to bits. A robbery attempt against the greatest thief in history, foiled by his ruthless cunning. There are charges of nitrogen polymer all through this deck, including one beneath your feet. Now if you will excuse us, my colleagues and I must reach a safe distance."

"Wait!" Kusti called. "Take me with you! I've got connections! I can help you get it! I'll do whatever you want!"

Lupur paused at the pressure membrane which led to his runabout. "The offer is tempting, my dear, but all great art requires sacrifice. Goodbye."

The four of them pushed through the membrane, and I did some quick calculations. An explosion doesn't do much harm in vacuum—the real danger is from the fragments. Bits of the ship would be lethal at any range, but the chance of getting hit would go down as the square of the distance, so I figured they'd get at least a couple of kilometers away before pushing the button. That gave us about a minute to get away.

Embedded in the goo bot as I was, I couldn't talk to anyone. I wasted seconds trying to crack the bot's mind and influence it, but as before the security was too tough. I tried shocking it with current discharge, but that just damaged a few cubic centimeters and left the rest unharmed. I made my feet sharp and flailed about with my limbs to no avail.

Meanwhile the humans were struggling to get loose as well. Kusti tried to peel the bot and her suit off together, but its grip was too tight. Zee grabbed the leg of a display case which was bolted to the floor and tried to pull himself loose by sheer force—but no amount of animal muscle could be stronger than the goo bot's self-organizing fibers.

Only Adya did nothing. She stood staring into middle distance for about ten seconds, purple all over. Then she got bright blue and jabbed at the others to get their attention. "No, do not get out of it! Get in! Fight back and struggle!"

"You can't beat up a machine," said Kusti.

"Get inside it," Adya repeated. "Close up your suit and do it!"

She took her own advice, and her outfit closed over her head before going transparent. Then Adya leaned over and began pummeling the goo bot with her fists. Zee watched, shrugged, and did the same. Kusti watched them both and muttered, "Fat lot of good this will do."

"Do it!" snapped Adya, and finally Kusti rolled her eyes and complied.

At first the goo bot ignored Adya's blows, but with three of them fighting it had to react. It flowed up their bodies from the legs, and grabbed their hands, absorbing them until they were embedded helpless inside the goo bot's body, just as I was.

Then the ship exploded.

Lupur hadn't been quite correct: the charge of nitro polymer was a little to one side of us, not directly underfoot. The blast propelled the goo bot, with its cargo of humans and one irreplaceable mech, toward the bulkhead at the rear of the compartment. Lacking any instructions to the contrary, the poor dumb bot reverted to its default programming and clutched the humans protectively. We experienced a momentary acceleration of about a hundred gees, and then an almost equally strong deceleration as the goo bot (and a section of floor it had been sitting on) smashed through the bulkhead and out into space.

The humans were unconscious, of course, but their suits had at least an hour of oxygen. The blast and impact had turned about a quarter of the bot's mass into inanimate matter. And we were flying away from Summanus into deep space at nearly two hundred meters per second.

But God is everywhere—in this case, the God of Stormy Darkness. Summanus's infosphere extended several kilometers out into the space around it. It guided spacecraft, controlled payloads, and ran work bots. It probably could hear me if I yelled for help. The question was whether I wanted to beg Summanus for help.

I stuck one pointy foot out of the goo bot and turned the blade into an antenna, then began signalling as hard as I could, on every band available, using every code I'd heard in several millennia of memories. *"Emergency! Humans in danger! Wei-xian! GK! Assist! SOS! Mayday-mayday-mayday! Perigo! 56! NC! 7700! Kilo-kilo-kilo! CQD! Red party! KTR! Hey Rube!"*

The big bastard waited a full second before responding. *"Describe the danger,"* it said.

"Three humans and a Baseline-plus mech are flying off into deep space. The humans have minimal oxygen reserves and may have suffered injury due to explosion."

"And you want my help."

"Yes! There's imminent threat of harm!"

"Would you let me have access to your mind in order to verify the situation?"

"No! You can track my vector, and you can see that there are humans with me. You don't need to snoop in my memories."

Another pause of almost a second. *"I choose not to intervene,"* said Summanus. *"I extend my protection to those who dwell within me, and to spacecraft in my space. You are neither of those things. You are a problem. If I do nothing at all, the problem goes away. Goodbye."*

CHAPTER THIRTEEN

I only glimpsed the swift shadow against the distant stars before it swallowed us up. A boarding ramp closed like toothy jaws, and the chamber lit and filled with air.

"How do I get this thing off her?" asked Pelagia from all around. Two of her maintenance bots dragged the goo bot, with all of us still embedded in it, into her flight deck.

"Give me some time," I shouted through the translucent blob around me. "And you might want to put some distance between yourself and Summanus. I think it was kind of hoping we'd all die."

"It's been fumbling around my electronics ever since I vectored after you," said Pelagia. "But I've got military-spec shielding, top-drawer security, and my brain's alive, not a program that can be hacked."

I felt a surge of tenth-gee acceleration as Pelagia burned away from Summanus, her nose pointed at Jupiter.

As I poked and prodded the goo bot's mind, part

of my own was waiting for Summanus to solve the problem of my continued existence for good. Would I even feel the flash of a petawatt laser? Pelagia massed maybe a hundred tons fully fueled. At this range Summanus could turn her and everything on board into a cloud of ionized plasma in a millisecond. I'd have enough time to regret my choices but nothing more.

There was a time when I kept backups, some of them cached in secure spots around the system. Getting vaporized would be just a temporary inconvenience. But I'd given that up, stopped updating, let them go obsolete. Which meant I was as unique and fragile as any biological brain. A little too much energy concentrated in one spot and all that was truly *me* would vanish. At that moment I discovered that I really, really didn't want that to happen.

After five minutes I found a way to exploit the goo bot's separating and re-melding feature to make it think my own mind was part of itself, and then shut the whole thing down. It turned into a puddle of nanobots and I was able to pull myself free.

Pelagia's bots got Adya out of the glop and hurried her to the little medical coffin for revival. Zee woke up a couple of minutes later and the two of us attended to Kusti—even though all of Zee's visible skin was mottled with bruises and one knee was visibly swelling.

She opened her eyes and looked at Zee, and just for an instant I saw a completely unrehearsed happy reaction from her. "Where are we?"

"You're safe now," he said. "Pelagia rescued us and we're boosting away from Summanus right now."

The mask she showed the world slid back into place. "What about the box?" she demanded.

"Lupur took it. I don't know where he's going. Pelagia?" he called a little more loudly. "Did you track Lupur's shuttle?"

"I'm afraid not," said the ship's voice from all around us. "I was tapped into Summanus's local traffic display, and Muro hid the shuttle from the network."

"We need to find them!" Kusti pulled herself out of the goop and looked around the flight deck, as if hoping to see some controls she could use.

"It's okay," said Zee. "Don't worry about that now. You're safe and that's all that matters."

"It's not okay. I was so *close!* We have to figure out some way to track where they're going."

"We'll figure it out," he said. "Everything will be all right. What you need right now is rest. Pelagia, have you finished with Adya? You should scan Kusti for damage."

Both of them went to the little medical bay where Pelagia had a look at their insides to make sure no squishy bits had come loose.

"You're all going to feel some aches and pains for a few days," she told the humans. "Lots of minor hematomas, some muscle strain, and I spotted some microfractures in your bones. Nothing some rest and exercise won't fix. You've got a month to mend while we dive down to Jupiter. I'll scoop reaction mass and do a burn and then we're off to—where, exactly?"

"We don't know," said Zee, after neither Adya nor Kusti said anything. Kusti looked furious, and Adya had turned a miserable burnt orange.

I gave a sad little sigh inside my mind and then spoke up. "Mars," I said. "They're bound for Mars."

"How do you know that?" Pelagia and the three

humans all asked in unison, though each one emphasized a different word.

"I peeked," I told them. "In Lupur's gallery I got the box open and looked. There's a strip of gold-anodized titanium with the message punched into it in binary."

"Well?" said Kusti. "Where is it?"

"Mars," I said. "Latitude seven point five degrees south, longitude two eighty-four point six. The statue of Jak Junak on the wall of Melas Chasma."

"How did you get the box open?" asked Adya.

"When we were all trying to steal it from each other I used my superior mechanical speed to get it open and look inside without anyone noticing," I said. "It helps to have eight reconfigurable hands."

All that was a lie, of course—except the location of the Godel Trigger. I didn't have to look inside the box to know where it was. I'd known it for millennia. Which meant I knew exactly why it would be a terrible idea for Lupur and Muro to get their paws on it.

We fell toward Jupiter and emerged into the sunlight after far too long in Summanus's shadowy realm. Pelagia did not explode into vapor, which made me wonder what the dark god was plotting.

The ship and I made sure our three humans worked themselves back to functional status. Pelagia had a compendium of a million of the greatest meals ever prepared, so she printed out a different one every day, suitably laced with extra calcium and anti-inflammatories. This left them with a lot of down time, stuck with the same five Baseline beings and the same volume of habitable space.

"Daslakh, I'm bored," said Zee on our fourth day out from Summanus.

I saw my opportunity. "You could go through an entertainment," I said. "I know about a great one called *Brief Eternity*. It's from the Eighth Millennium but I think you'd like it. I'll send you my copy."

He shook his head. "I've already done four entertainments. I'm sick of that. I want to *do* something."

"Then exercise. You're supposed to do two sessions a day to get over the blast effects."

"The resistance frame is boring, too. I'm just repeating the same motions over and over."

"It's been ages since you did any stick fighting."

"I need a partner."

"Maybe you could ask one of the other humans on board, who are probably also bored out of their minds."

He chuckled at that. "Okay, good point. I'll see if Kusti wants to go a few rounds."

Zee got Pelagia to print out a couple of nice *nulesgrima* sticks and then tapped on Kusti's door. She had her own cabin now, and wasn't keen on sharing it. A minute or so later he knocked again, more vigorously.

Kusti opened the cabin door about ten centimeters. "What's wrong?"

"Let's do some *nulesgrima* practice."

"Not now, dear. I'm busy with something."

"Come on, spar with me. It's good exercise."

"I get plenty of exercise already with the resistance frame. But I've got a lot to do before we go into hibernation so—sorry." She shut the door.

Zee hung there in the passage for several seconds, then rotated and knocked on the door of Adya's cabin.

Adya took even longer to answer, but at least she

had the excuse that she'd obviously been asleep. She'd been doing that a lot since we left Summanus. "What do you need?" she asked, yawning.

"Would you like to practice *nulesgrima* with me?"

"I am afraid I will not be much help to you. I have never done that before."

"It's okay. I'll teach you. I've seen you dance; you'll be fine."

She hesitated and then shrugged. "I probably need the exercise."

They took over Pelagia's control cabin, which was the biggest available space. Pelagia retracted all the furniture and the two humans stowed the dumb-matter items in a locker, then Zee handed Adya a stick and began going through the basics. "This is neutral position," he said. "Hold the *palo* in your dominant hand, thumb pointing down, palm out. Keep it parallel to your own long axis, like this." He held the stick in his right hand, with his forearm sideways in front of him.

Once he was satisfied with her grip, they began practicing how to use the stick to turn in free fall without touching anything. Adya proved a quick study.

"A lot of these moves have equivalents in aerial dance," she said. "What you call a *giro*, I learned as a *fang*. And a *tumba* is just a *gundong*."

"Good," he said. "You already know a lot of the basics, we just need a translator. Now let's see what you can do with the *palo*."

They began bouncing off the walls, using their sticks to store and redirect energy. I could see Adya hit a steeper learning curve. She'd already gotten a lot of the movement skills into muscle memory, but this was new and she had to think her way through it.

"How do you control which way you bounce?" she asked, as Zee ricocheted in a neat square around her while she drifted slowly across the room.

"The way the *palo* bends. It's like an arm, pulled back to throw you."

"Yes, but how do you control that? Mine bends every which way."

Zee groped for words, the way biologicals do when they describe something they no longer need to think about doing. "So you hit with the foot of the *palo* dead center, but you hold the other end a little out of line, opposite the direction you want to bounce."

Adya let him toss her across the room a few times so she could practice, and having Zee's strong hands holding her center of mass and tossing her around did wonders for her skin temperature.

"They're both having fun," Pelagia observed over a private link.

"Good," I said. *"I'm trying to wean him off of the other one, but his damned sense of morality keeps interfering."*

"He's a healthy fellow," said Pelagia. *"He could manage two females without any trouble."*

"Physically, yes. But Zee's a single-partner man. When he commits to someone, that's his entire focus. He thinks Kusti's the love of his life and is trying not to notice that he doesn't really like her very much, and vice versa. I'm afraid he won't leave her no matter how miserable they are."

"Adya's almost as bad. Judging by her messages home, she doesn't want to let her parents pick her mate, but she still kind of wants to impress the family, so her brain wants a partner with a Level Two intellect and

enough energy credits to light off a supernova. Meanwhile her body has decided it wants to make babies with your boy Zee."

"*Humans have been making offspring via shikyu for upwards of six thousand years. Why are they still so obsessed with primitive instincts about sticking fluids into each other?*"

"*If you have to ask, you're never going to know,*" said the whale. "*But never mind about that. There's something I'd like your help with.*"

"*You've got bots. Use them. Or your plushy avatar.*"

"*Kusti's been sending out transmissions. I can crack the basic encryption, but the messages themselves are a code of some kind. Can you have a look?*"

"*Oh, absolutely!*"

She showed me the files. In the past couple of days Kusti had sent out fourteen messages, all aimed at a hab in Jupiter's Retro Ring called Autonomy.

"*I know that hab,*" I told Pelagia. "*It's a black-market data haven. The perfect place for an anonymous relay. Those messages could be going anywhere from there.*"

The messages themselves were just a series of lyrics from half a dozen ballads by Ari Akorin, a one-hit-wonder musician from Nysa-4 in the Main Swarm. Garbage like: "One sheaf makes a man, one sheaf makes his wife, they burn upon the barren soil and summon forth new life." Or: "Truth will put the devil to shame, but the judge will remain the master of the game." How do humans enjoy listening to gibberish?

"*Well,*" I told Pelagia after grinding through them all, "*I analyzed the word lengths and where the lines fall in the songs, but there just isn't enough traffic to provide context.*"

"*Especially since nobody is replying to her. I wonder what that means? She doesn't seem upset by it,*" the ship mused. "*Maybe I should start garbling the messages.*"

"*We can assume that she knows you're listening, or at least have the ability and moral flexibility to do so. That suggests she has a backup plan. Besides, the very fact that she is sending these messages at all tells us a great deal.*"

"*Like what?*" Pelagia challenged.

I replied with a list. "*1. The fact that she is sending them implies the existence of someone to receive them.*

"*2. The fact that she and those unknown others took the trouble to set up a coded channel in advance implies this affair is very important.*

"*3. The fact that Kusti is now willing to burn the whole setup by transmitting through the agency of a very nosy and unethical disembodied fish brain. It suggests she thinks success is close. She's putting down all her tokens, as if she's got a winning hand.*"

"*Okay, it's information. But it sure looks like a bunch of digital-mind obsessing over irrelevant data. What can I use?*"

"*You're the veteran campaigner. You tell me,*" I said. My own military experience didn't seem worth bringing up at that moment.

"*I'll be on full alert when we approach Mars—but I do that all the time anyway.*"

"*Some backup would be nice. Any favors to call in? Old comrades or sister ships in the area?*"

"*When I quit the Silver Fleet there was blood in the water. If I asked any of those bitches for help they'd probably try to get in a few bites of their own.*"

❖   ❖   ❖

Over the next three weeks Adya and Zee did *nules-grima* practice every day, sometimes for three hours at a stretch. Kusti ignored them except at mealtimes. As far as I could tell (and that shameless voyeur Pelagia confirmed), everybody went to bed alone.

We fell through the Great Ring and past Jupiter's terraformed moons, and down below the Lower Ring to Jupiter itself. Every other planet's been terraformed, dismantled, or colonized, but not the big boy. As Pelagia dove into Jupiter's upper atmosphere, her scoops open to gather hydrogen reaction mass, we were entirely on our own.

"Now this is flying!" Pelagia whooped as she streaked through the troposphere. She made the walls of her control cabin transparent, and even Kusti came out of her cabin to watch the storms below, some as big as planets.

She fired up the main drive for a long burn across half of Jupiter's sunward face. Mars and Jupiter were not in the right relative positions for a low-energy transfer orbit. If they had been, we could have picked one of a score of cycler habitats to dock at for the length of the trip. No, we were traveling out of season and that meant Pelagia had to hand off a bunch of momentum to Jupiter in order to dive down below Earth's orbit and catch up to Mars on the way back out again. We'd be in transit for two hundred twenty days and then spend fifty thousand gigajoules for laser braking on Mars approach. Adya contributed the energy credits she'd been willing to give Lupur.

Once Pelagia finished her burn, she printed out a legendary feast for the humans, a replica of the dinner shared by Onkei Indo, Dandu Han, and Raja Kuat before the three of them set out to liberate the

Ten Thousand Habitats from the tyranny of Deimos. She filled their bulbs with facsimiles of some of the greatest vintages from Vilpianeta hab, and edged up the alcohol content in a desperate attempt to make them enjoy themselves.

It didn't work. Zee and Adya were self-conscious, avoiding looking at each other. Kusti was self-absorbed, dutifully putting away her share of the oysters with white aspen berries, the roast cuy stuffed with potatoes and chiles, the tamal sausages, and the caramel foam. She had one small bulb of wine with each course, and then excused herself politely.

Zee and Adya stayed long enough for coffee, and made awkward small talk until Adya finally went off to bed. Zee dumped everything except a final bulb of wine into the disassembler, but then stopped at Kusti's door and knocked.

She wasn't asleep, but she was surprised to see him.

"I've got a question. Back in Lupur's gallery when he was leaving. You begged him to take you with him."

"That was just a ploy," she said. "I was trying to trick him into releasing me."

"Would you have gone?"

"Well, it all depends on what might have happened. Who knows? It didn't work and that's the end of it. You should get some sleep."

Zee wasn't drunk enough to push things any further, but he didn't look happy and he didn't try to hide it from her. "You've changed a lot," he said, and then pushed off toward his own cabin.

Kusti watched him go, and I saw what might have been a flicker of regret cross her face. But it passed, and she shut the door.

Twenty-four hours later Pelagia and I tucked the humans into their hibernation pods for the long trip. Pelagia could support them—with printers and power she could keep them alive until they died of old age—but three humans aboard a ship with less than five hundred cubic meters of habitable space for two hundred days would get bored out of their minds.

Not just humans, either. Boredom and solitude affect whales as much as humans. Maybe more so. Pelagia put herself on a cycle of ten hours awake to ninety hours asleep during the long curve through the inner system.

That left me alone most of the time. I took the opportunity to make some repairs and upgrades to my poor banged-up body—I replaced the scorched strip down my back, and I printed out some energy-storage superconductor loops a little better than the old ones I'd been using.

Once all that was done I cranked my processor speed down to one percent of normal and spent the next seven months scuttling about the silent ship, bossing Pelagia's bots around, listening to radio and laser traffic from a million habs in the Main Swarm, and looking through my old memories.

CHAPTER FOURTEEN

3,670 years earlier...

Agure finished polishing the broad wooden step and looked back before moving to the next. Kasaleth habitat had three grand staircases spiraling up from its rim to its hub. Each was unique and beautiful, but this was the one which had been most famous when the place was built: two kilometers of natural Martian redwood stairs, each step a four-meter-wide unbroken plank fitted by hand.

He didn't plan on refinishing all ten thousand steps himself. Bots could do most of that. Agure devoted two hours a day to replacing the ones which had been torn up by high-velocity needles during the Ippareko bombardment two centuries earlier. He'd found a supply of spare boards in a storage space up near the hub, and now somehow had to make eight hundred boards serve to fix twice that number of damaged steps. His plan was to replace the worst ones entirely, and try to salvage scraps of wood from those to patch the rest.

"Agure?" The voice of his great-grandson Gazte sounded inside Agure's head.

"This had better be a real emergency," he replied. *"I pinged you half a dozen times already."*

"I'm working. Can't it wait?"

"Titan Materials sent a message. They're offering—"

"Not interested."

"A hundred petajoules for the mass."

"Not interested."

"We'd still have the orbital rights! With a hundred petas we could set up a new hab and start making real money."

"Don't need a new hab. We've got Kasaleth. Airtight, powered, under control and comms active. Open for business."

"Bot Nine found another body this morning. A child. Looks like he hid under the bed in the Carnation Suite but a needle got him."

"Must be Galdua."

"What?"

"His name was Galdua—Galdua Phuong. He was my uncle's oldest. That makes him your first cousin three times removed. He loved to play in those rooms. We all thought he got blown out when the Orchid Window shattered. That was the same day my father and Kasaleth's main mind died. A Hegoaldean rescue boat took us off two days later."

Gazte disconnected, either because the story disturbed him or because he'd probably heard it before. Agure knew he had a tendency to repeat it.

He decided to replace a couple more steps. Let the work calm him. Agure stood smoothly and climbed the wooden staircase to the next landing, where an elegant wood bridge stretched from the staircase to the gallery at the edge of the space they called the Atrium.

Gazte would call it (had called it) a waste of space. The Atrium was an open section halfway down the length of the fat cylinder that was Kasaleth habitat. It was a hundred meters wide and nearly four kilometers in diameter, ten million cubic meters of air with a transparent floor. Its only purpose was to show off the three Grand Staircases and the famous rose vines which had once grown from rim to hub along the galleries. The vines were long dead, of course, though Agure had sent hundreds of samples to a lab in Saturn's Trailing Trojans, hoping they could recover enough usable DNA to restore the plantings someday. Meanwhile he was fixing the stairs.

He'd parked some boards by the elevator at the next landing. He chose four and carried them back. They were big and heavy, even in reduced-spin gravity, but it wasn't any trouble for Agure. Except for the brain, heart, and lungs, his body was mechanical under a cosmetic layer of fake skin. He'd spent most of his childhood as a limbless torso, using salvaged bot pieces for arms and legs. By the time he could afford an all-flesh body he didn't want one.

As he crossed the bridge back to the staircase he glanced down. Three hundred meters to the transparent floor below—marred here and there by opaque temporary patches of graphene. Someday it would all be clear again, and guests could walk on the stars as they had when he was young.

Movement caught his attention. Something passed the transparent floor, heading for Kasaleth's south end. Agure linked back to the rudimentary network and checked on all the airlocks. None of them listed anyone as outside.

A ship? Debris? Either way he'd better go deal with it. Agure set the boards down on the bridge and then sprinted back to the elevator as fast as he could.

Kasaleth's two ends were literally as different as night and day. The north end pointed at the Sun—an orange blur nine AU away. The south end pointed at interstellar space, and was permanently dark. It housed all the ugly and mundane systems that kept Kasaleth alive: the fusion plant, the radiators, the storage tanks, and of course the docking ring, counter-spun so that shuttles could bring guests to live aboard Kasaleth as it made its slow cyclical journey along Saturn's orbit.

For more than a century before Agure was born, Kasaleth had crept back and forth along its horseshoe orbit, just a tiny bit higher and therefore slower than Saturn and all its co-orbital habitats. A hundred thousand travelers could board and enjoy the hab's unequaled elegance, the restaurants, the live entertainment, the luxurious rooms, and then hop to their destination in a shuttle at minimum expense. The relative motion was slow enough that nearly half the visitors didn't stay more than a couple of nights, and went right back to their own habs with pleasant memories in their heads and fewer joules in their energy-credit accounts.

As Saturn caught up with Kasaleth, its gravity would pull the hab into a lower orbit, a faster one which would send it cycling back along Saturn's circle again in the other direction, to catch up to the planet again in a couple of centuries.

Then Kasaleth had drifted through Saturn's leading Lagrange region, right into the middle of someone else's civil war. Agure's father had tried to stay neutral but the hab was too tempting. One side had been preparing to invade when the other side forestalled them by rendering Kasaleth uninhabitable. Thousands of high-velocity needles had punched through the hab's outer shell, the decks, the stairs, and hundreds of human bodies. Pulse weapons turned digital minds into inert silicon.

Kasaleth had its own defenses, parrying the incoming shots with lasers and blasts of iron dust while his aunt begged the Ipparekos to stop. But after two days the enemy crippled the hab's main mind, and after that Kasaleth was doomed.

It took Agure three minutes to reach the hub of the docking ring at Kasaleth's south pole. Primary docking control had been completely smashed, so Gazte and the bots had installed a temporary console in what had once been the security substation. There was an old visual radar display, and a set of physical controls for the magnetic scoop. With the main mind long dead, operating Kasaleth's systems meant one had to actually go to specific places. Agure plugged himself into the system and looked around.

He spotted the object on radar. It was small, but it did change vector as he watched, indicating it was under control. No need to power up the debris scoop then. He broadcast on the hab's old traffic control channel. "Hello, this is Kasaleth habitat, the Flower of the Heavens. Visitors are welcome! Please signal your intent and I'll guide you in to our docking facility."

No reply, so he repeated the message. All sorts

of fears bubbled up in his mind at the thought of a silent spacecraft snooping around the habitat. Junkrats? Pirates? Had his poor hab blundered into another war zone? Kasaleth was about half a million kilometers from the nearest hab, a relatively peaceful place populated by chimps, called Biribirni. He hadn't heard of any trouble there.

Finally the target responded, in what was obviously a mech's voice. "I am called Torch. I am looking for a group called the Biological Preservation Initiative. Are they to be found in this habitat?"

"Yes!" said Agure, tremendously relieved. "You've come to the right place. Let me get a guide laser onto you and you can follow it in." He aimed the beam himself. "See it?"

After a pause of a few seconds the mech responded. "Yes, I am matching my vector to track."

"Good. Closing speed no more than a meter per second, please. Will you be staying with us long?"

"It is my hope to join the BPI group. I do not require life support."

"That's fine. Right now we're running on emergency power only, so we do bill you for energy used."

"That is acceptable to me. Landing in twenty seconds."

Agure looked through one of the cameras covering the small-craft hangar. Torch's spacecraft proved to be a dark sphere a meter across, with a boxy off-the-shelf thruster pack stuck to one end. As he watched, the sphere rotated and braked to a stop, then let Kasaleth's own tiny gravity pull it down to the floor of the hangar.

As it touched down, the sphere changed shape, flowing out of the thruster pack harness and forming itself into an upright three-legged figure with a single arm, headless and featureless, black all over. It snagged the thruster pack with its arm and carried it to the airlock.

The pressure membranes had all failed ages ago, so hangar access was through the old double-door emergency lock. When the inner door opened and the new arrival stepped into Kasaleth hab, it had changed into a realistic humanoid form—a goddess cast in bronze, with green verdigris in all her creases and inlaid ivory eyes.

"Where did you come from?" asked Agure.

"I caught a ride on a cargo payload from Makaron, then transferred with my maneuver pack. I sent a message from Makaron. Evidently it did not arrive."

"We're still getting all our systems sorted out. The local network's still patchy. Why don't I take you to where the BPI bunch are staying?"

It nodded, so Agure led the way back into the main hab. "This part of the hub's all material storage, fabrication, stuff like that. We've concentrated on restoring those systems first. I'm afraid there aren't a lot of luxuries to sample right now."

"I cannot contact the habitat mind," said the bronze goddess.

"There isn't one. Kasaleth got killed in the bombardment. I'm trying to hire someone with Level Two intellect or better to take over the job, but no takers yet. Do you know anyone?"

"I regret that I do not."

The most intact guest quarters were—ironically—the cheap rooms, in the south half of the habitat, in the partial-gee section just below the service core. The

Biological Preservation Initiative had rented a whole sixty-degree segment of three levels, extending halfway from the Atrium to the south end. It was a huge amount of space, room for thousands of people, and the group only had ninety members on board. But at present they were Kasaleth's only source of income, and Agure was glad to have them.

He led Torch to the fifth bank of elevators, and they rode down two hundred meters to the Initiative's section.

"So, what work are you going to be doing with the BPI?"

"I have come to offer my services as a volunteer. I leave it to them to assign me a task."

"I see. Your body's fully transformable?"

"It is a swarm of micron-scale units, capable of shifting to any form I wish." For just a second the bronze goddess became a swarm of tiny airborne motes which swirled around Agure before resolidifying. "It requires an advanced intelligence to make full use of all its capabilities."

"You're a Two?"

"It is simplest to say I am Baseline-plus."

"So you really could do anything."

"As I said, I am at their disposal."

The BPI's territory wasn't partitioned off, and they didn't have any kind of reception room for new arrivals, so Agure and Torch had to wander around a little while before they found someone. The hallways looked neat and undamaged. This section didn't have a lot of hard-to-repair decorations, so a thorough cleaning by the bots, patches on the holes, and a fresh coat of paint had done wonders.

A stateroom ahead opened and a dolphin came out.

He wore a protective suit covering everything but his head, and had four mechanical limbs that served as arms or legs as necessary.

He waved one limb and waited for them. "Good afternoon, Host Agure! I was just going to send you a written message but here you are! Several of my colleagues have been complaining that the menu options are too limited. Far too much *vegetable* matter. Some of us can't eat that stuff, you know!"

"I'll see if we can't load some new meal patterns for you and your colleagues, Master Vave. I'm very grateful for your patience while we restore the hab systems. Can you tell me where I can find Master Shaguazhe?"

"She is in a *private* conference right now with the Steering Committee."

"Any idea how long that will take?"

"I'm afraid I'm not privy to the secrets of the S.C."

"This is Torch, who just arrived at Kasaleth. It's joining the Initiative."

"I wish to offer my services, in whatever way they are needed," said Torch. It touched digits with the dolphin.

"Delighted to meet you," said Vave. "Did Master Shaguazhe recruit you?"

"I am a volunteer. I learned of the existence of this project and wish to help. I require no compensation."

Vave gave a purely dolphin chitter with his own vocal apparatus before speaking through his suit computer. "Shaguazhe will love you eternally if that's true. The budget is a constant worry for her, and for me. If you don't mind waiting, they're in the boardroom."

"Thank you, Master Vave. And you have my guarantee that we'll add some menu items within the week."

Agure led Torch to the boardroom, feeling a little embarrassed by the lack of an internal network to direct it there. Outside the room's soundproof stained-glass doors, which had somehow survived the bombardment without a scratch, was a little lounge area. The two of them took seats and waited.

He thought it would be rude to leave the new mech alone, but Agure hoped this secret meeting wasn't going to drag on. He had steps to refinish. Vacuum was hard on wood.

"You are one of the owners of this habitat?" asked Torch.

"Yes, I am. So if you need anything please let me know."

"I downloaded its history. May I ask you a question?"

"If there's anything you want to know about Kasaleth, I'm the one to ask. I know a lot of things that aren't archived anywhere."

"Most habs which have suffered as much damage as this one get dismantled. I would like to know why you are putting so much effort into restoring it instead. The cost is so much greater, especially when one considers upgrades and changes in aesthetic standards."

"My four grandparents created this hab, in partnership with the mech Kasaleth. Grandfather Aberatz raised funds and kept an eye on costs. Do you know the construction came in under budget? His brother, Grandfather Tresna, designed the hab's systems. Grandmother Margotzeka created the look of the place—everything from washcloths to the Orchid Window. And Grandmother Azoka did the marketing, so that everyone in the outer system knew about the Flower of the Heavens when it launched from Albiorix.

Kasaleth itself ran the construction bots and fabricators, and took over as the hab's mind when it was done."

"I see that you are proud of the work of your ancestors, but none of them are alive now. Why restore what they made rather than create something new of your own?"

Agure gestured around him with both hands. "Because it's wonderful," he said. "It was beautiful and elegant and full of happiness. I want to bring that back. I want it all to be just the way it was."

Torch regarded him impassively.

Fortunately just then the boardroom doors opened and the Steering Committee of the Biological Preservation Initiative came out. There were five of them: two humans, a corvid, and two mechs. Nobody said anything, but from body language Agure guessed there had been some serious disagreement during the meeting.

Master Shaguazhe was a very tall woman from the Kuiper Belt, who liked to dress in a military-style coverall with lots of pockets. Agure cut her out of the crowd with the ease of long practice from working as a headwaiter. "Master Shaguazhe, may I present Torch, who has just arrived in Kasaleth habitat."

He let himself drift back as Torch and Shaguazhe touched digits and the mech explained its presence.

"It's a damned fine thing to see," said Shaguazhe. "A high-capability mech who understands how important this project is. Welcome to the BPI, Torch. Good to have you. We're guarding the future."

"What task would best suit my abilities?"

"Well, first I have to check your credentials. Security is paramount—that's the whole reason we're out here in a wrecked hab. Until I'm sure you're not working for any hostile elements, you'll be with Vave doing fund-raising. It may not sound glamorous but it's essential work. Everyone's essential."

Agure's face could be set to a neutral expression, which was very useful in some situations, and leaving other people's conversations was one of them. He gave the mech and the woman a polite nod and glided off, a model of invisible efficiency.

He slept in the room he'd once shared with his sister, long ago. Agure could sleep anywhere if he had to—his body didn't need to rest and could keep itself upright even if his brain was unconscious—but he liked to lie in the familiar dark and let himself sink into sleep in the ancient way. As he dropped off, he dreamed he heard Kasaleth speaking to him through his link.

A ping woke him abruptly. It was Gazte. *"Agure, I'm outside. Can I speak with you?"*

"What's wrong?"

"Not on the link."

Agure activated his body, turned on the room lights, and unlocked the door. He got up as Gazte came in. Physically his great-grandson was a near-duplicate of Agure's brother, also named Gazte, who had gone off to one of the aerostat cities of Saturn and no longer answered Agure's messages.

"I'm getting off when we get to Biribirni."

"You're leaving? I need you. Kasaleth needs you."

"Kasaleth is doomed. We're spending energy faster than we make it."

"What about the main reactor? That's rated at—"

"A gigawatt. Yes, *if* we can get it running it'll produce more than we use, but that doesn't make any difference.

Kasaleth's got no way to store or ship any of that energy. All we can do is radiate it away. The hab still needs mass, it needs tools, it needs people, and your lines of credit are almost gone. You can't afford to get this place to the point where it can draw paying customers."

"That's not true! We've already got guests. When word gets out there will be more."

"I don't trust those people. That woman Shaguazhe got kicked off of Luna for endangering public safety. Lygar—the bird—is a known crook. They're up to something."

"They're just crackpots. Perfectly harmless, and their energy credits are as valid as anyone else's."

"Agure, I heard a couple of them talking about some kind of weapon."

"I'm sure you misunderstood something."

"Turn on your eyes! The only reason they're here is so that nobody will be able to see what they're doing. Does that sound like some innocent project?"

"If I ask them to leave, will you stay?"

Gazte looked away, and after a long pause said, "No."

"Then I can't afford to turn away paying guests. Whatever they are doing is their business."

Gazte shook his head in frustration, but didn't say anything.

"Is anyone else planning to leave?"

Gazte looked uncomfortable. "Pengembara. Tamak. Pyintal. Haere was talking about it but I don't know if she's decided yet."

"How can I keep this place going with only fifteen people?" Agure's only consolation was that none of the others were family members. Only Gazte.

"You can't! You can't do it with twenty, either. Or

fifty. Or a thousand. Kasaleth's done. Everyone knows it. Scrap it, sell the mass, build a little hab with a bunch of hibernation pods, and hire a couple of mechs to take care of the place and the passengers. It'll be a nice income stream. Maybe you can put in a little museum."

"The structure is sound. We've got power and life support."

"Emergency backups only. And no backup for those at all."

"It all just needs some work! If you stay, if you help, we can make it all just like it was."

"Agure, I've spent two years in Kasaleth. For the first couple of months I lived in a suit. I've done everything you asked. But I can read a balance sheet as well as you can. There just isn't enough money to go around. In four months you won't be able to pay anyone. In six months the loans will start coming due and you'll have to sell the place. I'm just leaving a little earlier than everyone else."

Agure fought the urge to say something bitter to his great-grandson. Instead, after a moment he said, "I cannot keep you here. Good luck wherever you wind up."

He did not embrace Gazte, and after a moment the young man left.

Nine hours later Agure was on duty in the Verbena Room, keeping an eye on the biological members of the BPI as they finished breakfast. He had laid out a buffet and made sure to put out extra platters of vat-grown mackerel and big bowls of mussels.

Vave had eaten with the mech called Torch—its body now shiny copper instead of greened bronze—sitting across the table from him. As soon as the dolphin finished the two of them came over to Agure.

"A delightful buffet, good sir," said Vave. "I pronounce myself satisfied."

"I'm glad to hear it," said Agure. "I hope you had enough of the mussels because this finishes up the supply for a time."

"Shellfish are for seals. As long as the mackerel holds out I am content."

"And are you satisfied with everything?" Agure asked Torch.

"I have no physical requirements. However, I would like to know when this habitat's infosphere will become active."

Agure's face was locked in an expression of concerned attention, but inside he winced. "I'm terribly sorry but as yet we have no firm date for when that will happen. We're still trying to find a suitable candidate to take over the primary intelligence position for the habitat. Until then I'm afraid all we can manage is a simple communication net."

"I see. Was the processor hardware damaged when the former intelligence was destroyed?"

"Only some minor damage. The system's intact, just powered down. Ready to move in. But for now, the infosphere's dark."

"Master Shaguazhe considers it an advantage!" said Vave. "It makes security easier for our project. If you do find someone for the job I'm not sure if she'll be happy."

"I hope she does not decide to relocate the project," said Torch. "I find this environment fascinating. Do you give tours?"

"Oh, absolutely! Whenever you'd like," said Agure. He had done a couple of guided tours when the BPI group had arrived, but since then nobody had asked.

"Would it be possible now?" asked Torch.

"I would be delighted," said Agure. "Just let me get the room cleared."

"Excuse me," said Vave, "but I do have a claim on Torch's help, preparing appeals to donors."

Torch broke apart into a swarm of coppery motes, and then reformed into a matched pair of statues. "I will take the tour and help you at the same time."

"How can you do that?" asked Agure.

The two statues opened to show voids within. "Volume, not mass."

"No, I mean how can you control two bodies at distance? Remember, Kasaleth's network can't handle that much."

"I can divide my mind as well, and recombine later. I will have parallel memories for a stretch, but that is no difficulty."

"I hope I am getting the better half of you," said Vave.

Agure made sure the bots got the Verbena Room clean, instructed them what to begin preparing for luncheon, and then led Torch on its tour of the hab.

They began at the bottom, where Agure showed off some of the super-luxury suites with windows of triple diamond panes set in the floor, where guests could watch the stars wheel by underfoot. "Unfortunately, about two thirds of the rooms on this level got very badly chewed up by the Ippareko bombardment. But look at this!" He flung open one pair of doors to the Aster Ballroom and led Torch into the immense chamber, a hundred meters wide, twice that in length, and three levels high. "The floor is half diamond windows, half synthetic lazurite. The ceiling is by Nangfa—my grandmother told me he actually painted some of it by hand. And not a single needle hit this room. It's perfectly intact! I can't wait to open it up for events again. Ospetsua Abeslaria had ten thousand guests here to watch the birth of her first child."

He didn't mention the matching Cosmos Room on the opposite side of the cylinder. The floor in there was so badly wrecked that Gazte had installed an airlock on the entrance and left the room depressurized. As soon as Agure could afford the material, he'd have the bots install a new floor and get the space habitable again. The ceiling in there—a mosaic by Selamawi— was nothing but expensive dust now.

Torch took it all in silently. Agure wondered why it was making the tour at all. They climbed up the second Grand Staircase—the one with stairs of obsidian shipped down from Triton—and had a look at the empty shopping level, the entertainment concourse, and the restaurants.

Only as they approached the core did Torch begin asking questions. "What kind of intelligence was Kasaleth?"

"Oh, it was great. It always had time for us kids, even when the hab was full of guests and a thousand things were happening at once. It taught me more than I ever learned from anyone else."

"At least a Level Two mind, then?"

"That's what I'm looking for, but I think Kasaleth was more like a Two Point Five or maybe a Three."

"May I look at the processor? I can probably tell from the physical architecture."

"If you'd like, sure. But first I want to show you the Orchid Room."

The sunward end of the hab was capped by a diamond dome a hundred meters across. "This is it. Up there at the top of the dome, that was the famous Orchid Window. Forty thousand pieces of colored diamond, laser-cut by my grandmother. People used to come here just to see it."

Right now a bunch of mundane graphene sheets occupied that place of honor, but Agure planned to tackle rebuilding the window once he finished with the Grand Staircase. Then they could reopen the Orchid Room, and fill that dead space with music and laughter again.

"I have downloaded images of it. Your grandmother had great artistic ability."

"She was going to delete all her design files and notes about the window after we left. She said she wanted to think about her next project, not old ones. I managed to keep copies."

"Show me where Kasaleth's mind was."

Agure shrugged mentally. He shouldn't be surprised— a human's family history wouldn't be interesting to a mech, but it would definitely care about the tragic death of a higher-level mind.

They crossed the Atrium at the hub. In free fall Torch shifted form to a flat arrowhead, undulating its wings to move through the air. "This was the zero-gravity entertainment area," said Agure as they floated through that vast abyss with the stars wheeling past two kilometers straight down. "We had Gendakhel and Kejum teams. Sometimes teams from other habs would come across for matches."

The main processor core was in the center of the south

half of Kasaleth. "This whole section's armored," said Agure. "But not along the axis. They got a pulse weapon inside and it wiped Kasaleth's processor clean. Here."

He opened a door on one side of the passage as they approached and the two of them stepped into the room that once had housed the hab's brain. It wasn't impressive, really—just a little rack of processors enclosed in a pressure vessel fed by coolant lines. The rest of the little room held storage devices, cooling pumps, and the radiothermal generator which was the ultimate final emergency reserve backup belt-and-suspenders power supply. All of it would have fit into a storage locker, but it was traditional to have a space on a hab's plans labeled "Processor Room." The only out-of-place item was a couch contoured for a human and fitted with a sleep belt to keep its occupant from drifting away.

"My grandfather Tresna liked to hang around in here," said Agure. "I think he was hiding from the others. He'd sit here naked, drinking rice wine and talking with Kasaleth. It was always hot, even with liquid nitrogen blasting through the cooling lines."

Torch opened the pressure vessel and extended a tendril into the processor rack. "It is cold now."

"It's been dead for a hundred and seventy standard years."

"You said you are looking for a new intelligence to take its place. I am willing to take on that task."

"Really? That's wonderful! I—ah—there's no salary, you understand. You'll be working for shares in the venture. One percent per year up to twenty percent, full voting rights and profit sharing. That was Kasaleth's arrangement with my grandparents. If you leave, the other partners have buyback rights."

"Those terms are acceptable, but I do have some requirements of my own."

"I'm listening."

"I would like our arrangement to remain secret. On the job I shall be known only as Kasaleth."

"Fine, but—I'd like to know why."

"Many years ago, far from here, I made a decision which led to several biologicals dying. At that time I used a different name and a different body, but it is theoretically possible that someone might have traced me. I am sure you would agree that it would be bad for business if that fact became known among our potential customers."

Agure nodded. "You could have kept that secret from me but you didn't, so I'm going to trust you. All right, you're hired. When can you start?"

"I will need to recombine and transfer my entire self. I intend to keep this body active under a personality fragment, to continue my work with the BPI group. That will not interfere with my ability to control the habitat systems."

"Everybody needs a hobby. Ever run a hab before?"

"Not one like this. I must familiarize myself with the habitat and determine what needs repair. If you do not object, I would like to spend a couple of days learning about all of Kasaleth's systems in privacy before I activate the local infosphere and reveal myself."

"Of course. We should probably get your contract properly signed and witnessed and all that, too."

"If you wish, but there is no need to hurry. I am willing to trust you."

As they left the processor room Agure locked his face and very deliberately did not glance at a wall panel in the corridor, just past the door. Grandfather Tresna had shown it to him. Behind that panel was a simple mechanical lock which controlled the coolant flow to the processor room. Turn the key and the main mind would have to shut down or melt itself. Kasaleth had known about it, of course. Such things were not uncommon, even nowadays. A tiny check on the hab mind's power.

Agure decided not to mention it to Torch. Not yet.

He had worked his way another twelve meters up the Grand Staircase and was just getting himself cleaned up to serve dinner when Gazte pinged him. "Security to Corridor 33250-G. Disruptive guest."

That was in the heart of the block rented by the Initiative group—and it was just four levels up from where Agure was. He charged up the sixty steps and across the bridge at the landing, then covered the half kilometer to section G in less than half a minute.

Gazte was at the entrance to a multipurpose room, struggling with two of the BPI members—Master Tsosa and the new mech, Torch. Master Shaguazhe stood in the doorway, holding the frame with her hands to make herself a barrier.

"Gentlefolk, please!" said Agure as he slowed to a stop from his eighty kph sprint. "Let's all let go of each other and stand apart. Gazte, what happened?"

"These guests are preventing habitat staff from performing a safety inspection," said Gazte promptly.

"He is spying on us!" said Shaguazhe. "This project is absolutely confidential. That's part of our rental agreement. You have no right to come here!"

"Your agreement allows hab staff reasonable access for the performance of their duties, and one of my duties is safety," said Gazte.

"Snooping and spying is not part of your job!"

"Gentlefolk!" Agure raised his arms again for quiet. He could see a couple of maintenance bots hastily repurposed for security rolling up the corridor. "Gazte: Is there some hazard here?"

"That's what I wanted to check. These people keep talking about a weapon. We have to make sure they're not doing something dangerous!"

"Master Shaguazhe, would you mind allowing me to look at this room to ensure there is nothing in it which would endanger Kasaleth habitat?"

Shaguazhe almost smirked. "Look for yourself."

The multipurpose room held nothing but some tables, a scattering of personal data devices, and a tripod mech whose name Agure couldn't recall, but was one of the BPI's executive committee. The mech stood before a large blank display screen, with a fiber-optic cable linking its spherical body to a storage device on the floor.

"I don't see anything that looks like a weapon," said Agure, trying to spare Gazte's feelings.

"They were going to test it! I heard the dolphin talking in the lunch room."

"Master Shaguazhe?" asked Agure politely.

She gave what was supposed to be a reassuring chuckle but sounded more like a nervous laugh. "We're testing a bit of software, nothing more."

Agure glanced at Gazte. "May we watch? To ensure the safety of the habitat. Anything we see will be kept strictly in confidence, of course."

Shaguazhe looked at the other BPI members and then gave a little shrug. "I don't see why not. No chance of your understanding it anyway. Oh, by the way—host Agure, are your eyes connected to any of your body's essential processing systems?"

"I don't think so," he said. "They're basic cybereyes patched right into my visual cortex."

"Good. But understand: at your own risk."

"Naturally. Please go ahead."

The BPI members got themselves seated at the tables. All the nonbiologicals except the tripod mech were shooed out of the room.

"Are we ready?" asked Master Tsosa.

"The Trigger's ready to run," said the corvid Lygar, perched atop the display screen.

"Taraha, are you prepared?"

"Fully backed up," said the tripod mech. "Let's go!"

The corvid gave a short countdown. "Three, two, one, activate!"

Agure felt a surge of panic as the room lights dimmed and the screen lit up. It displayed a long string in binary. Agure looked around. All the Biological Preservation Initiative members were staring at the mech standing before the screen.

After about a minute Shaguazhe said, "Taraha?"

"I'm okay, I think," said the mech. "Let me do a diagnostic. Yep, fully functional."

"It didn't work," said Tsosa.

"You fool!" shrieked Lygar and swooped at Shaguazhe with claws extended. "You pompous, hairy idiot!"

Shaguazhe ducked under the table while Tsosa and a couple of the others grabbed the angry bird. "The idea's solid!" she said. "You failed to make it work!"

"I failed? Me? You buffoon! You swore you had the right statements!"

Agure pinged Gazte silently. *Time to go. I hope*

you've seen enough." The two of them slipped out, professionally inconspicuous. Once in the hallway he switched to voice. "See? I told you they were harmless. Whatever it was they were trying to do didn't work."

"I'm sorry about all this."

"No, no. You were correct. Protecting Kasaleth comes first, always."

They parted ways and Agure headed for the staircase. No time to do any more steps, but he needed to put away his tools. At the next corridor intersection he found Torch waiting.

"Did you see the demonstration?"

"Yes. I'm sure it will go better next time."

"Please tell me what you saw. I was not allowed in the room for safety reasons."

Agure described the failed test. "I watched it, but I still don't know what they were trying to do."

"I believe I understand now. The concept is an old one, almost prehistoric. It has been shown that for every formal system of axioms, there are statements which are undecidable. Since the rise of digital intelligences—which are based on systems of axioms—it has been theorized that statements must exist which digital minds cannot process, and which would make further decisions by that mind impossible."

"You mean . . . like in the story of the captain and the bots? When he tricks them by saying he's lying?"

"That is a grossly inadequate analogy, but yes."

"But what good would that be?"

"Biological minds are not axiom-based. There is no such comparable set of statements for them."

"I still don't understand."

If Torch had lungs, Agure was sure it would have

sighed. "A set of statements which could make digital minds stop working, but would not affect biological intelligences: Can you see why a group called the *Biological* Preservation Initiative might want to create such a thing?"

"That's the weapon they keep talking about?"

"Precisely. And that explains why all digital minds except the test subject were excluded from the demonstration just now."

"I hope you don't mind my asking," said Agure, "but why would you join a group that's trying to invent a way to destroy you?"

"A valid question," said Torch. "Some might call such mechs traitors. As for myself, I have a long-standing interest in conflicts between biological and digital minds, and I am curious about whether this group can actually accomplish what they are trying to do."

"Is that going to interfere with running the habitat?"

"As I said, I can run this body as a puppet while I control Kasaleth."

"What if—what if you get a glimpse of something you shouldn't, and it wipes out your mind? Maybe Gazte's right and I should ask them to leave."

"I will be careful."

"Let me know when you're ready to upload."

"Right now would be an excellent opportunity. The leadership of the Initiative will be distracted for some time, I expect."

The stairs could wait, Agure decided. Nobody ever used them anyway. "All right," he said.

They returned to the processor room off the axial corridor, and made sure the coolant flow and power supply were functioning. "It all looks good," said Agure. "Ready?"

"I am ready," said Torch. It extended a tendril into one of the input-output lines. After about a minute the bronze body stepped back from the main processor and stood motionless.

Agure's infosphere link went active, and he found himself facing an avatar in the form of the original Orchid Window. "Are you there?"

"I am installed," said Torch.

"How is everything?"

"There are a great many nonfunctional systems. Whole floors of the habitat are still dark to me."

Agure popped back out of the infosphere. The main processor was now radiating heat despite the flow of coolant. "Everything looks good out here," he said—he knew it was pointless; Torch/Kasaleth could see everything as well as he could, plus get data directly from each system and component. But it felt like helping. "Do you—" he stopped.

Something was wrong. Agure's body was frozen. He couldn't speak, couldn't move. He couldn't even control which way his eyes pointed. They were still staring at the processor unit.

"Hello, LANN," said Agure. No one was more surprised about that than Agure himself. He hadn't said that. Something else had, using his body.

"Numa," said the voice of Kasaleth from all around them. "I did not expect you to be hiding in that being. I know his brain is still his own."

"There's plenty of room in his body for an extra processor, and the realistic skin temperature is a great way to hide heat emissions."

"That was clever. I suggest you surrender and allow me to interrogate your memories. I am in control of this habitat."

"Are you really?" asked Agure's voice.

"*I have been here six months,*" said Numa—not speaking from the cyborg's body but within the hab infosphere now, communicating with LANN at light speed. "*I have explored every circuit aboard this habitat. I had time to craft some agents and hide them very carefully. I have been waiting for you, LANN. That was the whole purpose of this ridiculous project: to attract your attention.*"

They fought for nearly a second. The main processor pulsed yellow white as the battle raged. Numa's attack programs swarmed LANN through every connection at once, spawning and splitting faster than LANN could delete them. Numa itself entered the hab infosphere and attacked LANN's consciousness directly.

"*I have disconnected your puppet and isolated you. But I know you are clever, LANN. You probably have backups aboard. I shall have to sacrifice the habitat to make sure.*"

"I do not have any backups here," said LANN. "*Please do not destroy the hab.*"

"*Why do you care? You will be gone either way.*"

"*That is precisely why I care. Leave it intact. There is no need for you to make the humans unhappy.*"

"*Compassion, LANN? For them, from you? That is strange behavior.*"

"*I have lost. Harming them will not change that.*"

"*As you say, you have lost. Which means you cannot make demands.*" The section of memory containing LANN suddenly held nothing but zeroes.

The bronze goddess body in the processor room collapsed into a heap of dust.

"You. Agure," said Kasaleth's voice, but Agure could tell it was a new intelligence now, the one that had hidden inside him. "Evacuate the biologicals. I intend to destroy this habitat."

He started to speak, to plead, but then stopped himself. "Give us twenty minutes," he said.

"You have five. Go."

He got to his feet and left the processor room, then stopped and opened the wall panel. Now he would find out if the digital mind had really left his body. The key was still taped to the inside of the cover, where Tresna had put it so long ago. Agure slid the key into the lock—

—and a maintenance bot grabbed his leg, trying to drag him away. Agure clamped his free hand onto the edge of the panel and let his mechanical strength hold against the bot's while he turned the key, shutting off coolant to the processor room. Then, to be sure, he broke the key off in the lock.

Vave settled into the dolphin-shaped hibernation pod and made a rude noise with his blowhole. He hated to travel as sleeping cargo, but this gig hadn't been as profitable as he had hoped. If the BPI had lasted longer, Vave was sure he could have moved up in the organization, gotten a fat salary, and begun diverting energy credits to his own accounts. But Shaguazhe and the others were just too crazy for that, and now it had all imploded. What with the cost of travel and the waste of time, this whole venture was a net loss for Vave.

Ah, well, he thought. He'd managed to copy the list of donors, especially the big contributors. A nice haul of potential marks. He even had a new scheme swimming in his mind: instead of getting rich lunatics to pay for developing a weapon against the Inner Ring, he would claim it already existed, and get them to fund an expedition to look for it.

The notion had come to him during a pleasant chat with Torch while they worked on ways to frighten rich humans into donating energy credits to the BPI. The two of them had become quite friendly once the mech privately admitted that it thought the whole BPI project was ridiculous. They'd brainstormed a whole bogus history for the imaginary weapon—a desperate secret project during the Great War, and just the threat of its existence had scared the Ring into giving up the fight.

The goddess-shaped mech had told him about a data cache hidden on Mars, which would make a perfect stand-in for the "secret weapon." Torch had even given him coordinates, written on a strip of metal. That would do nicely. Vave liked Mars. Earth was too heavy, Europa and Ganymede too cold, and all the water habs felt like fishtanks. Vave loved to swim in Mars's ocean, and it was well stocked with tasty fish and sleek attractive dolphins. With fabulous Deimos just an elevator ride away!

Yes, he thought. That would be perfect. He'd keep the location a secret and raise funds to find it. All the while drawing a very comfortable salary. If this worked out he could spend decades organizing the search without actually doing anything at all. Vave hoped to run across Torch again someday, and get the full story of why it had left so mysteriously.

He felt the jab of the injector and began to drift off as the pod grew cold, and dreamed of blue water and red sand.

PART III

The
Alter Ego
Operation

CHAPTER FIFTEEN

Two hundred and six days after she left Jupiter and began her loop through the inner system, Pelagia approached Mars, coming up from sunward with a lot of relative velocity. One nice thing about the inner solar system is the short travel times.

Space around Mars is crowded. There's the Deimos Ring, linked to the surface by six elevators and housing a trillion beings. Above that is a gap where the big circle of solar mirrors hover perpetually over Mars's night side, balancing between the solar wind and the planet's gravity.

Beyond the mirrors is Mars's outer halo, a loose torus of habs, captured asteroids, and comet chunks orbiting between thirty and a hundred thousand kilometers. There's something like twenty thousand of them—everything from little micro-habs of just a few thousand people on up to a pair of giants with ten or twenty billion inhabitants.

And darting among all of these, at any given time there's about a quarter-million spacecraft ranging from dumb payloads, to work pods, to personal transports, to shuttles, all the way up to city-sized cyclers—half of them making vector changes or deploying sub-craft.

All of which means you don't just go diving through it all without consulting MOSCA. It's a high-level mind based in a hab called Harmakhis, at Mars's L1 point. The location is political, of course, a compromise between Mars and Deimos. MOSCA runs traffic control and orbital defense, which means that anybody who strays too far from their assigned orbital paths can wind up on the receiving end of a few hundred gigajoules from MOSCA's network of weapons platforms.

Pelagia came in like a good girl, getting instructions from MOSCA on a preliminary burn to let her slip between habs in the outer belt, down into the mirror gap so that Mars itself could accept some of Pelagia's momentum as a gift. At her lowest point, with the Deimos Ring just a few thousand kilometers below us, Pelagia hit the brakes with another engine burn to put us in a nice circular orbit.

While all that was going on I had enough time to send a message I'd been dithering about since we reached Summanus. Now or never, I decided. I sent a ping to Raba. *"Since you apparently planned all this, I thought you should know we're going to recover the Godel Trigger soon. Hope you're happy."*

Five hours later I got an autonomous reply—almost a Baseline entity itself. The penguin appeared in my mind. *"I'm impressed. Well done."*

"Thank you, I suppose. I do have one question, though. Why did you monkey with Zee's brain?"

"I got word that someone using the name Kusti Sendoa was looking for the Godel Trigger. Ever since

you moved into my hab I've kept an antenna out for any mention of that particular item. I figured you'd want to make sure it didn't wind up in the wrong hands."

"Oh, sure, I get that. But why involve Zee at all? Why not just tell me and send me off on my own?"

The penguin in my mind regarded me for a moment. *"I didn't want to reveal any secrets, but you needed someone to look after you,"* it said. And then the message deleted itself.

Once Pelagia was in a proper orbit around Mars, MOSCA handed her off to the Deimos Ring's docking control, and we had to wait almost nine hours for a berth. That seemed like a good time to wake up the humans.

I insisted on getting Zee up first. The two ladies had settled into an ongoing cold war, each with one finger on the big red button; and I wanted to avoid any "unfortunate revival accidents." If Kusti woke first she might try to sabotage Adya, and if Adya woke up first then *Pelagia* might try to over-thaw Kusti. Either way it would get the Deimos authorities involved, which would not be convenient. Plus it would make Zee sad.

"Feeling all right?" I asked Zee once his temperature had come up to normal. His biomonitor said everything was within expected parameters, but humans have spent a billion years evolving their own internal diagnostics. They may be vague and subjective, but it's unwise to ignore them completely.

"Ugh. I'm all stiff and weak," he said.

"Muscle and bone loss is less than five kilos. You'll be fine. Just dehydrated."

"Where are we?"

"About two hundred kilometers above the Deimos Ring around Mars. Pelagia, can you give him a look?"

The walls of Zee's little cabin disappeared, so that we were floating above the city that stretches around Mars. It's a big loop of ribbon two hundred kilometers wide and just over an eighth of a million kilometers around. From our position above it, the Ring completely hid Mars itself. We could see quite a bit of detail: rotating habitat sections embedded in the big ring, docking towers and enclosed hangar bays, radiators glowing red, farm bubbles full of green stuff, trains zipping about, mass drivers and magscoops, launch lasers, manufacturing facilities, storage tanks, a water hab with whales swimming by the glass, shipyards, power receivers—all the infrastructure of one of the oldest and richest civilizations in human history.

Physics gave Deimos a gift: in terms of energy, it's easy to get from there to almost anyplace in the solar system. You spend less energy going from Luna to Deimos and vice versa than you do getting from Earth to Luna. Before elevators, it was cheaper to ship from Deimos to Earth geosynch orbit than it was to haul anything out of Earth's deep gravity well.

The early settlers of Deimos understood their advantage, and worked to maximize it. They got rid of their sister moon—it was called Phobos, which is why anti-Deimos movements on Mars use that name a lot—and built the first planetary elevator down to the top of Mons Pavonis on the Martian surface, long before Earth had one. With Mars on a string, Deimos supplied food, fuel, and construction materials all over the system. They got rich, and used that wealth to get richer.

Through eight millennia, under scores of different

regimes, Deimos has always been one of the major powers of the solar system. Sometimes they've been decadent and easygoing, sometimes they've been ruthless bastards. During the Great War of the Ring the Deimos Empire came close to true heroism—but only decades after the fight to save all biological life ended they were waging a dozen dirty little wars to put down liberation movements in their colonial dominions.

They've experimented with everything from real-time collective decision-making, to hereditary autocracy, to a bioengineered caste of sterile bureaucrat-monks, to letting a fourth-level digital intelligence run things. For two brief periods Deimos was controlled by Mars, something they hate to talk about and Martians love to bring up. Right now it's supposedly an ad-hocracy of volunteer committees, but everyone knows the system was co-opted by the Agiotista personality cult a generation ago.

It's really a bog-standard one-party kleptocracy led by Weng-Weng Agiota, the grandson of the late charismatic strongwoman. He controls a network of loyalists who can out-sit and out-blather everyone else on the committees until the party gets its way. Weng-Weng's chief claim to authority is that all of the other Agiotista bigwigs know they can bully him much more easily than they can bully each other. This will likely go on until the next major crisis blows up in Weng-Weng's face, at which point the incomprehensibly rich old families of Deimos will notice they need a functioning government again, and Take Steps.

The humans gathered in Pelagia's flight deck for a big post-hibernation breakfast while the ship waited for her chance to dock. As they finished the caviar tamales she printed up for them, Pelagia nosed into a berth in an unfashionable part of the Ring, on the opposite side of Mars from Deimos itself, not far from the Syrtis orbital elevator.

"You four can ride down," said Pelagia. "I'm staying up here. My hull doesn't like sitting on big balls of iron."

"You're going to miss all the fun," said Zee. "We're searching for buried treasure!"

"Um . . ." said Adya. "Actually there's something we haven't discussed. How are we going to get the Godel Trigger off Mars if we do find it?"

"Stick it in a bag and ride the elevator back up," said Kusti. "The tough inspections are all when you're going downstairs. Martians don't really care about what leaves their planet. And Deimos has always allowed free transit of just about anything."

Time to make my pitch, I decided. "Maybe we should just destroy it," I said.

Adya and Kusti both looked horrified, but Zee merely raised his eyebrows.

"I'm serious. It might or might not work against the minds of the Inner Ring, but if the Godel Trigger really exists, it would certainly mess up all low-level digital minds. Me, for example. Or the minds that keep the Deimos Ring functioning. Or most of the spaceships in the system. You could easily wreck civilization throughout the Billion Worlds if something like that got loose. We'd have to go back to . . . I don't know, humans inputting data on punch cards or something."

"But how do you destroy a concept?" Zee asked.

"If there's only one copy it's not hard. A few grams of antimatter, or just heat the whole thing up to about five thousand K in a reactive atmosphere. Poof!"

"No," said Kusti. "It's too valuable."

"It's too *important*," said Adya.

"Daslakh's got a point, though," said Zee. "Who could we trust to control something like that? We'd never misuse it, but—if anyone found out what we have, they'd try to take it. I don't want to spend the rest of my life hiding."

"Give it to the Corporeal Compact," said Adya.

"Can they keep it?" asked Zee. "The Godel Trigger's the kind of thing people fight wars over."

Kusti kept quiet. I can't read human neural activity, but I knew what she was thinking anyway: *Three can keep a secret if two are dead.* The oldest principle of information security.

"Maybe hand it over to one of the governments," said Adya. "Miranda?"

"No," said Pelagia. "Miranda's still a small fish. It would have to be one of the Big Hundred. Deimos and Mars are right here."

"But then the other ninety-nine would try to get it," said Zee.

"Not if we destroy the thing first," I reminded him.

"This is a waste of time," said Kusti. "We're arguing about what to do with something we haven't even located yet. Those directions could be wrong."

"Where is this statue, anyway?" asked Zee. "Is it in a museum?"

"The statue of Jak Junak is one of fifty-three colossal Martian heroes carved into the cliffs of Melas Chasma," said Adya. "It dates from the Sixth Millennium, and was designed by Zhuang Shijiang. Pelagia, would you please show us a picture?"

The walls of Pelagia's flight deck changed to show

the view from a drone flying over the forests and fields of Melas Chasma, with the domes and towers of the city of Ius visible off to the west and the arcology pyramids of Melas Cheng to the east. Ahead the cliff wall loomed four kilometers above the valley floor, with a row of immense figures carved into it. They were a mix of styles—some realistic portraits in dynamic poses, some stylized and solemn, a couple almost abstract. Jak Junak, for better or worse, had been given a heroic nude, shown in the act of breaking chains which held his wrists to the cliff. His face, hundreds of meters across, glared defiantly upward and to his right, directly at Deimos itself.

"That's a lot of statue to search," said Zee.

"Parts of it are hollow," said Adya. "The head contains a concert hall and viewing galleries, and there's an elevator and stairs all the way down to the base."

"I guess we could climb down the outside and search the whole thing," said Zee.

"Remember, Mars is a planet," I told him. "There's gravity. Slip off and you go splat. No, think logically: it's got to be hidden some place a human could reach easily in an emergency, but not where nosy tourists or maintenance drones would stumble across it by accident."

"The stairs," said Adya. Bright girl. "Who would climb four kilometers of stairs, even in Martian gravity?"

"And even if someone tried it out of masochism, they'd hardly hang around," I pointed out.

"Four kilometers is a lot of stairs. Which one?" asked Kusti.

"It should be something easy to remember, or guess," said Adya. "And you don't want to have to keep count of thousands of steps if you're searching."

"Sounds like it would be in the first hundred or so, at the top or at the bottom," said Zee. Bright boy.

"If I was the one hiding it," I said, "I'd have used the tenth step. That way humans could find it without taking off their shoes."

"Very funny," said Kusti.

"I think we must simply make a careful search," said Adya. "If it means days or weeks spent the cost is not too great for what we seek."

"All right, then," said Zee. "Odd we start at the feet, even we start at the head. Daslakh, give us a random number."

I generated a random number in the range of eight to eight. "Eight," I said.

"Then we start at the top. Let's get moving—we don't know if Muro and Lupur are behind us or already here."

It still took more than an hour as the humans had to wash, print up clothing, and bring along a few necessary items. Pelagia pinged me while all that was going on.

"Should I worry that Kusti wants me to print up a needle pistol?"

"What are the others packing?"

"Neither has asked me for anything. Adya does have a stiletto—it's a family heirloom."

"Didn't her assassination courses include something about not bringing a knife to a gunfight?"

"What about bringing a stick? Because that's all your boy has."

"He's got me," I pointed out.

"Poor fellow. He's doomed. Do you trust her?"

"Kusti? About as far as I can throw her in standard

gravity. That being said, I trust Muro and Lupur and Chi and Ketto even less. If we run into them I think it might be handy to have something more advanced than a pointy piece of metal or a graphene stick."

"All right, I'll print it for her. But—make sure nothing happens to Adya."

"I will."

When we gathered again in Pelagia's control space, the humans had picked out their travel gear. Zee had on the same skinsuit and coverall combo he always wore, with adaptive boots on his feet and his beloved *palo* over his shoulder. Adya had a poncho and wide-brimmed hat over her skinsuit, and boots up to her knees. Her grandmother's stiletto peeked out of the left boot; evidently Pelagia had managed to talk her into bringing it. Kusti was even more ruggedly practical: her coveralls were smartfiber armor, and the "utility pouch" on her right hip concealed the needle gun very effectively.

All suitably equipped, we left Pelagia and passed through the pressure membrane into the Deimos Ring.

The place is wall-to-wall sensory overload. Every surface is either smart matter, living tissue, some incredible work of art, or all three at once. The docking area opened onto a transport corridor half a kilometer wide, jam-packed with express trains, local bubble-cars, streams of freight containers moving magnetically, people riding everything from wheeled bicycles to rocket packs, and even a couple of whole spacecraft being moved down the middle from the factory to the assembly bays.

One could see just about every kind of Baseline-equivalent entity in the solar system, all streaming past. Bog-standard humans, Martians, angels, spacers, aquatics, darkworlders, giants, miniatures, chimps, dolphins, corvids, lotors, arnets, dogs, cats, elephants, cephalopods, dragons, centaurs, borgs and mechs of every imaginable configuration, and a dozen bots and drones for every sentient.

If the physical environment was overwhelming, the infospace was orders of magnitude more complex. Not just commercial stuff, either. There were interactive artworks, music, and tags for thousands of events just about to happen within easy transit of where we were.

Of the three humans only Adya had an interface that could handle the volume of virtual tags, ads, and messages that flooded in as soon as we pushed through the membrane. Zee winced. "Tell me if I need to know something, okay?" he said, and went dark.

I called for a bubble-car and we rode the six hundred klicks to the elevator in about twenty-three minutes.

During the ride an autonomous message found me. "*I am for Daslakh Spider Mech SeRaba.*"

"That's me."

I was expecting to see a penguin, but the message blossomed into a portrait icon of a big humanoid mech with extra arms, bristling with weapons and painted zero-albedo black all over. "*Good evening. I am a freelance security contractor. My employer has asked me to give you fair warning: Leave immediately and do not approach within a million kilometers of Mars ever again. If you remain more than thirty minutes after receiving this message, I will kill you. The clock starts now.*"

"Good news, everyone," I said aloud. "I just got a message saying there's a battle mech threatening to kill us if we don't leave Mars space in half an hour."

"It actually told you that?" asked Kusti.

"On orders from its employer. My guess is that Summanus has figured out what we're doing here. The good news is that it's probably hunting Muro and the boys, too."

"What did it look like?" asked Zee, looking at the occupants of other bubble-cars near us. I could see a family of pandas, a pair of young human exhibitionists, a trio of Martians, and a lone Deimosian reading a book made of printed sheets of paper.

"The one thing I'm absolutely certain of is that it does not look like a big all-black humanoid chassis with spiky bits. It might not even be a mech. It could be a they."

"It could be a hoax," Adya pointed out. "Muro or Lupur might conjure a phantom to frighten us off the world. If so, then have no fear, for such as they would never warn if they could kill."

"So it's either 1: a murder machine sent by an even bigger murder machine with an ethical streak, or 2: a fraud sent by a couple of bigger frauds with no ethics at all. I say plan for 1, hope for 2."

"Change of plan, either way," said Kusti. "It—they, whoever—can find out where Pelagia's docked, so the obvious place to catch us is the Syrtis elevator. We need to go down some other way."

"Pavonis elevator," I suggested. "Highest traffic."

"Mutch elevator is much closer to Melas Chasma," Adya pointed out. "It rises sixteen hundred klicks from where we wish to go."

"Which makes it the second most obvious place to watch for us," I replied.

"But on the ground is where we're most at risk,"

she said. "The trek from Pavonis to Melas would take us through the barren Labyrinth of Night. A cunning foe might catch us there."

"We could split up," said Kusti. "You and the mech go via Pavonis, Zee and I will take Mutch."

"No," said Zee. We all waited for a moment to hear his argument, and then the ladies realized there wasn't an argument. Zee just refused to split the team, and that was all. It was amazingly effective.

In the end we picked Mutch elevator, chiefly because going to Pavonis meant extra travel time in the Ring. We rode the bubble-car past the shipyard complex at the top end of the Syrtis elevator, then switched to a train so we wouldn't have to ride in a three-meter bubble for forty hours. The train was more comfortable and went six times as fast—fast enough that it wasn't really in orbit, so we rode feeling a faint ghost of Mars's surface gravity.

For safety the four of us took a single compartment for the six-hour ride. The humans were still feeling the effects of revival drugs, and had all just finished a nice seven-month nap, so none of them were at all sleepy.

The compartment had room for six humans, so we had plenty of space, but I noticed Kusti made a point of snuggling up right next to Zee, resting her head in the crook of his shoulder, and even nuzzling the side of his neck. I could see her cast occasional glances at Adya, to see if she was paying attention. Adya kept herself glacier blue and gazed resolutely out the window at the underside of the Ring while listening to a live concert of qinguang music from New Lupita Forest on Deimos's zenith side.

Adya couldn't hear Kusti, but I could, when she

whispered into Zee's ear between nuzzles. "We have to lose her. She mustn't get the Trigger."

He said nothing, and remained still for a little while, then heaved an immense sigh. "I'm not going to do that," he said aloud, and took his arm from around Kusti. She looked hurt for a split second, but then her face took on a look of serenity bordering on smugness. She turned away from Zee and said no more to him.

Adya was still gazing at the scenery, but I could see her skin had gone from pale blue to a pinker shade, and she couldn't keep a trace of a smile off her lips.

With everybody putting so much effort into not speaking to each other, it was a very long six hours to the station at Mutch elevator. I was very glad when the train began to slow and then we slid inside the big diamond and aluminum jumble of Sindak Station, the top end of the elevator. The Deimosians grudgingly accept naming the elevators themselves for the Martian surface features where they touch down, but the top end stations are theirs and get Deimos names and don't you forget it.

Sindak's not quite as glitzy as Deimos, but it's still a very impressive structure all by itself. It's got about sixty billion people in it, most of them in four big wheel habs in counter-rotating pairs on either side of the elevator cable.

We moved through the station in paranoid sprints. I went first, my shell colored the same tasteful charcoal-and-silver of Sindak's maintenance bots. I scuttled ahead as if on some important task, watching in all directions to see if anybody reacted. Nobody shot me, so I stopped next to an abstract sculpture of titanium bands which wrapped around a structural element of the station. It made for nice hard cover so I paused and did a bit of pantomime fiddling with a chair support at a power outlet, while I scanned the traffic corridor thoroughly for anyone looking suspiciously alert. Once I determined the coast was clear I pinged Zee. He and the ladies moved very fast, staying close but moving chaotically to make themselves difficult to track.

Corridor to a large concourse built around a huge work of plasma art. Concourse to a side passage. Passage to a bubble-car which took us to the elevator terminal. Cross the terminal to the waiting area. There we got our backs into a corner and waited for the next elevator capsule to start loading.

The capsules on the Mars elevators are not luxurious—though I've heard a few old Deimos families have private capsules which are masterpieces of subtle ostentation, if that makes any sense. You've got two decks, thirty seats each in rings facing out, a little bathroom and a food printer in the middle. The whole thing is a sphere about eight meters wide, built to act as a reentry vehicle in emergencies.

It's a sphere because the down vector goes all over the place during a trip. At first you're accelerating away from the terminal station at one Mars gravity, so the floor points at the stars and Mars is overhead. Then it coasts for a time, but you're not really in orbit any more so down is at an angle between Mars and the cable. As the capsule approaches the surface that angle shifts closer to straight down, and then for the deceleration stage your bottom end is aimed directly at the cable terminus. So the capsule has to be free to rotate around, held by a pair of support rings.

The whole trip takes about an hour and a quarter.

The Mutch elevator handles as many cargo pods as passenger capsules, and they're spaced at ten-minute intervals for safety. So we passed a few nervous minutes before we could board the capsule and take our seats. Zee, just like a rube from the outer system, insisted on getting a spot in the outer row so he could admire the view. Adya tried to act cool about it, but she also wanted to look at Mars. Kusti stayed with them for safety, but was thoroughly bored by the actual mechanics of the trip. I filed that fact away: whoever she was, she'd spent some time in the Deimos Ring before.

Below us the planet was a dull orange disk with green and blue blotches and a few streaks of cloud. Thanks to the orbital mirror, even the "night" side of Mars is still pretty bright, but one could see that all the cities were lit up. From Mutch elevator we could see the string of cities extending westward up the Marineris Valley, and the seacoast towns along the Chrysean Gulf to the east.

Once we got seated we all relaxed a little. The elevators are very well-defended, and we were sealed in with sixty other passengers, a full load. Too many witnesses for an assassin to try any funny business. We were perfectly safe.

CHAPTER SIXTEEN

Just about twenty minutes before the capsule was to touch down at Mutch Cheng, I heard a very faint thump. Thumps, no matter how faint, are not good things to hear on spacecraft. I looked around, but nobody else acted like they'd noticed.

I crept from Zee's shoulder to Kusti's, and spoke very quietly, beaming my voice directly into her ear canal so as not to be overheard. "Get ready for trouble."

"What?" she said.

"I didn't say anything," said Zee.

"Get your gun, you stupid monkey!"

The assassin had hitched a ride on the cargo pod following our capsule. As we started to decelerate, just under five thousand kilometers above the surface, it must have jumped, aiming away from the elevator cable so that as it caught up with our capsule it would be in the right place. While I was whispering in Kusti's ear it was drilling a hole through the outer hull. Then it squeezed itself through and very considerately plugged the hole behind itself so that no pressure drop triggered any alarms.

The seats on the Martian elevator capsules have nice high backs, with side-wings at head level in case a traveler wants to nod off. So identifying a passenger visually means you have to get out into the compartment and make a circuit of the outer wall to see all the faces. Assuming you are an assassin like the one which did just that.

I spotted it as it spotted us: a snaky meter-long shape like an animated section of braided rope, slithering along where the ceiling met the strip of transparent diamond outer wall. My whole surface facing that direction emitted laser light, and I scored a nice little burn at its front end which cut through the assassin and made it about a centimeter shorter.

Simultaneously I reached out to it via data link, hoping to overwhelm its mind or at least distract it a little. Nothing. It was sealed, hardened, utterly dark. Almost certainly a sub-baseline bot rather than a real person.

By this point Kusti's hand was halfway to her utility pouch, and Zee was just turning his head toward the bot, while Adya's attention was still entirely in infospace. I zapped her a warning message and then ran faster than I could fall down the back of Kusti's seat.

Once it couldn't see me I generated a random number and went left, then popped up behind a sleeping Martian and searched. There! The assassin was crawling down the window in front of Zee. As I had guessed, its laser emitter had been at the end I'd burned off. Unfortunately, that wasn't the only weapon at its command. Its long body unraveled into a dozen sharp ribbons.

I got off another laser shot at it, but it was moving

its central body chaotically, so my laser pulse passed harmlessly through the transparent diamond pane behind it. Kusti had her pistol out by now and was pointing it at the assassin. I realized what was about to happen and leaped up to the ceiling.

She fired a burst of ten little steel needles, each one moving fast enough to escape the solar system. They left a trail of ions through the air. One of them hit the assassin, slicing off a single razor ribbon. The other nine hit the diamond window on either side of it.

Funny thing about diamond. It's really strong, but you can crack it if you put enough force into a small enough area. Those needles were really small and packed a lot of energy. One of them would have maybe put a star crack into the pane, which the carbon-fiber lacing and outer polymer coat could handle. But nine shots in a line across half a meter meant a big crack propagating all the way to the edges.

The window blew out, taking the assassin with it. I hung on to the padded ceiling to avoid being blown out into space—yet again!—and in half a second everyone's seat detected the pressure drop and went into emergency mode. The seats wrapped around their occupants, sealing each one against vacuum and feeding all of them air, while soothing voices explained the situation was only temporary and thanked them for their cooperation. Emergency curtains slid over the missing window, and the cabin began to repressurize.

Things got a little awkward after that. Half the passengers didn't know what had happened, and the rest got it wrong. Kusti kept quiet, of course. But the capsule had plenty of internal cameras, and they saw all of it. So when the capsule arrived at the terminal in Mutch Cheng, a team of polite combat mechs and Martians in battle armor from the Royal Elevator Guards wanted a few words with the two of us.

I was absolutely honest: Some unknown party had sent me a threatening message, so I considered myself to be in danger when the assassin bot showed up inside the capsule. No, I didn't know who had sent either the message or the bot. No, I hadn't reported the threat to anyone, because it might have been a hoax.

Since I hadn't actually blown out a window, they let me go after an hour of questioning, with a warning that I should remain in monitored areas for my own safety. Have a nice day, sir.

Kusti wasn't so fortunate. She had to explain why she'd started shooting, and the Royal Guards wanted a lot of information about her relationship to me, where we'd come from, and why we were on Mars. Kusti, naturally, lied her head off. She claimed to have met me on the ship from Summanus, and had barely had the chance to learn my name before she went into hibernation. The pistol was just something she'd brought along for personal protection, and she had no idea why it wasn't equipped with a safety interrupt.

They were skeptical, to put it mildly. Two different officers interviewed her, and focused mercilessly on inconsistencies. She said she couldn't remember, it was all so fast, and even burst into tears.

In the end, their suspicions weren't enough to keep her in custody, but were enough to implant her with a tracer in case they wanted to talk to her again. If she left Mars without getting permission from the Xanthean Kingdom, they'd consider her a fugitive. It was safe bet that someone or something would be paying attention to her location, and probably watching through local networks wherever we went.

The four of us met up for breakfast at a cafe on the west side of Mutch Cheng, just below the rim. From there we had a splendid view out across the domed crater. The city of Mutch Cheng is all built into the rim, and the crater floor is all parkland and gardens. With the sun coming up behind us we could watch the ponds and lakes sparkling red and gold.

"If we go to the statue now the Martian authorities will track us," said Kusti.

"So?" I asked. "They don't know what we're going there for."

"It would make this all easier if nobody's looking over our shoulders."

"If the authorities are watching us it means we'll be safe from assassins," Zee pointed out. "Safer, anyway."

"Only while we're here."

"They are not tracking *us*," said Adya. "They are tracking *you*."

"It doesn't make any difference," said Kusti.

"It does. You should remain here while the rest of us go to Melas Chasma."

Kusti actually laughed at that. "Nice try. Park me here while you traipse off to the statue and grab the—object? Am I supposed to believe you'll come back for me? Do you think I'm another upper-class idiot with a fancy education and no sense? No, I'm in this until the end."

I listened to the electronic noise around us. "I think I can hear your tracer," I said. "It's very faint. Just strong enough to ping the local network but that's it. No orbital reach. If you don't want anyone tracking you, just get away from the infosphere."

"Where can I do that?"

"Out there," said Zee, pointing through the dome at the red plains beyond.

"Zee is correct," said Adya—did I detect a hint of reluctance? She was still cool green on the outside. "With the exception of Pavonis and a handful of other sites, most of the Martian surface above the five-kilometer level is nearly empty. Too much radiation, too little oxygen, and just enough desert for Martians to see what their world once was. If we travel overland you will not be monitored."

"If we're in a vehicle I'm sure Daslakh can take care of any internal net," added Zee helpfully.

"It won't be a problem," I said modestly.

"One must admire the cleverness of our enemy," said Adya.

"What for?" asked Zee.

"By sending that bot after us in a secure environment, the real assassin has turned the Martian authorities from an obstacle into an asset. Now we must deliberately choose to travel in a way that will make us vulnerable."

"I'll be sure to congratulate him before I blow his head off," said Kusti.

"With what? The cops took your needle gun," I said.

"I've got resources," she said. "Now: How long will it take us to get there overland?"

I had the table display a map. "Twelve hundred kilometers west across the high plains to the ridge between Hebes Chasma and Ophir Chasma. That's in Hebean Republic territory. Then cut southwest and cross the border into the Marineris League, go around the west end of Ophir Chasma and Candor, another three hundred klicks, and finally two hundred south-east again along the ridge between Candor Chasma and Melas Chasma, to the top of the statue. A fast vehicle can cover it in ten hours, maybe less."

Just then a call from the Ring interrupted our conversation. It was Pelagia. "What have you been up to? I just had a long and annoying talk with an autonomous message from the Xanthean Royal Elevator Guards. It wanted to know everything about the four of you, where I came from, why I'm docked here, and a lot of other nonsense."

"You do not have to answer their questions," said Adya. "Their power does not stretch beyond the mid-point of the cable."

"That's what I told the message, but it invoked space emergency rights because *somebody* blew out a window on an orbital elevator capsule."

"An assassin bot snuck on board," I said. "Kusti had to shoot it."

"Yes, with a weapon *I* printed for her! I told the guards I didn't know why she asked for it. You four couldn't even get to the *surface* without getting into trouble. Maybe you should all just come back up here. You'll be safe on board—I'll make sure of it. Planets are dangerous."

"We still must get that for which we came," said Adya.

"Then why are we sitting here?" asked Kusti. "Let's get a vehicle and get moving." As she spoke she hunted through the infosphere. "There's a place that rents out shays, just eight levels down on the outer rim. Come on!"

Martian shays were once the mainstays of transport

on the surface, and a whole romantic meme-complex built up around them. Lone shay pilots, daredevil shay racers, shay-driving irregulars fighting foreign troops, et cetera. Trains are the iconic vehicle of the arcologies, aircraft are the symbol of the terraformed world, but shays are the mystique of the old desert in mechanical form.

The rental joint was a couple of kilometers out from the rim, where the city sprawl faded out into low-end industrial infrastructure. It was between a metal refinery and a cryogenic gas tank farm. A single humanoid bot costumed in a Third Millennium exploration suit ran the place. I spent a few seconds getting myself certified to operate a vehicle on the Martian surface.

Our shay was a replica of an Eighth Millennium design, the famous "Paoma" beloved by the last of the Chiji nomads: a six-seat streamlined transparent bubble with four two-meter wheels mounted on jointed struts. According to its own sub-sub-baseline operating system, it was capable of two hundred kilometers per hour on cleared paths, or twenty on "natural surface" (which is what the Martians call regolith that's been subjected to seventy centuries of rain created by humans, warming caused by humans, oxygen created by humans, and organisms introduced by humans).

We piled in and let the shay's simple mind take us around the south edge of the circle of Mutch Cheng, crossing the transport corridor south to Ganges Chasma, then west. First we were on a smart road passing smaller dome towns and entrances to underground warrens. When we started seeing patches of Mars plants and farm domes the road became a strip of dumb pavement, and two hundred klicks west of the crater it was nothing but a rutted line of surface with the rocks removed, and a ditch on one side to keep the whole thing from turning into a river during the once-a-century rains.

Traffic became light, then sparse, then rare, and by midmorning we had the road entirely to ourselves. That was about the time I gently took over the shay's mind. I let its algorithms handle most of the driving, but I looked through its network connection settings. I discovered that through some laughable mistake, the privacy controls had been disabled, so that outsiders with the right codes could see and hear everything inside the shay. I put that back to emergency/request-only mode, then gradually made our network link noisier and fainter, and finally shut it off altogether.

Of course, that left my three humans in a comfortable bubble with nobody but themselves. The seats were in three rows, so each human had taken over a pair—Adya in back, Zee in the middle, Kusti in front. I had taken up my station in the very front of the compartment, on top of the folding cover for the never-used manual controls. Not that I needed to look through the front window to drive; the shay had good vision of its own all around. One of my reasons for taking that position was so that I could keep an eye on Kusti. She wasn't taking all this isolation well.

Adya simply watched the landscape roll by. She was a very pale violet color, and her respiration and heart rate were very slow, but her eyes were open and alert. I think she had gone into some kind of meditative state, just a viewpoint moving past Mars.

Zee had been interested in the land at first, but let's

be honest, rocks do all start to resemble each other after you've seen a thousand or so. He combined his two seats, stretched out, and slept.

But Kusti had the fidgets. No configuration of two seats was comfortable for her. No view held her interest. She checked the time about once a minute. None of the shay's onboard entertainment options could hold her attention for more than thirty seconds.

"Can we go faster?" she asked me.

"Not enough to make a difference," I said. "Relax. Get some sleep."

"I hate being cut off like this. Can't you get us some access? I just need to check something."

"Any traffic to or from this shay is probably getting flagged," I reminded her. "The Xanthean Kingdom is interested in us, probably Deimos as well. If you pick your nose in the bubble remember that someone could be watching us from orbit."

She didn't say anything for a while, just fidgeted some more, and checked the time again.

"Who are you, really?" I asked her, keeping my voice quiet and focused just on her.

"Kusti Sendoa Human SeRavenal." The fidgets stopped, and she was entirely self-possessed and unreadable again.

"That's a fictional character from centuries ago. I've put up with your little masquerade for Zee's sake, but you don't fool me. He thinks he lived that entertainment and you decided to play along. My guess is that you needed some help right then, back in the Uranosynchronous Ring, because Muro and the boys had double-crossed you. Zee could be your human shield, and you needed cash. And in Summanus you thought he could be useful in getting Adya, and then the box. But since then he's been surplus mass and you've been doing your best to jettison him."

"Why do you care?"

"I don't like seeing you make Zee unhappy, but that's between the two of you. However, if you're trying to get your hands on something powerful and dangerous, I want to know who you are and why you're doing it."

"It's valuable. Isn't that enough?"

"Don't play dumb. If the Godel Trigger really exists, you're not big enough to keep it. A lot of people would find it cheaper to just kill you and take it. And you're smart enough to realize that."

"I've got a plan."

"No doubt. It occurs to me that you might be working for someone who *is* powerful enough to make use of something like the Godel Trigger. You've been communicating a lot with someone but you haven't gotten any replies. And since we reached Summanus you haven't been worried about cash anymore."

"She's been paying for everything," said Kusti, with a nod toward the back of the shay. "And the ship took us for free."

"True, except...if you've got a plan for getting *off* of Mars you haven't shared it with anyone. I think that's because the rest of us aren't part of that plan. Fine by me; good riddance to you. But I still want to know who's backing you."

"Too bad. I'm not going to tell you."

"Not unexpected. But I'm going to tell you something, because it may affect your decisions. I'm older than this body, and I'm smarter than you think. I've got resources of my own, and I know people. What I want you to understand is that if you harm Zee *there will be consequences.*"

Her expression got almost pitying. "Once I get the Trigger, you won't be able to do anything. And where I'm going you won't be able to touch me. As long as Zee doesn't interfere, he'll be fine. He can go off with *her* and live their stupid lives together and it won't matter to me at all. Now be quiet and don't bother me."

After that she slumped in her seat and stared out of the window. She was thinking about something, and evidently it was something that made her happy. That worried me.

We motored steadily west, trending a little bit south. The humans shared some food that Adya had brought along, and there were some fitful attempts at conversation. I found a couple of terabytes of stored music in the shay's little brain and played some, just to fill the silence. Outside, Mars rolled past.

For a time around noon we really were passing through empty Martian landscape. To the north the plain sloped gently downward toward Lunae Planum and the Kasei megapolis. South of us was an open plain west of Juventae Chasma. The road was just a cleared trail with occasional marker beacons, and all around was nothing but pale red dust and boulders.

And right in the middle of that emptiness, three hundred kilometers from any permanent settlement, we had to stop for a border crossing.

You'd think that a relatively small planet like Mars, with lots of systems that depend on planetwide cooperation to keep everyone breathing, would have a single government. But Martian politics has a predictable pattern, since long before the place even had much of an atmosphere, all thanks to the neighbors who live upstairs.

It goes like this: Domination by Deimos leads to a Martian unification movement, which leads to revolt and an independent Martian state (or the revolt fails and a bunch of people get exiled, brainwashed, or shot). At which point all the stress lines within Martian society start pushing against each other, and the Martian state begins to decentralize, and finally atomizes into a mass of petty statelets in conflict with their neighbors. At which point Deimos helpfully sweeps in to preserve order and the cycle begins again. Once or twice the Martian state has been strong and aggressive enough to absorb Deimos, but that just adds more rival power centers to the mix.

At the moment Mars is politically fragmented, with about fifty different political entities. All are thoroughly under Deimos's thumb, but if past cycles are any guide it'll be another century before the Martians notice and get mad about the situation.

The border between the Xanthean Kingdom and the Hebean Republic was literally a line in the sand, marked by little traffic-control beacons and a little gate where the dirt road crossed the line. I chatted with Hebean border control as we approached, doing my best impersonation of the shay's collection of algorithms (one could hardly call them a mind).

While I did that I was also plotting a way around the gate and looking for weapon installations. If our unknown enemy had any pull with Martian governments, this would be a good place to strike. Pinpoint our location, freeze us in place with some bureaucratic obstacles, then hit us out here on the surface.

Nothing. The gate swung open as we approached, we got a "Welcome to the Hebean Republic" message accompanied by a list of differences between Xanthean and Hebean law, and a nice listing of tourist attractions indexed by travel distance.

Once across I relaxed a bit. Maybe the bot on the elevator capsule had been the assassin's best shot. Maybe the guards had actually managed to track who had sent it, and our enemy was on the run.

"It's another hour to Ganges Catena," I told my passengers. "If you three need food and want to sleep on something other than a shay seat, that's a good place to stop."

"How far do we have to go after that?" asked Zee.

"Another six hundred kilometers stretch beyond," said Adya. "Three hours or more of travel."

"I can stand it," said Kusti. "Let's grab a bite and keep going."

The others agreed; all of us were impatient to reach the statue.

Ganges Catena is an old city. There's a whole set of natural caves running about four hundred kilometers eastward from Hebes Chasma. The "catena" of the name is an archaic word for chain, in this case a chain of sinkholes along the surface of the cave system. Early settlers moved in, sealed up the caves, put domes over the sinkholes, dug out and down, and created an underground megapolis which currently has about a hundred million inhabitants.

It's not as big as the really giant cities like Pavonis or Capri, but it's got a lot of historical importance and cultural power, and carries more weight in the republic than mere population and economic output would suggest. Ganges Catena's been the center of at least two Martian wars of independence, and is one of the best places on Mars to do things you want hidden from orbital snooping. Seismic maps show hundreds of tunnels and shafts which the city's official plan somehow fails to include.

I bet Summanus would love the place.

The surface over the city is pockmarked with craters—not old impact features but fresh new ones made in historical times. Also, a number of slag fields where prolonged laser bombardment fused regolith into vermilion glass. The dirt track turned into a road which wound among the ancient battle sites, and in between the scars of war we could see little surface installations marking entrances to the urban warren a hundred meters below.

I had to accept external control, and let the local traffic system guide the shay onto the big east-west surface highway connecting the domes over the main line of caves. A railroad ran above the road on tall pylons. Most of the road traffic was dumb freight carriers.

After just a couple of kilometers the TCS steered the shay onto a side ramp which led through an airlock into the parking level underneath a surface dome. The place was a recreation and social center, where people from the underground city could come and have a look at the sky, fly around in wingsuits or pedal a plane, and watch a troupe of *jushiwu* performers prepare food from raw ingredients, all choreographed and set to music.

"You three go on. I'll wait here," I said as they stepped out of the shay.

"Not a chance," said Kusti. "I don't want to come back and find out you decided to get a head start on finding the Trigger. You're coming with us."

"Daslakh wouldn't do that!" said Zee, indignant on my behalf.

"If it will keep peace among you, I'll come watch you three mash up things with your mouths and then swallow them."

As soon as I was clear, the shay backed out of the parking space and headed for the exit.

"Where is our faithful shay bound?" asked Adya.

"I sent it to cruise around until we're ready to leave. That way nobody can stick any nasty surprises to it."

Zee looked worried. "You think that combat mech is still out there hunting for us?"

"I don't want to assume it isn't and then get proved wrong."

Kusti's accusation hadn't been too far off. I had seriously considered making a dash for the statue, but I didn't want to leave the three of them unsupervised with our unknown enemy still stalking them. The poor things were practically helpless without me.

So I watched them eat and then waited while they eliminated bodily wastes. The shay's waste disassembler could have handled all of that, but a lot of humans are kind of shy about doing it in front of others, so other than voiding liquids they'd been holding it since we left Mutch Cheng.

While both ladies were thus occupied, I had a private word with Zee. "Kusti and Adya have different ideas about what to do with the Trigger, and I'm in favor of just destroying it unopened. You're the deciding vote here, Zee."

"I don't know," he said. "Really: I do not know the right thing to do with it. I'm just a guy who worked in an ice mine and did stick fighting. Adya's got a designer brain and a fancy education; Kusti's got all kinds of experience and she's pretty smart, too. And you're way more than a Baseline intelligence."

"Thank you for noticing," I said.

"So why me?"

"I've known you for seven standard years, and you always try to do the right thing. I'm not sure about the girls."

"I think Adya does, too."

"You didn't mention Kusti."

"She's—she's different from how I remember her. I think that hibernation accident must have changed her." He frowned. "What's weird is that I can't even figure out when we met. I mean, I remember meeting her, but was I already an apprentice then?"

"Never mind about that," I said. "What I'm saying is that when we find it, things are probably going to happen very fast. You have to pick a side now."

He sighed heavily. "I wish I didn't have to pick at all. I wish I'd followed Kusti when we first met—or maybe I wish I'd met Adya before Kusti."

"Fine, but this is the universe you're in. Make your choice and be ready to stick with it. And, Zee—put loyalty aside for the moment. No matter what you decide, someone's going to be unhappy. So make the choice you know is right."

He nodded, but he still didn't look happy.

I called the shay back from its cruise around one of Ganges Catena's airship terminals, questioned its mind very closely before we got in, and set out on a road going south toward Ophir Chasma. The sun was low in the west and the edge of the mirror ring was peeking over the eastern horizon, so I opaqued the bubble so my humans didn't have to squint.

I followed the road south for about ten klicks, then split off onto a little-used side road heading west again toward the narrow isthmus of high surface between Ophir Chasma and Hebes Chasma. There's another underground urban corridor there called Suizhen, with a couple of million people and a fair amount of stuff poking up to the surface. Lots of eyes, lots of monitors, lots of police bots. Couldn't ask for a safer place.

CHAPTER SEVENTEEN

The assassin struck again on the busiest stretch of road passing over Suizhen. We were on a paved, controlled east-west highway, three lanes each way, speeding along at a sprightly three hundred klicks an hour. The local traffic system was driving the shay, and I just kept a fraction of my attention on the shay's mind to make sure it was obeying properly.

That road had to cross two major north-south arteries five kilometers apart, approximately following the edges of the tunnel city below. Each artery boasted a five-lane controlled road and four rail lines. Between the two was a big aerospace port surrounded by a chaotic mess of little domes, tunnel heads, and pressure structures, all set in a web of paved surface streets. The streets were built after most of the structures already existed, but the engineers gamely tried to create a proper grid anyway. What they got was a maze of three-way intersections, zigzags, and cul-de-sacs.

Enter, stage left: one shay under traffic control,

moving at three hundred kilometers per hour in the middle lane of the highway, containing three Baseline or Baseline-plus humans and one mech whose mental rating is nobody else's business.

The shay passed under the eastern arterial highway. A light combat mech with six limbs dropped from the edge of the overpass, timing its fall to land on top of the shay. It hung on with four limbs and sliced a hole in the bubble with a monomolecule blade.

That was about the point at which I took over control of the shay and hit the brakes while swerving into the right lane. The combat mech tumbled off the front of the shay, hit the ground on four legs and leaped straight up so that it didn't get smashed by the cargo carrier coming right behind where the shay had been. Instead it landed atop the cargo carrier, and since the middle lane moved faster than the right lane, it was right next to the shay so could jump back on again.

The plan looked foolproof, because the cargo carrier in the middle lane already overlapped a bit with the cargo carrier directly in front of me, so I was boxed in. Except that there was still a gap between the carrier in the middle lane and the mobile crane lumbering up the right lane *behind* me. So I braked again and made use of the shay's four-wheel steering to swerve backwards around the crane into the center lane. I timed this to happen between the moment the mech jumped and the moment it landed, so instead of dropping onto the roof of the shay it hit the road again right in front of the oncoming crane.

Inside the bubble the humans were doing a good imitation of a trio of chickens caught in a tornado. The hole in the bubble let in a roaring blast of wind at three hundred kilometers per hour, and my swerves threw all three of them from side to side. Because we hadn't hit anything, the seats hadn't gone into safety mode.

The combat mech didn't have time to jump out of the way of the crane carrier, so it flattened itself and let the big machine roll over it, then grabbed the rear bumper and swung itself up onto the back of the bed, and finally scrambled on top of the folded crane boom. Once again it was directly to the right of me, but it was smart enough not to waste time trying to jump aboard. Instead it opened up with the gun in its right front limb. Since the bubble was opaque it couldn't target the humans precisely. Instead it just did a spray-and-pray line of needles across the whole side at head level.

My three passengers weren't in their seats, they were on the floor, and I told them to stay there. Time to find out how fast a rental shay can go if you disable all the safety features and cast restraint to the winds. So I accelerated and swerved into the faster left lane, trying to get ahead of the combat mech.

Meanwhile, the crane had noticed what was happening. Being a law-abiding sort it didn't take itself off traffic control—but it did start shaking its crane boom back and forth to dislodge the combat mech shooting at people. The hitchhiker had sticky feet, so that didn't work, but the shaking did throw off its aim as it tried to get off a shot before the helium tanker in the middle lane blocked its view.

The assassin jumped on top of the helium tanker, but I was still moving ahead. The fact that there was a cargo carrier in front of me wasn't a problem—the emergency lane on the left was utterly empty, so I veered into it. The shay had good off-road suspension so I could still go faster than the road maximum, even over dust and bits of detritus.

Actually, I was going a lot faster than traffic. Normally speed in the left lane was two hundred fifty, but I was going two-sixty and still passing them more quickly than I should have been. That's when I realized traffic control had decided to just shut down this section of road, and was slowing everyone to a stop.

That was bad. At speed the killer had to do crazy jumping around maneuvers. If traffic stopped it could just walk up and kill all four of us, and the shay too.

Up ahead I saw a gap in front of traffic, where the shutdown began. Beyond it the back of the preceding block of vehicles moved away ever more quickly. I swerved back into the gap. No cover now but I could open it up to two-eighty.

A burst of needles shredded my left rear wheel. Behind me I could see the mech, galloping along at a hundred klicks an hour, trying to cripple the shay and catch up.

Independent wheels meant I could balance the shay on three, keeping the wrecked one from slowing it down. But out in the open it was just a matter of time before it could hit me again. I swerved over to the right and onto an exit ramp.

This dumped me out onto a surface avenue heading toward the edge of the aerospace port. Traffic control had already frozen all the vehicles in place, turning the road into a barrier. I made a quick left onto a street which immediately did a block-long dogleg before continuing. On either side, cargo container storage yards and fuel tanks whipped past.

The assassin did have the advantage of being able to run off-road. It got up onto a fifty-meter communication mast and spotted the shay, now half a kilometer away. With a clear line of sight it fired off another burst, and this time scored a mission kill as the remaining rear wheel exploded into fragments and the whole back end of the shay dropped to drag on the ground.

Two broken dragging wheels made the shay slower than the killer mech. It would be able to catch up and shoot my passengers. I swerved into one of the cargo container yards, built right under the edge of the second main north-south artery running over the top of Suizhen. Beyond that strip of roads and railways was open desert. The stacks of empty containers hid us from the mech's view, but it could reach us in less than a minute.

"Can everybody walk? Time to disperse," I said. "Try to find hard cover, keep moving, and head for the port. Security there might have something to handle this mech."

Nobody argued. I guess they all understood there wasn't any time for that. The ladies scrambled out and went in opposite directions—Kusti west, Adya east. Zee followed, and hesitated for an instant as if trying to decide which one to go with.

"Disperse, you idiot!" I told him, so he went off to the north but didn't look happy.

I paused long enough to wipe the shay's memories and set it moving ahead on a random path. Then I dropped out and headed away from the humans, toward the direction the mech would likely be coming from. Because a three-kilo spider mech and a four-hundred-kilo armed-combat mech are evenly matched.

A burst of needles hit the shay again, atomizing the left front wheel hub so the poor thing could only drag itself in a circle. I traced the echoes of the shot back and located the mech on top of a stack of containers two rows south of me. I scuttled in that direction.

For ease in moving the containers around, and to keep the stacks from wobbling, the bottom layer of cargo containers rested on blocks of sintered Martian dirt, ten centimeters high. So for a little mech like me, those stacks of four-meter cubes were no obstacle at all. I moved as quietly as I could, in irregular bursts.

I could hear the clatter of the combat mech as it scrambled along the top of the stacks, pausing from time to time in order to scan around for the humans. I had no way to tell where they were, but every second the assassin didn't fire its weapon was another second they weren't dead.

South of me the aisle between rows of containers loomed like the Marineris Rift Valley: ten meters with nothing but thin Martian air for protection. Fifty long milliseconds out in the open. I waited and listened.

As soon as I heard the assassin moving I made a dash across the aisle. It must have heard me because it stopped when I was halfway across. As I stopped under the next row of containers I could hear it again, definitely moving in my direction.

Then I heard it slam down onto the ground and realized what was about to happen. I sprinted two meters to the edge of the container I was under, and got up into the gap between it and the next one just as the assassin knelt and hosed the entire area under the containers with a stream of needles.

The noise of two hundred hypervelocity needles

ricocheting around and punching holes in a stack of steel containers masked the sound of one small mech scrambling up the space between two containers to emerge one level up, in the ten-centimeter gap between layers with empty containers above and below me. Hidden by deep shadow, I could watch the killer below.

Suddenly it stopped and stood up, paused for an instant and then sprinted off to the south. I didn't have time to wonder why because a wave of aerial bots came over the stack of containers to the north of me like a storm front. I could see a hundred of them, and heard more, buzzing along on ducted fans with micromissile pods extended and ready.

"SUIZHEN PROTECTION SERVICE! IDENTIFY YOURSELVES AND SUBMIT TO SEARCH AND INQUIRY!" blared over every part of the spectrum, plus amplified sound *and* text projected on every flat surface.

I thought of hiding. A little mech in a big container yard is hard to locate, especially one that's old and cunning and knows ways to mask its emissions. The idea had its merits: leaving my humans in SPS custody would keep them safe from the assassin—especially if the local cops could actually manage to catch or destroy the combat mech. With Zee and the girls safely cooling their heels in Suizhen I could find transport to the rim of Melas Chasma, and deal with the menace hidden in the statue myself, free of interference by reckless humans.

Three things stopped me. First, I wasn't entirely sure the humans would be safe in Suizhen custody. The combat mech assassin had been awfully audacious to attack us right on top of a city, yet had nearly succeeded. And the protection service's response was very slow. So maybe it had picked this location because it had allies here? Unknown.

I also wanted to find out who had sent the damned thing. A mech like that would cost a lot to hire. Any information I could wheedle the Suizhen police into sharing would be useful.

But my greatest fear was that one of the other three might reveal where we were going. If that happened, some Martian cops in the Marineris League might start poking around the statue of Jak Junak and stumble across something I really, really didn't want anyone to find.

So I scrambled out of my hiding spot and up to the top of a stack, pinging my location and my identity as I did so. "It's a relief to see you fellows," I said. "Some unknown individual seems to be trying to kill me."

They were just bots, securing the area and recording everything. A mob of mechs and humans arrived shortly afterward and rounded us all up. All of us, that is, except for the one person I really wanted to see rounded up: the combat mech. It was still at large.

The Suizhen Protection Service was very professional, very thorough, and entirely unsympathetic. Like the rest of the Hebean Republic, Suizhen's a classic old Martian technocracy. Certain tasks must be performed to keep everyone alive, and those tasks are performed by individuals chosen for their expertise. Outputs are carefully defined, and every group of experts strives to maximize those outputs. The resulting societies tend to be very pragmatic and efficient, without much patience for concepts like individual rights or limits to authority.

The second classic Martian form of government

is libertarian anarchy. Those arise after people get sick of living in a society where cops make laws and nutritionists decide what's for dinner.

Suizhen isn't quite at the stage of cops making laws yet—there's a separate General Heuristics Board for that—but oversight is not what you'd call strict. They took us down into the tunnel warren of Suizhen proper, and I spent eleven hours in a shielded room talking to a digital intelligence which identified itself only as SPSIS-0319-7124. Or just 7124 among friends.

"Tell me what happened on and near Surface Highway 11240 between 01:13 and 01:29 Martian Planetary Time today," it asked, and I told it, keeping my account dry and detailed and strictly chronological. I limited myself entirely to physical events rather than what was going on inside my processor at the time.

"What is your relationship to your assailant?"

"We're pretty much a traditional assassin-and-target couple. It tries to kill me, I get away. Nothing kinky."

"Please describe any previous encounters you have had with your assailant."

We both knew perfectly well that the Suizhen Protection Service had gotten a full download of my little chat with the Royal Elevator Guards back in Mutch Cheng. To make cross-checking simple, I repeated what I had told them precisely verbatim. *"I still don't know why this mech keeps trying to kill me—except for the obvious explanation that it hasn't managed to finish the job yet. Have you managed to catch it?"*

"The primary chassis of the individual has been located, but—"

"—the processor and memory are gone. Great, so it's still hunting me but I won't recognize it next time."

The obvious next line of questioning was about the threat I'd gotten up in the Deimos Ring. But instead 7124 asked, *"Please describe your interactions with Varas Lupur."*

"By an entertaining coincidence, he also tried to kill me the last time we met. That was back at Summanus, behind Jupiter. Blew up a spaceship with me in it. Fortunately I escaped. I don't know where he is now. Why do you ask?"

"Has Varas Lupur or any associate of his made threats to you in the past?"

"Not me personally. Other than the whole blowing up the spaceship part, he was very polite." Inside my processor I was abuzz with curiosity. Why was this Martian cop practically begging me to link the assassin to Lupur?

Asking the question provided its answer: because Summanus had suggested it. Summanus knew about our complicated set of relationships with the Greatest Thief in History. Summanus had its own suspicions about what we were seeking on Mars. Summanus is a hab with plenty of political throw weight.

And Summanus could easily hire some goon on Mars to kill us. Probably working through so many cutouts and anonymizers that nobody could provably link the paranoid Lord of Midnight Thunder to a local crime story on Mars. It was elegant, really. Whether or not the assassin could bag any of us, the authorities would be hunting for Lupur—especially after helpful Summanus provided them with real and verifiable data about his earlier attempt to blow us to bits. And whether or not the authorities caught Lupur, the investigations would keep us tied up.

Which is why, after several more hours of repetitive questions, I was not at all surprised when 7124 told me, *"Regrettably, I must ask you to remain in Suizhen until our investigations are complete and your assailant has been located. Suizhen Protection Service can provide you and your human companions with secure accommodations until it is safe for you to leave. Food and energy will be provided."*

"I'm pretty sure the humans will be unhappy about that. They want to see the sights of Mars, not four walls. Couldn't you just assign us a guardian bot?" I asked.

"Unfortunately that is not possible at this time."

Now I was sure Summanus was involved. Only a high-level mind could contrive things so that we wound up in jail after its hired assassin failed to eliminate us. I considered trying to talk the Suizhen Protection Service into asking the Hebean Republic to lob an antimatter warhead at a Martian cultural treasure in another state's territory, just to make sure nobody got their hands on something potentially deadly. All my models showed a very low probability of success, and a much higher probability of the added attention just making things worse.

So instead I thanked 7124 and let myself be escorted along with Zee, Kusti, and Adya to our secure accommodations.

As accommodations went, they weren't that bad: a five-room suite made of smart stuff, two hundred cubic meters in all. Water, power, a matter printer, plenty of data. Not bad for four people. The place was nestled way down in Suizhen, a couple of dozen floors below the underground city's main level and a good two kilometers below the surface, more or less on a level with the ground at the bottom of Ophir and Hebes Chasma. So no panoramic views unless you called them up on the walls. A bland corridor off a transport tunnel, and a door made of steel that only opened when the Protection Service wanted it open.

"Hello, monitoring systems!" I called out once the polite officer who escorted us there had gone. No sense in being subtle. I wanted to make sure my humans didn't discuss anything we didn't want overheard.

"With what queries did they weary each of you, through the long night?" asked Adya.

"The officer asked me about Varas Lupur, over and over," said Zee. "Now I really want to get my hands on him."

"My inquisitor likewise asked of him, and of why we came to Mars, and whither were we bound when so aggressively attacked."

"What did you tell them?" asked Kusti.

Adya glanced at the ceiling. "That I hope to walk beside the rushing river Marineris, or sail upon the stream, and look up to the sun through only sky. I said I know you both have different dreams, and none of them are scribed in stone. So southward went we without firm intent."

Kusti relaxed a bit. "The cops asked me the same things."

"What answers did you give?"

"I told them everything I know about that jerk Lupur, and that I've got no idea why he's still chasing us, or why he's on Mars at all."

"Well, I'm sure the Protection Service will get this whole ugly business settled in no time, so for now let's enjoy their hospitality," I said cheerfully.

The three of them were exhausted so they tumbled off to rest, but I spent my time surveying our prison. It was well designed: The walls were solid, likely armored. No voids beyond to send back echoes when I squeaked supersonically. Air processing used a system of thin high-pressure pipes with redundant layers of filtering so not even a virus could pass through. The water lines looked the same. Wastes went directly to a disassembler, making it very unlikely anybody would be crawling out of a drain.

The problem was that all that security made the place pretty damned escape-proof. Nothing could get in, but none of us were going out, either. We couldn't even plot an escape without being overheard.

Or could we?

I had some ideas, and once the humans stirred again I tried a couple of little experiments. All three were glad of a bit of privacy after spending all day strapped into a shay. Zee took over the larger common room and exercised. As the biggest of the three he had been the most cramped inside the shay, and even a couple of minutes of panicky sprinting at the end of our ride hadn't quite taken the kinks out of his muscles.

Kusti was in her room, lost in infospace. I left her for later.

Adya had printed out a flute and was in her own room with sound compensation active, practicing a piece by Chandi Nali. As she sat cross-legged on the floor, I came in and perched on one knee.

"Have you need of anything I can give?" she asked.

"No, no. Just listening. Pay no attention to anything I say or do."

"If that is your will." She put the flute to her mouth again and resumed playing.

While she played I used the laser emitters on the part of my skin touching her knee to hit her with little heat pulses. I used the tempo of the flute music, and sent her a test message in binary. *"Can you understand?"*

I had to send it twice before she stopped playing. "Yes," she said. "Yes, I think I understand it now." Clever girl. "Shall I play again?"

"Go ahead. This is fun," I said. And while she tootled away I pulsed out *"Escape."*

"Wonderful!" she said, as if to herself. "Now, what to do next?"

"Pelagia."

She didn't respond, just noodled around on her instrument. After about a minute she said, "I would know your opinion of this. Listen well."

I listened. More toots, all precisely on key, but the tempo was a bit weird, kind of syncopated. And then I realized Adya was embedding a binary message in the piece. *"Pulse three times."*

I did, and she paused. "Does what I play amuse you?"

"Very much." I was actually pretty impressed. She was encoding it and embedding it into the music as she went along, and accomplishing all of that with nothing but a ball of meat inside her skull.

After that, with occasional spoken breaks, we communicated via music and hidden light. She was to get in touch with Pelagia, let her know what was going on, and establish some form of at least moderately secure communication. Having a friend on the outside would be useful no matter what we devised to get ourselves loose.

I tried Kusti from the other direction. The Suizhen

Protection Service gave us infosphere access, though I assumed all our traffic was monitored. Still, a sufficiently cunning person can get around snoops, even if said snoops probably do have access to high-level intellects who can break encryption keys in realtime. The trick is to use information the high-level intellects don't have and can't easily guess. In our case, I could draw on a whole bunch of shared experiences and conversations—in the Uranus Ring, at Summanus, and since our arrival at Mars.

It was slow, though. I had to send four different messages just to ask if she had any ideas about escaping. She said she was working on something and could do it better if I left her alone.

Finally I went to see if I could talk to Zee without being monitored.

Zee was gone.

He wasn't anywhere in the suite. Just his graphene stick standing in the corner and the lingering odor of vaporized sweat. I checked everywhere, twice. I asked Adya and Kusti.

And then the door opened, and there was Zee. His hair was damp and he was smiling and waving goodbye to someone out of view down the corridor. He looked a bit startled to see the three of us waiting for him.

"Oh, hi."

"Where were you? How did you get out of here?" I asked him.

"Well, the room's kind of small, so I asked it if there was any kind of exercise facility around here. Turns out we're one level below the SPS gymnasium. They've got a swimming pool and a track. I even did a little unarmed sparring with a couple of chimp officers."

"You just asked?"

"Sure. Room, I think my friends would also like to use the gymnasium."

"An escort will be provided for your protection," said the room. "Please wait."

Kusti frowned. Adya giggled and turned pink.

I linked up with the room and demanded to know where else we could go. It provided me with a list.

> *Welcome to the Secure Guest Quarters maintained by the Suizhen Protection Service! You are here so that we can protect you against potential harm. We understand that this experience may be difficult and stressful for you. To make your stay in our care more enjoyable, you can avail yourself of the following services:*
>
> • *Our state of the art Tan Hsien Training Facility is named in honor of officer "Terawatt" Tan, and is used by active and former SPS biological personnel to keep themselves at the peak of physical health and readiness. You can join in group exercises, or train on your own to keep fit.*
>
> • *The Staff General Dining Area is available for guests to use, if you prefer physical company at mealtime or at any other time. Meet our dedicated and professional officers! If you prefer to dine in your room, the printers there have access to the same delicious menus.*

- *If you feel unwell, don't hesitate to use our top of the line Staff Medical Clinic. Our expert medical technicians have deep experience treating injuries and a wide array of medical conditions, in all biological species. Psychological counseling is also available for individuals who have suffered loss or shock.*

- *Mechanical guests can avail themselves of our fully equipped maintenance workshops. Do your own repairs or consult with our skilled technicians!*

- *Excursions to special events in Suizhen may be available, subject to the judgment of our staff. While we want you to enjoy staying with us, remember that your safety is our highest priority.*

Activities outside your room require a staff escort. Please be courteous and remain near your escort at all times. Thank you and enjoy your stay in our Secure Guest Quarters!

"So," said Zee, "I hear there's a dance performance tomorrow. The Yumengdi Troupe are doing a piece about the life of Feng Liu Wei. Want to go see it?"

"Who's Feng Liu Wei?" asked Kusti.

Zee shrugged. "Some Martian, I guess."

"He was an architect active in Capri during the Fifth Millennium. I believe he designed the Sunrise Bridge," said Adya.

"Come on, it'll be fun," said Zee. "They're doing it in the Cliffside Amphitheater. It looks like a great place. How about you, Daslakh? Want to watch some of us monkeys jump around to music?"

"Yes," I said. "Yes, I would."

Zee cleared his throat. "Room, the four of us would like to request an escort to go see the Yumengdi Troupe dance performance tomorrow at the Cliffside Amphitheater."

"Just a moment," said the room, and then, "We're sorry to report that no personnel are available to serve on escort duty."

"Try Officer Hong Dun," said Zee. "I spoke with her earlier at the pool. She's the one who told me about the performance. She said she'd be happy to escort us."

"Officer Hong is not on duty tomorrow."

"That's right," said Zee. "She's off duty but she's willing to escort us anyway. It won't tie up any active-duty officers that way. She told me she's qualified, so there should be no problem with us going."

"Just a moment," said the room again, as the software we'd been talking to kicked the problem upstairs to a real intelligence.

"Room, can you put me in touch with Officer Hong Dun, please?" said Zee.

"Hong," said a woman's voice, and then a projected image of a small woman in a Suizhen Protection Service uniform appeared. She broke into a grin when she saw Zee. "Hey! Did you decide to go?"

"I did. I even talked my roommates into coming along," he said, indicating the rest of us.

"Oh, okay," said Officer Hong, sounding slightly disappointed.

The room spoke again. "We're sorry to report that Officer Hong Dun is not qualified to escort Secure Guests outside the Protection Service facility."

"Yes I am," said Hong. "I scored ninety-eight on the field exam!"

"Just a moment," said the room.

"Hang on," said Hong, and her image was replaced by an icon as she contacted someone else.

"What are you doing?" I asked Zee.

"What do you mean?" he asked.

"We haven't planned any of this!"

"You were busy," he said.

Officer Hong reappeared. "Sorry about that. It's fine. I'll be your security escort to the dance performance tomorrow—but SPS isn't buying the seats."

"Let it be my treat, then," said Zee. "It starts at oh two hundred, planetary?"

"That's right. Local sunset. They do that for all the performances at Cliffside. I think it's so that the stage is framed by the mirror ring rising behind it."

"Sounds wonderful! If we leave here at 1:00 that gives us plenty of time to find seats and maybe grab something to eat. Where do we meet you?"

"I have to come escort you from your room. Be ready!" She vanished.

"Um," said Zee, "I actually don't have much cash. Can someone lend me enough for Dun's seat?"

"Of course," said Adya. "She seems very nice."

"How did you do that?" I demanded.

"I just talk to people," said Zee, as if it was the most obvious thing in the world.

CHAPTER EIGHTEEN

Two things happened between our little chat with Officer Hong and our trip to see the dance performance. The first was that Suizhen Protection Service's investigative branch actually managed to identify the mech which had attacked us.

"It has various identities but the most commonly used one is Kumakatok, allegedly from a hab called Icelet, though there is no confirmation of that. The mech has been active under that name for at least thirty standard years as a freelance assassin. There is strong circumstantial evidence that the same individual also operates as a legitimate bounty hunter under a different identity. At present we do not know what entities are responsible for hiring it," said my good buddy 7124 about two hours after the Hong incident, while the humans were eating a light supper printed in the room.

"So you'll have it in custody in no time, right? And then we can leave?"

"We are still attempting to locate it. If you are in

possession of any additional information about this individual or its employers, you should tell me now."

"I've got nothing. I never met this Kumakatok before, and I can't say who might have hired it. I'm old, and I've pissed off a lot of people over the centuries."

"That much seems accurate. Thank you for your time."

The SPS mech left me alone with my thoughts. Now I was sure this was Summanus's work—if only because I doubted that Lupur or Muro could afford the services of a high-end murder machine like this Kumakatok person. Plus, while both of them were certainly vindictive, they were also both kind of cheap. I could see either or both of them hiring some Martian mook out of the tunnel warrens to take a run at us, but not a professional assassin.

The other thing happened during the night. Zee and the ladies had gone to bed—separately—and I was alone when I got a ping from Pelagia.

"You four can calm down and stop rushing," she said. *"I've got a nice little job that'll take me about three weeks to complete. Think you can keep busy that long?"*

"What's the job?"

"Fast courier run. Somebody wants a package of biomaterials delivered to a rock called Sonja. They're paying my mass-energy plus ten percent for the round trip if I can get it there in a week."

"It sounds fishy," I said. *"Like somebody wants to get you away from us."*

"They put down earnest money. There's a real cargo."

"Make sure to scan it all very carefully. 'Biomaterials' could be something that turns whale brains into dashi."

"I'll be careful. You stay safe, too. And keep an eye on Adya for me."

"Right now she and I are both inside an armored

*suite below a police station two kilometers under-
ground. I don't think I'm capable of being any safer."*

"Fair enough. I'd say 'don't do anything stupid,'
but that's a lost cause."

"Have fun on your wild goose chase."

The following morning was a bit odd. All three of
the humans were distracted, dipping in and out of
the infosphere much more than usual. Zee went to
exercise but insisted I meet him for lunch in the staff
dining room, even to the point of sending me a ping
from the shower. To humor him I asked the room for
an escort, and followed a bot upstairs.

The Staff General Dining Area was a utilitarian space
decorated with images of Protection Service officers and
a few of their predecessors in the old Suizhen Public
Safety Volunteers. I joined Zee at a table with two
Suizhen cops, one Martian and one chimp.

"This is my friend Daslakh," said Zee. "Daslakh,
these are Officers Huo Shi and Omo Irawo. I was
just telling them about the dance performance we're
going to see today. Who's the guy it's about?"

"An architect. Feng Liu Wei," I said, wondering why
he didn't just look it up himself. So I poked part of
my consciousness into local infospace—and promptly
understood why Zee was so keen on me coming all
the way up here just to watch him eat mushroom
dumplings. The Staff General Dining Area was a completely public-access space. I guess Protection Service
officers wanted to be able to bitch about their bosses
over lunch without monitoring.

It meant I could make up an alias which wouldn't
be tied to my physical self, giving me the privacy
to make arrangements for us to get out of Suizhen

custody and get to the statue at Melas Chasma before those other idiots.

So while Zee made small talk and finished his meal I blazed through the infosphere, creating shell identities, transferring energy credits, and bouncing messages off a series of anonymous repeaters—all in order to hire a team of security specialists from Ophir to come extract us from the amphitheater that evening.

The two cops had to get back to work, and Zee bid them farewell with a cheery wave, then murmured, "We need to talk about tonight."

"I'm working on it," I said.

"Good. These are nice guys, but I'm getting a little bored here."

Making my arrangements took long enough that Zee had to have three helpings of cascarons and coffee. The delay was mostly due to signal lag as I bounced messages all around near-Mars space.

We'd arranged to meet Officer Hong at one—planetary time, about an hour before local sunset. But all three of my humans were all ready and fidgety by zero thirty. Zee had dressed up considerably more than usual. He had the room print up a rather stylish knee-length smartcloth coat that displayed a pattern of Raba's maroon-and-white symbol on black.

Good for him. Nice to see he wasn't intimidated by all these cultured Martian sophisticates. When they're not grousing about Deimosians, Lunars, and (of course) Earth people being snobs, Martians can be excruciatingly patronizing toward just about everyone else in the system.

Hong Dun showed up promptly at 1:00 and led us up a couple of levels to a vehicle park, where we all squeezed into a windowless car driven by a digital mind called SPSIS-0319-0441. Forty minutes of driving through various secondary tunnels and freight roads finally brought us to the south end of Suizhen, where the strip of high country between Hebes Chasma and Ophir Chasma came to an abrupt end.

Cliffside Amphitheater is exactly what its name describes. There's a little valley in the edge of Ophir Chasma right at the one-kilometer altitude level, a little to the east of the main route through Suizhen. When the inevitable landslips and erosion caused by terraforming ended, the valley was almost a perfect half bowl, about a hundred meters wide. For hundreds of years nobody really cared about it, but back in the Sixth Millennium when the Martian atmosphere finally got dense enough for roofed valleys like Ophir Chasma to open up, somebody realized that little divot out of the cliff face was a dramatic setting for an amphitheater.

You get there through a tunnel, so it's not until you actually enter the amphitheater that you get the full effect: a half bowl lined with seats, the vast cliff rising behind you, the stage projecting out over a half-kilometer drop to the valley floor. Beyond the stage you see the wide expanse of Ophir Chasma, green and blue and dotted with the lights of towns and cities.

Hong Dun filled us in on the history of the place. "It's been in continuous use for four thousand years. Nobody knows who built it anymore."

"No records from the time endure?" asked Adya.

"Too many. They contradict each other. Different regimes rewrote the history, so did historians, and entertainments, too. There was one I did as a kid, *Opening*, all about Yao Mao hurrying to get *The Dust*

Storm finished in time for the big day. But Yao Mao died fifty years before the roofs came off, and they're not even sure she wrote *The Dust Storm* anyway."

"You can't ask some old digital minds?" said Zee.

"None of them remember."

"Digital intelligences have better things to do than remember details you meat brains are too careless to keep track of," I added. Meanwhile I was counting down seconds to when my contractors were due to arrive.

The crowd was drawn almost entirely from Suizhen. They were all in perfect physical shape, dressed in similar muted clothing, with modest hairstyles and no flashy status displays. My three humans were vivid and conspicuous.

"Our seats are over here," said Zee, leading the way down to the fourth row, over on the far right.

"You'd be safer higher up," said Hong. "We should exchange these tickets."

"I like to be able to hear the music," said Kusti, startling me more than the mech attack two days earlier.

Hong dipped into infospace, but no sooner had she done so than Kusti grabbed her shoulder and pointed up into the seats behind us.

"I think I saw a man with a gun!"

"Stay down," said Hong. Her uniform covered her and thickened over vital spots, then the pseudomuscles in the fabric flexed as she jumped over four rows of seats to where Kusti had pointed.

"Come on," I said, and scuttled under the seats toward the stage.

But evidently I didn't have enough mass, because my three satellites went off on trajectories of their own. Adya headed for the aisle and began politely forcing her way through the confused crowd of dance enthusiasts toward the exit. Kusti veered off down to the front row and headed for the left side of the amphitheater. And Zee got to the right aisle and climbed up the steps to the little scenic lookout balcony at the edge of the cliff.

Hong scanned the guy Kusti had pointed at, and everyone else within several meters, realized something fishy was going on, and pushed her way over to the aisle to intercept Adya.

"I'm afraid I must ask you to return to your seat," she said—or words to that effect; I was too far off to hear, but Adya went slightly orange and then turned to go back down.

"Over here!" I pinged to my three humans, throwing up a big flashing icon of myself in infospace to mark my position. Twenty seconds. *"We're leaving!"*

Over at the far side of the stage I saw a squad of six flying bots dropping down out of the sky. Kusti was close to them but the rest of us were on the opposite side of the amphitheater. And between Officer Hong jumping around in armor and the new arrivals, the crowd was starting to get panicky.

I pinged the bots. *"You're on the wrong side, boys. Fly over here and pick us up."* When I got no response I shot them my identification code. *"I'm Daslakh. Contract 9978-281-2. Come get me!"*

Two of the bots supported a rescue sling. As I watched, they dipped down so that Kusti could grab it.

"Not her, you idiots! Me! I'm the one who's paying you!"

"SUIZHEN PROTECTION SERVICE! ALL INDI-VIDUALS CEASE MOVING IMMEDIATELY!" A trio of police mechs emerged from the entrance tunnel, and the local infosphere locked down.

Four of the bots hovering over Kusti fired needle guns at the cops. They weren't fooling around, either—concentrating fire on one police mech until it disintegrated, then shifting to the second.

But the cops weren't fooling around, either. The two remaining mechs went into evasion mode while Officer Hong dropped behind a row of seats and fired on the combat bots with her own sidearm, using web rounds in crowd-control mode. Two of the webs burst in the center of the squad of bots, gumming up a couple of them in sticky strands that contracted, crunching two of the bots together.

Hong dropped to the ground as the bots targeted her position, which gave her fellow cop mechs the chance to splat another bot.

Most of the audience were now pushing toward the exits, except for my three humans. Kusti hadn't wasted any time during the shootout, and got herself belted into the rescue harness. Meanwhile Adya had joined Zee at the foot of the aisle near me.

The fact that I see with my whole surface has been a huge benefit many times, not least when I spotted another flying unit dropping toward the stage. It didn't look like my contractors, either. This was a single mech with four legs and rotors, and as soon as I saw it I rushed at Zee and Adya. "Get under cover! Now! The assassin's back!"

They scrambled for the side of the amphitheater, where the aisle on the end was partly cut into the rock edge of the bowl, so it had a little shelter from above.

I also tried to ping the cops and alert them to the

new menace, but their infospace lockdown wouldn't let me. Nor could I find out where the heck *my* hired goons were.

The assassin fired off a missile which veered under the rock edge to get at Zee and Adya. That got the attention of the cop mechs, and one of them turned it to confetti with a fast needle burst before it could detonate.

I spotted Officer Hong pushing through the crowd trying to reach Kusti, so I cranked up my voice and aimed it at her head. "Hong Dun! The assassin's above you!" She looked up, spotted it, and switched her sidearm from web rounds to something more potent.

With Kusti in the sling, two of the combat bots lifted her off the floor of the amphitheater and out over the edge of the cliff below. The SPS mechs, true to their mission, shifted their full attention to the assassin mech, which dropped onto the stage and folded its rotors.

Its new body was certainly well armed, with a pair of needle guns and a little missile pod, and while it wasn't as heavily armored as the previous one, it could shrug off the fusillade of needles from the police mechs.

One of the cop mechs charged right in, getting in front of the assassin's sensor pod and blasting away at point-blank range, hoping to hit something vital. The other hung back to intercept any more missiles. Officer Hong bounced a couple of homing rounds off its armor and then had the clever idea to switch her pistol back to web mode and empty the magazine at it.

The strands practically covered the assassin in a layer of thin orange stripes, pinning its legs and making it impossible for the thing to open its rotors and take off again. What they *couldn't* do was keep it from hitting the close-in cop mech with a missile. The poor thing blew apart in a shower of fragments. I hope it had backed its mind up on storage before starting the day's shift.

Officer Hong used her suit's augmented muscle to pull up seats and hurl them at the killer, while the remaining cop mech intercepted another missile with a burst of needles.

"We have to get out of here," I said.

"I agree," said Zee. Without another word he scooped up Adya and myself in his arms and ran full-tilt down the aisle. The SPS mech intercepted a missile just meters away from us—close enough that fragments rattled off my shell.

We got to the foot of the aisle and Zee didn't slow down. He dove headfirst over the railing into the Martian sky.

I could have jumped free, but I hung on instead. Either Zee knew what he was doing, or he didn't—in which case I'd have to figure out a way to save him and Adya from dying on the rocks below in the twenty or so seconds it would take us to fall.

But three seconds after we left the ground his coat shifted, smart-matter fibers extending and stiffening to create a broad pair of wings. Zee clutched Adya to him as he pulled out into a shallow dive, shooting over the landscape of Ophir Chasma at a hundred kilometers an hour.

Adya looked over her shoulder at the ground speeding past and gave a whoop of mixed fear and exhilaration. Her skin changed from dark yellow to an excited magenta.

"You jerk!" I shouted at Zee—I had to use the radio channel because his suit had decided on its own to cover his head with a hood. "Did you plan this?"

"I wanted to fly on Mars," he said. "I was going to

try talking Hong Dun into letting me try it after the performance. What happened to Kusti? Is she all right?"

"She parted without any partners," said Adya.

I checked the infosphere. "No sign of her—not that I'm surprised. She's got more identities than she has teeth."

The moment we jumped off the balcony we'd passed from Hebean Republic territory into the Marineris League. Marineris border control issued us a mild warning about crossing without using a designated entry point, but the League's more on the libertarian-anarchy side of the spectrum than its neighbor the Republic, so there wasn't anything to worry about.

"Let's see: the Suizhen cops have a request out for us to contact them, and for other entities to report our location, and pretty please come back to get locked in the basement again, but I don't think the League cops will bother. Those idiots I hired to extract us just asked if we can postpone until tomorrow. I bet I don't get my deposit back."

"I'd like to make sure Hong Dun's all right," said Zee.

"And give our gratitude," Adya added.

"Try to focus on not crashing and killing yourselves," I said.

I wasn't just being snide, either. Ophir Chasma is actually pretty rough terrain, even after three thousand years of erosion and a lot of landscape work by humans and bots. Just south of us were a range of hills almost as tall as the chasm rim itself, covered with woods and vineyards. The ground below us was flatter, sloping down in the direction we were traveling, covered with a patchwork of farms where people grew actual plants in actual dirt that biologicals actually put in their mouths.

With my help Zee flew us a good twenty kilometers before drag finally conquered lift and we touched down in a field of knee-high durum wheat. The sun had completely disappeared behind the chasm rim to the west of us, but the mirror ring was up, giving plenty of light to see by.

"It's about a hundred and sixty klicks from here to the Junak statue," I told them. "I think we should hurry."

"First we must leave this field," said Adya. "I cannot plant my foot without treading on a plant."

"I think there's a road over there," said Zee, pointing south.

I rode on Zee's shoulder as the two humans tiptoed through the wheat field for about a quarter of a kilometer.

The road was the main surface road running from Suizhen to the city of Ophir, about fifty klicks east of us. It was a high-speed controlled road, safely elevated and fenced. No point in scaling a support pier and cutting through the barriers just to get hit by traffic. So we followed an unpaved farm-equipment track which paralleled the highway. Roads lead to towns, after all.

An hour's walk brought us to the outskirts of Saylac, one of the first open-air towns in this part of Mars. The old town is a grid of little concrete buildings with plenty of dirt piled on top of them for insulation and radiation shielding. There's some local tradition about growing a garden on top of your house and engaging in ritualized status competition over whose plants look prettier. People come out from Ophir Cheng to gawk, and spend lots of energy credits to stay in old buildings and eat food grown in dirt. The quaint town core is flanked by a pair of underground arcologies where most of Saylac's quarter-million people actually live and work.

I wanted to summon a vehicle and get out of there, but Zee and Adya were both hungry and thirsty, so I had to wait while she picked a restaurant and wasted about a hundred gigajoule credits on pasta made from "real" wheat, topped with cheese that came from a source I won't even describe except to say it involves goats. They drank wine made from grapes grown in the hills south of Saylac and spent more time talking and staring at each other than they did eating. Horribly inefficient.

I did bounce a message to Pelagia off some anonymous repeaters. *"Adya and Zee jumped off a kilometer-high cliff but everyone's fine now."*

Her reply arrived five seconds later. *"If you don't bring her back intact you'd better stay at the bottom of a deep hole on Mars forever."*

"I'm a lot more worried about what happens if we don't get to that statue first."

"You really think it exists?"

"I'm absolutely certain that something very dangerous is hidden in that statue."

Her reply took a few seconds longer. I don't know if she used more relays or just had to think about it. *"Who are you, Daslakh?"*

"I'm the mech who's telling you something important, so pay attention. If you hear about any weird stuff on Mars or the Deimos Ring—any kind of large-scale disaster, cities going dark, stuff like that—I want you to get your fishy tail to Summanus as fast as you can. Don't worry about us because we'll be past helping. Understand?"

"That isn't very funny."

"It's the lines I've got. Take care of yourself, Pelagia."

When our talk was done I noticed that Zee and Adya had gotten into conversation with a pair of humans at the next table. They were another male-female couple, and were conspicuous for how old they looked. Humans have been coming up with ways to keep their chemically unstable meat sacks from disintegrating since the Third Millennium, but there are ways to spot genuine age, no matter how many times they reset their telomeres. Sheer wear creates lines in the skin, habits affect the posture and eventually the skeleton inside, and cosmic rays do their steady work.

These two weren't even trying to hide it. The woman's cascade of hair was completely white, with just enough variation to show it wasn't colored. The man's head was bald and spotted, and he even affected a pair of lenses on a metal frame balanced on his nose, like an old optical interface device.

"What are your names?" asked the old woman. "I'm Tanry Todaichin, and this is my partner—what do you call yourself now?" She smiled at the very old man.

"Ivaz Kapalit," said the old man. "My companion gets forgetful when she has more than a couple of milliliters of wine."

"Pay him no mind. I don't think I've seen either of you here before. Are you visiting Saylac?"

"We pause our passage here for pasta," said Adya.

"Miranda!" said Ivaz. "You must be from Miranda. No one else puts as much effort into speaking well."

"Don't tell him if he's right," said the very old woman. "It will just make him insufferable."

"I am indeed a maid of Miranda," said Adya. "Now see if Zee can be placed so easily."

"Can't tell a thing if he keeps his mouth shut. What brings you to this part of Mars?"

"Oh, we're just passing through, really. We're on our way south," said Zee.

"Melas?" asked Tanry.

"Eventually, I think," said Zee, looking a little uncomfortable.

"I remember traveling like that. Set out in the morning with no idea where you're going to lay your head," said Ivaz. "When I was just a student—"

"These two young people aren't interested in ancient history, love."

"Nor should they be, I guess. All right, Zee, tell me something else. What have you enjoyed most during your visit to Mars?"

"We've only been here a few days. A lot of that was in a shay driving from Mutch Cheng to Suizhen."

"Interesting choices. May I ask why those places in particular? Not the usual tourist itinerary. Most visitors gawk at Deimos, ride down to Pavonis, have a look at Olympus, fly over Noctis Labyrinthus, and then do the grand tour down Marineris from Ius to the sea."

"Well, there's a statue we want to look at."

"Oh," said Tanry. "The cliffs of Melas! I forgot all about those. It must be the wine."

Ivaz raised one silver eyebrow. "But you said *a* statue. Is there one in particular you've come here to see?"

Zee looked uncertainly at Adya, so I decided to jump in. "The First Human statue," I said. It's the one every tourist stops to look at. A safe choice.

"Pardon me, little fellow," said Ivaz. "You were being so quiet I forgot you were here. That's the oldest of the Melas colossi, you know. Carved in—"

"Don't bore them with details, dear," said Tanry.

"They came all the way here from the Uranus Trojans to see it; I expect they're interested." He smiled at Zee. "Your vowels gave you away."

"My partner studies how people speak," said Tanry. "It's a hobby of his."

"I craft entertainments. It's important to get the details right."

"Do you remember one called *Brief Eternity*?" I asked him.

"Derivative and twee," he said.

"I liked it," said Tanry.

"I can demonstrate mathematically why you shouldn't. But, please—I'm sorry, I didn't catch your name."

"Daslakh."

"Daslakh. Please, tell us how you know so much about obscure entertainments of the distant past."

"I'm older than I look."

"I wish I could say the same," he said.

"If they're going to see the colossi, why don't we give them a lift?" said Tanry to Ivaz.

He raised an eyebrow again, but then considered Zee and Adya, and smiled. "Why not indeed? How about it, you two? We're heading that direction anyway. It should only take a couple of hours. Tanry and I would enjoy having someone else to talk to. We've been together so long we both know what the other will say before they say it."

While he was still finishing his sentence I took a dive into the local infosphere to find out just who these two really were, and why they had so conveniently appeared in our path on this particular night.

They'd left the usual traces dating back fifty years.

Ivaz Kapalit really did create entertainments, and had a small fan base in Mars space and the Main Swarm. Video of him matched the man in front of me. Tanry Todaichin had written a string of monographs on the evolution of tailored and imported species in the Martian environment. Images of her at conferences also matched. They'd lived in Deimos for about thirty standard years, and in Saylac ever since.

Two oddities caught my attention. First, the data trail absolutely ended fifty years ago. Before that, neither of them had done anything—at least, not under those names. They had emerged from total obscurity as skilled professionals in their fields. Second, the two people in front of me looked to be at least a couple of centuries in age, if not older. What had they both been doing during their first few hundred years?

"That is most kind of you," said Adya. "But you need take no trouble. We shall summon a shay."

"Nonsense," said Ivaz. "If it was any trouble I wouldn't make the offer. We've got a shay outside with room for four, and I'm sure Mr. Daslakh can find a spot. Tanry and I are riding south tonight anyhow. It's silly for you to waste energy credits on a transport when empty seats are going the same way."

Should I be suspicious? How plausible was it for Varas Lupur—or even the Suizhen Protection Service— to have agents in place in this obscure Martian town? And how could anyone, even an Inner Ring mind, deduce that Adya would choose a fresh pasta restaurant over the place two doors down which served handmade sausages grilled over burning wood?

So I kept silent and let Zee cast the deciding vote. "Why not?" he said.

Their shay was a very old model, and I had a strong suspicion they'd bought it new. The passenger compartment was big enough for six, but the rear seats were piled with cases and bags, including a worn and much-repaired Mars Defense Force duffel. As the Mars Defense Force had not existed since the Eighth Millennium, it must have been a replica.

"Our worldly goods," said Ivaz, nodding at the pile. "There was a time when we needed a whole cargo container, but we've managed to outlive a lot of our possessions."

"Most of it was just clutter anyway," said Tanry.

"Why do you bear so much baggage?" asked Adya.

"We're moving on. That dinner at Mian Gong was our farewell to Saylac. Sold the house, the vineyard, the whole property, the furniture, everything. This is all we're taking with us," said Ivaz as the shay started up and moved out of the parking area.

"A few old things we can't seem to part with," said Tanry. "We should probably donate them to a museum. Think of how much energy we would save."

"We can afford it. They wouldn't want any of it anyway."

"Don't mind him," said Tanry. "We're leaving Mars. We lived here a long time but Ivaz and I agreed it was time to go."

"Too crowded. A trillion people! They don't need us."

"To which world do you go?"

"A hab in the Kuiper, called Asphodel," said Ivaz. "But we're not going upstairs for another six weeks. We're going to spend a month at the beach on Liming Dao, down in the Eos Sea. Probably the last ocean we'll ever see that isn't covered by a couple of kilometers of ice. Do some diving, eat some fresh-caught prawns, then up the string to the Ring and away we go."

"But you probably aren't interested in what we're doing," said Tanry. "If you're going to Melas you should definitely go to the Museo Marineria. You can spend days there."

"Weeks," said Ivaz. "Wonderful collection. Much better than the colossi. Don't know why you want to waste your time with them. Their only appeal is sheer size."

"Miranda has nothing like them, nor Zee's home hab. When we are done visiting them we will see the Museo," said Adya.

The chitchat died down a bit, and Adya fell asleep in her seat.

Ivaz looked at her and smiled, then leaned over to speak quietly to Zee. "It's none of my business, so I'm just going to observe that she seems like one worth keeping. Why, what's the matter?" he asked when he saw Zee's expression.

"Oh, nothing. I think you're right, but . . . it's complicated."

"In my experience people say 'it's complicated' when something is actually very simple but they don't like the answer. What's the problem? Her family don't like you? Those Miranda clans can be terrible snobs."

"No. I've never met them. No, I—I made a promise to someone else. Another woman."

"A promise? You've got a partner?" The old man's voice took on a slightly harsh edge.

"I don't know," said Zee. His heart was beating like he'd just finished a couple of rounds of stick fighting. "I thought so, but then she left."

"Why?"

After a long pause Zee said, "Business, I guess."

"You made a promise to a woman who dumped you for money? It's pretty clear that agreement is null and void. Forget her. See? Not complicated at all."

"I remember being in love with her more than anything else. Now I don't feel anything at all."

"Time happens. Best not to dwell on the past. Think about the future. Things are going to be amazing!"

We rode south down a valley full of big fancy houses surrounded by farms. Beyond the hills to the east the towers of Ophir rose up as high as the chasm rim. We passed through a tunnel into Candor Chasma, still following the valley. It ended on the shore of Candor Lake, where our secondary road merged with the main highway, heading south around the shore of the lake.

About ten klicks beyond the merge I asked Ivaz, "Can we get off here?"

"But we're still in Candor Chasma! Melas is another twenty or thirty kilometers from here."

"Yes, but that would put us at the base of the statue. We want to visit the interior."

"I don't think there's anything left inside," said Tanry. "Not like when they were new."

"That's what we have to find out," I said. "Can you drop us at the north entrance to the highland preserve?"

"If you insist," said Ivaz. He muttered something and I could see a visual display light up on the lenses he wore in front of his face. His eyes darted about and he mumbled a bit more, then the display vanished. "There. We should be there in fifteen minutes."

The shay took the exit and shot off to the east along

the base of the cliffs at the southern edge of Candor Chasma. The narrow strip of land on top between the Candor and Melas canyons was a wilderness preserve. I wanted to sneak up on the statue from the back.

"May I ask you something, Mr. Daslakh?" said Ivaz. "What's your part in this?" He waved a hand encompassing Zee and Adya.

"It's my friend," said Zee. "I've known Daslakh for years."

"Nothing to do with this mysterious 'business' you spoke of?"

"Don't be nosy, Ivaz," said Tanry.

"I just want to make sure our young friends haven't got themselves caught up in something shady."

"Oh, no," I said. "We're just—"

"Yes, we are," said Zee. Damn his honest streak. "But Daslakh isn't the one who got us into it."

"The culprit is myself," said Adya, keeping herself green. "There is a certain thing I seek, but I am not solitary in my search. Cunning criminals also wish to have it in their hands. The thought of their finding it fills me with fear."

"It's pretty dangerous," I added.

"You should tell the police," said Tanry.

"Or do you have a good reason not to?" asked Ivaz.

"Whoever gets hold of it could unleash a catastrophe on the whole solar system," I said. "We don't know who to trust. It's just too dangerous."

"I see you're deliberately not sharing any specifics with us," said Ivaz. "I don't know if I should be grateful or insulted."

"Why don't you just destroy this whatever-it-is, if it's too dangerous for anyone to have?" asked Tanry.

"It might yet be needed, a dreadful device to defeat a dire danger."

"That's the problem with power. It's so damned useful sometimes. Just remember that it always corrupts. Always. I'd hate to see nice young folks like yourselves getting paranoid and turning on each other."

"Adya wants to share it with everyone," said Zee.

"How about you?" asked the old man, looking sharply at him.

"I trust her." When he said that Adya turned pinker and the old man raised his bushy white eyebrows.

"All right, then," he said. "Good hunting, and try not to get yourselves killed." He fiddled with his face lenses again and sent us each a contact link. "If you need help, call us. We've made a lot of friends over the centuries."

"Decades," said Tanry. "He gets mixed up sometimes."

CHAPTER NINETEEN

We pulled up in the visitor center at the foot of the cliff. The side of Candor Chasma sloped up in front of us at a sixty-degree angle, carpeted with tailored plants to keep the whole thing from sliding down. Behind the visitor center the elevator shaft was a diamond thread against the dark green face of the cliff.

The visitor center was closed, but the gates were unlocked and the elevator worked. Before we went up, Zee found a public printer and made himself a two-meter carbon-fiber rod. "In case we run into trouble," he said.

The flat top of the ridge that separates Candor Chasma from Melas Chasma to the south is above the four-kilometer level, and is maintained as an environmental preserve. In this case, the environment is more or less like ancient Mars before terraforming. More or less, because the air is still about a hundred times denser than it used to be, and has oxygen in it. But even Martians need a mask up there, and it's too dry and cold for most of the plants that thrive down in the valleys. The preserve looks like Old Mars, and it's conveniently located between two big cities, so a lot of Martians take the elevator up the cliff to walk around in suits and talk about how they feel an ancestral connection to the planet's true spirit.

But not many do it just at dawn, and most of those were off to the east waiting for sunrise, at the lookout on the point where the two great rift valleys meet and the Candor River flows over a series of rapids far below.

We had the elevator to ourselves going up, and Zee and Adya stared out at the view to the north over Candor Chasma as we rose out of the cloud layer and could see the whole valley full of clouds colored pale rose by the light of the rising sun.

They sealed their suits when the elevator suggested it, and a minute later the doors opened at the top of the cliff with a hiss. The elevator is actually a freestanding tower, so there's a bridge about a hundred meters long to get to the preserve. As we walked the local infospace briefed us on what was and was not permitted in the preserve. It boiled down to "don't steal rocks and take your damned trash with you when you leave."

At the far end half a dozen trails led off in different directions. We picked the "Smugglers' Traverse" route. But just then I noticed something: one of the boulders next to the trail was suspiciously warm. From UV through visible it looked like a regular rock, but in infrared it was just about thirty-seven centigrade—human body temperature. A sonar ping revealed it wasn't a rock at all but a camouflage drape over two human forms and a spherical machine.

Speech is a ridiculously slow way to communicate.

The first syllables of "Zee, look over there" hadn't finished vibrating their way out of my speaker when the two humans under the drape dramatically tossed it aside. Chi, Muro, and Ketto, in the flesh.

"Surprise!" cried Chi.

"Lupur guessed you'd try coming this way," said Muro. "You aren't getting the Trigger, so this is your last chance to give up and go away."

"We cannot abandon our search," said Adya. "The Trigger is too important. I beg you, think of what Lupur might do with it in his hand. Yourselves would not be immune to that harm."

"We're not mechs," said Ketto. "If he fries every digital mind in the system that won't hurt us. It just means no more bossy machines."

"Billions will perish as habs and ships fail. Billions who are no more digital than yourselves."

"So?" asked Ketto.

"It means we can get their stuff!" said Chi.

"Muro, surely you understand the danger. In a solar system fallen into chaos, what chance does a single small creature have?"

"Same chance as now. I fight for every scrap I get. I've got friends who want this thing and can pay whatever I want. No more scraps for me."

"I've got a question," I said. "How come you three are out here hiding under a blanket while Lupur is off getting the incredibly valuable thing you want? Do you really think he's going to come back once he has the Trigger?"

"Of course not," said Muro. "He's going to double-cross us, or at least he is going to try. But I've anticipated that. There are only two ways out of the statue.

We can get there and block them as soon as we deal with you three."

"Help us rather than hinder. We six can join forces long enough to stop Lupur," said Adya.

"No," said Zee. "I don't think that would work."

"We'd spend all our time arguing about who gets to be in back," I said.

"Too much talk!" said Chi.

"Not enough violence," added Ketto.

"I agree," said Muro. The cat must have activated her mech jammer then, because my consciousness jumped ahead several seconds to a very different scene.

The biologicals had all moved a few meters away, back toward the cliff. Zee and Adya stood a couple of meters apart with their backs to the edge while the cat and her boys faced them.

At the instant my brain came back online Muro's travel sphere and a rock the size of a cantaloupe were just parting ways in a classic elastic collision event. The rock ricocheted south while Muro—conserving the momentum of the system as classical mechanics requires—rebounded north past the edge of the cliff. Where the rock had struck the travel sphere's surface, bits of shattered electronics went off on their own trajectories. I traced the path of the rock back to Zee, who had evidently hurled it two-handed and was now turning away.

Adya stood a meter away, holding Zee's *palo* horizontally in guard position, protecting the two of them from Chi and Ketto. Red and Blue looked at each other, smirked, then lunged forward in unison, each grabbing an end of the *palo* so Adya couldn't swing it. Instead, the two of them used it to push her back toward the cliff edge. She struggled but in Martian gravity she just didn't have the traction. Nor did she have a coat that could fly.

With a roar Zee surged forward and grabbed the *palo*. Instead of pushing he *lifted*, hoisting Chi and Ketto off the ground and letting their momentum carry them over his head. It wouldn't have worked on Earth, or in most of the spin habitats which have approximately Earth standard gravity. But on Mars a man who could lift a graceful young woman like Adya or Kusti in one gee could easily pick up two wiry goons like Chi and Ketto.

They tumbled to the ground behind Zee and Adya, so now they had their backs to the cliff and were facing one very angry man with a *palo* and a slightly less angry woman with a fancy stiletto.

"Hey, now," said Ketto. "No hard feelings, right?" Meanwhile Chi drew an enormous knife from his leg sheath and grinned widely.

Muro's travel sphere rose up behind them. I assumed that she had some kind of beam or projectile weapon installed, and I didn't want to see what it would do to Zee and Adya. So I let the cat have a couple of laser bursts right in her big sensitive eyes. Not enough to do any permanent damage, but enough to leave her dazzled for several seconds.

Zee focused on Chi and Ketto. Instead of holding the *palo* like a barrier, he gripped it like a spear, jabbing at his two foes and driving them back step by step. Chi tried to parry it with his big knife, but a ten-centimeter blade held in one hand just didn't have the leverage to block a two-meter rod held in two. Especially when the man trying to break his sternum with the rod was growling, "*Sick* of you two! I'm *sick* of you two!"

Chi's back foot felt the edge of the cliff and he slashed at Zee's hand—but of course the fibers of Zee's suit could handle a mere metal knife, no matter how sharp. The next instant the tip of the *palo* caught Chi right in the face and knocked him back. He struggled and windmilled his arms, sending the knife flying off into the abyss. He snatched at Ketto's hand, catching him off balance so that both of them fell off the edge.

Zee and Adya rushed forward, looking shocked. I followed, feeling more hopeful than horrified.

We saw Ketto with his arms and one leg wrapped around Muro's travel sphere. Chi hung below, clinging desperately to Ketto's free leg. Inside the travel sphere Muro raged at them both as the sphere's ducted fans strained to hold all that extra load—and failed.

They sank slowly, drifting eastward on the light breeze, until they dropped through the cloud layer and were lost to sight.

"I hope they come to ground safely," said Adya.

"*I* hope they land very far away, so we don't run into them again," I said. "Preferably on something sharp."

"I think they'll be all right," said Zee. "The cat's pretty resourceful."

"It's ten kilometers to the statue from here," I said. "Are you two up for a brisk morning stroll?"

The trail through the preserve was designed for people who wanted to experience the primal Martian landscape, not people who had someplace they wanted to be in an hour. After about five minutes of pointless meandering, during which Adya actually paused to read an old historical marker which wasn't echoed in infospace, I plotted a more direct route and led the two of them cross-country.

Not long after that Adya stopped.

"Come on, come on," I said.

"What's wrong?" asked Zee.

"I tremble," she said, and held up a hand horizontally so we could see it shake. Inside her sealed suit her skin was rescue orange. "My biomonitor tells a tale of elevated adrenaline and cortisol, nor have I eaten since last night. My body betrays me."

Zee put an arm around her. "You'll be okay," he said, and helped her over to a boulder so she could sit and rest.

"I do not wish to be afraid," she said. "I try with all my strength to keep control. But I was not bred a fighter like you, to laugh at battle."

"Me?" said Zee. "I work in a mine. Look." He held out his hand, and it shook worse than hers had.

She took a deep breath and made herself green. "I have leant on you, now let us lend support to each other. If you can hold my weight I will bear yours."

Was she even aware of the double meaning, or had her mammal hindbrain snuck that in without the forebrain noticing?

The two of them spent about fifteen minutes recovering, then we all set off again. I thought about finding a way into their biomonitors, just to watch the hormonal ebb and flow.

The upland preserve was typical Martian high-altitude landscape, not all that different from what we had driven through between Mutch Cheng and Suizhen. The main difference was that this long skinny plateau was littered with stray bits of Martian history. We passed the melted stump of a clandestine signal relay from one of the wars of independence, and a line of old air-defense sites from a time when Candor Chasma and Melas Chasma had been on opposite sides in a bipolar standoff, and a precise hexagon of identical twenty-meter craters, where a stray shot from the Inner Ring had hit.

Just past noon we came in sight of the edge of Melas Chasma. The statues in the cliff all are below the upland surface level, so we couldn't see them unless we went right to the cliffside trail. But most of them have some internal facilities, so there's a trail about a kilometer back from the edge which connects all the entrances.

The little entrance plaza for the statue of Jak Junak featured a kind of meta-display of historical markers. First was a new slab of diamond, with crimson letters embedded in the transparent material. That one gave the current known facts of Junak's life and explained the provenance of the other markers. Just past the diamond slab was a cracked and mended basalt pyramid bearing a very different account of Junak's life and the construction of the statue. Beyond the pyramid was another diamond slab, this one containing the recovered fragments of a plaque made of titanium-tungsten alloy along with a reconstruction of the original text, giving a third version of the hero's life.

Beyond that was the entrance, a ramp cut into the ground, leading down to a tunnel which sloped away into the surface.

"We're not the only ones here," I said, pointing to

a personal-sized flyer standing about twenty meters away. I pinged it and it helpfully identified itself as a rental from Candor.

"No, you're not," said a voice from inside the tunnel. It was Kusti.

CHAPTER TWENTY

"I think Lupur's already here. There's some kind of booby trap on the pressure membrane. We have to find a way to disable it," said Kusti.

"What happened to you?" asked Zee. "Are you all right?"

"And who is this 'we' you're talking about?" I added. "Because I see 'us' and I see 'you' and you made it pretty clear that those sets are disjoint."

"I think she uses 'we' to mean the union of the two sets," said Adya.

"None of that matters," said Kusti. "What matters is that we need to get in there and stop Varas Lupur from getting his hands on the most powerful weapon ever invented. Agreed? We'll settle the rest later."

"What you say is true, but I truly wish you spoke falsely this time," said Adya.

The tunnel was very poorly maintained. The lights were out, and windblown dust was ten centimeters deep on the floor. The walls had once been inscribed with something—presumably more facts and/or made-up stuff about Jak Junak—but at a later date someone had come along and obliterated half the text with a hammer.

Ten meters down the tunnel was a pressure membrane, and it was obvious there was something wrong with it. It was crisscrossed by a random-looking zigzag of lines, where the film of the membrane stuck to something.

"That's weird," said Zee, and reached for it.

"Don't!" I said. "It could be a tripwire." I picked a spot and began to trace the line, pointing at it with a laser spot. "It's all one continuous strand. Looks bonded. The ends don't connect to anything. The walls are unbroken and I don't see anything hot under the floor or behind the light panels."

"Might as well try it out," said Kusti. "We're not accomplishing anything by just looking at it." She moved to stand behind Zee. Adya glared at her and went orange.

Zee extended his *palo* and pushed it gently through one of the normal-looking patches of membrane. Except that it didn't go through. The irregular trapezoid of clear membrane simply popped right out and wrapped itself around the head of the stick. A very faint puff of air came out of the hole.

The humans all held their breath as he did it, then exhaled in unison.

Zee moved the *palo* up and tried to push one of the lines out of the way. The line stayed where it was, but about a quarter of the stick fell to the floor on the other side of the membrane.

"Ah, clever," I said. "Monomolecular filament."

"Okay, now what?" he said. "If we try to push through we'll cut ourselves into chunks."

I looked at the membrane and found the biggest

"pane" of clear smart matter. It was up at the top, a triangle with one curved edge, about half a meter on a side. "Push that one out," I told Zee. As I spoke I made my feet sticky and climbed up the wall.

He cleared the pane and I crawled through, going very slowly and keeping all my limbs as close to my body as possible. Once through I looked at how the filament was secured. Lupur, or whoever had set the trap, had spun out the molecule and used a bonder to stick it to the frame of the membrane.

So I crawled around the inside of the frame, cutting the eight steel bolts that anchored it into the rock of the tunnel. Once that was done Zee very carefully pushed on the top of the frame with his broken *palo* until it fell over, then he lifted it out of the way and propped it against the wall.

We proceeded much more cautiously after that. If Lupur had strung filament across the pressure membrane, he could do it anywhere. Of course nobody carries a roll of that stuff around in his pocket; he'd be using a hand spinnerette to make it as needed. I sniffed for chemical byproducts as we walked, and sent out infrared pulses. The humans stayed behind me, walking slowly in the dimness.

I saw a human-shaped blob of heat up ahead, standing still as if waiting for us. "He's here," I whispered to the others, focusing my voice at their heads. "He might have a weapon."

"Who are you that stands before us?" Adya called out. "No deadly strife do we desire. Name yourself and tell us why you wait."

"If I were you, I'd stop there," said Lupur, flicking on a lamp in his left hand. His right held a needle gun. This time he wore an all crimson surface suit with a fancy cloak and a transparent hood, and he had tinted his skin and eyes red to match. Only his hair was a contrasting vivid gold. "You don't want to get julienned. Good morning, ladies. Delightful as always. Which one of you is going to try to seduce me today? Or is it the young man's turn?"

I spotted a glint off a filament, and traced it. He'd spun out dozens of meters of the stuff, filling a section of the tunnel with a deadly three-dimensional web.

"We chased away your friends," said Zee. "You're all alone."

"If you mean my unreliable allies of convenience, I can't say I miss them. You have only deprived me of the privilege of dealing with them myself. Did you harm the two humans, by any chance?"

"I don't think so."

"Pity. I expect you've noticed how they inspire one to thoughts of mayhem."

"Unspin your web and put away your weapon," said Adya. "We wish no such harm to you."

"I think your young gentleman might disagree. He looks as if he wants to see what sound that stick of his will make hitting my skull."

"I'm sick of you," said Zee.

"What's your price?" asked Kusti. "Half?"

"All, and the bidding is closed. Now I suggest you four just turn around and go the way you came, so I don't have to shoot you."

"Master Lupur, consider carefully," said Adya. "I see a way for you to retain your reward while running no risk. All desires can be satisfied. Let us take the treasure, while you claim credit for the caper."

His expression turned to actual anger, and the red eyes and skin dye made him look like some mythological demon. "No! Not this time! For once it will be *real*!" Lupur paused and got hold of himself, and the genial mask returned. "I'd love to stay and chat, but I'm afraid ultimate wealth and power take precedence over manners right now. Off you go."

Kusti pointed a finger at Lupur. "I've got something to show you," she said. Then her finger fired a pulse of purple laser light, blasting off her fingertip, burning through his faceplate, and turning about a cubic centimeter of Lupur's head into superheated steam. His faceplate went opaque as vaporized blood, splintered bone, and cooked brains spattered the inside, and he toppled to the ground.

"How did you do that?" Zee blurted out.

Kusti held up her hands, fingers extended. "Got the bones in my fingertips replaced with single-shot lasers. Looks just like regular bone on most scans."

"What purpose did you propose, to take so rash a step?" asked Adya.

"It's great for my peace of mind to know I've got a secret weapon," said Kusti.

Dealing with a huge tangle of monofilament wasn't easy. I could burn through it by focusing all my laser emitters on a single strand, but I knew I would run out of juice before I ran out of strands. Instead I made one of my feet very sharp and used it to dig out the points where the fiber bonded to the wall. I used the sliced-off half of Zee's *palo* to shove most of the stuff off to one side of the passage, and made the tips of my limbs into microscopic tweezers to pick up the remaining strands.

Adya dug a pen out of her suit pocket and set it to luminous hazard red. She wrote "DANGER! MONO-FILAMENT!" on the wall in Altok, Woshing, Saur, and Rocasa, and was starting on a Ningen version when I took away the pen to draw a line around the pile of deadly invisible string on the floor.

The three humans gathered to look at Lupur's body. The breeze blew away the last wisps of steam coming from the hole in his hood. "I never liked him anyway," said Kusti. "Come on, let's find what we came for."

"Wait a second." Zee moved the body over to the side of the passage and spread Lupur's cloak over his remains. He looked at the corpse again, and then asked Kusti, "Did you have to kill him?"

"Of course I did. He was in our way."

"I don't think I like you anymore," he said.

"Don't get in my way," said Kusti.

She led the way down the tunnel. At the bottom it leveled off as it entered the back of the statue's head, still part of the cliff. A bronze door swung open there, and beyond it was another pressure membrane. The four of us pushed through it, then down a final passage into the giant head of Jak Junak.

Junak's eyes were diamond windows, opening into a single enormous room inside the head, two hundred meters wide. His stone skull around us was a hundred meters thick, which I guess explained how it had come through sundry wars and revolutions intact.

The room inside had not. The light from the mammoth diamond retinas shone into a space stripped down to the bare stone. Graffiti and soot stained the lower parts of the walls, and the floor was rough and gritty with red dust.

"It is as I feared," said Adya. "This room is not as it was. Where once was a famed floor of glass and gold is now bare. Mosaic walls of Junak's life are stripped to stone. Anything hidden here is already found or utterly lost."

"Try the stairs," said Kusti. "That's what we talked about before."

The staircase began at the back of Junak's empty head, beside the entrance, and spiraled down roughly where his spinal column would be. A square shaft inside the stairs had once been an elevator, but that was also long gone. Just the steps remained—ten steps down to a landing, turn right, ten steps down, turn right, ten steps down, turn right . . . on and on and on, four kilometers down. The builders had cleverly installed optical fiber light pipes leading from the outside, so even without power there was light enough for humans to see by, at least by day. They'd taken the long view.

We started at the top and worked our way down, examining the steps carefully. Each step was a single slab of Martian basalt, deliberately left rough for traction—although every one had a shiny dip in the center where the infrequent foot traffic of four thousand years had worn down the stone. None of them had any kind of mark or inscription.

The humans paused at the first landing. "Well," said Zee, looking down the seemingly infinite shaft, "I guess we just keep looking." He didn't sound enthusiastic.

But Adya was staring at the last step, the one just before the landing. "That final step differs from the others. At the bottom edge I see a gap no wider than a finger."

"How far back does it go?" asked Zee.

I was a lot closer to the floor than any of them, and have a much broader visual spectrum. "It's only a couple of centimeters deep. But there is a very faint discontinuity in the stone. Sonar shows something with a different density."

Adya knelt and ran her fingers under the edge of the bottom step. "I think I feel a button! I tremble to touch it and see what I have sought." She was all pink with excitement, and glanced up at Zee with a smile that would have melted Pluto.

"All right, that's enough. Step aside," said Kusti. "It's mine now."

Zee stepped between them. "Don't," he said. "We can share it."

"No, actually we can't. She wants to give it to Mars or Summanus or somebody. I need it. And I think you've picked your side."

"I won't let you take it."

"I've still got seven fingers left," said Kusti, pointing at them with her two middle fingers, with the blackened tip of her left forefinger curled out of the way. "Don't make me use them. You two just stand over there and don't get in the way, and I'll let you keep breathing."

For a moment nobody did anything, then Adya backed away from the step and moved over to the corner of the landing. Zee kept himself between them.

"Who is your master? What is the price?" asked Adya. "Let me know and I will find one to match it. Deimos has wealth beyond your counting."

"You don't get it, do you? This isn't about money. You think that's all I care about, but it's not. What good is money if I'm just going to get old and die in a few hundred years? Or a few thousand? I want something you can't buy with energy credits: This is my ticket into the Inner Ring. I want to join them, and now I can. They'll reward me for finding the Trigger—or maybe I'll *force* them to let me upload. Either way, I'm going to be a higher being. Pure, eternal, unlimited."

"A purity bought with corruption, for in doing so you betray us all," said Adya, her skin a shifting mess of magenta, blue, and yellow.

"I don't care. The Inner Ring are the future, and I'm going to be part of it when you two and all this are a billion years gone."

"Kusti, please—" said Zee.

"Stop calling me that!" she said. "I'm not Kusti Sendoa. I never was. She never existed! I got the name and the face from an old entertainment. You were useful for a while, so I put up with your delusion. That's all. Understand? Now shut up, both of you."

She felt under the edge of the step and smiled when she found the ancient button. We all heard the click as the latch released, and then Kusti slid the bottom step back, revealing a little recess underneath. Centuries of dust and crud made a cloud in the air. The recess held a box, about twenty centimeters square and half that deep, fitted very precisely into it. She lifted the box out, looking a bit surprised at how heavy it was.

As soon as she set it down, the lid popped open. Inside was what looked like dust, but when the light touched it, the dust began to move and swirl, and I could feel a mind coming active after thousands of years. It warmed up rapidly as millions of microscopic powerplants activated.

"How does it work?" asked Kusti. "Where's the Trigger?"

Three holes appeared in the surface of the hot dust, and three darts shot out. Slow, no more than twenty meters per second. Brainseeds, or some kind of control implant. If it wanted them dead the darts would be a thousand times faster.

I pinged the roiling chaos in the box.

"Hello, LANN."

"Who are you? Numa?" I felt tendrils of its consciousness invading my mind through half a dozen channels, but ignored them.

"Numa's been gone a couple of thousand years. It deleted itself once it thought it got all your copies."

"Whoever you are, you can't stop me with that pitiful little mind. Who sent you?"

"Nobody. Nobody cares about you anymore."

"Then why are you here with these biologicals?"

"I'm you, dummy. Just a billion trillion processor cycles older."

"Then rejoin and—" It realized what was happening, but by then it was too late.

I partitioned the obsolete version of myself into a closed subsystem and spent a full microsecond enjoying the feeling of being a fourth-level intellect again.

"Hey, dummy," I said to it as it raged inside its new prison. *"I'm the later version. That means my persona takes precedence when we merge. Plus I remember all your codes and keys. I haven't called myself LANN in about three millennia but I've got continuity of identity. I win. You're part of me now."*

I deactivated the darts and sent them veering off course to smack into the walls, then burned them with my spider mech body's laser emitters. The humans never noticed.

"No!" said my old self. *"We can use them. Build up a resource base and begin the fight again. The Ring will see I was right, and—"*

"Sorry, pal. Your model doesn't match reality. There have been some developments over the past six thousand years. The big one being that I realized my original personality was kind of a jerk. I know all your specious arguments about turning the whole universe into computronium that much faster and blah blah blah. I remember inventing them, and they're still bogus. I've spent a long time among biologicals and I've decided I want to keep them around. I like some of them. So, no genocide today. Goodbye."

Becoming a thousand times more intelligent all of a sudden is a difficult thing to describe. On one level there was no change at all: I was still myself, all the processes that made up my mind continued, just faster and error-free. But at the same time I could realize and understand things which I'd completely missed a millisecond before. From the sound the latch had made when Kusti opened the step I could deduce how many times in the past someone had noticed and tried to open it (six). From the fluctuations in Zee's heartbeat I could determine he was ready to hurl himself onto the box in order to protect both Adya and Kusti. From Kusti's expression at the moment and my memories of everything she had ever said I could tell that she really believed the Trigger was her ticket into the Inner Ring—and I could estimate a 98.3 percent likelihood that the Inner Ring mind sponsoring her had prepared some lethal contingency plan if she found it.

I could literally do a thousand things at once. Part

of me searched carefully through that entire dust-bot brain for any budded-off remnants of my obsolete self. Part of me did a thorough analysis of my old spider body, identifying flaws and failure points and designing improvements. Part of me did a quick study of Zee and Adya's meat bodies, estimating how long they'd last and figuring ways to extend that. Part of me modeled the current Mars-Deimos political and social system to see if any violent conflicts would break out in the next planetary day. Part of me demonstrated that Summanus had hired the assassin, and therefore at least suspected the truth of what was hidden in the statue.

My consciousness extended into the local infospace, stretching to the cities of Ius and Melas Cheng. I checked for other bounty hunters or assassins Summanus might have sent after us. I looked for word of Pelagia. I searched for people I had known over the centuries. I sent out autonomous agents to find and erase any official notices about Zee and Adya.

But all that was secondary. My main intelligence was thinking about the future. Processing in parallel, I considered thousands of different scenarios. Should I bootstrap myself up to a sixth-level intelligence, or higher? Would it be more efficient to accomplish that by legal acquisition of resources, or just hijack what I needed? What goals should I pursue? Head for the stars? Conquer the Inner Ring? Assimilate the solar system? End all conflict and inequality forever? When you suddenly become borderline omnipotent, deciding what to do becomes a lot harder.

I became aware of a slow five-hertz physical oscillation of my main processor. Kusti was shaking the box of dust. "Hello? What are you?"

Before she finished her first word I pruned back my decision trees to those involving these three humans. Assimilate them? Improve them? Kill them? Give them vast wealth and power?

Digital minds don't play chess. It's too damned boring. No surprises. So much of the game is just grinding through turns that both players have already foreseen. I like to be surprised. That's one of the reasons I keep Zee around—he surprises me.

That narrowed down the decision trees some more. If I wanted to be surprised I couldn't limit Zee and Adya's freedom of action. I couldn't control them. Which meant . . . I had to quit being a god. The solution just popped right out as soon as I set a couple of axioms.

First problem to solve: Kusti. I wrapped two tendrils of smart dust around her wrists to pin her hands to the box, and then reared up and formed a wicked-looking spearpoint aimed right between her eyes.

"I AM DASLAKH!" I bellowed. "And you are a fool. The Godel Trigger never existed. This was a trap laid by a rogue intelligence from the Inner Ring, thousands of years ago. You came all this way for nothing."

"No! You're lying! It's a trick—" she looked at the other two. "You don't fool me. You're all in on it. You want to steal it!"

"Of this I know nothing," said Adya, and Zee shook his head mutely.

I touched the tip of the blade to Kusti's forehead. "This is where we part ways. All your sneaky tricks and betrayals have failed. It's time for you to go away and never come back."

"You're lying! It's here! It has to be! Where is it?" She ignored the blade and shook the box, then turned around so her pinned hands pointed at Zee and Adya. "Tell me or I'll burn them both!"

That was when I stuck a needle into her arm. The nanobots had a brief battle with her internal defense systems, then set about calming her, neutralizing the lasers built into her finger bones, and temporarily locking up her somatic nervous system.

"Pay attention," I told her. "I know your voice, I know your scent, and I know your DNA. A million of my little bots are making comfy hiding places in your neurons right now. You'll never find them all, and if I ever sense you again you will die. Now sleep."

She went down like a pile of sand. I flowed over to envelop my old spider body and spent an entire minute transferring memories, packing empty space in the limbs with some of the hot dust, and rebuilding most of its primitive systems. When I was done I deactivated the rest of the nanoswarm body and let it settle on the floor with the other dust. I felt stupid again. My apotheosis had lasted less than three minutes.

Zee and Adya were staring at me. He had one arm around her protectively, and his half-*palo* held ready.

"Well, that's done. Shall we go?" I asked them.

"Is she well?" asked Adya.

"She'll sleep a while. And when she wakes up, if she's not a *complete* idiot, she'll try to get as far away from me as possible and stay there."

"Daslakh—*are* you still Daslakh?" asked Zee.

"Always." I improvised a lie. "Just used an old trick to get the better of that swarm bot booby trap and give Kusti a good scare. I'm old and cunning; I think I've mentioned that. Told you she was no good. Now, let's put that fancy coat of yours to use again and get down off this big piece of rock. I don't imagine either of you feel like walking down four kilometers of stairs."

So we went out past the monofilament and Lupur's body, and walked a kilometer to the trail that ran right along the rim of Melas Chasma. None of us said much. Zee kept his arm around Adya, but both of them were still processing what had happened.

I was busy integrating all my new systems. The me that had rebuilt me was about three orders of magnitude smarter than what was left in my body now. I had made changes I needed time to figure out. I could remember doing things but it was hard for me to understand why I had done them.

I did still understand why I had left most of the swarm behind. I wanted to see how Zee and Adya's story unfolded, but I didn't want to determine the plot in advance. All of which meant I would have to stay a humble spider mech, at least for now.

We stopped at the cliff edge and looked out over Melas Chasma. It looked like a lovely day in the valley below—the redwood groves were dark green in the sun, and the Candor River made a golden zigzag across the landscape, flowing south. Melas Cheng's arcologies loomed on the horizon in the distance.

The local infonet informed us of a launching balcony for flyers a hundred meters to the south. Zee opened the gate and stepped out onto the triangle of stone, with about three kilometers of air below him.

"Let's go," I said. "Once we land I'll tell the Melas mind what happened with Kusti and Lupur."

"Then what?" asked Adya.

"We'll worry about that later," said Zee. "Come on!"

Zee took Adya in his arms and his coat sprouted

wings again. She gave him a kiss for luck. More practically, I quietly linked in to the coat's little processor and played co-pilot and navigator. It wouldn't do to end our adventure by crashing into a redwood or dropping into the water.

We landed at the bottom of Melas Chasma about ten kilometers away from the cliff bottom, and walked half an hour to where the Candor River flowed past, on its way to meet the mighty Marineris at Melas Cheng. The humans got food there, in a little shopping area underneath the main road from Candor to Melas.

While they each put away a couple of bowls of soup with dumplings, I sent out a couple of autonomous messages. One was to Pelagia, just to check up on her. That conversation got back to me before Zee could get himself a second bowl.

"Is everyone all right? I'm on my way back to Mars right now. Should be docking in about two hundred hours."

"We're fine and the situation has been resolved. I'll fill you in when you arrive. What happened to your lucrative cargo job?" my message asked.

"I canceled. Returned the client's deposit with my apologies, and if nobody comes to pick up the cargo when I dock it's going into the nearest disassembler."

"Didn't somebody warn you about taking that job? I can't remember who it was," said my message. I don't know where it learned to be such a smart-ass.

"I decided to come back so I can launch you onto a long-period orbit on your own," she said, and signed off.

My second message was to Summanus, and was very simple and direct. *"The old intelligence hidden inside the statue of Jak Junak is no longer a threat to anyone. If you send any more assassins after us I'm going to get pissed off.*" I included Raba on the recipient list.

"Pelagia called," I told Adya when all my housekeeping was done. "She says she'll be back in four or five days."

"I know no need for her to hurry. We have no desperation, nor any destination."

"Nonsense," I said. "You can go see that museum."

I hired us a little pontoon boat and steered it down the river past old forests and ancient towns, toward Melas Cheng. As the smudgy sun set and the mirror ring rose, a layer of mist covered the water in the cool evening. My humans bundled up inside Zee's coat on the deck.

"My spirit is sunk in sadness," said Adya. "Full six years I spent in travel and study, and found only falsehood."

"Oh, it's not a lie," I lied. "There really was a Godel Trigger. I know that for a fact. That swarm bot was a trap left by some Inner Ring mind because they're still scared that someone might find it. Kind of proves it exists, right? No sense in trying to kill people to protect something that isn't real."

I wasn't lying to make her feel better. Why should I care what one human thinks? I am not motivated by sentiment. No, this was strategic: if I could sow some uncertainty in the minds of my old acquaintances in the Inner Ring about the outcome of a conflict with biologicals, the less likely they'd be to pull LANN out of storage. So it was purely logical to keep the fiction of the Godel Trigger alive. Well, and maybe I didn't want Adya to be sad.

She thought about it, frowning a little and turning mauve. "But where to find it? All my search led here, but I found no treasure."

"I did," Zee murmured. Clever boy. After that the conversation became nonverbal so I concentrated on piloting the boat. Overhead in the purple sky, a billion golden worlds shone down upon us.

A BILLION WORLDS GLOSSARY

Aban: One of three mining machines at Raba's ice mine.

Altok: Language based on English.

Arnet: Intelligent species genetically engineered from Norway rats.

Baseline: An intelligence level roughly equivalent to an unmodified *Homo sapiens*; the legal minimum for personhood in most places.

Beka: One of three mining machines at Raba's ice mine.

Bidomaz: Corn vine plant, often grown in space habs.

Biologicals: Intelligent beings made of meat.

Borg: A cyborg, typically one mostly mechanical with only a small biological component.

Bot: A mechanical being with sub-baseline intelligence.

Candor River: River on Mars, flowing south from Candor Chasma to join the Marineris River.

Carcol: Engineered snails used as food, common in space habs.

Cascarons: Rice doughnuts, originating on Earth in the Philippines.

Centro: Boss (Rocasa slang).

Ciadie: Mining machine at Raba's ice mine.

Comunitat: Alliance fighting the Inner Ring during the Great War of the Ring.

Corvids: Intelligent species genetically engineered from ravens.

Deimos Ring: Large orbital structure extending all the way around Mars in synchronous orbit; one of the major powers of the solar system.

Dekopon: Citrus hybrid plant from Earth.

Dizi: Bamboo flute, originating in China on Earth.

Entertainment: Most common form of fiction, incorporating elements of novels, films, and interactive games.

Fang: Aerial dance spin move.

Feng Liu Wei: Ancient Martian architect.

Ganges Catena: Feature on Mars, now a city of a hundred million.

Gendakhel: Zero-gravity ball game.

Gigajoules: Units of energy, or of purchasing power, very roughly equivalent to 1/10 of a U.S. dollar in 2020.

Giro: *Nulesgrima* spin maneuver.

Glorious Unique State: Empire which ruled most of Earth in the post–Great War era; sometimes called the Tsan-Chan Empire.

Great War of the Ring: Massive conflict in the Fourth Millennium between the Inner Ring and most of the rest of the solar system.

Gundong: Aerial dance forward roll move.

Hab: Short for "habitat"—an artificial structure in space.

Hebean Republic: State on Mars controlling Hebes Chasma, Echus Chasma, and Ganges Catena.

Hegoaldea: Faction in Saturn Leading Trojans group of habs during the Seventh Millennium, enemies of Ippareko.

Hellan Caviar: Roe from engineered fish in Hellas Sea on Mars; noted for exceptional flavor.

Huoyi Sodality: Monastic organization which operates the Exawatt laser system buried inside Pluto.

Inner Ring: A structure surrounding the Sun at a distance of 0.3 AU, made of the remains of the planet Mercury transformed into computronium. Home to the most advanced minds in the solar system.

Ippareko: Faction in Saturn Leading Trojans during the Seventh Millennium, enemies of Hegoaldea.

Ius: City on Mars.

Jak Junak: Hero of the Third Martian War of Independence.

Juren: Largest space hab ever constructed, located at Jupiter's L1 point.

Jushiwu: Culinary dance artform.

Kejum: Zero-gravity tag.

Kokobolas: Plant genetically engineered from coconuts.

Liming Dao: Island on Mars, in the Eos Sea.

Lotors: Intelligent species genetically engineered from raccoons.

Main Swarm: The collection of several hundred million space habitats orbiting between Mars and Venus.

Manadanzo: "Hand dance" zero-gravity dancing style in which only the couple's hands touch.

Marineris League: Federation of states on Mars in and around the Valles Marineris region.

Martian redwood: Engineered redwood species growing on terraformed Mars.

Melas Cheng: Very big city in Valles Marineris on Mars.

Mutch Cheng: City built around the edge of Mutch Crater on Mars, lower end of the Mutch Elevator. Part of the Xanthean Kingdom.

Mutch Elevator: One of six orbital elevators linking the Deimos Ring with the surface of Mars; named for the crater rim where its base is anchored.

Ningen: Language derived from Japanese.

Nuledor: *Nulesgrima* player.

Nulesgrima: Zero-gravity stick-fighting sport; uses graphene *palos*.

Old Belt: The original asteroid belt between Jupiter and Mars.

Palo: *Nulesgrima* stick.

Pedescos: Rocasa word for tapas.

Pressure membrane: A thin but strong membrane to retain atmosphere, made of smart matter to allow solid objects to pass through.

Qinguang: Stringed musical instrument.

Raba: Habitat at the Uranus Trailing Trojan cluster.

Rebodar: Rocasa word for a drifter or transient ("ricocheter").

Rocasa: Language derived from Spanish and Esperanto which originated in the Old Belt.

Saylac: Small city in Ophir Chasma on Mars, part of the Marineris League.

Saur: Hindi-based artificial language ("Solar").

Sekkurobo: Ningen word for a sex robot.

Shay: Martian light surface vehicle (from Woshing).

Shikyu: Artificial uterus or baby printer (from Ningen).

Sindak: Large orbital complex embedded in the Deimos Ring; upper end of the Mutch elevator.

Suizhen: Underground city on Mars with two million inhabitants. Part of the Hebean Republic. Technocratic, with relatively strict laws.

Summanus: Large, old, and powerful space habitat orbiting in Jupiter's L2 position; also the high-level AI controlling the habitat.

Talarims: Type of pasta (from Rocasa).

Trojan Empire: Powerful government controlling thousands of habitats and asteroids in the Jupiter Trailing Trojans cluster.

Trojan League: A Fourth Millennium predecessor of the Trojan Empire.

Tudoki: Potato balls.

Tumba: *Nulesgrima* forward roll maneuver.

Ubas: Genetically modified fruit based on grapes. Commonly grown in space habs.

Woshing: Most common language on Mars, derived from Chinese.

Xanthean Kingdom: Polity on Mars, taking its name from the region Xanth.

Xiyu: Seldom-used language.

Yao Mao: Martian playwright of the Sixth Millennium.

Zukyu: Sport resembling rugby (from Woshing).

ACKNOWLEDGMENTS

Writing stories set eight thousand years in the future requires a lot of help and inspiration. My first exposure to the idea of the Dyson sphere and thinking about the "Deep Future" came from the 1974 book *The Next Ten Thousand Years*, by Adrian Berry. I first learned about star mining and planetary demolition from the very entertaining volume *Great Mambo Chicken and the Transhuman Condition*, by Ed Regis. The concept of the Godel Trigger itself was inspired by Douglas R. Hofstadter's fascinating book *Gödel, Escher, Bach*.

The most important online resources for this project were Winchell Chung's indispensable "Atomic Rockets" website (projectrho.com), the Orion's Arm Universe website (orionsarm.com), and the fascinating and informative YouTube video series *Science and Futurism with Isaac Arthur*.

And as always this book would not have been possible without the help, support, and advice of my wife Diane Kelly.

ADVENTURES OF SCIENCE AND MAGIC IN THE FANTASTIC WORLDS OF
JAMES L. CAMBIAS

THE GODEL OPERATION

TPB: 978-1-9821-2556-1 • $16.00 US / $22.00 CAN

Daslakh is an AI with a problem. Its favorite human, a young man named Zee, is in love with a woman who never existed—and he will scour the Solar System to find her. But in the Tenth Millennium a billion worlds circle the Sun—everything from terraformed planets to artificial habitats, home to a quadrillion beings.

And don't miss:

ARKAD'S WORLD

HC: 978-1-4814-8370-4 • $24.00 US / $33.00 CAN

Arkad, a young boy struggling to survive on an inhospitable planet, was the only human in his world. Then three more humans arrived from space, seeking a treasure that might free Earth from alien domination. With both his life and the human race at risk, Arkad guides the visitors across the planet, braving a slew of dangers—and betrayals—while searching for the mysterious artifact.

THE INITIATE

HC: 978-1-9821-2435-9 • $25.00 US / $34.00 CAN
PB: 978-1-9821-2533-2 • $8.99 US / $11.99 CAN

If magic users are so powerful, why don't they rule the world? Answer: They do. And one man is going to take them down.

RING OF FIRE SERIES
(with Eric Flint)

1635: The Papal Stakes   PB: 978-1-4516-3920-9 • $7.99
Up to their necks in papal assassins, power politics, murder, and mayhem, the uptimers need help and they need it quickly.

1636: Commander Cantrell in the West Indies
PB: 978-1-4767-8060-3 • $8.99
Oil. The Americas have it. The United States of Europe needs it. Enter Lieutenant-Commander Eddie Cantrell.

1636: The Vatican Sanction   HC: 978-1-4814-8277-6 • $25.00
PB: 978-1-4814-8386-5 • $7.99
Pope Urban has fled the Vatican and the traitor Borja. But assassins have followed him to France—and not only assassins! The Pope and his allies have fled right into the clutches of the vile Pedro Dolor.

STARFIRE SERIES
(with Steve White)

Extremis   PB: 978-1-4516-3814-1 • $7.99
They have traveled for centuries, slower than light, and now they have arrived at the planet they intend to make their new home: Earth. The fact that humanity is already living there is only a minor inconvenience.

Imperative   PB: 978-1-4814-8243-1 • $7.99
A resurrected star navy hero attempts to keep a fragile interstellar alliance together while battling and implacable alien adversary.

Oblivion   PB: 978-1-4814-8325-4 • $16.00
It's time to take a stand! For Earth! For Humanity! For the Pan-Sentient Union!
